THE
LIES

To Nang,
Enjoy the ride

J. MICHAEL KOPPEN

June 2022

ISBN 978-1-0980-6998-8 (paperback)
ISBN 978-1-0980-8357-1 (hardcover)
ISBN 978-1-0980-6999-5 (digital)

Christian Faith Publishing, Inc.
832 Park Avenue
Meadville, PA 16335
www.christianfaithpublishing.com

Printed in the United States of America

CHAPTER 1

The cold steel of the .38 felt strange against his temple. This new episode was without precedence. Never had it gone this far. This was the first time with the gun in his hand.

Holden Jeffries closed his eyes and leaned back against the soft leather of his Thomasville chair. He had everything he had ever wanted...ever dreamed of...it was all here. It was worthless... *Where in the hell was the satisfaction...the peace?* He pushed the barrel deeper into his temple. *Where had the dreams gone?* He had done exactly what they told him—followed the plan. He worked hard, went to college, married a beautiful woman, worked harder, had kids, bought stuff, worked harder, climbed the ladder, bought more stuff, and on and on. None of it really lasted most of it just rusted. In high school, Mr. Edwards said he had potential...but what if they saw him now... Holden knew the truth...he was a performer...a chameleon. It's what he did best. Not impressive as a man...but particularly important in business...it buys success...and Holden knew about success.

At fifty-two, he was CEO of one of the largest computer programming companies in the Midwest. He was married to his college sweetheart. He had three children. His salary was well into seven figures, and the new house was testimony to his position. He had toys and property that made associates drool and control of most of what mattered in the Twin Cities. Why, then, was he facing the finality of this new possibility?

It began months, maybe years before. Somewhere, in the midst of contentment, a crack began to emerge.

"What was the meaning of life—his life?"

They told him success brought happiness. And of course, success was measured by dollar signs and driveways, by titles and deeds, and by what others thought and stated.

Was he happy? Who was really happy anyway? If the year-end was positive, and shareholders spoke highly of accomplishments... happiness would follow. That's what they told Holden, and he believed them.

The fragrance of gun mixed with the pungency of the Crown Royal in his glass almost nauseated him as much as the lie he had sold out to.

"What the hell... I'm dead anyway...just as well make it reality." Holden slurred his words. *Could he be drunk? What had he had, three... maybe four drinks? He used to drink that before going out!* Another truth he resented; he was beginning to see age in the mirror. The future was looking shallow. *Get some guts, do something real once...*

It would be easy. The end would be quick...probably almost painless.

Pull the trigger. Who would really care? They'd question why but another performer would slide in behind his desk at Litany...most would be happy that one more step on the ladder was gone. The family would have plenty to cover their needs.

*Go...ahead pull the trigger...*he tightened his grip, squeezed his eyes tightly and waited...nothing.

God...you truly are pathetic Jeffries!

"God"...another problem for Holden. Somewhere where he wasn't even certain existed...somewhere deep inside of him there was a fear of death...a fear that seemed to make more sense than all the arguments he could bring against it. *What was death anyway? Was it an ending or the beginning of something that his mother preached about for years? Would God forgive him if there really was a God? Would he go to heaven if there really was a heaven? Would he end up in hell if there really was a hell? Where would he spend eternity if there really was an eternity?* Holden was not a religious man. Why then did all these questions seem so important? He slammed the gun down marring the top of his mahogany desk. It was all too much for him to chance.

CHAPTER 2

The cold steel of the .38 felt strange against his temple. Jack Grayton had been here many times before. Life wasn't getting easier. Not like the old days. *How long ago was that anyway?*

Downtown Minneapolis had changed a great deal over the years. The all-night casinos and convenience stores on every corner made life easier. He didn't have to find a hot air vent to keep warm on winter nights, but the employees were far too knowledgeable of his background…less than understanding of his "role" in the city. He spent a lot of time in jail. Not for the big stuff…little things like public intoxication, beating on a prostitute now and then, a few drug sales. He'd never owned a car, never had a job, he'd never paid a cent in taxes. That made him proud in the early days…not now…he was without pride, actually without much of anything.

Things had begun to get out of hand. Jack had run out of answers. He was always the one in control in younger days…he was "the man." Now there was little left to control—most of those days were memories at best.

The fragrance of the gun brought fond memories. While he had few opportunities to use guns, he had been around them all his life. Nothing could bring about compromise like cold steel. What about the finality of this all-too-familiar possibility? What kept him from finishing the job? He had nothing to lose, he had lost more than he could ever repay. He'd been married once. The memory was less than vivid. *Sometime in the sixties*, he thought.

Much of the sixties had been a blur for Jack. Much of life had been a blur for Jack. The drugs and booze, the days that blended into nights and the years that blended into decades all had left their signature on his life. Again, he was contemplating death… *As if it would matter.* He knew the truth, and that's probably what hurt the worst. He didn't really exist as the world defined it. He was six-foot-four, weighed about 230. He was fifty-three years old and nearly all his life he had hated everything. Nobody had ever given him anything. He had to take what he wanted. He had always been strong and tough enough to survive. Now the thought of another winter was debilitating. Summers were no picnic, but the winters in Minnesota seemed to last a lifetime. He had no one. He had no expectations of change. He stared down at his boots—cowboy boots—the only thing he ever bought new…even they looked like they needed a change. He took off his cap and adjusted the bill. He could smell his greasy hair and filthy clothes. As if he gave a rip…as if anyone did. He could smell the cheap vodka he had spilled when he dozed off. Dozed off…he fell asleep like some old man, his chair propped against the wall in this hellhole. He was pathetic. Everybody had seen it for years…now he knew too. Jack had been stepped over by most of the people in downtown Minneapolis. The truth was…they were right…he wasn't worth stopping for…not worth noticing. His finger pressed harder on the trigger. This would be quick. All the pain would be over soon. He closed his eyes waiting.

It always happened. In anger he used his gun hand to pound the table. The dirty dishes clamored on the wood, then exploded into the darkness as he cleared the table with an angry arm. Jack wanted to scream. He couldn't even finish this! He was hopeless. Somewhere deep inside of him, somewhere he really wasn't certain existed, there was a fear of death, a fear that seemed to make more sense than all the arguments his mind could bring against it. Jack could never pull the trigger. Was it the voice of his mother that brought the fear?

She had always said, "There is no place in heaven for those who choose to kill, especially if it was your last act on Earth."

What was this crap about heaven anyway? Why should he care? She certainly hadn't offered much comfort for him over the years.

She was all about rules and laws and right and wrong. Where had it gotten her? She died at thirty-six, looking like she was sixty, a Bible in her arms and a smile on her face. Her last words were something about God loving him, but Jack knew better—God was supposed to love his mother too, and what good had it done? God…what a joke! God knew the truth about him too. He'd never gotten anything from anyone…including God.

Someday he'd find the courage to finish the job, someday.

CHAPTER 3

Kate left the club and headed for home. Home, a euphemism, it was simply a house, a large house, a new house, a beautiful house, an extraordinary house, but not yet a home. *Why did it seem so cold?* She loved the idea at first, moving to the lake, moving to the "neighborhood." It was what they'd dreamed of—given up their lives for— yet for some reason it lacked the joy that she had anticipated. She had noticed the disappointment in Holden too. He seemed to love the chase, but rarely was satisfied in the end result. *Where had their lives gone?*

It seemed like only yesterday that they struggled with payments. They had dreamed of the day when money would not be an issue. Now the issues were far deeper than dollars.

Kate's had always been popular, and beautiful. She had been born into a family that was neither rich nor poor. Her parents were high school graduates and farmed the rich black soil of southern Minnesota. Her parents were religious people, but not outward about their faith. They believed spirituality was a personal matter not to be shared. Kate was taught God was to be worshipped. He was responsible for taking care of lives. He was to be trusted and followed. He loved all and would do what was best for His people. He was God. It was His job to keep things together. She should not worry about anything.

Kate was a good person. She always tried to do what was right and had excellent academic skills…college was her future.

Her mother was diagnosed with breast cancer in Kate's freshman year. Of course, there was hope. The pastor had assured her God was in control—He had plans for her mother. She had only to trust and believe. She prayed and trusted and believed. She had faith and prayed some more. She visited her mother every weekend. Each weekend she looked weaker, but Kate had faith and prayed and trusted and prayed. Yet each week she seemed to be getting worse.

Going to class was torture. It was impossible to concentrate on lectures when her mother was going through the fight of her life. She would find herself angry with the others.

Couldn't they understand? What was the matter with them?

It was like she was alone. It was like no one cared about her pain, her future, her mother, her life.

Where was God in all of this?

He must be just testing her to see if she really did trust Him. Nothing was impossible for God. And oh, how she needed to trust God. There was no one to talk with. Spiritual matters were personal. She prayed and trusted and prayed and trusted.

On a Friday in April 1968, Kate was called home to the hospital. God seemed to have lost control. Her mother was gone. Gone without reason. Gone after only forty-one years of life. Gone from Kate's plans. It was not supposed to be like this. It was not fair. Now all Kate had was her father. He was not a strong man. His entire life revolved around her mother and the farm. Now his wife was gone. The farm that had brought him joy and warm memories became a burden.

Kate remembered the weekends, finding her dad with an empty bottle of the booze of choice, dressed in the same clothes she had left him wearing on Monday morning. She had asked for help, not from outsiders (these things were personal), from his family. But of course, everyone was busy, and *he was an adult*—he should *get control* of himself.

In the winter of her junior year, January 1969, her father finally did take control. He took a shotgun and ended the pain. Kate dropped out of college for the rest of the year and tried to get the farm and her finances defined. She had inherited two hundred and forty acres of the best farmland in the midwest. Her father left her with fifteen thousand dollars of life insurance so she could at least finish college. She found herself a different person in 1970 than she had been in 1966. She was certain of one thing. Blind trust was for idiots!

Kate returned to college in the fall of 1970. She met the dashing Holden Jeffries. He was strong and self-reliant. He had plans and places to go. She was ready to leave for nearly anywhere someone else would lead. The whirlwind romance lasted nearly three months and ended with a Saturday night wedding in a Lutheran church with a few friends and family. After a one-night honeymoon, back to school and a final exam on Monday.

Holden was hired to create a new system of programs for IBM compatible computers for Litany Systems Corporation. It would be necessary for them to move to Minneapolis/St. Paul. Kate would wait to get her degree.

Holden had never slowed down. He now was CEO. Kate had graduated and worked in her field of teaching for several years, until the children came. She spent her free time with the kids but needed the diversion of working out of the house. She found that her taste in fine gifts and artwork attractive to the management or her favorite department store. She became their department buyer for fine gifts. The part-time position turned into a career and now Kate was the head buyer for the chain. Money was not a problem, but problems were not a thing of the past.

CHAPTER 4

Matt Roth entered the ministry in his second year of college. In the first ten years of his practice, he began to realize that the desire to serve the Lord was not enough. Disillusionment, dissatisfaction, disrespect, disdain, and disappointment were his closest friends.

From the beginning all he wanted was to make his life count for something. The Bible says to store up treasures in heaven where moths and mildew don't destroy them. It is exactly what he wanted to do.

Matt first call was pastor of a small church in rural East Central Minnesota. He was shepherd of fifty-six active members in a church with a roll of about three hundred. Matt was determined to find the needs, settle disputes, promote love, and serve God. Parishioners were quick to point out their feelings and expectations. Some wanted two hymns sung; others wanted three, or one or none. Some wanted contemporary services; others were appalled at the idea and would tolerate only a traditional service. There were threats of leaving and taking others with them.

Many times, the least Godly place Matt visited was the church. He was not prepared for this. This was childish bickering among people that should have better things to do. How could believers be manipulative and mean? How could believers get angry about petty jealousies? How could church people gossip about others in the flock? How could money and materialism be the topic of nearly every board meeting? How could the spiritual side of the church— the faith side of belief—be downgraded to the next dollar?

He had studied of miracles and tongues, and healings and spiritual warfare. He had never imagined the depth of darkness within the heart of the church.

The final blow came after nearly a decade of service. Some of Matt's flock became "Spirit-filled" at a conference. Matt prayed the "awakening" was beginning. Within months a new set of problems arose.

The Traditionalists were suspect of anything that the Charismatics would suggest. The Charismatics would rhetorically label the others as second-class believers. They wanted to be able to wave their hands and dance in the spirit. They wanted to pray in tongues and prophesy in tongues and interpret the prophecy. The Traditionalists wanted nothing resembling chaos in their worship. The "love of Christ" was absent in all.

Matt felt he was working with a pack of wolves, not a flock of sheep. Matt walked away. He became a deliveryman for the local bottling company. It fed his family and rarely raised his blood pressure or lowered his expectations.

Matt Roth still felt a need for a ministry. He spoke with the County Sheriff and after several days of contemplation the jail would have its first Bible study compliments of former pastor, deliveryman Matt Roth.

Matt had never felt more at home. From the first evening, he was hooked. The prisoners were refreshing. Most were transient men from the Twin Cities, on their way to bigger places. The study was strictly optional. It was a time to read, question, talk, and learn about a man called Jesus who Matt said was a friend like no other.

"God really works in that jail. I truly need only to be there. He does the rest."

"Sounds like an excuse not to prepare." Connie teased from across the kitchen table. She loved his innocent outlook on this very guilty world. It was her responsibility to be the sounding board.

"It's not like that! He really wants to control this ministry. I'm only a sort of vessel, a vessel that needs only to be obedient. The church seemed like a job, a responsibility. This seems like—a call."

"Wow, you're starting to sound a little like some of the fanatics you used to question. Remember the 'God told me,' 'God said' group?"

"I know it's hard not to be cynical about this stuff, but you almost have to be there to see it. I go, He uses me, and I walk out of that place about three feet off the ground. In all the years of preaching and working as a pastor, I can't remember any experience that compared to this."

"You've never really talked like this before."

"Connie, you remember when I used to complain about the lack of love in the church? I used to tell you that I had expectations. That congregation should have certain principles and work from biblical perspectives." Matt tilted his head and watched his wife's expression. She had her back toward him, but she nodded to continue.

"Well the church and the believers have left these guys behind. Many of the men have rarely heard of The Lord or experienced love of any kind. They are angry and tired and lost, and well aware of it. They are broken, not pretentious. They are the ones I've been searching for, the ones that He has been searching for. I only go there with the story. He changes lives."

"I love the fact that you care about these guys but be careful. Try not to get too involved. Remember, they aren't in there because they skipped church."

Matt noticed the concern in his wife's expression.

"That's the tough part. If I really believe God sees all of us the same, and that we all need the saving blood of Christ or we don't go home. How can I tell them I won't get involved?"

"Tell them that your wife won't let you get involved. It really does frighten me that you are involved with criminals. Sometimes you can be a little...gullible."

"But if you were to talk to them, you'd see. Much of their past they did not choose."

Connie's expression had not changed, but she was listening.

"Who is going to tell them? I only see them for a couple hours on Monday night for a few weeks, then they're gone. They have no memory of anyone who ever cared. Why should they see me any different? It must be more than words—that's why He is calling for more. I feel that I have to listen to His will."

"That's great Matt but use your head. I'm just a little worried." Connie smiled and touched his hand. "It's because you mean so much to me."

CHAPTER 5

Holden was increasingly disenchanted. The old hurdles weren't providing the challenges. The whole software business had changed. Kids right out of college expected a position that had taken years to earn.

The corporation had gone public. Holden had lost most of his control. A board of directors saw the bottom line as the only real issue. The board had some specific expectations from both the corporation, and its officers. Officers were expected to be highly motivated.

It really wasn't the work that troubled Holden. It just made him realize how far he had come, and how far from it he wanted to be.

The voice on his intercom startled him

"Mr. Willers is waiting to see you, Mr. Jeffries."

"I will be available shortly."

"Thank you, Mr. Jeffries, I will alert him."

Frank Willers was a snake. He had slithered his way from a sales position to executive vice president in six short years. Litany had gone public due primarily to his urging, and Holden's voice was not enough to halt the progress. Holden was wary of the man. He stood, then walked to his office door and opened it to the waiting area.

"Frank, thanks for waiting. Please come in."

Frank smiled as he walked past Holden and entered the huge office.

"I was surprised at your call, is there something I can do for you, Mr. Jeffries."

"Call me Holden…please. I just thought I might have a chance to clear the air. We have not always seen things in the same light, and in some ways, I find that unproductive for the future of Litany."

"I am sorry to hear that, Mr.…ah… Holden. I have always respected your opinion, even when, especially when it was contrary to my own. That's the beauty of the system, many voices, one focus—the future."

"I received a phone call from a source that will remain anonymous. He tells me there have been some interesting media leaks about our upcoming software release. Someone is blowing the package totally out of proportion and the stock prices are inflated. Since you are the head of Litany Marketing, is that surprising to you?"

"Litany has a great name in the marketplace. Everyone is always talking about the new and wonderful things we are planning. I am not certain if I should be offended by the tone of your questions. Is this accusatory, or just my imagination."

"Listen, Frank, this is not just accusatory, it's flat out truth. I know you have been selling something we don't have, and if that damn stock falls apart a lot of people are going to get hurt."

"Holden, didn't you just liquidate two hundred thousand shares of stock. If what you are saying is true, maybe it's not me that should be careful of how this looks."

"That liquidation was part of the settlement from the public offering. I have given my life to this place, and the shareholders bought out forty percent of my holdings. There is nothing illegal about the liquidation."

"Perhaps not illegal, but it does have a certain odor if the bottom falls out of Litany now doesn't it."

Willers smiled a wry, youthful smile.

"It might just be difficult to maintain your radiance in this light. But I am certain this is all just superfluous gossip."

Holden wanted to tear his heart out. Frank Willers was far more than some snot nosed whiz kid. He was the future.

"Be careful, Frank, I may look old, but I'm not quite dead. I still have friends and a great deal of power in this town."

"I've never doubted your resume, Mr. Jeffries. I have enjoyed our meeting. I'll just let myself out."

He walked from the room without a glance at Holden. The final act of defiance…dismissal.

Holden sat in silence. He needed to talk to someone, but who? Kate was no help. He really believed as they grew the barriers would melt…he would find the confidant for whom he had longed. It was a ridiculous notion, but he was young then.

Now he understood. Women and men were naturally separated. He had long since given up childish expectations.

In the absence of an understanding ear, suicide again crossed his mind.

Not an option. But leaving had its advantages.

*****

The internet had always fascinated Holden. As he considered new options, he realized he would need to leave the country to find peace.

He would need a new identity. *How can you become someone new?* He found the net chat rooms a great place to start.

"Have you ever been hired to find someone that had run? How'd you find them? Had they changed their names, or identity? Social Security number—that must be hard to change?"

CHAPTER 6

The sun broke through the dingy windows at 6:17 AM. The Starbrite Inn was less than bright, but it *was* cheap. Jack had lost track of the places he had frequented for a night or two over the last fifteen winters. He had learned early that you never wanted to stiff these places, "'cause they all talk, and once the word gets out...you are out!"

It was a good idea to get out of the place early. The police made rounds by seven thirty...checkin' who might be using or holding. Sometimes it got a bit rough.

Jack had paid for three days. He had never had a job, but he wasn't "without means." He was well known as a runner for some of the boys in the "downtown club." Now and then he would help to get someone's attention. The pay wasn't much, but he was able to exist. Jack didn't need much. He was connected.

He also knew the ropes. Whoever said there was no free lunch had never lived in the inner city. The downtown mission was a pretty good place to get fed. When times were tough, you could even stay over if you got there by 3:00 PM. It always filled up by four, especially in the winter. He didn't have to worry about that now. He paid for three nights.

The Citgo station on Second Street had free coffee in the morning. They liked Jack, so his 7:00 AM ritual began there.

"Hey, Randy, how they hangin'?"

"Jack, you still alive? I was wondering if you'd be by for coffee."

"Can't start the day without your coffee. The gas fumes give it that extra kick, makes my day. Where you been? Nat said you'd been talking 'bout religious stuff. He thought maybe you were headin' out for good."

"Jack, you know better than that. The city is my home, but there certainly is more to life than this job. What are you going to do in eternity, or don't you know about eternity?"

"You're not gonna start preachin' to me, are you, Ran?"

Jack stirred his coffee with the little plastic stick.

"The last person to do that stuff died. She gave it a try, but this God thing doesn't pay that well. My life isn't about all the rules. I just would never fit into your little box. Especially if you have Jesus in there too!"

"Well, Jackson, God isn't quite ready for you, but he has got his eye on you!"

"That's good, Ran, hope he keeps what he sees to himself."

*****

Jack had heard all of this before. God's got a plan for you, Jack. His mother had told him that a thousand times. *Well, this God must have quite a sense of humor if this was his plan.*

Jack really was without importance—he knew it, and most of all...he knew... God knew it.

CHAPTER 7

The busy time was over, the product had been shipped and the display artists had worked their magic. All that was left was to watch it sell. Kate told herself that she was doing the people a service. They always smiled when they walked into the fine gift department. It was far from reality, it was fun, and wasn't that what life needed, some fun?

"Kate, the new Swedish Crystal is exquisite. It should sell through at least twice in the fourth quarter. You really have an eye for the best."

"Thanks, Roxy. I just really like what I do."

"It shows, Kate. What are your plans for tabletop?"

"You'll see, there were so many patterns to choose from. You'll love the looks."

"Kate, are you going to take some time off before the spring buying starts? You really have earned it."

"Guess I haven't thought about it much. Seems like the shows just come too often. Then there's the reading and the advertising ideas and follow up on the displays and training. I'm not certain there's time. Holden is busy too, and we don't vacation without each other."

"Well, the time is yours when you want it. It's not that we want you to leave, but everyone needs some fun now and then. That's what keeps life interesting."

Time off frightened Kate more than working too hard. Home seemed the loneliest place in her life. Holden was distant and self-absorbed. She really wasn't much better.

She wasn't sure when it had started, maybe when her father quit trying…maybe after the wedding and the truth about marriage became evident, or maybe she had always been like this. *Whatever… it didn't matter.* She'd never get it back anyway. *Life is supposed to be disappointing!* Life is tough, so you must be tough, and she was. One thing her life wasn't anymore was fun.

CHAPTER 8

Slueth@AOL.com was on line and a bundle of information and Holdem@AOL.com was interested in all he or she had to say. He had no clue who he was talking to. It could be kid or an octogenarian. It could be a man or a woman. It could be your next-door neighbor.

"How do you find them…if they don't want to be found?" Holden typed and sent.

"They are always stupid. They tell someone."

"Tell them what, their plans?"

"Their plans, their ideas, the whole story."

"Why…why tell?"

"They're idiots. When they take off, the friend can't keep a secret, or someone puts heat on them, and the trail gets hot fast. Or things don't work out, or they get scared, or it's not what they had planned…whatever…sooner or later they blow it."

"Can't they just get a new identity?"

"They can try. It's not quite like in the movies. It's not that easy to do it right."

"Do it right?"

"You have to find someone who has an ID but doesn't really exist."

"Doesn't exist?"

"You know, someone who doesn't have a job, doesn't pay taxes, doesn't own property or owe on a mortgage. He can't even have a bunch of parking tickets or driving problems. He probably shouldn't even have a driver's license, and should be single—you know, some-one who doesn't exist?"

"Great idea but…where can you find someone like that?"

"Exactly!"

"The guy would have to be a bum or dead?"

"Dead isn't good. That's one record they track…but a bum, yeah! You thinking about leaving? Who knows, maybe they'll hire me to find you!"

"Yeah, right! Thanks for the information!"

Holden signed off and began to think. He had to find someone who existed, but just barely. What about some of those street people he saw on his way to the office, or the bums that spent their lives in and out of the Hennepin County Jail. That's it…

CHAPTER 9

The rays of light were too dim to make the sounds that Jack heard real. It was far too early to be having the *"blues"* doin' bed check. He jumped up and took another glance at his watch.

"Oh, God, it was almost eight!" It couldn't be true, and he was still holding. The stuff had to be dumped before they got there. He dug frantically in his pocket, "Nope, that's not it!"

"Where in the hell? Under the mattress? No!" It came to him at exactly the moment the police hit the door. They saw his shoes at the same time that he remembered putting the stuff in them for safekeeping.

"Hey, Jack, nice kicks! Amazing the new liners they're putting in these...these must be those new ones that form to your feet."

"They ain't mine." Jack nodded as he spoke. "Someone must have left them in here last night!"

"Right, Jack, I suppose they belong to the Butler."

"Go to hell, Riley, they could."

"Well, why don't you call him in here to watch us read you your rights and fit you with this jewelry? It'll go nice with the rest of your outfit."

Jack was familiar with the process. He was held without bond, as if it mattered. Any bond over twenty bucks was out of the question. Guys like Jack were destined to serve out their sentence. Defense Lawyers were handpicked by the system to fail. They were underpaid, and basic underachievers. Jack would hope the sentence would be fair because he'd be doing all of it.

CHAPTER 10

"You say his name is Jack Grayton, and he lives around here?" Holden tipped his head down as he questioned the waitress at the counter.

"It's Jack Gray...something. I think he lives wherever he is at the time," she half growled.

Holden wondered why the women that served in these places seemed to have the same voice. She wasn't helping him much in finding someone who would fit his "barely existing" criteria.

"Jack ain't around right now," the voice from behind him added.

Holden immediately turned to see a grease monkey with a Citgo shirt standing close.

"So you know Jack?" Holden asked.

"As well as anybody knows Jack, I guess! The name's Randy."

"Well, Randy, can I buy you a cup of coffee?"

"Sure, but I can't help much, Jack's in jail."

"Doesn't matter, the guy I'm looking for is supposed to have a job and a family."

"You got the wrong Jack. The Jack I know never had a job. Don't think he's ever worked a day in his life. He did have a wife once, but never a family."

"This guy drives for one of the trucking companies."

"Drives? Not our Jack. Strictly a bus man, taxi if someone else is paying for it, but never a driver!"

"Hey, listen, thanks for your time, guess I got some bad input. Maybe I'll catch you later."

"Stations right around the corner if you ever need gas or a mechanic."

Holden could hardly hold back the smile as he considered Randy working on his Lexus.

CHAPTER 11

The Vikings were playing the Cowboys on Monday Night Football, that made it a rough night for the Bible study. The guys would have to choose between God and "The Vikes" and that was a tough call for the best of believers.

Matt always prayed before going into the jail. This was much different than church. There was no agenda, and no set program. Since attendance was optional, Matt was never certain how many if any would show up. Some weeks there would be as many as fifteen, other times nobody.

The story was plain and simple, "Love and forgiveness."

"Lord, prepare me to be used in your work. Spirit take me and empty me of me. Fill me with you so that I can be used. Help them see you and not me. In the name of Jesus, amen."

Three men came: Bill, a forty-year-old man with drug and alcohol problems, Thomas, a black man that had been in and out of the system for his whole life, and Jack, a very angry man in his early fifties. He was just was there to listen, he stated bluntly.

"So where are you spiritually, do you know about Jesus and the Bible, or is it new for you?"

Silence. Several moments passed. Matt knew the Spirit would do the work.

"My mother was a Bible-thumper," Thomas blurted out nervously, "She prayed all the time, and was always preachin', and singin' somethin about Jesus Loving Me or something like that."

"Yeah, mine too!" quipped Bill. "My Mother was a real fanatic. She loved me even when I hated her or said I did."

"That's bull!" Jack snapped. She couldn't love someone who hated her. "That's flat out bull!"

"She said she did! She never quit coming to see me, and always tried to bail me out. She sure acted like she loved me!"

"So that's what you think love is, a broken-down woman who couldn't help a bit? Sorry, believe what you need to believe but she did that for herself. She felt guilty for being a loser. That's not love... that's bull."

"She gave all she had!"

"She had to, she's a mother! That's a job description! She did it 'cause she had to. It was guilt."

Transparency was rare in the church, not here. At times, the expletives were disquieting but the honesty refreshing. Matt would rarely interfere.

"Guys let's take a look at the book for a bit" Matt interrupted. "Turn in your Bibles to John, chapter 15 beginning at verse 13: *'Greater love has no man than this, that he lay down his life for his friends.'*" It wasn't quiet long.

"So what's that supposed to mean? Is that supposed change us? Just who in hell would give up *anything* for me? I've been stepped over by more people going to church than going to work. They make it clear, we're worthless. The world doesn't want us in or out of jail." Jack snarled.

"You're right, Jack, no one in hell would do a thing for you. We aren't talking about hell here. This is about God the Father, the true Father."

"I hated my father, still do! I hate the word father! I hate what it stands for! I would never want to be called father, and I will never be one... Never!"

Bill and Thomas nodded their agreement.

"Turn to John chapter 3 verse 16: *'For God so loved the world that He gave His one and only son, that who ever believes in Him shall not perish but have ever lasting life.'*

"See, men, God is a real father, a loving father that will never stop loving you."

"Gave his son for what? I didn't ask him to send his son, or even to send me to this world. I didn't ask to be born into a slum, to be given a mother that never married. It wasn't me that met some scum she slept with. I was just one more thing in her life that she didn't need. We're supposed to be forever grateful to God? For what?"

"Jack, the life you've been dealt probably is not fair. But God can use even this terrible stuff and make something good out of it."

"God had his chance, he created us. Now we're supposed to give him another try."

"Do you really believe that you have done a good job with what God has given you."

"Hell yes! I'm a fighter, and most times I'm a winner. You can think whatever you want about my life. You ain't got a clue of what my life has been."

"But do you really think you are what you were born to be? Do you think you have accomplished anything worth living for?"

"Are we supposed to feel all guilty about the past, and get all broken up over the loss of our potential? I'm not about to take this crap. Isn't God responsible for some of this too? Shouldn't he be the one to make us into something to be 'proud of'?" Jack leaned in close to Matt.

"Why should we care about this Jesus anyway?"

"Because He died for you!"

"Hey, man, you don't get it! I didn't ask him to die for me!"

"No, Jack, His father did."

"Why?"

"If Christ hadn't given his life for you, you really would be without hope. We all would be lost."

"Lost? I've been considered a lost cause all my life! The words sound pretty but spare me the canned stuff! 'You'd really be without hope.'"

Jack was mimicking Matt in a snotty voice.

"That's pretty, but I don't need anything that you or He offers."

"The wage of sin is death. Do you understand what that is saying? All of us sin, even you Jack, so we deserve to die. There is no way out. Jesus died without sin, so we'd have a way out!"

"So we all can go to heaven, because of him? Right!"

"Think about it this way." Matt stood and walked to the mirrored window in the back of the room.

"If tomorrow I come to the jail and say, 'Hey, how much time does Jack have left, and they say six months or a year or whatever. Suppose I say I'll change places and do the time, let him go. Then they come to you and say, 'That guy says he'll do your time if you accept his plan. You say, 'Let me think about it. No thanks I'd rather pay it myself.' No matter what I have to offer I can't set you free."

"Would you do that?" Thomas asked.

"Probably not, but that's what Jesus did."

"Ain't nobody ever offered to do anything for me. Don't need to start now."

"If you choose not to follow Him, the debt is owed by you. It's a gift. It's free, but you must accept it. If you want to be free."

"Our time's up, guys. Read in the book of John, chapters 1 through 3, and we'll talk next week. Bill, Thomas, Jack, thanks for coming. Let's end in prayer…"

"Father, thanks for bringing out the truth in each man tonight. May your Spirit go with them through this week, and may you touch them with your word as they take the time to read and pray."

"Hey, Pastor, or whatever you are, you may be coming back next week, but I'm not. I don't need this Jesus stuff. I can do fine without it."

"No problem, Jack. God calls those whom he desires. The choice to follow is up to them."

12

The third quarter was nearly over when Matt got home. He really didn't care whether the Vikes won or lost. He was still back at that jail. Jack was right; Matt probably would have or had walked over him at some time in the past. He had to do something that could begin to bring life to those who wanted hope.

He turned in his Bible and read James 1:5, *"If any of you lacks wisdom, he should ask God who gives generously to all without finding fault, and it will be given to him."* And James 2:14 *"What good is it, my brothers if a man claims to have faith but has no deeds?*

*****

The coffeepot was on early, much earlier than Connie had come to expect. She rose to find Matt in prayer and in anguish.

"What's going on, Matt?" she asked. "Are you in trouble?"

"I guess so, Connie. I guess the truth is I'm a fake. I never followed. I just took the Word, not the love to the people. I couldn't figure out why they didn't respond," Matt said with his head in his hands.

"I don't get it, Matt. What's this about, those convicts again?"

"No, Connie, it's about men that need help. They're in pain just like you and me. It's about men that I need to try to help because I say that my life is centered in God. God calls men to get dirty!

"You're getting a little preachy Matt. Get dirty?"

31

"To be a little uncomfortable for the sake of somebody else, to take this 'dying-to-self' stuff seriously."

"Aren't you being a bit hard on yourself? How many other people even care about those people in the jail, or about anybody? Most people want their jobs, their family, success, and weekends off. That's the meaning of life to them."

"All my life I thought it was about being, being a believer, being a minister, being a nice guy. It's about doing. If you aren't willing to get involved to the point of discomfort, it's just not ministry."

Matt stood and walked toward the sink, then looked out the window as he continued.

"It's not enough. The call is about submission to God and His will in my life. I know this is preachy, but I really need you to understand. I can't keep living the old way. This is a crossroad. I have to turn right or left."

Connie walked over to Matt and placed her hand on his shoulder.

"Okay, Matt, I don't get it, but I'll try to help. I'll try to understand. I'm a bit afraid. Promise me it will be His plan, not yours, and I'm in."

Matt turned and looked directly into Connie's eyes.

"It's got to be His, Connie, I can't do anything without him. I have no money, no power of my own."

Matt kissed her lightly on the cheek and touched her face with his hand. They walked back to the table…to their coffee.

"I need much more help than I can afford with the men in the jail. I believe that God has shown me how to begin. I'm going to ask corporations to get involved in a new endeavor to put people back into the work force. The economy is so strong that they are struggling to cover the jobs. They just might be interested in helping if we can get a program started."

"But how, Matt?"

"He will bring the people if we keep humble and let Him lead."

CHAPTER 13

"Holden, are you going to have coffee before you leave," Kate smiled as she asked. "Sure, Kate, let's enjoy the lake a bit."

Kate wasn't sure what had come over her husband. *Could it be another woman?* she wondered.

She knew that was always a possibility. Some women were always looking. Something was different. He even seemed a bit interested in her. Maybe he had gotten through the mid-life crisis about who he was or would be or whatever it was.

"What are you reading?" Holden asked.

"A letter from this Christian guy that wants the large corporations to get behind his idea of rehabilitating inmates into decision makers."

Kate lifted the coffee cup toward her mouth.

"What does he mean 'decision-makers'?"

"He says that he wants to start a program that teaches convicts the difference between right and wrong, and good decisions versus bad. Start from the beginning, I guess. He dropped the information off at the head office, and I just happened to get a copy."

"Is this guy's name Tom or Matt or something, because I think we got something like that in our mail?"

Holden sipped his coffee and continued.

"I only have one question. What does he know that hundreds of others haven't tried? Those guys in jail are a sorry mess. Lord knows Litany has enough set aside for work in the community. We just haven't found the right place to put it."

Holden smiled as he contemplated using this guy's ministry to get Jack out. He knew there could be a conflict when he needed to get the Social Security card copy if Jack stayed in jail.

"I'm going to look into the possibility of helping this guy. We certainly could give a bit to help those who are less fortunate. For some reason, this hits at an interesting time. I have felt a real desire to get involved in the lives of the down and out."

"Maybe you are starting to grow, Holden. They say that beginning to care for others is a sign of maturity."

"Who knows, maybe I am. This could be the beginning of a whole new way of life."

CHAPTER 14

Matt couldn't believe the response from his few mailings. Two of the largest corporations in Minnesota and one national firm replied and offered their support when the format was worked out.

"Format, what format?" he just knew that something had to be done. He began to feel small. *What could he offer?* These companies were going to demand a plan. He was just a driver, a delivery boy. How could he talk to major corporate types?

Lord, I'm not sure that you got the right guy, I have little to offer.

He had to talk to Connie. She had a much better feel for this stuff.

Matt was home early, and supper was nearly finished when Connie arrived from work. She was pleasantly surprised, and a bit suspicious when they sat down to eat.

After saying Grace, Matt filled his plate and sat quietly for a while.

"Connie, can you help me get some plan together for this new idea. I sent out the feelers to the corporations, and they responded. I really don't feel qualified to set something up that will fly."

"Matt, you're fine. You aren't the head of this thing, remember?"

"I know, but I just need to talk this out with someone."

"Let's start at the beginning. What are you trying to accomplish with this idea?"

"I just want to have something to offer those who want to try a new way of life."

"So would it help to work on getting them out on bail? Maybe they could put up bail for the ones that you feel have potential."

"I really don't want to oversee choosing. I'm a sucker for a slick story." Matt stirred his fried potatoes with his fork.

"Well, someone's going to have to be in control. Maybe you can find a way to tell which ones He really is calling. Whatever—you can't worry about these things until they become a reality. This is about a plan, His plan."

"Okay, I'll start with the bail idea, and having a weekly study after release. I'm not certain that I can offer much more time at this point. My job takes five full days, but nights are free.

"Maybe you could talk to the church. They may have some people that would want to help. We just need faith, Matt. How many corporations that replied are local?"

"There are three that are in the cities. Their corporate offices are right downtown. Maybe I could meet with them all within a couple of days, or even in the same day."

"Maybe, you only need one right now, until you get the rest of the plan up and running. You'd better talk to all of them, or at least send them a letter of thanks and the agenda."

"Wait a minute, what did you say?

"You need to thank them?"

"No, before that, did you say maybe you only need one?"

"Yes, but…"

"That's it! Maybe I should start with one guy, and build on that? Maybe that's what God's plan is about. How did Jesus do it? He picked them one by one, and the Father brought them to him."

"Well, Matt, do you have someone in mind?"

"Yes, but he said he wasn't coming again."

CHAPTER 15

The cell seemed to be shrinking daily. Jack hardly slept since that stupid Monday night Bible study. He really felt that he had made some good points, and that he was right about how people felt. This Jesus stuff had angered him since he was old enough to remember.

He was over it and then this preacher came in and started it all over again. This stuff about owing a debt for the sin in your life, it was just one more way of trying to control the crowd. Most people wanted to be led by someone. Jack wasn't one of them!

He had read the first three chapters of John every day. He would be ready to take this guy apart on Monday night. There was stuff in there about another thing that angered him… "Born Again"! The "club" that every one of these fanatics joined; the "Born Again Christians."

The guy was right about some of the stuff. Jack really hadn't done a great job with his life, but whose fault was that? *Sure, he had made some bad decisions. He had to! He wanted to eat and survive.*

How many times had Jack walked the streets wishing that he could experience a real family, a real home? He had no rules to follow. He had no one to care. He hated rules in school! The fact that he had nothing did not go unnoticed. The kids with homes had clean clothes and money for pencils and notebooks, they noticed. Jack pretended he didn't care. He was stuck as Jack. He had learned to make do.

He learned intimidation had merit. The rest of the kids feared his don't give a damn approach to life. They were afraid of getting caught…so he controlled his own little world with fear.

What troubled Jack most, he had no friends. There were those that followed, but none he could trust. Jack realized he had never really trusted anyone. He never really loved anyone. He was sure that no one ever loved him. Well maybe his mother, but that was only because she felt guilty.

The guy said that God loved him. That's what his mother said too! Well it's a strange way to show love. Jack continued to pace the cell. The other men had long decided to steer clear of this man, nobody asked him anything.

Jack's picture of God was this huge king with a set of rules. Eventually, when men didn't meet His expectations, he'd lower the boom.

What if I buy this Jesus stuff, and I don't measure up? What if Jesus can't help me? What then?

He was thinking like a crazy man. This had to stop!

CHAPTER 16

There was enough cherry wood in the office to make Matt realize that the cost of computers had more than a small profit built with the 56K Modem. The Metro Building was without equal in the Twin Cities. The exterior was Italian marble with gold trim and black glass.

Mr. Jeffries's office was on the forty-second floor. The appointment was at 10:00 AM. Matt dressed for the occasion, but his dress Dockers and loafers from JC Penney's didn't seem to fit in with the silk suits and Italian shoes he encountered in the elevator.

Now he knew how Moses must have felt when he went to see Pharaoh. As he watched the floors pass by through the glass Matt felt ridiculously small.

He made a valiant effort not to look like a tourist when he entered the front office. The cherry panels, gold signage, Tiffany lamps and two-inch thick carpeting, were something he had never experienced. The beauty took his breath.

"May I help you, sir?" the lovely voice from behind the desk asked.

"I am here to see Mr. Jeffries. My name is Matt Roth. I believe I have an appointment."

"Mr. Jeffries will be with you in a moment. May I get you something to drink, coffee...a soda?"

"Coffee would be nice."

When the coffee arrived, he was amazed; the flavor was fresh ground, and the finest he had tasted. It was served in a gold embossed English China cup.

"Mr. Jeffries will see you now."

"Thank you," Matt said and followed the young lady through the labyrinth to the back of the forty-second floor.

The office of Holden Jeffries was intimidating. Matt was certain that his first church had less floor space.

The carpeting was white plush with a fifteen-by-fifteen-foot Persian Rug centered in the sitting area. The mahogany desk was at least seven feet long and had a carving of Holden and the company logo centered in the front. There were personal photos of Holden with some of the wealthiest people in the world. Matt recognized three presidents.

The walls were decorated with prints and tapestries from all over the globe. Many had small brass plaques noting names and dates of the gift. There was a six-foot wide cabinet in the corner that displayed awards won for each new program developed by Litany since 1970. To the left of the desk Matt saw a stone fireplace and two leather sofas.

On the wall above the fireplace was a fifty-inch Sony plasma television. There was a full-size bar to the left of the fireplace that extended into the room. Beneath the bar Matt noticed refrigerated drawers for cans of soda and mix. The entire west wall was floor to ceiling windows. The view of downtown Minneapolis was spectacular.

Holden entered and took a seat on the leather sofa, motioning for Matt to join him.

"I must say that I am interested in hearing about your plan to make something out of men in the jails of Minnesota."

Holden smiled and waited.

"Well, sir, I do a Monday night Bible study at the Moss County Jail just north of the cities."

"I know where that is, but what's the plan. You say that you want to change these men. Do you think a once a week Bible study will do it? I guess I was expecting something a bit more...extensive."

"Exactly...these men...not all of them...but some of them... come to find out about a new way of living. Some have never considered spiritual things. The problem is that I can tell them what the

Bible says, but I have little else to offer them. I leave them with no more of a future than they had when we met."

Matt sensed that Holden was not buying this. He continued.

"Even with faith, men need the basics. They need to know that when they begin to make good decisions, good things start to happen. Unfortunately, the police mark many of these men because they have past problems. The added stress and surveillance make their potential for change poor. So their basic scenario is to learn to get by, not to get better."

"I don't understand, Mr. Roth. What are we at Litany being asked to do?"

"Actually, sir, I really want to start slow. I'd like to choose one of the inmates—one that I think has potential—sort of like a disciple. I would need to be able to post his bail, and of course there would be specific rules and consequences for non-compliance."

Matt watched Holden's eyes, but got no clue.

"I am only planning on getting involved part-time. I intend to continue my delivery job during the day and working with this in evenings or on weekends."

"Are you certain that you want to take on this kind of responsibility? What do you gain?"

Holden shifted his weight and crossed his legs.

"That's a good question. The truth is, I would rather not get involved. I like my life simple, but Jesus is my Lord. That may sound fanatical, but He's calling me to make some tough decisions."

Matt caught the thin smile on Holden's face. This man was not a believer.

"I believe God loves these people as much as He loves you and me. Wouldn't it be wonderful to see some of these guys become productive citizens? It probably sounds unrealistic, but it really is up to God whether it works or fails."

"Can you really be certain what God wants you to do? Do you hear His voice or something? I have a Board of Directors. They are very vocal. Even with that, many times I am uncertain."

"I guess I just have to have faith."

"Well, Matt, this meeting was about how we can help, not whether we would. Do you have some idea of what kind of budget you will need for this?"

"Actually, I have no idea."

"I can make decisions of under $25,000 without the approval of the Board, so let's say that we put aside $15,000 and keep the other $10,000 for future needs."

Matt was speechless.

"We will never need all of that, Mr. Jeffries. I will keep records of any expenditures and I will not abuse your generosity. You can trust me."

"I must say, I may not understand you, but I certainly do trust you. Maybe someday I'll come along on one of your Monday nights."

"I'd be honored by your presence any time, Mr. Jeffries."

"I'm sorry, Matt, but I have another meeting in fifteen minutes, and I have some preparations to finish."

"I will keep you informed of our progress, Mr. Jeffries. Thank you so much! And God bless you, and your future."

Holden wondered where these people learned this stuff. This guy seemed to have some education, some common sense. He was making a conscious decision to throw it all away on something that had little potential for success.

Holden smiled but was more amazed than amused.

The chance of Matt Roth ever making a difference with even one of these losers was minimal. How many treatment centers existed just in Minneapolis? What gave this guy the idea that he was special?

Holden was disappointed. Matt had little potential to help him with his predicament with Jack. Matt was a nobody who was committed to remaining one. But the corporation could use the write-off, and it would look good in his obituary.

CHAPTER 17

Fifty thousand dollars in small bills was a pile of money. Holden was familiar with large numbers, but even he was a bit taken back when he saw the money in the suitcase.

He had made withdrawals of $10,000 from five different accounts acquired over the years for just this purpose. Holden had saved this money as insurance in the case that his marriage had ever failed. It certainly would come in handy now. It would provide cash for the interim when he would be out of sight while the trail cooled.

Holden and Kate rarely spoke of money. Kate was totally confident in Holden's ability to handle their financial affairs. This was a great comfort to Holden especially since he had not been totally honest.

On the anniversary of his first year as CEO, Holden opened the first of several numbered accounts in the Caribbean. Throughout the next several years he had transferred nearly five million tax-free dollars into foreign banks. The family still maintained ample funds spread in many different areas; stocks, bonds, gold, Certificates of Deposit, mutual funds and cash, but Kate never knew just how wealthy they really were…or he was.

Holden was certain that he had covered the transfers well enough for divorce lawyers, but what if the Fed's got into it after he was found to be missing? Why would they if he kept his head?"

There was so much preparation needed. He had to get to work on this new identity. He needed to buy a car and store it for future use. He had to find a place to hide out. He had to stash the cash and clothes. He had bus tickets to buy, and canoes to purchase and hide. He had fishing-trips to plan and none of it could be done in the name of Holden Jeffries.

How could that idiot Jack get picked up? He was supposed to be a street-smart slick. Holden could see that he needed to look for another possible identity. There had to be another Jack out there. He felt betrayed by this loser. Now he'd have to start all over.

CHAPTER 18

It was dark when Matt pulled up in front of the jail. He couldn't help but wonder what he was doing at this place.

Why would God, the Living God, the Omnipotent, the Omniscient, the Father of All Mankind, call Matt to submit to following Him to this place? Matt began to feel a bit ridiculous. Why couldn't he just accept life as enough? Why did he have to get so preachy, and melodramatic?

He had failed in the ministry. He had failed in almost everything he tried. This whole idea was probably self-contrived to make him feel important. He would go inside and get over this idea that he could make a difference in the world.

He would offer them *"the Word"* and get back to realism. He was embarrassed to think of just how far he had taken all this "called" stuff. He had even visited corporations. They must still be laughing about his plan.

"Lord, forgive me for my self-serving attitude. Forgive the way that I tried to use your name and your call to bring glory to myself. As I go forth tonight please take control."

Matt hesitated, then continued,

> *"Forgive me for trying to lead. Take this ministry to those you call. In Jesus's name, Amen."*

45

Jack had told himself all day that he wasn't going to the Bible study. He would just tell the jailer that he had changed his mind. It was useless, and there was lots of stuff on TV worth his time.

Jack knew that nothing could really be done for someone that had lived opposite the law. Still, when they called "Bible Study" Jack got up and headed for the library. It probably was just to see this guy squirm when the tough questions came out.

Jack reached the library and realized he was the only one who had come. *What about Thomas? What about Bill?* There was no way he was going to stay, but he sat down.

"That's it for tonight," the jailer said.

"Thanks. I'll let you know when we're finished," Matt nodded at the jailer.

"Jack, its great to see you again, I have thought about you every day."

"Right! I'll bet you could hardly sleep."

"Before we start, let's bow our heads and pray."

Matt prayed some stuff Jack didn't really understand. Then he began.

"Jack, did you get a chance to read the passages we talked about?"

"I looked at them a bit," Jack said, "just what are you trying to get me to see with this stuff?"

"Let's turn to John 1:1. What do you see in these first few verses, anything that gives you some idea of God? Why do you think that the word "*Word*" is capitalized? What does that usually signify?

"It's the name of somebody."

"Exactly. '*In the beginning was the Word and the Word was with God and the Word was God. He was with God from the beginning.*' See Jack, whoever this was, this Word person, he has always existed, and not only was he with God, but he was God.

Jack sat expressionless, staring at the wall to his left.

"This shows us that there are just going to be things that are above our understanding. I have no choice but to believe it by faith or reject it as impossible."

"Why even worry about it? Why should we care?"

"You know, Jack, that's a really good point. If it is true, then we must deal with it because our entire future in eternity depends on what we do with it. You see if it's true, then we must either accept it or reject it. There is no place to hide. There is no middle of the road. He either is or isn't. If He is, we have to follow or walk away. One way is life, the other is death and darkness, hopelessness."

Jack sat looking at the wall. *Idle chatter, that's all it is.*

"There's more, let's go on, *'Through Him all things were made; without Him nothing was made that has been made. In Him was life, and that life was the light of men. The light shines in the darkness, but darkness has not understood it.'* I think you are very much aware of what that darkness is like, Jack."

"You got no right to say stuff like that. You're not any better than anybody else."

"You're exactly right, Jack, but I don't have to carry the weight of it anymore like you do."

"You really are full of shit! I'm not carrying anything that I don't want to carry. I have a right to my own life."

"You can keep any of it you want, Jack. But doesn't it get tiring, walking around without any answers, without any way out of the hole."

"What hole?"

"Jack, God knows everything about you. He wants to help; He really wants to set you free from the darkness."

"Darkness... I'm telling you that's bull?"

"Jack, be honest, wouldn't you like to begin again, to be free to start over, with hope and a future? God can give you that again."

"What if he doesn't think I deserve a new beginning."

"None of us deserve it, but all of us can receive it. God doesn't say 'clean up your act, and I'll come in.' He says, 'Let me come in and I'll clean up your act.' He only knows what you are meant to be, and what He can make of you if you will believe and accept His love."

"How can He love me? You really don't know me—what I'm like—where I've been—how far from your life I live. What if He doesn't want me? No one has ever wanted me, not my father, not teachers, not school, not the city. I'm not sure my mother would have stayed if she didn't feel like she had to."

"Jack, turn to Revelation 3:20."

The library was silent as Matt helped Jack find the passage.

> Behold, I stand at the door and knock. If anyone hears my voice and opens the door, I will come in and eat with him, and he with me.

"See, Jack, the words are in red, which means that Jesus spoke them. He says that he stands at the door of your heart knocking."

Matt took a chance and placed his hand on Jack's shoulder.

"The reason that I can come and tell you that you are welcome is the next part. If *anyone* opens the door, I *will* come in. See, it doesn't say that God checks you out to see if you are okay, all He asks is that you open the door."

The tears welled up in Jack's eyes, but the burning was a welcome relief from the bottled-up anger that had plagued him for years. Fifteen minutes earlier he would rather have died than started crying. Men just didn't cry in Jack's world.

As the tears streamed, Jack felt warmth enter him that seemed to fill a hole that had existed for decades. Jack was experiencing emotions unlike anything he had expected. Where had this come from? Had Jesus really entered his heart? He actually felt like praying. The pastor had tears in his eyes too. Jack realized that this guy really did care, possibly the first person that had cared in all his life.

"Can I say a prayer, Pastor?"

"Sure, Jack, do you want help?"

"No, I'm okay. *God, I have been running from something all my life, probably from accepting the life that you gave me. I feel like for the first time that it's okay to be me. I want to tell you how sorry I am for the terrible way that I have lived my life, for the many times that I made fun of you and those who talked about you.*

He was forced to stop and swallow and wipe his nose and eyes.

I'm sorry for the way I turned away everyone you sent my way. I have cussed at them, spit on them, even hated what they said. I want you to forgive me, God, please forgive me of this stuff.

The truth was floating to the top, years of darkness were experiencing light.

I don't ever want to feel that empty again. Please don't take the warmth away from inside me. You have filled the hole for the first time. Help me do something with what's left of my life.

And thanks for sending this guy here and giving him the strength to keep talking even when I didn't want to listen. So many times, I have wanted someone to care, thanks for bringing someone.

Jack was sobbing through the prayer. Matt wasn't certain what to do, he'd never experienced anything like this before. *What a God we serve. This guy was a nobody, yet the "Author of All Life" stopped and touched him in this tiny room in the middle of nowhere.* "Jack are you aware that you just made one of the most important decisions of your entire life? You have just begun a new life. You are a new creation."

Matt smiled investigating the face of the man before him. Red eyes and all, something about him really did look new.

"I just want to feel this way forever!"

"What way?"

"It's like everything is brand new. I feel like I am free. I feel like I have a future."

"Jack, I'm going to see if I can get you out on bail. I have found some funds that I can use to help. Would you be interested in working with me when you get out? I would want to study with you at least once a week."

"Pastor, right now getting out isn't as important as it was a couple of hours ago, but sure, if you can work it out. Whatever it takes—I can't believe I'm even saying this, I sound like Randy."

"Randy?"

"Yeah, he's a guy I liked to make fun of because he was getting' religious. Now I really can see why he smiles a lot."

CHAPTER 19

The message his machine played seemed almost like a bad joke. "Bible Study Matt" was requesting money for bail for his first disciple. Holden could not have cared less until the end, "he's a guy from the city named Jack Grayton."

It was impossible! This guy was about to get Jack out without any manipulation. His name wouldn't be involved. Maybe this God had a sense of humor.

He threw the last of the stuff in the back of his car. Kate was visiting her friend across town and knew he was heading out for a business trip. Holden was on his way to the BWCA. Holden had driven it a hundred times usually with friends and great expectations. The Boundary Waters Canoe Area is a labyrinth of lakes and rock, which has been nationally protected as a true American wilderness. Over one million acres of water, portages, trees, campsites, and hiding places...it was perfect.

The area has changed little since its unveiling when the glaciers melted ten thousand years earlier. The fishing was great in the spring, and most of the summer, but this was winter. It was a five-hour drive and anything but a pleasure trip. Holden had airtight packs with clothes, shoes, and other items he would need in the future. They must be placed where he and no one else could easily find them.

CHAPTER 20

The bail hearing went without incident. Matt found a lawyer who was willing to look at the case. When he read the report, he laughed. The police had been so confident of the outcome they had cut corners to the point of idiocy. The attorney found no less than twelve legal loopholes. Jack would never face the charges. There was no chance that Jack would see the inside of a courtroom much less a jail.

To Jack the last few days had seemed much more like a dream than reality. What had happened? Matt had told him that he was a new creation. Like so much of the religious talk he had heard before, Jack wasn't certain of the meaning. But there were new feelings inside.

Jack woke with a smile. He had no money, no job, no future. He found meaning in just living. How could he explain? Jack was free to return to his street life, but he wasn't certain that his street life still existed. It was almost as if the darkness of the street couldn't exist around him anymore.

He was afraid he would return to the old ways. He never dreaded this life before. It was as if he had been cured of some lifelong illness. He was afraid to go back to downtown, but he had nowhere else to go.

"Hey, Jack, where the hell have you been?" Willie the beggar whined. "I can't get nothin' done alone you know. The jobs just don't come like they do when you're around."

"Willie, I'm not sure that you're going to be that happy that I'm back."

"What the hell are you talkin' about, Jack? I always am happy when you come back." Willie smiled…it was a worried little smile.

The word "hell" had a new ring to it. Jack couldn't remember being bothered by someone using it before. He had noticed guys using Jesus's name as a swear word in the jail. It was as if he heard the words for the first time. Now the same words, especially Jesus, or Christ, or God, bothered him.

"Willie, you probably aren't going to believe this, but I learned something that changed my life in that jail."

"Well you sure got out early. You must have learned something that you didn't know before."

"It's not about getting out. It's about a whole new meaning to life. See, Willie, I found someone that really cares and can make a difference even in a crummy place like this."

"Crummy? Jack, this is where you live. It's all you got." Now Willie really was worried.

"I don't think so, not anymore. See, Willie, I'm not the same old Jack. I've got a life to live. I've got to help others see that there really is something worth living for—something that we are all born to do. God really wants us to find the purpose in the life he has given us."

"Geeze, Jack, you sound like the preachers at the Mission. What the hell happened?"

"God touched my life, and I learned to love—love life, love God, love even you, Willie." Jack tried to reach out, but Willie backed away.

"If you got religion, how you going to live out here? You know what I mean. Jack, you gotta eat."

"This Bible says that God will provide. He'll just have to provide for me. God loves us all and knows what we need so I'm just going to wait and see."

"Wait and see? You really mean that?"

"I don't remember ever feeling happiness. It's here now, and it is far better than food, or a room filled with darkness. I can't explain it. I think that God really does care. I've never had a friend that I could trust. Jesus is my friend." Jack's eyes were watery, it seemed to be happening often.

"Jesus is in church. You are out here in the street. Jack, this is about livin' and starvin'. I like you, but I can barely take care of myself. I ain't going to be able to help you too."

"Watch, Willie. You may find that you want to get to know Jesus too. Just watch, I know I don't have to worry anymore."

"Well, you got me worried! And what about the job? If they hear you got religion, they're gonna get real worried. Might want to give you a reason to keep your mouth shut. Ya' know what I'm talkin' about?"

"Willie, you worry too much! This God I just met can take care of it all. I'm not about to start running. I'm certainly not going back to the old way, so guess I'll just have to trust God for the answer."

"Great, Jack, but when they find you with your head beat in I ain't about to feel sorry. I did my job. I told you to be smarter. I ain't takin' no blame. If gettin' to know God makes you this stupid, I can tell you right now it ain't for me!"

CHAPTER 21

The news of his death shook the corporate ladder. Holden Jeffries had been well liked and an innovator for nearly three decades. The accolades poured in from some of the wealthiest and most powerful businessmen in the United States and around the world. He was gone.

Kate took the news badly. The life they had grown into took much of the luster off their marriage. Why had she waited to tell him how tired of the whole money thing she had become?

Two weeks had passed. There had been a steady stream of helpers and friends. Many of them came from the world that had consumed her life. The corporate world would put on its best face for the next few weeks then all would be back to normal. Kate found it incredulous that Holden's position had already been filled, his office cleared and boxed up. His picture was posted in the hallway and the boardroom—all neat and finished. This was the legacy Holden had worked to develop. History would remember—but not often.

The police never found the body. They found a canoe on a lake somewhere in the Boundary Waters Canoe Area. Holden's friends had told her that he had gone fishing at ten o'clock at night. She knew little about fishing. It seemed strange, but the guys had assured Kate that Holden loved night fishing.

When Holden did not return by 7:00 AM, the rest took out their canoes to search. At 10:00 AM on June 10, they found the empty canoe capsized on a large lake in the middle of nowhere. There was no sign of Holden. They found some items when they dragged the lake: a fishing pole, his life vest, a tackle box, a jacket with his keys and wallet, but no body.

The search lasted ten days, then they just called it off, and the coroner declared him officially dead. The currents could have swept the body all the way to Canada by now. They never really expected to find Holden, but someone with his position deserved their best attempt.

Kate put the house up for sale on July 1, sold it on the tenth and vowed never to look back. Life had to be more than this. The farm was empty, and she would try to heal there.

CHAPTER 22

Healing is a painful process. Kate had hoped that hiding from her world would spare her from the memories and the questions. It did not. She moved into her childhood home and immediately began the process of bringing it into the nineties.

Wallpaper had to be peeled, carpeting was ripped up, new cabinets in the kitchen, shingles and siding, all made the days livable. The nights came too early, and the tear-ridden thoughts of the past and a future alone came like waves on an empty beach.

She hadn't spoken to anyone other than the carpenters for nearly six weeks. Haunted memories and guilt were her only companions as the darkness descended on the farmhouse.

The lack of sleep made little difference. The questions would roll through her mind like thunder during a summer rainstorm. The answers and sleep eluded her. Perhaps there were no answers. Perhaps there would be no comfort.

Kate had wonderful memories of the early years when Holden seemed to love her more than life. She found him to be easy to manipulate in those days. His needs and wants were simple. Holden hadn't experienced business success, and Kate's attention was the barometer of his importance.

She used his desire to obtain her wants. When she wasn't happy with his actions, she would merely withhold intimacy until he saw his error. It worked so easily...but?

Eventually he sought attention from other sources. In the end, he rarely looked at her with those adoring eyes that she had loved in their youth. The marriage seemed hollow even before Holden died.

Where had she learned to use love rather than to just love? Was she really a cold person?

Holden had fallen in love with success, and she became his possession rather than his passion.

"What's the difference?" she cried. "He had to die before I saw myself. We would never have changed. It would have been far too difficult to experience this pain."

The clarity was amazing…how little it mattered. What kind of a God could bring all this pain into the lives of his creation? She realized she hated God more each day. He had never lived up to his billing—he was never in control.

CHAPTER 23

Winter's chill remains in the water of the BWCA far into the summer months. Early June can be deadly to the unprepared. Holden had swamped the canoe quietly, but the icy water had been reluctant to give up its prey. The hypothermia and the intake of large volumes of water had nearly cost him his future. He dragged himself onto shore and ran in place for ten minutes to get the circulation back into his body. The change of clothes and the other canoe were right where he had left them. He paddled and portaged the six miles to a small bay just outside of town. He found the rotted dock of the abandoned campsite and dragged the Grumman ashore. There were many small cabins and old homesites along the shoreline. Holden had chosen carefully. He placed the canoe upside down and leaned it against the moss-covered woodpile at the rear of the cabin. The sun was beginning to rise in the eastern sky as Holden slipped out of his wet clothes and put on the Wrangler jeans and red cotton Eddy Bauer shirt. He slipped on hiking boots and placed the wet clothes into a Ziplock bag, then tucked them into the bottom of the duffle bag. He was careful to walk out of sight of the road until he was near the edge of town. As he rounded the corner and sat outside the Greyhound stop, he kept his head down. Nobody seemed to care. He was just another nobody on the way to nowhere. All the way to Chicago, not one person even acknowledged his presence.

He arrived in early in the morning on June 12. He went immediately to the subway, then directly to downtown. He had booked a room at the downtown Holiday Inn at Mart Plaza. The registration desk was on the Fifteenth floor, so the street riffraff was kept at bay. The chance of Holden being recognized was minimal since the hotel catered mainly to gift-buyers, airline pilots and flight attendants.

Holden had paid in advance for two weeks and would rest up for the next phase. He could leave for good in five to six weeks.

He let his beard grow and saw no reason to trim his hair. He walked the streets of Chicago and smiled as the corporate world melted away. There was no remorse, no looking back. The dream was on the horizon.

Holden entered a Starbucks, ordered a Café' Mocha, took a corner table away from the window and read the newspaper while he sipped. A young professional woman entered, purchased her coffee and sat reading nearby. Holden caught the scent of her, and Kate appeared in his memory.

He tried to read faster, but the memory wouldn't fade. He really didn't want to deal with this. She had offered him little of her life in the last few years. He certainly didn't need her tainting his present or his future.

Did he ever love her? He loved a different Kate, a Kate that needed him, or needed something in the early years. She seemed enthralled with his insight then. While she was never subservient, she was interested in him. She held his arm and snuggled against him and put her nose near his neck.

She made him feel as if he was important. He wanted to win the world for her. She was a beautifully soft woman, and he adored her. Somewhere it had been lost. The television, the newspaper, almost all of life replaced their conversations. Their life together became a shell.

Holden had made success his lover. He had no remorse. The true love of his life had turned cold and he would not beg for attention. There were plenty of sources for satisfaction in the corporate world. *Then why did I want to kill myself, why wasn't it enough?*

The business world is like a prostitute. It is willing to give whatever fantasy the buyer desires if the payment is high enough. There is nothing real about it. The corporate demands are insatiable. Fanaticism becomes a necessity.

The saddest realization for Holden came when the prize lost its glitter. The money, toys, and trappings just began to rust. He was left within another shell of a love affair. This one nearly cost him his life.

"Are you finished?"

He nodded and smiled as he handed the paper to the voice.

If you only knew?

It had been five weeks and four days since he had gotten off that bus. Tomorrow he would begin the final phase. He was tired of the city. He smiled at the thought of the millions waiting in that bank in Grand Cayman.

The next morning, he arrived in Merrillville to find the car in the rented garage just as he left it. The suitcase and the bag with the fifty thousand dollars were in the trunk just as he had left them. The '94 Regal was no Lexus, but it wouldn't turn any heads. Holden rolled down the windows, took a deep breath and smiled like he hadn't done in years. Jack Grayton II was free!

One stop, then on to Midway. The Super America would do fine.

He filled the tank and headed inside to pay. When he walked out, he heard the screaming of the tires, and caught a glimpse of the Regal as it sped out of the lot. He had no idea who was at the wheel, but as quickly as it had begun, the dream died.

The car was gone. Gone with the new life.

Holden's heart pounded in his chest, and instant pain imbedded itself in his brain. The sun felt hotter than he had ever experienced as he was immediately drenched in perspiration. He caught himself as he was about to scream out…he had to be careful. He couldn't make a scene. He walked weakly back to the front of the station and tried to find a shady spot to sit for a moment…he needed to think.

What now? How could I be such an idiot? All the money…the clothes, the briefcase with the account numbers, the passport…all gone.

He hadn't locked the car, but all the stuff was in the trunk, why would anyone think it was worth stealing?

Why didn't I keep some of the money in another place, or the tickets in my pocket, or the account numbers in my wallet?

He was alone. He was a nobody with nothing. No one knew or cared. He was Jack Grayton!

Holden had one hundred eighty-six dollars and some change in his pocket. He had to forget the anger building inside him.

Where should he sleep the night?

He had enough money for a couple of nights if he didn't get to fancy, but what then?

The Wayside Rest Motel wasn't the worst Holden had seen, but it was several notches below his taste. The office was a converted room, with a computer table, a phone, a board on the wall with some keys, and the filthiest, fattest, greasiest, receptionist Holden had ever experienced. He was in his forties, and his Cubs hat probably dated back to the time when they were winning—it was tilted to the right just above his eyes. The bill was bent but not like it had been planned, just bent.

"Got a room?"

"Yep, one bed or two?"

"One will do. How much is it?"

"You want my cheapest room?"

"What's it like?"

"It's not a bad room, got a bed, a dresser, TV, you know pretty much got it all?"

"How much is it?"

"Thirty-two bucks in advance."

"Do you have something a little better?"

"You want my best room?"

"What makes it your best room? I mean…what's it got that the other room doesn't have?"

"'It's got color TV, a phone, and a clock radio…real nice."

"How much?"

"Thirty-five bucks."

Holden tried not to smirk. "That's probably the one I want. Is there any special price if I stay longer than a day?"

"Can let you have it for thirty if you stay a week. Gotta know soon, 'cause weekends get pretty busy."

"Yeah, I'll bet this place is a weekend retreat for lots of folks."

"I can let you know tomorrow. Is there a place to eat nearby?"

"So you're stayin' then?"

"At least for a night."

"Rusty Skillet."

"What?"

"Rusty Skillet—the place to eat. It's about a block to your left. Not bad food. Don't let the name scare you. Uh, I'll need the thirty-five to hold the room though."

The Rusty Skillet wasn't quite as bad as its name. The coffee was fresh, the clientele not. The ventilation system was pathetic. Everybody walked out smelling like cigarette smoke that had been fried in bacon grease.

He took the corner booth. Even in his work clothes he looked overdressed. He had to get a plan together while he still had some cash. He had to get a job. How—with his identity? He couldn't turn in wages. He would have to find odd jobs for cash. He needed to find something soon. Even at thirty bucks a night he had to have some money in four to five days.

"Can I get you anything with your coffee?" the voice asked politely.

Holden hadn't even noticed her when she had brought his coffee, but the voice got his attention. It was soft and feminine. As he turned toward the voice he was taken by her eyes, they were deep and peaceful. She was beautiful yet it was understated—her fragrance was fresh, soapy, she had shoulder length dark curly hair, an oval face with an olive complexion, full lips and a dainty nose, but those eyes…

"I'm sorry, miss, I have just been so engrossed in thought that I have ignored you. Do you have a menu?"

"It's right there against the wall in the holder. We serve breakfast all day, but the morning special is done at eleven. My name is Angela. I'll give you a couple of minutes and get you a refill on your coffee."

"So are you staying close by?" Angela asked.

"Yes, over at the Wayside. How did you know?"

"You walked up…no car. Thought you probably were either staying somewhere, or that you got dropped off by your wife or something."

"So are you watching me, or what?"

"I watch everybody. I'm always interested in a stranger that looks out of place. You look really down." Angela tilted her head then smiled.

"I just got into town. It's hard to fit in when you don't know a soul, and the money is running out."

"You don't talk like most men. I've heard a lot of losers. They don't have your vocabulary."

"Angela, that's a pretty name. Have you always been a waitress?"

"You're good, don't answer, just change the subject. So you think you could help around here if I could get you a job at the restaurant? You're going to need someplace to stay. If I know the Wayside, you gotta be paying at least $25 a night."

"Thirty-five."

"That's ridiculous. Did you pay him yet?" she asked with and edge to her voice.

"There weren't any other options. Without the money he wouldn't hold the room."

"I can try to get some *options* for you to consider, but I need to do some calling. I'll have a little more information for you if you come by here tomorrow for breakfast. Now what can I get for you to eat?"

Holden was hungry when the burger arrived. For some strange reason things seemed to be better.

Curious…

He took another bite of the burger and looked around the restaurant.

Small town USA.

Holden had worked with people that had a net-worth in the millions. The wealthy never chose to get close to someone. Their money could always cover their obligations. Distance was a great insulator from personal involvement.

"Can I ask you something, Angela?"

"What?"

"Why are you doing this?"

"You need help," she said, then her eyes turned a bit serious. "Why, what would you do?"

Holden didn't answer. If he had nothing to gain, he probably wouldn't have considered helping God himself."

He realized years ago that decisions like this wasted time of the common people and kept them from getting ahead. Angela and others like her would spend money and time they didn't have to help someone that could offer nothing in return.

No wonder she's still working in this dump.

"You think I'm stupid for helping, don't you?"

"I just have never figured out people." Holden lied.

"You mean that you aren't sitting there wondering why I am wasting my time? That's not what your eyes just said."

"Oh, so you now read eyes as well as being a student of the down and out?"

She laughed and made a statement that Holden should have expected. "God wants us to love everyone. No matter whether rich or poor, sick or well, old or young. He asks us to be a servant to all by being a servant to Him. Maybe it's God you need to understand."

There it was. The curse of the ignorant—guilt. He should have known...another "believer."

"If God were going to help, he probably would have started long before I met you. I think He's getting quite a laugh out of all of this."

By the time Holden reached the motel, it was getting dark, and the neon certainly helped the looks of the place. It reminded him of the memories of the county fair. It always amazed him how a gravel parking lot with a bunch of tin sheds and empty barns could be transformed into a four-day long, arena of excitement.

The transformation was never quite so evident as when daylight turned to darkness. The half-painted, broken-down carnival became ablaze with neon. It was as if brand new. Holden was always a victim of facade.

As Holden turned the key in the paint peeled door, he struggled to define his feelings. He went to sleep without watching TV. Tomorrow had to be a better.

CHAPTER 24

"*K*ate? Kate, is that really you? What are you doing in town?"

Kate nearly tripped as she turned toward the unfamiliar voice. As she focused, she recognized one of her closest friends from her school days, Tony Minelli. She had not seen or talked to him since before her wedding.

"I guess I'm trying to find the past a bit. I came home to put the farm back together, and maybe myself with it."

"Kate, you could have looked me up."

"Tony, it's about me. Holden died in a fishing accident. He drowned! I have lost so much of what I used to be, that I guess I can't be certain that I want to even relate to anyone, even my old best friend."

"I'm alone too. Jen and I split nearly ten years ago. Seems she found someone who would listen and care more appealing than someone who paid bills. Really, I was pretty bad as a husband."

Kate looked down the aisle of the grocery store. She was a bit uncomfortable by Tony's openness.

"Guess I've always been much more committed when commitment wasn't mandatory. I've never been much good at anything mandatory. I have no desire to make this a relationship…we have a relationship. We've had one since third grade.

Tony never seemed concerned about perceptions of others.

"It's about caring. Sure, we lost touch, but look at us, nothing has changed, you probably haven't been this honest with anyone since Holden died, have you? Well, have you!?" Tony grabbed her arm and smiled.

Kate turned her head and smiled back. She realized that she hadn't laughed much lately.

"Tony, why can't you at least sympathize with me? Why can't you be like the others and let me be?"

"Let you be what, miserable? You didn't kill the guy. I know all about the guilt and the second-guessing. Most of the time, I was quite sure that everything was my fault."

"You just said that it was your fault. You weren't being attentive enough."

"No, I mean everything, not just the marriage—my job, the kids, the economy, the rain, the drought, Russia breaking up, the price of gas—absolutely everything."

Kate knew the feeling, but certainly hadn't realized what it had been. "So what changed your attitude?"

"Actually, lots of stuff, but what about you? Are you ready for a friend?"

"Tony…" Kate hesitated, "I'd like that."

"Let's find a cup of something and talk about it."

CHAPTER 25

There was no window in the door. Holden opened a crack and was immediately blinded by the morning sun. Angela stood there with a cup of hot coffee and a bagel. She was dressed in her uniform, but the curves were evident in the bright light. It was a pleasant wake up call.

She stood approximately five-foot-seven and probably weighed 145, not skinny, but not plump—nice, just nice. Holden was suddenly aware that he was standing in his boxers and backed around the door, so his head was the only visible body part...at six-foot-four and 240 he was hard to miss. His face flushed and he could feel the warmth. He hoped that Angela wasn't too observant...her smile said otherwise.

"I'm sure you don't have a robe. But maybe I should come in or come back a little later, the neighbors would probably be happier."

"Why don't I just put on some clothes, and then you can enter... Uhhh...be right back."

He closed the door and scrambled to get dressed, wondering why he hadn't just asked her in. Was he that much of a prude? He hadn't had a woman alone in a bedroom...other than his wife...ever. Yep, he was.

Angela was still smiling when the door reopened. Holden was relieved that she hadn't left.

"So can I come in now?"

"Sure, but I hope you'll forgive the mess, I was remiss in my cleaning duties, and you sort of surprised me. I guess I'm not used to a lady in my life."

"So you're not married?

"Not anymore."

"Divorce?"

"It just sort of died. How about you?"

"Oh, I'm still married, but we kind of come and go. He kinda comes and goes anyway…has for years. He's never really been the stay at home type. Sometimes will bless us with his presence."

"Us? Do you have kids?"

"Yes, a son, Thomas Lea. In fact, that's why I'm here. There was really nothing at the restaurant for now, so I got you a job at least for a day or two. It's cash by the hour. Thomas says they need someone else to help in his delivery job, and that you'd probably do. I also got the room rate changed to $25 a night, a couple of free coffees a day for a couple of weeks and he saw the light."

"Wow, you really got pull around here."

"Let's just say I know some folks."

"When am I expected to be there?"

"Tom will pick you up here about seven o'clock or so. Can you be ready?"

"I think, unless I don't look good enough to you, that I'm ready now."

"You look fine, but do you think you really want to wear Tommy Jeans and a Polo shirt to a delivery job? Don't you have something a little more…every day?"

Kate glanced around the room, then directly at Holden.

"Just what is your story anyway? You're no drifter. Your hands are way too soft to be a bum."

"Listen, I got to be honest with you. I have no need for a relationship in my life. While I appreciate the help you have given, I'd rather not get involved. If I give the impression that I'm available, I'm not."

"Available for what?"

Holden never answered—their conversation was interrupted by the knock on the door.

"It's open," Holden stated, and the knob turned.

"Hey Mom."

"Thomas, this is Jack Grayton... Jack... Thomas."

"You can call me Tom."

Thomas was about six-foot-five, with nearly black hair. He looked like a middle linebacker for the Vikings. He didn't seem too surprised to find his mother in a motel room with a man.

"We need to get on the road. Are you ready to go Mr. Grayton?"

"You are welcome to call me Jack... I'll call you Tom, ok?"

"Let's hit the road."

Thomas wasn't much of a talker. He just didn't seem to care much about having losers along...especially losers that his mom picked up at the restaurant. Holden had been wrong about Thomas's lack of concern about the motel room. Things were certainly not warm in the truck on the ride. There was not a noise for the first twenty minutes.

"Been working this job long?"

"Couple of months full-time, about six months if you include the part-time stuff."

Silence...

"Where are we headed?"

"Chicago, East Side"

Silence...

"So why is my mom so interested in helping you? What'd you promise her? You know she's married. She's not the "hot-pants" type. She and God got this thing—you probably won't be interested much once she lets you in on that stuff. She ain't about to change, and you ain't about to get much outa her.

Thomas turned his head and gave Holden a frozen stare.

"She hasn't got much money, and she works most of the time. Sooooo...maybe you best be looking some other place for a good time. Understand?"

"Hey…? The lady offered to help. I'm not looking to knock-off anything. I got a cash crunch right now and she offered to find me a job with no strings."

"That's another thing, why the cash thing? You got somethin' to hide?

Tom hesitated giving Holden another angry glance.

"See, I just don't want her hurt anymore. She's been through enough. You don't look like you are going to be much of an answer for her."

"Hey, there is nothing that impresses me more than some snot-nosed, fuzz-faced cretin, judging the world through eyes that are barely opened."

"Up yours!" Tommy seethed.

Holden wasn't finished.

"It's not just me you've misjudged. Your mom probably hasn't gotten many breaks, but she still lives life her way. You don't have a clue of who I am, and worse…you really don't know much more about your mother."

"If you weren't so old, I'd stop this truck and kick your ass. You're a lousy bum in jeans and a shirt you probably stole. You're so old you're nearly dead, and you ain't got ten bucks to your name. I got no reason to try to impress a loser like you. As if it would take much."

The kid had fire.

"Okay, so you can turn the truck around and take me back to the Wayside, or we can tolerate each other and maybe make a buck or two. I can handle it either way…it's your call?"

"Just shut up, we got a lot to do."

CHAPTER 26

It was 4:00 AM when Kate finally hit the pillow. Since meeting Tony, life had become tolerable, even exciting.

The last two weeks had been a whirlwind. Tony either came to the farm, or she went to his place, but they had been together every day. Tony seemed to need everything she offered. He seemed vulnerable. He certainly could make her laugh—something she had missed for so many years. A smile crossed her lips and she drifted away. Morning was not far off.

The room was ablaze with sunlight, yet her eyes would not open without a fight. The phone was ringing but not registering. Kate grabbed the receiver and covered her eyes.

"Hello?"

"Good morning. Is Kate Jeffries available."

"This is she."

"Kate, this is Matt Roth. I don't really think that we ever met, but I worked with your husband on a project just before he died."

"Matt, forgive me, but my husband's work was rarely discussed in our home."

"This was not about the office. It was a project to bring the Gospel of Christ to those in prison. He probably never mentioned it to you."

"Actually, Matt, we did speak of it. Holden said he had met with you and you were going to try to get it off the ground."

"Well, it certainly is off the ground. Men in jail are being challenged by the dozen to change their lives. It's unfortunate that Mr. Jeffries never got to see what he started."

"I am happy for you, but I am also terribly busy. Is there something that you wanted to speak with me about." She lied.

"I'll be brief. The new corporate leaders are not as inclined to be altruistic. We have been turned down for funding for the next year. I was wondering if you would be kind enough to put in a good word for our program with the new CEO. Perhaps he would consider meeting with me to go over the successes and details."

"I really don't know Mr. Willers. I'm certain if you call the office, he will be happy to speak with you."

She knew Willers wouldn't give his mother coffee money without a guaranteed return. He was less spiritual than Holden, but she hoped this would get rid of Mr. Roth.

"I have repeatedly phoned. He just won't see me. Are you certain there is nothing you can do?"

"Please realize that this is Corporate USA. My husband was in a rare mood when he agreed to meet with you Mr. Roth, but I will see if I can at least leave a message."

"Thanks for your time, and you have our sympathy in the loss of your husband. He truly was a good man. Please be assured that we would be happy to help with anything at any time if need arises."

"Thanks, Mr. Roth. Holden spoke highly of you and your vision."

As the phone clicked Kate's heart felt pain again. She remembered that morning. It was one of the last times that they had spoken. Had she given him the impression that she really didn't care?

There it was, just like Tony said, guilt. She hadn't killed him; he died in an accident. All the guilt and remorse in the world wasn't going to change that.

This Matt guy had a lot of nerve to contact her wanting favors. She would do what she had said, but she didn't need a bunch of convicts messing up her plans.

Kate was again startled as the phone rang.

"Kate, are you up?"

"I certainly am, Tony. I've already been a busy lady. Got a call from an old acquaintance."

"Really, anyone I know?"

"No, just a guy that Holden worked with."

"A guy, huh? So you have some other men interested in your life. I thought you had left all of that behind."

"Tony, it was just a phone call. The guy is married and a pastor. I really don't like the insinuations."

"Hey, Kate, it was just a joke! Friends like to make each other laugh. Let's start this conversation all over. Are you up yet?"

"Sorry, Tony. Guess I've always been a bit guarded when it comes to my private life. I need to learn to trust friends."

"Well, I hope you know you are what matters to me. It was one of the luckiest days of my life when I saw you. I guess my life had become a bit empty before I met you. Do you have any plans for the day?"

"Well, I have to make a couple of calls, and the house needs a bit of work. Maybe we can meet, say about four, for coffee. We can talk about the evening. I really need to get some sleep tonight. This four in the morning stuff is for kids, and I am really beginning to understand that I am no longer a kid." She laughed lightly, but hoped he got the message.

"Well, you still look rather good to me. We'll make an early night of it, remember, it's all about you. See you at four."

The smell of coffee and the toaster made the spacious kitchen feel like home. Kate remembered hundreds of mornings in this exact room. The stove was always hot when she got up. The house had a furnace, but it must have been marginal. Her bedroom walls were frost-covered on some cold winter mornings.

Those days were so much easier to understand. The family ate meals together. Decisions were made right there at the kitchen table. Victories or defeats were celebrated or overcome right there at the table. Now, families sent each other e-mail messages and spoke on cellular phones.

Tony was right. It wasn't her fault. She had work to do.

"Is Mr. Willers in, please?"

"May I say who is calling?"

"Kate Jeffries."

"Oh, hello Kate, I'll check his phone. I hope you are well."

"Quite well, thank you."

"Kate, what a surprise, I hope everything is okay."

"I'm fine, Frank. I just have a favor to ask of you."

"I hope that I can help. What do you need?"

"This morning I received a phone call from Matt Roth. You may not recognize the name, but he was an acquaintance of Holden's. He has a group that is trying to reform some men in jail and get them back into the work force. Holden had supported them in the past. Apparently, the corporation has changed its view lately. Matt would like to speak with you about his plan. He phoned to ask if I would speak with you as a friend."

"Kate, I am so glad that you called. I am aware of Mr. Roth, and frankly his work has merit. He is however a very…religious man…a Christian, and while I am fond of spiritual matters, we must be careful not to endorse one belief over another. You realize, Kate, that it is not as simple as the beliefs of you and me. There are thousands of employees in this corporation. We must treat all views and religions with equal value and respect."

"Frank, how is helping Matt Roth any different than giving to the American Legion, or to the Boy Scouts? The man is trying to help others. The corporate world could take a lesson from those like Matt. Am I to understand that you won't see him?"

"Kate, we've been friends for a number of years. Please try to understand, the world has changed, and we must change with it."

"So you won't see him?"

"I simply can't help you with this matter, but please don't hesitate to call me if I can assist on something less political."

"Thank you, Frank. You can be assured that I will keep that in mind."

Kate hung up the phone. Nothing was as it was in her early days. People with fortune were so busy protecting it, the plight of others had no merit. Was Kate like that? Probably, but those days were over.

"Is Matt Roth available?"
"No, this is his wife Connie, can I take a message."
"Tell him to call Kate Jeffries."
"I'll give him the message. I hope it's nothing serious."
"Tell him I'm about to begin to get better."

CHAPTER 27

IT WAS 7:00 PM when they pulled into Wayside. Tom and Holden had been working together nine hours a day for three weeks. Holden had nearly nine hundred dollars and a stiff back. Holden lay on the bed trying to put the thoughts of the day together. He had nearly drifted off, when he heard what seemed to be the creak of a door, and he felt a gloved hand around his throat.

"Keep your mouth shut, and I'll let up on your throat. Don't even think about fighting, 'cause there's three of us, and mine just might be the last face you would ever see."

"You guys must have me mixed up with someone else. I've got nothing and know nobody here. Just don't get all upset. There has to be a mistake."

"Really?"

"That's right, I got a little cash from a job I been working. It's yours if you just leave me alone."

The guy with the gloves kept his hand at Holden's throat, and grabbed his wallet from the nightstand.

"Jack Grayton, huh? From Minneapolis? What are your doing down this way?"

"Just passing through. Got a little help from a couple of people. I got a job to make a couple of bucks, then I'm gone…got no people here, got nothing to pack, could be gone in seconds. Just tell me to go, I'm gone."

"Oh, but Jack, what would Highland Deliveries do if you don't show up tomorrow... I hear you really been putting your back into the job...they're pretty impressed."

This must be coming from the damn kid, or the kid's father, probably thought Holden was sleeping with his wife...

God, he was going to get shot or beaten for nothing. The irony was laughable. All the stuff he did as a CEO the world applauded.

"Hey, I'll stay if you want. I'll even work a bit harder. I didn't know you were with Highland."

"You really think were just a bunch of hicks out here?"

"I haven't got a clue who the hell you are. I'm just trying to keep from being your next victim."

"Too late, Jack."

Holden felt a needle prick his arm, a warmth in his body, then only darkness.

*****

"So are you two getting along any better?" Angela asked Tom.

"We just don't talk much."

"That must make the days just fly by."

"It's not so bad. The guy really wants to prove he's not old. He almost runs to make sure he does his share. He sure acted like a rear end the first day, though."

"Unprovoked, I'm sure."

"I really didn't trust him. It really made me mad that he was hitting on a married woman."

"He wasn't hitting on me. I'm the one who was making the suggestions, and they had nothing to do with what you are worried about." Angela paused and looked at her son.

"While I am flattered by your concern, I just wanted to help him find some answers. He truly looked like a lost soul that first night at the restaurant."

"But mom, you know how jealous Dad is about stuff like that. If there is ever going to be a chance to get together, that might just spoil it. This is important."

"Tom, your father and I are about as far apart as East is from West. He has no need for a spiritual life. The only tie that we have is you. It's still the best gift that I have ever received, but he just doesn't care."

Tom stood and walked to the window.

"He cares! Doesn't he send money? And call to see how everything is going?"

"He sends just enough to keep us from total starvation and calls when he wants something. He cares for himself. Nothing but a relationship with Christ will ever change that. He wants nothing to do with change."

He turned facing his mother.

"Why do you always have to talk about Jesus? You sound like some fanatic. It's like you are trying to drive Dad away with all this religious stuff."

"It's not religious stuff. It's a way of life."

"I love you, Mom. I always will even if I'll never understand you."

"I love you too, Thomas, so does my best friend. Someday, He'll be yours too."

Tom could never stay mad at his mother—but she did annoy him with all this Jesus stuff.

"I'll try to be a little friendlier to Jack. He seems too smart to be a bum."

"I guess we never know what's inside until we look deep and take some chances. Life is so boring without living all the minutes to the fullest."

CHAPTER 28

It was nearly 3:30 PM when the phone rang. Kate was already a bit behind and needed a shower. She let the phone ring.

"Kate, this is Matt Roth, Connie said that you called. I suppose you are out for the day, but thought I'd get back to you in case you needed something. I'll try later."

Kate really needed a shower, and Tony was due at the house soon, she grabbed the receiver.

"Matt, this is Kate. Tell me about your project."

"Actually, the project is still small. We use the money for legal fees and finding help for those on the inside. The Bible studies are all volunteer."

Kate sat quietly.

"We have helped those who show potential for change, those who show remorse, or a changed attitude, by offering legal assistance. Usually the cases are so poorly litigated a single hearing with a competent lawyer can get them out on bail."

"So who decides the men who are worthy of these efforts?"

"Actually, that's a really good question. This is a lot like life on the outside, lots of people try to fake a belief in Christ; some even get others to believe in them. Does God only offer love and help to those who are totally ready? Not the way we see it."

Matt paused and waited slightly for some sign of disagreement from Kate. There was none.

"God offers his love and his hand to all who profess an interest. I'm a bit cynical at times, but a changed heart comes from God, not from our program. God must decide who to use and who to move and who to put in what position. We must only be available when He is ready to work."

"So you're getting these guys out of jail. What happens to them after that?"

"That's where Jack comes in. Jack Grayton is a born-again Christian who just happens to have a very colorful background. Jack helps the men locate housing, and hopefully a job. He heads Bible Studies and prayer groups to help them grow. He also has an insight that is priceless. He can spot the con-job, and he is extremely comfortable in confronting it."

"Who pays Jack? Who is funding all this work?"

"Well, I have a good delivery job, and we are getting by."

"But who pays Jack?"

"Oh, I'm sorry. Jack lives in our home, and he works at anything that he can find, odd jobs, McDonalds, anything. God has provided for our needs. We never go hungry. But the lawyer fees are paid by the corporate checks. Now they aren't coming, so I hoped that you could help to keep that part intact."

"So you are funding this with your job as a delivery man, and the part-time salary of an ex-con? Aren't you married?"

"Yes, Mrs. Jeffries, to a wonderful woman, and please don't be concerned with all of this. We are doing fine. It's just the money for the legal advice that is an issue. God has always provided the rest."

"I have decided to take over the funding of your project. Holden's corporation has been kind enough to turn it over to me. If this was important to Holden, then I would like to continue to be a part of it in his memory. Where can I send the check, or how would you like to handle this from now on?"

"There's no need for a check. All we do is have the lawyers bill you and you can pay them. That way we know that you are certain that the money is being used correctly. Mrs. Jeffries this is not what I had in mind when I called. I didn't plan to add another burden to your life."

"Actually, you have offered a place to give something back for all that I have."

"Someday I'd like to meet you and thank you personally for this generosity. The men really need someone who cares. Thanks!"

"Actually Matt, you haven't added a burden. I think I've just begun to get rid of some of it. Thanks for your call. I too look forward to meeting you someday soon."

Kate was in the shower when Tony arrived. "Just pour yourself a cup of coffee, I just made it. I'll be down in ten minutes."

Tony poured the coffee and sat at the kitchen table. He had been in this house hundreds of times as a kid. He remembered Kate's mother baking and the smells of cinnamon rolls and cookies. This place was a welcome haven from the hell of his own home.

Tony's dad was an alcoholic, and his mother was a very angry woman. He was never certain if the alcoholism caused the anger, or if the anger caused the alcoholism, but they both caused him pain. His mother was into herself—she was an exceptionally beautiful woman who liked makeup, perfume and other men. She spent hours on herself, was constantly on a diet, (Dexedrine every morning, Valium every night). She managed to spend most of the money that his father didn't drink up on clothes, shoes, etc.

Tony was an afterthought for both. He was not athletic, which mattered little to his parents. They had no desire to enter his life. He excelled in the theatre, which is where he felt most at home. There was something wonderful in becoming someone new. His parents attended one of his performances in his junior year. He shuddered as he recalled his father causing a scene because he couldn't find a decent seat after stumbling down the aisle less than three minutes before curtain. His father left at intermission for his favorite bar, leaving Tony's mom to find a ride home…she had already chosen a potential suitor as he exited. At breakfast, his father told him "acting is for faggots." They never attended another function, and Tony never acted again.

College was a bust; he finished his third semester with a 2.2 GPA and just walked away. His marriage was a joke. She was fooling around on him in their second year; something that he expected from women. He didn't care if she shared her bed with other men, in fact he didn't care much about her at all. The divorce was uneventful.

"Sorry I wasn't ready; I had a late phone call. I see you found the coffee."

"No problem. It's like I'm seventeen again, the smells, the sunlight through the window, the sound of the leaves rustling in the wind, the neighbors fresh mown hay. All we need is the 'Everley Brothers' and I could be right back there."

"Would you really want to go back? I mean…if you get past all the reminiscence and romance of all of it, would you like to start again?"

"Hey, that's a little deeper than I wanted to go right now. I was enjoying the sensory memoirs. I'm not certain that realism has a place in the past."

"I'm not joking, Tony. Have you ever contemplated what life would have been like if things had been different?"

"Like if Julie had actually said yes when I asked her to the prom, or if Mr. Johnson had a better sense of humor and didn't take grades so seriously?"

Kate stood up and got the coffee pot, a bit less than amused.

"Tony be serious. What if Mom hadn't died, would I have married Holden? Would my dad still be alive? Would I be as strong as I am now? Would I be stronger because of their presence? What if your parents had been different?"

"Gee Kate, this certainly is fun. I was hoping that we could dig up some old wounds. They've healed, and I'd rather put my hand in boiling water than to live them again, especially if it was not a necessity."

"Maybe it is a necessity. Maybe it's like a coral wound."

"A coral wound?"

"When divers in the ocean brush up against coral and it breaks the skin. Many times, the wound will heal, then periodically the body will attack it again, and it will fester and open, then heal, fester and heal, on and on and on. The only way to rid yourself of the problem is to get help from a professional to surgically remove the coral. A very painful process is involved, but it's better than having to deal with the pain time after time."

"No wonder I never wanted to swim in the ocean."

"Tony, I know that you tell me that most of what I feel is guilt, and that guilt is wrong, but I'm beginning to think it has its own purpose. If I turn my back on the cause of some of the pain, I learn nothing. What is to keep me from experiencing the exact same pain again?"

"Kate, what if it's not your fault? What if you didn't ask for the pain? What if you didn't ask to be ignored? You still think that we should go through all that again? Sorry, I don't! I want to change the subject. I didn't come here to be analyzed or to be healed, or to be cut open by some amateur surgeon. Maybe we should just call it a night. I'm a bit tired, and you seem wound up about something."

"Tony, if you want to leave, I understand, but you've been telling me to forget it since we met. I'm just trying to give you another outlook. Why does that make you so uncomfortable?"

"Kate, get some rest, I'll call you tomorrow."

Tony was seething when he got into his car. He slammed the door and thrust the key into the ignition. The rearview mirror gave him a glimpse of his eyes. He reached up and ripped it off the support. He tossed the mirror into the rear seat, with little acknowledgement of the blood from the cut in his hand. He hated women. They were all the same…weak and stupid. It would never change—and Kate was the worst. The past ran through his mind like a spring grass fire.

"You self-righteous witch. My life has been a disaster. I never had the family you had. My mother was a slut, and my father a drunk. Who the hell do you think you are in trying to bring all that back up? You had everything you ever wanted—one silver spoon after another."

The tires squealed as the car cut through curves in the darkness.

"You acted like we were friends, but most of the time I knew what you thought. I was just the 'token poor kid.' Sorry, Kate, but I don't need to dig it out. It's all right here."

She could have her guilt. He had overcome his past—she could live in hers if she wanted.

"To hell with Kate Jeffries!"

Kate tried to cry herself to sleep. She knew she had offended Tony, but she hadn't intended to hurt him. She had really hoped that Tony would be her answer.

She closed her eyes and prayed, *"God, I've been angry with you for a long time, I have blamed you for nearly everything that hasn't met my expectations. Forgive me and help me start again. I need a friend so badly, and there is supposed to be hope in you. Will you take me back? Will you love me again?"*

Kate drifted off and slept like a newborn…exactly what she was.

CHAPTER 29

The room was dark, damp and cold. The air smelled with mold and something else that Holden couldn't place. There definitely were memories that went with it. Suddenly he recognized it…it was blood. He remembered the smell of the slaughter-house he visited as a boy. He remembered the sticky floors. He remembered the red footprints in the snow. He remembered the smell, that pungent odor of death and the utter hopelessness of the animals. He wondered what went through their minds in the final seconds.

"I think we got off to a really bad start, Jack? All we really want is the truth. Who are you, and what are you doing in Merrilville? These questions aren't that tough, certainly not worth dying for."

"Dying?! Geeze, I don't even know what's going on here, I ran a little short on cash. I stopped at a motel, then a waitress helped me get a job."

Holden felt the tape over his eyes, and the ropes around his wrists. He could see little, but faint light filtered through the tape. He knew the men weren't far away because he could smell the scent of sweat and cologne. His eyes felt like lead—the hangover worsened as he tried to think.

"Jack… Jack… Jack. We're not stupid."

He was lifted off the floor by his hair and a giant hand around his throat, then dropped into a cold steel chair. *These guys are serious. What do they know, or think they know?*

His back felt the cold of the steel chair. There was a slight breeze on his face as he sat waiting.

He had to think. He couldn't panic. Never play any cards you could hold. He had to get on the offensive.

"Okay, so you guys know about me, so what?"

The punch lifted him off the chair, and he felt his rib cage nearly collapse. It took what seemed like minutes to get his breath, the pain on his left side continued after he began to breathe. As the man pushed him back up in the chair, he smelled his cologne—it was Aqua Velva—Geeze how long had it been since he wore that stuff? He didn't even know they still made it.

"Just answer the questions, we'll decide whether we like the answers."

"We know you're not Jack Grayton. We ran your prints. They don't match."

Ran my prints; who the hell are these guys?

Holden had never been printed in his life, but of course Jack had been, he had been in jail several times. Holden hoped he had been gone long enough that there hadn't been any recent pictures in the paper. This was never supposed to happen.

"You're right, I'm not Grayton, but there are a lot of folks that aren't who they say they are… I'm telling you guys, I got no agenda… I just want to make a few bucks, then get out of town."

"So why are you driving a car registered in the name of Jack Grayton, if you aren't him?"

"I'm not driving anything."

This time the punch not only lifted him off the chair, but he was certain that it broke his ribs. Holden nearly passed out from the pain. These guys had short fuses, and nothing to lose.

It was beginning to be difficult to think…the pain was excruciating. He had never considered himself a tough guy…but he had to keep his mind and his wits about him… Aqua Velva man was standing awfully close to his chair.

Concentrate…concentrate.

"You drove a Buick Regal, 1994, black with silver trim, gray leather interior, license plate, Illinois 7BJ9868, odometer 49,876 miles. Anything else you wanted to lie about?"

He had to get ahead of the game, to buy some time to think.

"The car got stolen along with probably the rest of my life. I had a bunch of money in the trunk that wasn't mine."

"That's better Jack. How much money was in the trunk?"

"You're not going to like the answer, but please don't hit me again... I never counted it, but it looked like a lot."

"It was fifty thousand, Jack. Where'd you get the money?"

"FIFTY THOUSAND! You got me all wrong; I'm not some hit man or something. I'm just a guy that got in a little too deep to some people that I never even met in Minneapolis. I had some gambling debts that I couldn't pay."

He was waiting for the next punch, but nothing came. He tried to sit up a little...to get his breath.

"Actually, I was going to pay them off...they just wouldn't wait for me to get my feet on the ground. They wanted it NOW! There were a bunch of threats. I knew that I had to do something, or wind up getting the hell kicked out of me...so I asked if we could work something out. A bookie named Randy in the cities set up this pay-back. I was supposed to come to Merrilville, pick up the car that was parked in this storage garage, and drive it to Chicago. I was supposed to park at the Hilton Hotel on Michigan Avenue, and leave the car. Three hours later, I was 'sposed to go back, get in it and drive it back to the garage here in Merrilville and leave it."

He heard some movement to his left and braced himself. He hesitated only for a moment...nothing.

"Then I was to take the bus back home and I get credit for the $5,000 I owed. It all seemed so simple. Now the car is gone. I'm trying to get enough money to put as much distance between me and Randy's friends as I can."

He was buying some time to think.

"If you guys know about the car and you're responsible for it being stolen, maybe we can work something out? I got nothing if I don't get that back. I'm not so concerned about the gambling debt, but the $50,000...that just could get me killed." The story was getting better—stronger.

"So that's why you didn't call the police. Why'd you stick around here? Didn't you think they'd start looking for you if the deal fell apart?" This was a new voice—not so throaty, less gruff.

"I figured they'd be watching the buses for sure, but I really didn't know what to do. I'm just a small-time car salesman that got into something I wish I could get out of. I thought you guys might be them when you were in the room."

"We'd love to believe you Jack, but there were clothes and books in the trunk that give us the impression that whoever was using the car had some long term plans—it just doesn't seem like a trip to Chicago was the only part of the plan."

"Hey... I was just supposed to deliver the car. I didn't inventory the trunk."

"What are all the numbers in the books, and why do the clothes seem to be your size? See, Jack, we are a bit cynical about strangers here in Merrilville." This was a third voice, higher pitched and nasal...sounded older, a bit tired.

"I'm tellin' ya... I got no idea about anything in the trunk. I just knew there was supposed to be money in it. I checked for the money, and never looked at anything else, didn't even count it. I just wanted it over. It was just a job. I didn't want to know the specifics."

They ripped the tape off his eyes, and the bright light felt like a stiletto to his brain. When he finally began to focus, tears were running down his cheeks. He saw the shadows of at least two men behind two bright halogen lights. "So you don't recognize this stuff?" They threw his Polo slacks and a bright red Polo shirt into his lap. Aqua Velva man grabbed the back of his neck and forced his head in the direction of the clothing.

"It's not mine, but I sure could use it."

"You're telling us that you didn't even pack a bag,"

"Hey guys, it was just 'sposed to be down and back."

"Don't know anything about this stuff either?" The man with the older voice, the shadow to the right of center, tossed the remainder of the items on the floor directly in front of Holden's feet.

He saw his Day-Timer in the light. The account numbers in Grand Cayman were coded in the *Notes* section. Now there they lay in his lap. He never thought he'd be this close to them again. He had to get out of here with that book.

"This book and its numbers aren't yours...you don't know how to read this? Jack, is there something you're not telling us?"

"I have never seen them before right now. I'm telling you; I was just supposed to drive it, leave it, and return it. These guys didn't seem like the type who wanted to share their secrets."

"So it wouldn't matter if this stuff got lost or destroyed? It's not yours?"

"Not mine, but it must mean something to them. After all, fifty thousand."

The hand behind the light, grabbed the book, ripped out several pages, and with his lighter, set them on fire, dropping them into the suitcase on the floor. He watched helplessly as his dream went up in smoke. Would this nightmare *never* end?

He didn't change expression. He didn't move a muscle. The years at the head of table at the Board meetings paid off for something. He never flinched.

Holden couldn't see the men, but he knew he was being watched. There was some mumbling. He feared what was about to come. He expected to hear the cocking of a hammer.

"Are you married, Jack?" the voice asked.

"Divorced...no kids, not even a dog."

"Nobody waiting back in Minneapolis?"

"Nope."

Would he hear the shot, or just feel the bullet?

He heard muffled whispering. There was some movement, and there were two large shadows now behind the light. He could see their shoes. They offered nothing in the way of a clue.

Holden tried to concentrate on the darkness. The whispering was over. He felt their eyes boring holes in him as he sat saturated in his own sweat. The smells and the heat had become so mixed he wasn't certain which he found to be the most agonizing.

"What was that?"

It was…it was the cocking of a hammer." He felt the force of the bullet before he heard the shot. It entered and shook the wall just to the left of his ear.

"That was a great story, Mr. Jeffries. We had a feeling you'd be good at telling lies."

Holden closed his stinging eyes and dropped his aching head until his chin hit his chest. His ribs burned as he tried to inhale. His lungs ached each time he exhaled. His eyebrows and eyelashes felt hot from the irritation of the tape.

"Who did you call me?" Holden whispered.

"Mr. Jeffries, or would you prefer 'the late Holden Jeffries' or the 'Executive of the Year, Mr. Jeffries, or 'husband of Kate Jeffries? That's right, Holden, we know exactly who you are."

"You knew about the money? How did you know it was in the trunk?"

"Sorry Holden, we don't answer questions, we ask them, or… we decide to end the conversation, sometimes with a bang."

There was a faint snicker from the voice. He had known many men like these. They usually spoke for someone else—someone who had the power to control their speech, and the money to control their lives.

He wasn't dead yet. Someone must want something. He had to hold on.

"Actually Holden, we have a proposition for you."

"Assuming that I am Holden Jeffries, what could I possibly offer you?"

"We have a growing little business here. It could use some-one with the corporate talent. We like your quick thinking. We enjoyed your performance this evening. And above all, you offer something that we just can't find in the workplace. You are already dead, so killing you if it doesn't work out will be almost redundant."

"Why not kill me now?"

"You have so much to offer…we feel you'll be a real asset. You already have provided both entertainment and a nice membership fee. We're going to say good-by for now, but we'll be in touch. Sleep in tomorrow." The hand grabbed his arm, the needle sunk into his flesh, and welcomed darkness followed instantly.

CHAPTER 30

Kate had expected the days to seem long without Tony's presence, but she was amazingly upbeat, almost happy. She remembered her prayer but was suspect as to whether God could really change anyone. Didn't God have enough to do without having to get involved in the life of every woman who was trying to sort life out?

She did feel different. Something was changing, but what? Tony certainly wasn't the answer for these questions. She considered calling a Pastor in town but had no idea who. She'd just have to rely on God to send someone if He wanted her to know more about Him.

About two hours later the doorbell rang. Kate was dressed in her old "Lauren" jeans and a lavender tank top. Her hair was streaked with wallpaper paste and perspiration. She considered not answering it but went to the door anyway.

"My name is Jack Grayton, ma'am, Matt Roth is my best friend. He gave me your name and told me what you are doing for the ministry. I'm here to share a story with you. If you're busy now, I can come back later."

"Jack Grayton? Yes, I think Matt mentioned that you had found some answers, please come in."

Kate led Jack into the kitchen, moved the pan of water, and the wallpaper from the table, pulled out a chair, and motioned for Jack to be seated.

"Do you like coffee, Mr. Grayton, I have soda if you prefer."

"I love coffee...used to drink it lots when I lived downtown. But don't go to any trouble."

"No trouble, I was just about to brew some for me...time for a break anyway."

Kate was amazed at this weathered leathery-faced man. He looked physically worn out, but his eyes had life and almost fire. There seemed to be a peace within his voice.

He wasn't extremely tall, probably just over six feet. He still looked solid, with broad shoulders and large hands. His hair was dark with streaks of gray that extended into the ponytail in the back. Some older men looked foolish with long hair, but it definitely fit Jack.

He certainly didn't look like someone to fear. He was dressed in khakis and a black T-shirt, and cowboy boots. She knew clothes and these were not expensive, but he managed to look well dressed.

She glanced at him periodically as she prepared the coffee and got out some cookies. He seemed to be taking in the house with wonder.

"This place is beautiful. Did you do all this decorating yourself?"

"Well, it's a long way from finished, but I guess I'm the decorator, if you want to call it that. Nice of you to notice."

"I never had a house. We lived in a rundown apartment when I was a kid. The rest of my life I lived on the streets of the city. I hope that doesn't scare you. It seems like a long time ago. Almost like another life, I guess."

"Sort of like born-again, I guess?" Kate stated flatly. She wanted to get right to the point if there was to be one.

"That's what the Bible says in John 3:3, and lots of people like to spread that around and some I guess abuse it. Kinda like joining a special club. But for guys like me, it's so much of a change that I know only God could do it. I've been changed, not just in the way I act, but in all of my life." He looked directly at Kate and smiled.

"The most amazing thing about this, I want to do it. I don't want to go back. I found love, and all of us need to be loved by someone.

Jack dropped his head and breathed deep.

"Sorry, I don't want to preach to you, I just came here to thank you and tell you why this ministry means so much to me. I always get going and talk way too much."

Kate smiled slightly as she watched Jack shake his head with self-reproof. What if God really had sent him?

"It's okay, Mr. Grayton. I know about God, and I guess I've needed some answers in my life too. What do you mean lived on the street?"

It was all Jack needed. For the next three hours he shared his early life with all the pain. A father that was never known, a mother that wanted the best for her son but was incapable of supplying any-thing above the bare necessities of existence. Jack spoke of his moth-er's faith and how many times she had prayed for him.

He wept when he shared the stories of how he ridiculed her for her belief in a God. Kate noticed his smile when he spoke of her read-ing her Bible, and how he hoped someday to find it. She noticed his eyes and the change in his tone when he told of the rules and rights from wrongs as his mother had put it.

She could nearly see the two-room apartment and feel the win-ter cold and summer heat as Jack shared his memories. His life on the street was far from easy to understand. Kate had never known hopelessness, or worthlessness. Jack had lived it and brought it to life with his stories.

Kate felt the fear, the anger, the violence. She was enthralled with the stories of young people with no way out. She began to understand some of the reasons behind street people and kids in trouble. Kate had always blamed them for their situation.

She wanted none of the responsibility. She had worked hard and made something of herself. She had overcome pain and loss. She had made good choices. She didn't need any more baggage, or to be dragged into paying for someone's lack of a work ethic. It wasn't her fault.

As Jack's voice filled the room, she began to realize the change in her heart. Three days before, Kate would never have allowed this man into her home. They had nothing in common. She would have seen nothing of value in his life, his background or his future. Now it was as if she saw him as someone just like her—someone with pain and needs and ideas and hopes and dreams—someone with something to offer.

Could God really have sent him?

Kate stood and refilled the coffee for the third time, when she noticed that there seemed to be someone in Jack's car. She turned in fear.

"There's someone in your car!"

"Oh, that's Brian, just a kid from the streets. He wants to know what makes my life different. He doesn't have much, so he didn't feel like he was dressed well enough to come in. Said he'd wait in the car."

"Jack, are you serious? This kid's been sitting in the car for nearly four hours in this heat? At least let him come in and watch TV or something. He's got to be thirsty, or hungry."

"He isn't bothered by heat. Where he lives he only sees the backside of air-conditioners and furnaces. He just happens to have a driver's license—I don't yet, so I asked if he could drive here. He told me to take my time and not worry about him."

"Jack, you will go outside right now and insist that he come inside for a Coke. I won't hear of it any other way. Now go tell him!"

Jack heard Kate's tone. He had heard it from his mother. He stepped out into the heat and motioned for Brian to come to the door. After some debate, Brian sheepishly followed Jack into the kitchen.

"Brian, my name is Kate, welcome to my home."

Brian was a young black, about six feet tall, very thin, with Nike look-alikes, and baggy pants. His clothes were clean but worn. He wore a lean troubled look. His eyes never met hers as he nodded. He was careful to stay behind Jack.

"Would you like a Coke…maybe a cookie or something?"

"He'll have a soda, maybe save the cookies 'til later." Jack stated as if he could read Brian's mind.

Kate opened the can, and put some ice in a glass, then led Brian into the family room, turned on the big screen TV. He might be a street kid, but he was male, she and handed him the remote. As she left the room, she glanced back and watched as Brian panned the room and smiled ever so slightly. He began to watch ESPN with his Coke.

"The basics," she thought, "aren't the same for everyone."

Jack got into the final episode, the change. He told about how Matt had challenged him to think differently, and how it had angered him. He told about how God wouldn't let him go…how he felt he must attend the next Bible study even though he didn't want to… how he felt a war inside him.

"Part of me wanted to hold onto all that anger…all that hatred. But something inside me knew the truth."

"What truth?"

"All that resentment was killing me. I was blaming God for everything. I wouldn't have to look in the mirror. There was something inside of me, I call it my spirit that told me to quit lying to myself and be honest. I was dying little by little. That's what is odd, the part that wanted me to stay angry didn't care about the pain…it only wanted to stay in control."

"In control of what?"

"In control of everything. That part of me, my flesh I call it, wanted nothing to do with God or giving up."

"So what made you change your mind?"

"It was like I finally saw it… I finally understood the truth. It was almost like magic. One moment I was fighting, the next moment I was a new person. I think all it took was to say okay, and it was done. I felt love of Christ flow into my body, and all the darkness flowed right out with my tears. I never want to be without that love again."

"Has your experience lost some of its spark over time?"

"I just keep getting better. I resented God for the life I had been given. Now I see that God had a plan…my life is centered on bringing others to Christ. I just had to let go and watch Him work."

"Do you go back into the jails? Is that the call you feel?"

"It's absolutely amazing. God uses me to touch others that have never known much more than trouble. They are finding the light. Many of them are finding jobs and making a difference. God opens the doors. People like you Kate… God calls people like you to help… and you do."

As Jack spoke, Kate felt the warmth deep inside as if something were melting. Tears streamed from her eyes, but there was no burning, only warmth.

She could feel the walls around her heart tremble. The anger, the pain, the guilt, the resentment…each brick…melted with the warmth of her tears. She was not embarrassed…she was renewed. *Could God really have sent this man?*

When Jack finished, Kate looked at his face; it nearly glowed. She glanced at the family room and realized that Brian had been listening and watching as Jack spoke. There were tears on his cheeks and his eyes and face were different. He looked directly in her eyes and smiled.

Jack whispered, "The Holy Spirit can work miracles that man won't even dream. Did you feel His presence… His touch?"

Neither Kate nor Brian spoke.

"Kate, this is the beginning of a new life, but just like when you were born the first time, you will need some nurturing. You can help the growth with prayer and reading of God's Word, but you will also need some other believers to share with you. Just pray, God will provide."

"I think He just did. What about Brian? I think God touched him too."

"We will get someone in touch with him. We have about twenty guys that we are discipling now in the city. They know God…now they need to find how to make better decisions."

"Twenty? How can you keep it all going?"

"It's tough. It truly is like war, but we have amazing weapons if we use them. You happen to be one of them. That's why I came, to say thanks."

"I am flattered, but that's not why you came."

Jack smiled.

Kate made hamburgers and French fries for supper. There was lots of laughter… Kate had found two friends for life.

After dinner Kate took them for a walk around the farmyard. She was amazed at the questions and interest as she explained the farrowing pens and the milking areas of the barn. They loved the hayloft with its huge door and hay rope. She wasn't sure she would ever get Brian off the tractor.

As they walked into the fields of soybeans and corn, she was surprised to find city people with a true love for the country. Maybe it was just a love for a place to find people who care, but it was evident.

The sun was setting as Jack prepared to climb into the car, and Brian took his place behind the wheel. Kate gave Jack a hug and asked him to come again. Brian shook his head too. Then they were gone. Kate gazed at the sky as she slowly walked back to the house. *Thanks, Lord, I love you.*

CHAPTER 31

It wasn't the Hilton, but it wasn't the Wayside either. Holden had no idea how he had gotten to Blue Roof Inn. It all seemed like a bad dream. They knew his name…he had no clue who *they* were or *what* they expected.

Holden only wanted to get the numbers of those bank accounts and get out. He knew the destruction of the book had been a sham.

There were so many questions. He wondered what was next. He had to find a new plan.

Holden showered with difficulty. His ribs were still on fire. A simple coughed had brought him to his knees. He found his closet filled with his clothes from the suitcase and his shaving kit in the bathroom. He dressed and waited. At twelve thirty, the phone rang. When Holden answered he recognized Tom's voice.

"They told me to call this number. Guess you got tired of the Wayside or something. I've stopped the last two mornings and there wasn't even a message, I was wondering if you were still working with me or what?"

"Who told you to call this number?"

"The guy at the desk. He also said to pick you up and bring you to the office sometime this afternoon. Something's different 'cause Wally said the info is coming from the big office, and I don't even know where that is."

"It has been an interesting last couple of days." Holden winced as he shifted in the chair.

"I'm at the Blue Roof Inn. When do you want to pick me up?"

"It's only a couple of minutes from here, but I haven't had lunch so thought I'd stop by after…unless you want to eat."

"Lunch sounds good, I can be ready in a couple of minutes. I'm in room 357. Just call when you get here. Maybe we can get a sandwich at the Rusty Skillet."

Holden finished dressing and waited for the call.

The Rusty Skillet was busy when Tom and Holden arrived. The smell of bacon and hot grease almost seemed comforting. Maybe it was the presence of Angela, or just the joy of being alive, but it surprised him.

"We were worried, Jack, nobody had seen you for a couple of days. I was concerned. You just didn't seem like the type to leave without saying good-bye."

"I came by every day to pick him up, I can't help it if he doesn't show. Anyway, it's not that big a deal, he's here now. No problems." Tommy took off his cap and tossed it into the booth.

"I really didn't mean to worry anybody, I just got tied up… unexpectedly." Holden smiled, then gritted his teeth as he slid into the booth. "Must have pulled something. Ribs are a bit sore." He rubbed his back with the palm of his hand, then smiled again.

"I guess you got tired of the Wayside. Thought you couldn't afford much better?"

"Can't say I'll miss the Wayside. The Blue Roof isn't far, just a bit cleaner and about fifty years newer. I still plan on eating here as much as possible."

Tom turned his head and mumbled something. Holden almost enjoyed watching the kid steam.

Holden ordered two eggs over easy, Texas toast and crisp bacon. He was famished. The coffee even tasted better than usual.

"So why did somebody else come and pay the bill at the Wayside? There's something strange about you Jack. I'm not so sure that I want much to do with you. I'm really sure that I don't want you around my mom."

"Tom, the woman's married, I'm not interested. Trust me on this one. I would never hurt her. She's probably the most honest person I've ever met. She cares about everybody."

"I don't trust you in the least. I'm not stupid… I see stuff. The guys in the office are all movin' fast 'cause of some meeting set up. I know something's up." Tommy squinted his eyes for affect.

"Nobody even asked where you were for two days. Now you're back and they tell me where to call and to pick you up. I'm not stupid, Jack."

"I really don't know about any meeting…right now I'm interested in those eggs. Let's eat while it's still hot."

The office smelled of Pledge and stale cigar smoke as Tom and Holden entered. Holden noticed the slight glances in his direction as he passed through the room. The meeting room was in the back. There were two large men in suits standing outside the room. They seemed unaffected by Holden's presence. They were far more interested in Tom as the two of them approached.

The larger one, the man on Holden's left, raised his hand and motioned for Tom to stop. "Sorry, he goes in alone."

"I thought we were to be reassigned."

"All I know is that nobody except this guy goes in. You want answers…ask the guys up front…but nobody goes in but this guy."

Holden felt small compared to this man. He was a mountain. Holden looked at his hands as he placed them on Tom's shoulders. The fingers were the size of a baby's wrist. The suit jacket sleeves looked like pant legs and the obvious bulges told Holden it was a tight fit. The guy had a neck like a tree stump, and his head was the size of a basketball. His face was pocked from acne, and he wore an untrimmed black mustache beneath a large crooked nose. His eyes were nearly black…angry. His medium length black hair was greased nearly flat on his head and combed back over his ears. Holden waited.

"Fine." Tom said like a three-year-old and turned away. The giant looked almost disappointed.

The guy on the right, a slightly smaller man, frisked Holden, then led him into the office. He was escorted to a worn folding chair at the left side of a tattered desk and told to wait. There were no windows. Bookshelves stacked with three ring binders of every shape and color lined back wall. A vintage fax machine that looked rarely used, and stacks of papers covered the four drawer file cabinets lining the wall on his left. The phone on the desk had three lines available, with the red light on the top one. He hoped this was not indicative of the technology level at Highland.

On his right was a door that led to the back of the building, possibly an exit, and to the right of the door was a cabinet with a Bunn coffeemaker and four or five assorted mugs, none too clean. The floor looked swept, but white hole-punch dots and a couple of paper clips were visible around the desk chair. The entire office paled in comparison to the state-of-the-art computer on the desk. Holden was stretching to get a look at the screen when he heard the door open.

"So Mr. Jeffries we meet at last."

CHAPTER 32

Tom was visibly angry as he reached Morgan's desk. He slammed his fist on the blotter and was nose-to-nose with his boss.

"What the hell is going on? One day this guy is some slob that needs to be told when to take a leak…the next day we can't even stand too close to him. This is —— and you know it. I been bustin' my butt for you guys, and you let these rear ends take over like this. Do you know what's up or not?"

"Keep it down, we got enough goin' on here without some idiot causing a scene and getting us all killed."

"Killed? What the hell are you talking about?"

"These guys don't play games, Tom, this is the real stuff." Morgan whispered. "You think you earn $50,000 a year driving around the country and pickin' up stuff 'cause you're such a good driver. Wake up man!"

"You're saying that this place is a cover?"

"You're finally getting this? I ain't letting these guys take over… they own this place. You got a much better chance staying healthy if you keep your questions to yourself and forget most of what you just saw."

"So who the hell is this Jack anyway?"

"I ain't got a clue… I don't want a clue… I don't ever want to want a clue. Are you getting' this? I don't even know who's in my office, or how long they're going to be in there or even if they're in there. Don't know a thing…don't want to."

"What're you going to do, Morrie…just sit here?"

"Hell yes, I'm just going to sit here, in fact, I don't plan on getting up from this here front desk 'til this place is empty. I don't want to be anywhere near the back of this place. The very last thing I want to do is to catch a glimpse of something or someone that could be hazardous to my health."

"You sure got an imagination, Morrie. These guys don't look that tough to me."

"You best look again there, Tom, 'cause it ain't just how they look. I'm tellin' you to shut up, and to quit making yourself so visible. Just take an old man's word for it."

CHAPTER 33

Holden saw the door open and watched as three men entered. It was obvious that two of them were there to protect the third man. They had no qualms about the visibility of the guns inside their suit jackets. Each of them had on a dark suit. One was navy with a very subtle stripe, the other was dark gray, nearly black. They had white shirts and ties, black socks and black wingtips, shined nicely. Holden was somewhat impressed.

The third man was wearing a black and white hounds tooth cashmere jacket, black slacks and a black mock turtle sweater. He was about six foot three, and in decent shape, with long dark hair pulled into a ponytail. He had a mournful face with aging eyes. The shoes were Italian. He wore dark socks with a pattern. His slacks had a one and one-half inch cuff and didn't have a wrinkle. He wore a gold bracelet and a gold bracelet band watch, not Rolex, but certainly not a Timex.

Holden watched as they entered. They seemed to know the routine.

"So Mr. Jeffries. We meet at last."

The two men took their place on each side of the office door and kept their focus on Holden and the exit. The boss took his place behind the desk. He slid the chair away from the desk, leaned back and crossed his legs.

"I feel so fortunate that your final journey included Chicago and Merrilville. I cannot tell you how surprised I was to cross your path. Sorry we never got the chance to meet before now."

"Should I know you? You don't seem familiar to me."

"Actually, I have never met you. I was away when you and Kate were married but your untimely death has brought new possibilities to an old relationship."

"Do you know my wife?"

"I have nearly always known your wife. She and I go back a long way. I was surprised when she married you. But...you are right...this has little to do with us. I want some answers...then we can talk about the future if there is to be one."

"Who in the hell are you? Kate never told me that she had friends in the mob. I know that she would have let me in on it."

"Kate and I have a friendship...a friendship from her past that she can use to bring healing through this trying time."

Holden caught the wry smile.

"My name is Tony, there really is no need for you to know more. I am a lot like you. I know how to play the game—how to be something for everyone. I've done some research on you Mr. Jeffries. You were good at negotiations. The New York Times called you a tiger during that last strike—a manipulator with an attitude."

Holden watched the arrogance before him and wished he had met this guy when he was a CEO...the tiger would have enjoyed the meal.

"We got lots of guys that want to be somebody in this place. Now we got a 'somebody' that wants to be nobody. We can use you, but I'm not buying the story."

"I have nothing to hide. I got tired of the rat race, the corporate jungle. I wanted to get out and not have the baggage. I wanted it clean and done. I guess I made some mistakes, but there's no way you could have known it was me at that gas station. You guys stole my car, and my way out."

"That was fortune for us misfortune for you, but it's done. You realize don't you, that this is where it ends? You either bend and become a part of this, or you don't leave this room alive. I'd threaten you with the health of your wife, but I already know how much you care about her."

Tony made a thumbs-down gesture with his right hand.

"There are others in your life, your children for example, that waitress, Angela, you've gotten to like a bit, her son, Tom. They all are expendable to keep you in line."

"Keep me in line? I got no friends, no car, and about three pairs of pants and three shirts. Do you really think I'm a flight risk?"

"That's what I mean. You can really tell a story. Maybe you think I'm just some flunky. Well Mr. Jeffries, you don't leave a million-dollar house, and a several-million-dollar job to hide away for the rest of your life in Chicago. You got money. It's stashed somewhere. I want to know where it is. I think it's got something to do with this notebook."

Tony threw Holden's planner pages on the desk.

"I thought you burned that a couple of days ago in the packing house."

Tony watched closely, no reaction.

"You wouldn't leave without the money, at least a good share of it. I know that Kate hasn't got it. She got some money for your death, and the house, but the investment accounts, the farm, and the cash can't be the full story of a workaholic in a major position in a top ten corporation. There's got to be more. You and I both know it."

"Didn't they tell you about the $50,000? I had $50,000 in a suitcase in the car. They got that too. That would have set me up for a nice beginning. I planned to keep a low profile. I learned the truth about all that materialistic stuff. It doesn't offer fulfillment, just empty promises." Holden almost smiled.

"If I had the money, what would I have been doing in that Buick in Merrilville? Why the Midwest, why not go far away?"

"That's exactly what I have been asking. Maybe you wanted to be sure the story had chilled a bit. Let things cool down, and it worked. I mean, if it weren't for me knowing Kate, I'd never have recognized you, even with the surprises we found in the trunk."

"So after you realized who I was, you went back to the cities and found my wife? And she hasn't seen right through that?"

"She doesn't live in the cities anymore. She moved back to the farm. And yes, it was an amazing coincidence that we met in the market. She is a very vulnerable woman. She has deep wounds from the memories of an unfulfilled marriage. She blames herself for most of it, but I think I'm starting to get through."

"You're after my wife's money?"

"Hardly, it's the challenges of life that bring value to living. She is certainly a challenge"

Tony hesitated for effect.

"And anyway, I had to know about her financial situation to get a feel for my suspicions about you. I know there's money. Eventually I will find it. I can make your life, or should I say after-life, very enjoyable. We have several sins available to our employees...especially the important employees. Life can be very unfair too if you make the wrong choices."

"Tony, I really have little to offer except my expertise. Since you are not going to let me go...you can have that. Maybe someday you will give me my freedom if I show you I deserve it. If I had something to offer to purchase it, I would do that. What can I do to win your trust?"

Tony smiled, and Holden wasn't certain if the smile was a sign that he believed Holden, or just the satisfaction of seeing him crawl. Neither mattered. All that was important was the notepad. It was still intact. Holden needed to get that book and not let them know it was gone. If he were right about them...running from the police was nothing compared getting away from these guys.

"I am going to give you a letter that puts you in charge of Highland Transfer. Your training will begin Monday. You will need to learn the operation. Don't take your time, there's a lot to learn, and we want you ready for the busy season.

Tony stopped and looked directly into Holden's eyes.

And...we are always watching so don't be stupid. This could turn out a whole lot better than you think. We want to trust you, never entirely, but at least a bit, so don't give us any more reason to worry. Just help us and we will keep you happy."

Holden nodded as if in total submission.

"By the way, you will still be Jack Grayton. Many of the employees are accustomed to your name. It's difficult to trace. And you are never to repeat my name outside these walls. It was certainly a pleasure. We must do this again."

CHAPTER 34

The meeting was over just before three thirty. Holden exited the office alone. He carried a large manila envelope. The two giants stood beside the desk arms folded as Morgan broke the seal.

> To all employees of Highland Transfer, Jack Grayton is now in charge of all operations Merriville Branch and will be in training beginning August 31. Please give him all your attention and help him get acquainted with both the position and his fellow employees.
>
> Sincerely,
> Morgan Whitman, Manager

Morgan was not surprised. This meant nothing to his position. He would be expected to work in the same capacity...just to show the new guy the ropes. The Big Guys wanted Jack to get acquainted so they could move him either into a new project, or into the main office in Chicago. At any rate, the next few weeks would be tougher... it was no fun training the new guy.

"What's that all about? Morgan, what's the letter say?"

"Geeze, Tom, give me a chance to get stuff together, you'll hear soon enough."

"So if it's not a secret why can't I see it now?"

"Jack here is taking over the operation in Merrilville…at least for a while."

"Jack?… This Jack?… He ain't even been here two weeks. He still doesn't know half of what I know. He's been gone two days without even telling us he was leaving, and then he gets a promotion. This is exactly what I was talking about."

"Hey Tommy, I don't make the rules. If they decide to make him President, I don't give a crap. Jack, you got a bunch to learn… did they give you any timetable."

"Nope. They just told me to bring out the letter."

"Who told you, Jack?" Tom jumped in.

"Hey, I don't think they want a lot of what was said in there spread around. If they wanted to be introduced they probably would have arrived and left by the front door."

"The thing's not even signed. How do we know it's real?"

Holden turned and faced Tommy whispering nearly nose to nose.

"Real? Are you serious? What about those two guys, do they seem real to you? Tell you the truth… I had little intention of moving up the ladder here but looks like none of us have a lot of choices at this point." Holden hoped Morgan wasn't listening. He seemed preoccupied with the two thugs who were packing up and heading toward the door.

"I don't trust you Jack, got that?"

"Yeah, and I'm real impressed with the job you got me. You're probably going to tell me you never knew anything about the upper management."

"I didn't have a clue until today that this was anything other than a freight company and transfer station. How in the hell did you get to be so important? You've been holding out on Mom and me. You said you didn't even know anybody here."

"I have some experience in running small companies that interests them. I'm not so sure what they expect myself. I just know that at this point I have little to say about the decision. You and your mom have been a lot of help. I need someone to trust. I hope I can count on you."

"I'm not about to let my mom get hurt again. I'll give you a ride back to the hotel, but I ain't about to trust you!"

"A ride would be nice."

As they drove, Holden watched Tommy. Holden was certain that Tom had never seen the truth of his job. He just trusted them to be honest with him. He was trying to keep the household afloat...so to him it was just a paycheck.

Holden noticed how troubled Tom seemed as he drove, running the events through his mind, trying to make sense of it all. He knew the questions because he had them too. Who could he trust? How deep was he? Was he in danger? How about his Mother? Would he still have a job? Would he still want the job? Should he leave? Could he leave? Just who were those guys?

The wheels turned, and conversation was nonexistent, which suited Holden fine.

CHAPTER 35

K ate awoke with a plan. There was a lot to do. She had to get moving. The shower was invigorating. She had more energy than she expected as she entered the kitchen to make breakfast. The suns warmth felt wonderful on her feet as she stood in the reflection of the window. Each day she seemed to love life more. Kate phoned Matt immediately after breakfast.

"I understand that you had a couple of visitors."

"Actually, I think we experienced more than a couple, Matt."

"Well, Brian certainly seems like a different kid. He just can't tell enough people about the tractor and the farm. It was his first time out of the city, and he has never seen so much open space. He loved the meal you made too. He said you did something special with the French Fries."

"I just used real potatoes, not the frozen stuff. Guess some of us take the country for granted. But…that's what I want to talk to you about."

"French fries?"

"No Matt, the farm. I have been thinking since the guys left about the excitement in Brian's eyes when he got outside of the house. I think this might be a special place for kids from troubled households to come for some education. Maybe even some of the guys from the jail."

Kate hesitated. She listened for some sign from Matt…quiet… she continued.

"We have two hundred and forty acres of farm here to work. I learned so much about a work ethic on this farm. Why can't others learn from this environment? I know that there are lots of questions to work out, but I want you to start to work on this. Ask Jack...ask whoever, but I want to use this place for what God intended...a place to learn to live."

"Kate, are you serious?"

"I've never been more serious. I think we should stop renting this place out and get back to farming it ourselves. When I was growing up, chores weren't always the most positive thing, but they made me learn responsibility. Work gave me a feeling of belonging and accomplishment at the end of the day. It's still a part of my life...that feeling...that need.

Matt broke in. "It's not that I disagree... I'm speechless."

"There are dozens of jobs to do. Each task demands a different skill...different gifts. It requires a family type atmosphere to make it succeed."

Kate walked to the kitchen table and remembered the many meals she shared there.

"What these kids are missing the most is a feeling of family? It can't have changed that much?"

"I do know things have changed, but by the look on Brian's face, the farm has something to offer some of the kids."

"We can get animals and chickens. We can plant, farm and harvest. We can build a bunkhouse, and all eat together. This place can be more than a camp for troubled kids...it can be a place to live forever if they choose. I want it to be a business that they run, a home where they are loved and respected. I just don't know where to start."

"We always start with prayer. Pray until we get the answers. Kate this is exactly what I've been praying for. I wasn't asking Him specifically for a farm, but I was asking for a place for people who had never experienced a family to start over. You just described it—it must be from God. He probably already has the answer, he just wants us to ask the questions."

"This is going to take a lot of work Matt, but prayer makes sense. It really does...much more than it ever did in the past. I will do just that. Pass the information on to Jack and ask him to pray too. Get back to me if any lights come on."

Matt hung up the phone and his mind began to race. Could this be true? This desire that he had expressed to God to make a difference, was it really happening? The jail ministry... Holden Jeffries... Jack Grayton...the closed doors...the misery of the loss of a husband...the number of times that Matt had doubted. Could it all swirl together and come to this?

Matt realized at that moment how little he really understood about God. God was in control whether he worried and fretted or not. He smiled as he pictured a Father with a knowing grin looking down. Matt was loved by a power that could shake the world and was willing to use the weak to help rebuild it. He dialed his wife's work phone.

"Matt, is everything ok?"

"Wait 'til you hear this one."

He told Connie the entire story. Tears flowed as she listened. Connie was a prayer warrior. She had never complained about the lack of things in their lives. She bought clothes at garage sales and stretched the food budget, never losing faith. They had never experienced children, and Connie had trusted God with that too. She had always wanted a family.

Now as Matt talked, she imagined the farm as a place to experience her own family, children were children. God answers prayer. Sometimes one person's answer also serves to answer another's. Connie was thrilled, and nearly overwhelmed.

"We must consider moving down there to help get the place in shape. Have you seen the farm? Does it need a lot of work? How much room is there to live?"

Connie walked while she talked.

"Does she expect us to live on the farm too? Matt, are you listening?"

"I'm right here, Connie. I don't know any of this stuff. I just told her to pray about the details. I think she just came up with the idea after Jack and Brian visited. There probably aren't any answers to the questions yet. But they are good questions. We need to talk about our part in this, and we need to pray too."

"Matt, do you think your dad might want to help out with this? You know he has some wonderful experience with the farm and all that goes with it."

There was a silence on the line. Matt had not considered his father...he hadn't considered him for years. His father as much as disowned him when he decided to go into the ministry. Gus Roth always had high hopes for his son. He wanted him to become an engineer or a lawyer, something to be proud of.

When Matt had dropped out of the University and headed for seminary it was almost more than his father could stand. He told Matt not to expect his help, and said he felt Matt was taking the easy way out.

They kept communications open, although strained, until Matt dropped out of the ministry and took a job at the Coke plant—that was the final blow. The "I told you so" attitude had driven a wedge between them. Matt felt he failed, and his father certainly agreed. They had grown apart, and death of Matt's mother added to the distance.

Gus had alienated himself from nearly everyone who cared. He had no grandchildren with the Roth name, another disappointment. His son was a failure, his life was as good as over, and he was willing to share his disillusionment with anyone who would listen.

"Matt, are you there?"

"I'm here Connie, I really can't say my dad came to mind in any of this until now."

"But Matt, it's what he knows. It's what he lived. He has nothing to do, don't you think it would be good for him."

"I think we need Christians to bring this about. He doesn't even like Christians."

"Matt, you said it was God who would lead this, right? Then think about it...it just may be part of His plan. You know...mysterious ways. When God has an impossible job, he sometimes uses impossible men."

"I'm not saying I won't consider it, it's just not the sort of thing that Dad seems interested in doing. In fact, it's his total lack of interest in much of anything that makes me wonder why you would even consider him."

"We all need to be needed, even the seeming independent and self-reliant. He needs to be a part of something again. This is a perfect chance. He loves the farm, though he would never admit it. He was happiest when he was farming."

"Happiness and my father were rarely seen together...at least in my experience. I promise to pray about it...but...not too hard."

CHAPTER 36

The two bedroom house in Madelia had never replaced the farm-house. A postage-stamp-sized lawn was a far cry from the half section farm Gus called home for nearly forty years. Life alone was a bitter pill to swallow after having a wife and family.

Gus Roth had never known much happiness in his life…retirement years were turning out to be no exception. He always dreamed of buying the farm from the landlords, but they always wanted more than he was willing to pay. Just about the time that the price seemed realistic, they raised it.

He rented the farm for forty years. He knew he was responsible for making the owners rich. It was Gus who knew about hybrids and fertilizer. It was Gus that kept the buildings like new…the fields without so much as a weed. Of course, the kids never wanted to walk the beans, or bale hay, or do the chores, but life isn't about what you want, it's about what is required. Gus was aware of what was required for most of life.

He had a daughter, his oldest child, must be about forty now. She was married and had two kids. Married a schoolteacher and moved to Kansas right out of college. He never got much of a chance to get to know those kids, and he wasn't shy about telling her how she was ignoring him in his final days.

They tried to come home at least once a year, but his house was so small that it wasn't very comfortable for them, especially with the kids along. Lately she had been coming alone, the husband and the kids stayed back home and made flimsy excuses. Gus knew the

117

truth…he really didn't care…probably best not to get too close anyway. It hurts less if you don't have any close ties.

His son Matt could have been somebody. He was smart, athletic, well liked in school. Gus had pushed him a bit when he was young, taught him a work ethic and the meaning of success, but it never really took.

The kid went to college and put forth a marginal effort. When he had blown his chances at becoming somebody, he used religion and talk about God to enable him to back out of his commitment to his father. He had become, of all things, a minister…a bible thumper…a man without a real job. Gus tried to persuade him to rethink his decision, but kids never listen to parents, even if they're right. So his only son went to the *cemetery* as Gus liked to joke and became a "man of the cloth" (another word for lazy).

As if that wasn't bad enough, after a couple of years, the kid got tired of it and quit. The only job he could find was driving a Coke truck in a suburb of the cities. His biggest claim to fame was going into jails and talking to ex-cons and jailbirds about God. It made Gus angry just to think of it. He had given his life to these kids. The ingratitude was almost unspeakable.

Gus tried to stay busy with a little wood shop in the garage, but wood was so expensive he didn't spend much time in there anymore. There was a coffee group at the café, (a bunch of old farts that spent most of the day with their noses in other peoples…business). When he first moved to town, after his wife passed away, he used to frequent the round table quite often. Not anymore. Something changed over time.

The last few years he sat on his porch and listened to WCCO, 830 on the AM dial. He would think about how it could have been. The preacher stopped by a couple of times and invited him to church…kind of a nosy guy, wanted to know if he was saved (all the bible-thumpers used the same lines). He told him in no uncertain terms that was personal and none of his business. Young people have little respect for people with experience.

Harvest time was approaching. He loved the smell of picked corn and bean fields. He could almost hear the picker working or the combine running. Gus had spent so much of his life listening to the machines it was almost part of him. He didn't tell anyone, but in the fall when it was dark, he would drive out in the country and just sit in the fields and remember.

Hell, he had no place to go, no place to be, and nobody cared if he was gone all night. Like the kids cared. The smells and the sounds of the night, and the cool air brought back memories so vivid that he could almost hear his wife call him in to supper. He remembered plowing in the late fall through the night. The 560 would change its sound as the night air cooled. The tractor had far more power at 10:00 PM than at any time during the day.

He remembered the fire that came out of the muffler as it worked its magic, turning stubble into black earth, so black it reminded him of a newly opened can Kiwi shoe polish. He remembered the ear corn moving up the elevator of the picker, and the husk getting caught in the rollers. He remembered the combine cutting the stalks of soybeans and watching the hopper fill with yellow. He remembered cutting oats with the binder and baling the straw. He remembered stacking the bales in the barn, and the feeling of accomplishment when it was all in and done. It was a wonderful time.

But most of all he loved plowing. He was in a world of his own when he was on that tractor, a world he wished he'd never left. He knew life was unfair, but he never expected it to end up this lonely.

He nearly tipped over the chair when the phone rang.

"Dad, is that you?"

"Who else lives at this number? Of course, it's me."

"It's good to hear your voice, how've you been."

"I'm surprised you recognized the voice, been so long since you heard it. I guess I'm doing ok, been pretty busy in the shop. You're lucky you caught me. I just sat down for a break."

"I was wondering if you were going to be there a while. I'm calling you from the car. I got a phone for my route. They let me carry it even when I don't work, so thought I'd let you know I was coming your way. Thought maybe I'd stop by if you are going to be there."

"I ain't plannin' on going anywhere, but I don't have much to snack on, so hope you've eaten lunch. Got coffee, but that's about it."

"I thought I might bring lunch along if you haven't eaten. Thought I might pick up come KFC. I know you always loved chicken."

"What's the score, Matt? Are you trying to butter me up for something? You need money or something? I barely got enough to get by myself, so no use trying to get blood from a turnip. If that's it, just thought I better tell you up front."

"I do have something to run by you, but I promise it won't cost you anything except a bit of your time. Can you spare a couple of hours, or would it be better to do this another time?"

"I must say I'm not surprised there's a catch. You haven't exactly been too interested in my life in the past…been pretty much ignoring me since your mother died…but I can find a couple of minutes, and the chicken thing sounds ok, even though I just ate. I can at least sit with you while you eat, maybe I'll nibble on a wing or something if there's an extra one. How far away are you?"

"I should be there in half an hour, see you then."

*****

When the doorbell rang Kate was just finishing up painting some of the woodwork in the three-season porch. She wasn't exactly presentable for company, but since moving to the country, she had lost some of the *neighborhood.*

She did not recognize the man at the door, but his age put her at ease. He was at least sixty. Although in fair physical shape, he certainly didn't look like someone to fear. She pulled her hair back into a loose ponytail as she approached the door and tucked her blouse into her jeans.

"May I help you sir?"

"I understand you want me to teach you the ropes, young lady. I ain't seen the whole place yet, but it certainly doesn't look like we got a lot to work with. I'm not saying we can't do it, but it's going to be spendy, and a hell of a lot of work."

"Excuse me, but I'm not certain you are in the right place."

"You're Kate Jeffries, aren't you?"

"Yes, but…

"Then I'm talking to the right person. Gus Roth's my name. How many tractors you got? How about machinery, you know, planters, plows, combine, all that stuff? That stuff will kill you if you got to buy it all."

"You're Matt's dad…come in, I'll put on some coffee. You do drink coffee don't you?"

"Love coffee, but not too strong. I like to see the bottom of the cup. Most women make coffee way too strong."

Kate thought about how both alike and unlike her father this man seemed. He was straight forward, nearly to a fault, but she was certain it was a facade. His eyes looked lonely. He had a round face with nearly white hair and a white beard. She was certain that he had been alone a while. She could tell by the wrinkles in his khaki pants that either he had no one to iron his clothes or he had worn these a number of times.

The flannel shirt collar was worn and wrinkled, and the cuffs were a bit threadbare. He wore tied work boots that had hooks on the top four or five laces. She remembered helping her father lace his boots in the mornings before school, and the feeling of just being close to him…he had worn boots like these. The boots were scuffed but not dirty and seemed to be fairly new. She noticed the T-shirt collar had a yellow tinge, another telltale sign of men living alone. Men were aggressive in so many things, but it always struck Kate as peculiar that they feared things like bleach and laundry detergent. She had watched her father build sheds, rooms onto the house, and fences, yet pale when faced with an electric iron, or a washing machine.

She wondered if this man cooked or ate in the café in his town. Few men cooked for themselves. Usually it was a combination of loneliness and laziness. Gus watched intently as Kate prepared the coffee and put some chocolate chip cookies on a plate. She set the table with two cups and saucers and two small plates. She sat while the coffee brewed.

"Matt mentioned that he had spoken with you, but I wasn't aware that you were planning on visiting."

"Are these cookies store bought or homemade, they look like you baked them?"

"Actually, I bought them at the bakery in town."

"Probably not much of a cook since you were kind of a businesswoman your whole life. It's okay, I buy pretty much everything myself. My wife was quite a baker in her time, though. She made bread nearly every day when the kids were growing up…sometimes baked cookies or pie if we had the money. Is that one of those Bunn coffeemakers with the water hooked right to it?"

"Yes, it's a Bunn built in. Just click a switch."

"Is that right? Does it have the coffee and everything in it too?"

Kate nodded.

"Didn't think so, thought I saw you put some in that brown basket. What's that little thing that growls then?"

Kate couldn't help but smile. "That's the coffee grinder. I use whole bean coffee so I get a fresh taste."

"We always just used Folgers, it tasted great for the first pot or two."

"See how you like this. I hope it's not too strong."

Gus took a sip from his mug, then closed his eyes lightly and nodded. "Didn't think it would be worth all the trouble…it's really good. I'll have to get me one of those grinders when I get some money. Now what's this about giving the farm to a bunch of jailbirds?"

*****

"I spent the afternoon with a man from Madelia. You wouldn't know anyone there would you?"

Matt winced. "My dad came by the farm?"

"He said you wanted him to take over, and he needed to get a handle on what was to be expected. He was full of great ideas and seems to love chocolate chip cookies and gourmet coffee. He also says you don't visit him much."

"Kate, I'm really sorry. I mentioned that you were thinking about starting up the farm again, and that his expertise might come in handy, but I never expected him to bother you. I'll call him and talk to him as soon as we're done. It won't happen again."

"You're probably going to have trouble finding him home, he's moving into the bunkhouse tomorrow. Wants to get right to work, lots of stuff to do. I can't wait to have him around…he's a great guy. I will get a phone out there as soon as possible, but you could come by and help a bit on weekends if you want to see him. Said he hadn't seen Connie for a long while either."

"How long was he there for cripes sake?"

"I really can't be certain, I enjoyed him so much that the time just flew. I learned so much about his past." Kate didn't really know Matt that well, but she was enjoying his discomfort and she truly had enjoyed his father's company.

"You're kidding about the bunkhouse, aren't you? You don't really have a bunk house, do you?"

"Actually, it was a little building that my father remodeled for our hired man back in the late fifties. It needs some cleanup, but what doesn't around here. Your father lit up like a Christmas tree when he saw it. I did offer to cook some meals and eat together with him while he's here. He really is a lonely man. I think he knows a lot about the farm too."

"You're serious?"

"Matt, he is exactly what we need, and I think we are exactly what he needs, even though he would be the last to admit it. God works in mysterious ways, you know."

"Jack and Brian would certainly like to help when you get a plan. Connie and I will be there too, just let us know."

"Let's get together Saturday, here at the farm. Time's a wasting."

"I'll try to get it together at this end. Don't let Dad get too much of a hold, he rarely lets go."

"Just let me handle that, Matt. You worry too much."

Gus could think of nothing else on the way home. That little bunkhouse was perfect. It had a kitchen with cupboards just like the ones he remembered from the farm, and the bedroom had a closet with a curtain for a door, just like when he was a kid. It had a queen-sized mattress…more than he needed, but it was great. There was kerosene stove for heat and a fan for cooling off.

He would get packed tonight and leave right away in the morning. Kate had given him a tour of the farm. The machinery was nearly non-existent, but used machinery was plentiful in southern Minnesota. He knew machinery and what they would need.

He had one tractor, a Farmall Super MTA…a great machine in its time. The reason International Harvester quit making them was because they never broke down. It had nearly sixty horsepower and could easily pull a three-bottom plow. It would be enough for a start. He found a plow and disc in the machine shed. They were rusty but would work for now. He would need a planter, some wagons, a cultivator, a corn-picker, a spring-tooth…what else, what else?

The barn was in surprisingly good shape. The milk parlor was a disaster, but he really didn't want to milk cows anyhow, so…no problem. The stalls need to be cleaned, the manure was probably twenty years old and about knee deep. They would need some kind of manure spreader too. If they were going to have animals, they would need to repair the fences and gates…what kind of animals should they have?

It was way too early to think about all of this. Where would the jailbirds sleep and eat? There wasn't a building decent enough other than the bunkhouse, and that was taken. There was a lot to do. He was almost relieved when he drove into his garage, but he hadn't enjoyed a day like this for a long time. He couldn't remember a quicker sixty miles. It was like he just left. He had to get packing.

CHAPTER 37

Angela and Tom met nearly every day at the Rusty Skillet for dinner. They rarely saw Jack since he had been declared boss at the transfer company. Today, the conversation had nothing to do with Jack or the company. Angela was in tears when Tom entered. He was concerned but not surprised. She had left a rather anxious message on his cell phone about needing to see him ASAP. She was usually not the type for melodramatic annoyances, but she was his mother and at times she worried more than necessary.

"Hey, Mom, I got the message, what's up?"

"Tommy sit down, we need to talk."

Tom knew it must be something she considered particularly important...she rarely called him Tommy unless she was upset or angry.

"Sure, did I do something wrong?"

"It's not you, Tom. They found your father this morning in a burned-out car, just outside Chicago. He was behind the wheel, and there was a bunch of money in the trunk. There aren't too many details, but they want me to identify the body as soon as I can bring myself to do it."

"Dad's dead? They're sure it's him? Who called you, the police or who?"

Tom sunk deeper into the chair.

"Do you really think it's him, Mom?"

"They said the body is pretty burned, but the ID in his wallet checked out to be him. They are going to try to check his prints if they can find them. They also want his dental records… Will you go with me to the morgue? I just don't think I can do it alone. Tommy, will you go?"

"Of course, but to what morgue? Where did they take the body?"

"That's sort of interesting, the body is here in Merrillville. They shipped it here because they knew his family lived here. How would they know us? He hasn't made any effort to include us in his life for so long, I can't figure how they knew about us." Angela stopped for a moment as if thinking. "At least it's close by and we don't have to drive into the city for this."

"Who called you, Mom? Do you remember who it was?"

"Yes, it was the County Sheriff here in Merrilville. They even left a message on the phone at home in case they hadn't caught me at work. How did they know he was my husband? It must be on record somewhere…it's probably no big deal, but the last name of Parker isn't so rare that it makes the world tie us together."

"I think the first thing we need to do is to make certain that it's really Dad. It is kind of strange the way it all played out, but we need to know if he's really dead. Can you stand going right away 'cause I'd really like to get it over?"

"They said I could do whatever I needed to do…take what ever time it takes. Let's head over now. Do you know where the morgue is?"

"I think it's at the City Hall, didn't they tell you?"

"They did say it was at the hospital, I think, not City Hall."

"That makes more sense, I'll drive."

*****

Holden had been learning the ropes for the past few weeks. The operation was seemingly small, although he wasn't certain if he was seeing the entire operation. At any rate, Highland Transfer was legitimate in some ways, and a front in others. The warehouse had a shipping and receiving area, but they were only a small part of the six-hundred thousand square foot building.

Tom had not been dishonest with Holden. He probably had no idea that he was working for a front company for the mob. Each day there would be legitimate business out the front doors. But the back doors were the busy doors, especially at night. The body shop as Morrey called it was in the back.

Cars were stolen in the area every day. They were chosen by a specific criterion. The license plate was usually from at least two states away. The cars were either luxury models or basic. The luxury models should never be more than one-year-old, the mileage must be low, and the car should be cherry.

The driver should always be a woman. The best place to find the perfect hit was at a strip mall. There of course were exceptions to these criteria, but most fit the list. The basic cars were chosen by a different set of rules. The cars should be late model, probably not older than five years. Midsize and above were fair game.

The base sticker price of this group should be in the midtwenties to low thirties. It made no difference if the driver was man or woman, if they went inside the store. The boys needed only seconds to move the car, and less if the driver left the keys in the ignition. There was always a market for wheels, but what was the mob doing, opening used car lots?

"Jack, I must tell you that passing through these doors and talking about what you see to anyone, even your priest, would be an unhealthy decision."

"Got it, Morrey. I think I picked that up at the employment interview. I am supposed to learn the operation, I think I already know the incentive program."

"Yeah, well sometimes even smart people make some stupid moves."

"You might say eternal, huh?"

"That'd be close…yeah, eternal." Morrey shot Holden a sleazy smile.

They stepped into an enormous warehouse, with hundreds of lights. It was bright as sunshine. Holden immediately began to take it all in, to his left were approximately sixty nearly new cars, every one of them a Lexus, Mercedes, BMW, Lincoln, or Cadillac. The workers wore white coveralls with no name, just white. There was no smell of painting, and only the hoods were opened.

Holden noticed that the windshields were removed from nearly every auto. Holden looked to his right and saw another group of autos; these were nothing fancy. There seemed to be no rhyme or reason for the brands, Taurus, LeSabre, Sable, Nova, Toyota, and on and on. The windshields were missing on these also, and the hoods were up. He also noticed that none of the cars had license plates. "If this is a body shop, or a chop shop, why aren't these cars being torn down."

"Don't have to. These cars are being remodeled in a different way. We get rid of the VIN numbers on each car, replace the plate, and voile, it's a new creation."

"You can't sell cars without a VIN number."

"Depends where you peddle them. Or…if you peddle them."

"There are no rules in third world countries, and the market is hot for luxury cars at great prices. Everybody likes a deal, and we don't put a lot of time in on these, so the price is right."

"Mexico?"

"Mexico, Russia, Central America, Cuba, there are markets everywhere."

"They want old Fords and Chevys, and Lexus's?"

"The Ford's and Chevy's are not marketed in the same way. Our guys use them."

"Our guys?"

"Yeah, we need to use cars to get our stuff done. We don't always want everybody to know who owned the car if it turns up somewhere where something bad has happened."

"Like, a death, or a robbery, or a kidnapping? That kind of bad stuff." Holden stated cynically.

"Exactly. Our customers prefer to remain in the background. They pay for anonymity, you know?"

"You mean, anonymity, don't you?"

"Whatever, you know they don't want anybody to know who they are. Anyway, the cars get a different license plate, and we file the numbers, and we sell them to the highest bidder. I think that's going to be your job, finding the highest bidder. I hear you got talent in negotiations."

"Where do you get the plates, without the police running a number and finding out its hot?"

"It ain't hot! We got lots of friends around the state that own used car dealerships. You wouldn't believe the pieces of crap people trade in, most of them got plates with at least a couple of months left on the date. We switch the plates and they are sent to the crusher, and bingo, we got a car that doesn't even raise an eyebrow if the police run it. Started out with the cheap ones, then it worked so well that somebody got the idea about the spendy ones, and just like that we got a whole new business. Just can't get enough inventory for the demand."

"If all these cars are being stolen around here, aren't—the police a bit suspicious."

"First place, very few cars are stolen around here, at least in Merrilville. Unless somebody leaves the keys in it or something," Morrey snickered, then continued, "second, we got some friends in the system, if you know what I mean."

"The police are in this?"

"Not the police, just a friend or two. It ain't something you need to worry about."

"So where are all the offices?"

Morrey pointed up to his left. "They been watching you since we walked in."

Holden had completely overlooked the windows above him. He could almost feel the eyes from behind them. He was relieved it was just theft. He could deal with that, much of what he did in his old job probably had similar demands, it was called business.

*****

Tom and his mother barely spoke to each other on their way to the morgue. It is interesting how death brings emotions rarely expressed in life. Angela spent the time questioning the last thirty years of her life. The highlight of her life was seated beside her, but the partner she had dreamed of had never materialized.

Mickey Parker was a handsome, daring stranger when she first met him in her junior year in high school. He had a reputation for being a mover, and Angela was very vulnerable. She knew little about boys as an only child in a single parent home.

Her mother had dumped her father two weeks before she was born, and he had never been allowed into her life. She was told that he was dead for the first fifteen years of her existence, and only through reading some hidden letters had she learned about the lie.

She faced her mother with the truth when she was sixteen, only after she allowed her mom to dig herself a big hole with her lies. She remembered pulling the letter out of her blouse pocket and dangling it before her eyes. She remembered the tears and the apologies, but Angela would have none of it. She packed her bag moved in with her friend Charlotte, leaving her mother shattered and alone.

Charlotte lived almost by herself about two miles from Angela's house. Charlotte's father was an alcoholic and her Mother died years before from an overdose of Heroin. Charlotte had it made. She had no curfew, no budget, no rules, no bedtime, and she needed a friend desperately. Life became fun again. They could go anywhere, and they didn't have to go to school every day…they got to choose…it was great.

Angela remembered her mother dropping by with peace offerings, something she may have found at a sale, or baked for them, but she never demanded that Angela return. The distance between them widened… Angela believed her mother didn't want her either.

One year later, when Angela was seventeen, Mickey entered her life. He was full of ideas and said nice things especially about her figure and looks. He took her to movies and held her hand. He told her that he loved her…she wanted that more than anything. She became pregnant and dropped out of school. Mickey married her in her seventh month and lost interest in her eighth. He had always been a shadow of a husband.

When Thomas was three, Mickey attempted fatherhood. Angela hoped having a son would be enough, it wasn't. He stayed for three weeks, four days, and seventeen hours. Then his next chance at making it big presented itself—a job as a bodyguard for some second-rate hood—and Mickey was off again.

Angela was devastated. She was still a child herself alone with a baby she had no desire to raise. She had no skills, no income. Her mother had her own problems with depression and drugs. Since Angela had become pregnant out of wedlock, her grandparents disowned her and her baby. She had nowhere to turn. In her darkest times she considered suicide and taking her baby with her.

After a year of struggle, unemployment, and welfare, she found a job in a small greasy restaurant called the Rusty Skillet. She was hired and trained to be a waitress for the four-to-midnight. They even allowed her to bring the baby in the early years because her pay simply wouldn't cover childcare. She loved her job and her boss, but she despised the late-night crowd. They knew her circumstances. They knew she was alone. Some saw her as one more item on the menu. She fought constantly to keep the losers from getting the wrong idea.

The owner Andy Marriotti was a heavy-set, jovial man who rarely seemed anything but content. She came to trust him, and even left Thomas with his wife and kids, as he grew older. Angela knew that he had a strong faith in God. She was amazed to see his faith in the dark times almost the same as in the best of times. She finally asked him about it.

"Why are you happy even when crappy stuff happens to you?"

"I'm not happy about it, but I know that I have a friend that will change it to something good in my life."

"You mean God, right?"

"God in the person of Jesus, yep. It's all about caring more about Him than all this stuff put together. I probably ain't gonna be here forever, but now that I know where I'm going and who it is that is leading me from here on out, none of this much matters. Took me a long time to get to this point though. Had to give up most of everything I had learned about getting ahead. Had to realize I'm already ahead if I just let Him do the leading."

"You really don't seem to worry too much, but then you got a business and enough money to get along, that helps."

"Hey, Jesus owns everything anyway, he just lets us use it. Why not give him a chance to help? If it don't work out, you can go back to worrying."

It was conversations like that that changed her outlook and her life. Oh, she still struggled to make ends meet, and Mickey never wanted much to do with her or Tommy, but she had a friend that loved her more than anyone else ever had, and it never changed. She could count on Him.

She regretted her mistakes, but found forgiveness for them, not always from the world, but from the creator, and that was enough. Now, as she felt the car pull to a stop, another chapter in her life was about to come to an end. Only God knew what the next one would bring.

*****

As Tom drove, he was lost in thought. His father was probably dead, and it looked as if he'd been set up. He knew finding a burned-out car with money on the scene was usually a sign from someone that it wasn't an accident. He couldn't help but remember the words of Morrey about keeping quiet. Had he done something that caused his father's death? He had no idea how they could even know that it was his father, but they had lots of inside information, and you could never be sure who was who, or how much they knew.

He looked at his mother and saw the sadness. He always hoped that his father would come home. He realized years ago it was only a dream. He was surprised he saw his father at all. Since his mother found God, there were entire seasons they never heard a word.

Tom wanted to ask him about his job, but he knew that his father would never be honest. He was always looking for the big score. It was always just around the next corner. It just never got close enough for him to grasp. He was a loser. Tom knew it. His mother knew it. But they never discussed it.

People find more hope in lies than in truth. It's better not to be too honest with yourself…less pain, less anger, less worry. Now he was gone. It was not as if it would be a lot different, but the finality of death brought different emotions than loneliness.

As the car pulled up to the hospital, Tom prayed he would not find his father in this place, but deep down inside he knew he would. At least he would not feel the loss that someone who had been loved would have experienced. He could handle this; it wasn't as if he was losing a real father.

Angela and Tom were escorted to the basement of St Mary's Hospital. The hallways were dimly lit, and narrow. The clean smell of the upper floors had been replaced with a musty underground odor. It wasn't unpleasant, but it was not comforting. The doors had been recently repainted—the windows still had forgotten masking tape around some of their edges. Tom recognized the fragrance of Latex paint and floor wax mixed with the dampness of the underground. Furnace and water pipes gave the ceiling a hint of their past, but they seemed without the dust found in most basements.

The nurse opened the outer doors and they entered a stark room with tables and several overhead lights. Tom knew this must be the place where autopsies were performed. He could smell formaldehyde, a fragrance he remembered well from high school biology.

Angela was not doing well; she was nauseated and perspiring and…the identification had yet to begin. The odors were overwhelming for her. The extremely bright lights were causing her to feel uncomfortably dizzy. The nurse was young, barely thirty, and seemed unaccustomed to her task. She rarely spoke but had a comforting smile. As they stood in the center of the room none of them seemed anxious to get down to business. Tom broke the ice.

"Will we be viewing the remains in this room?"

"The identification will take place in the adjacent room. Everything is prepared, but I would like to warn you that the body is severely burned. If either of you don't feel that you are ready for this, we can set it up for a later date."

Tom shrugged and shook his head. "I am not sure what to expect, but waiting doesn't seem to be an option. Mom, are you all right with this?"

"I have always hoped never to be involved in something like this, but God never gives us more than we can bear, so I will face my fears. Let's get on with it."

They were given face masks and led through the door into the next room. It was not much smaller than the examining room, but much darker. The gurney was in the middle of the room with one light shining directly on the white sheet. It was evident from the shape a body lay beneath the cover. It seemed to Angela it took an inordinate length of time to reach the viewing area. She was dreading what she would see in the next few moments. There was an oppressive odor of burnt flesh that added to her anxiety.

The nurse took hold of the sheet and pulled it quickly away from the body exposing the head and shoulders of the corpse. Even without hair and eyelashes and burned, it was evident that it was Mickey. Angela held tightly to Tom's right hand as they both nodded almost simultaneously then turned away. The nurse immediately replaced the sheet and the viewing was finished.

There was no need to extend their stay. They had answered the mandatory questions, signed the papers and passed quietly through the hallways and back into the night air. Angela collapsed to the curb into a flood of tears. Tom was not expecting this response. She had been so strong. She had not fainted at the sight of a burned corpse. It had nauseated even him. She had shown amazing fortitude in the paperwork, now this obvious weakness had him confused.

"Are you okay, Mom?"

"I'm going to need a minute, Tom. Could you find me a tissue in the car?"

She lifted her head slightly and then covered her eyes with her hands.

"I know I'm causing a scene, but it's not a real busy place. I just can't go any farther. I'll be better in a couple of minutes. You go on to the car I'll be there shortly."

"I'm not embarrassed. I've got a napkin right here, and it doesn't matter to me if you want to sit here all night. You did a great job back there, Mom. I know a lot of men that couldn't handle what you just experienced. I just wasn't aware that you loved him this much…to cry like this about his death. I guess I'm just surprised… I had no idea that you cared so much for him."

"I let him down, Tommy. He died without hope. I never got him to believe in Christ. I know that he is not in a better place. I could see the fear in those eyes. I never want to see that again."

Angela was looking directly into the eyes of her son.

"Tommy, you've got to promise me that you will not wait too long to make a decision. It's over for your father. I just don't think I could handle not knowing if I would see you in heaven."

"Mom… Geeze…this stuff is bull. You can't possibly know what happened to dad. Are you saying he went to hell?"

"Sorry, Tom."

"Nobody can know that. It's just a guess. He wasn't that bad of a guy. I know a lot worse, and you're not perfect either."

"He didn't know Christ, Tom. That's all that matters. Without Christ, there is no hope for heaven."

"I don't want to talk about this now. I thought you cared about him. You just want to use this to get me into the same religious stuff as you. I don't believe it. I don't want to be part of it."

Tommy's voice was escalating.

I really don't need some kind of sermon. This fanatical religious stuff is okay for you… I want to have a life."

Angela dropped her head in her hands and sobbed. She did not know what to do anymore, her husband was dead, and the memory of his horror filled eyes would be with her for the rest of her life. Now she was alienating her son. She silently prayed.

Tom turned and stomped to the car. Why had he been born into this messed up family. He had a father that never wanted to be a father, and a mother that never wanted to be a wife. Now she was preaching at a time when he needed some understanding. He hated what she stood for. What had it gotten her anyway? They lived in a dump, and always had. He barely had what he needed and never had known what it was like to just buy something that he wanted. There was never enough money, and never had been.

Angela arrived and took her place in the passenger seat. All was quiet. Tom seemed to be finished talking.

If this God had been taking care of them, he had done a pretty poor job. He worked harder every year. Where was the reward that his mother talked about? That was it…it was just one more fairy tale, just one more story like the ones about families that lived together and loved one another…never happens. He was going to find what life had to offer, and Jesus wasn't where he was going to look.

*****

Holden returned to his hotel suite at 6:30 PM. He had gone to the Rusty Skillet to have a sandwich, but Angela wasn't there. The other waitress mentioned that her husband had been in a car accident, and that she and Tom had been called to identify the remains. Holden had never met her husband, but Tom had spoken about him periodically.

He was fond of Angela as a friend, but she was a strong Christian and he didn't want to get involved with anything resembling that. He waited at the restaurant for an extra half hour just in case they returned, by seven he headed home. He had a company car that they were letting him drive, and an expense account, but he still enjoyed company at dinner. Tonight would be another lonely time with ESPN.

As he opened his door, he noticed a manila envelope placed perfectly on his pillow. "To Jack, with love" it said on the front. He was concerned about its presence in his room. He opened it carefully. The pictures were graphic and left no doubt as to the fire and the body within the car. The note said simply, "Recognize your Buick? Let's hope the police don't get too interested in the previous owner, because we're not sure if the VIN number was filed."

CHAPTER 38

"How much for that used spreader?"

"Three hundred bucks?"

"I'll bet it wasn't that much new. I really would like to work with you 'cause we are going to be needing a bunch of machinery, but there's got to be some workin' together or this just ain't gonna fly."

"Whose farm are you running?"

"Kate Jefferies place. You know the one just south of town."

"The old Daniels place? That's rented land. Nobody has lived on that farm since the sixties."

"Well, that shows you don't know much more about what's going on around here than you do about machinery prices. Kate's been fixing the place up most of the summer. You sure you live around here?"

"Hey gramps, I don't need your lip, and I really don't care much if you take all your big business somewhere else. The spreader is worth three hundred, but I'll settle for two fifty. That's bottom line though."

"Your sure the thing works okay. I mean, you do guarantee it for a couple loads to make sure it's not a lemon."

"I can tell you who traded it to us, and you can call him. We will stand behind it for a week, but you can't run a bunch of rocks through it or something. It's a manure spreader, so that's all we promise it will haul."

"You won't take two hundred?"

"Nope, two fifty, that's it. I'd rather burn it than sell it for less."

"I like the way you deal. I'll take it. We also need a four-row planter, kinda looking for a John Deere, so keep your eyes open for one."

"What kind of tractor are you using?"

"Super MTA."

"I'll watch for a picker too if you don't have one. Saw a couple of IH mounted ones on sales last month. You know you're not going to be setting any records putting in the crops with this kind of stuff."

"We really aren't in a hurry...it's more about being out there."

"You gonna be doing the farming?"

"Oh, me and some friends. Kate is letting us relive the old days."

"Maybe you can make a list of stuff you'll need, and I can kinda watch for it. I go to lots of farm sales."

"Here's your money. Can you help me hitch it up to the pickup? I just as well haul it home. The barn isn't getting any cleaner with us chattering."

Gus smiled all the way home. He hadn't lost a beat in his negotiating. There's just nothing like making a great deal. That New Idea spreader would last the rest of his life. They just didn't make spreaders like that anymore. He kinda liked old Marty too...felt a little bad about taking advantage of him like that, but that's what being a salesman is all about. Real nice how he offered to kinda keep an eye out for nice stuff. Yeah, he probably was an okay guy.

"Now who's here?" he muttered to himself as he drove into the yard. He kind of liked having the place to himself. Of course, Kate was the boss of the house, but the farm and such was kind of his responsibility. It was a lot like renting, but the owner was living on the place. It suited him fine. "Who the hell is the guy with the ponytail?"

Gus drove the truck down to the machine shed and unhooked the spreader. He lined it up just right. He could probably get most of that dried stuff off it and it could look almost like it did when it was new. It was in good shape. He couldn't help but smile.

He was still congratulating himself when he heard Kate's voice. "Gus, I'd like you to meet a friend of mine. This is Tony. Tony, this is Gus Roth."

"I'm pleased to meet you Mr. Roth. Kate has told me wonderful things about you."

"Huh, she hasn't mentioned a thing to me about you. Ain't you kinda old to be putting your hair in a ponytail. No earrings though, s'pose that's next."

Kate turned her head and tried to hide the smile.

"I suppose you don't see long hair much around here."

"Mostly on girls or gay guys, not much on men."

"You farmed most of your life. Was it around here?"

"Around Madelia. Rented a half section for forty-five years. Great farmland around there."

"Ownership didn't appeal to you?"

"You always wear a suit jacket, or are you going to a funeral or something?"

"I have some meetings this afternoon, but thought I'd stop and see how Kate was doing. I was surprised to hear she had a hired man."

"Tony, that's rude. Gus is a guest, not an employee. He has offered to help get the place back to a working farm. I must say that I'm surprised at you."

Gus watched old Tony's eyes spark and smiled ever so slightly. He was certain they would never be friends. This guy was a "slick"…a lady's man, someone who wouldn't know work if it bit him in the butt. On top of that he was touching Kate's shoulder and back of her neck as they walked… Gus didn't like him, never would. He probably was trying to horn in on the widow.

He did appreciate the way Kate had stood up for him. She was quite a woman. At any rate, she deserved someone a lot better than this jerk.

*****

Tony walked Kate back to the car, but he was not pleased. "Did I do something that has offended you, because you don't seem to be yourself."

"I'm acting strangely? Tony, you just insulted someone that could have been your father. What was your purpose in that? He may be a bit abrupt, but that doesn't give you the right to be offensive. At least that's what I have always believed. If you intended to impress me with your innuendo, it didn't. I thought it was rude, pure and simple. Gus has had a lonely life, and he has a lot to offer if we can overlook some of his brashness."

"He is an offensive, rude old loser. He came at me from the word go, and I don't tolerate that well. I frankly think he is the rude one, not me. What about the remark about my hair, was that a bit nasty or was it just me?"

"He's nearly seventy, Tony. He isn't comfortable with the new styles, and at that age many people become a bit obtuse and confrontational. It is normal, but you don't win their friendship by trading barbs. I happen to love this man and I really don't appreciate the way you acted toward him. I feel that you should apologize to him."

"Kate, I'm not certain that I would apologize if I felt I had been wrong, but I can tell you that it will be a cold day in hell that he will hear an apology from me. I do not share your feelings for the old geezer, and he can curl up and die for all I care."

"Perhaps you should leave, Tony. I'm having a difficult time with your attempt at humor."

"I have to be going anyway, but understand, Kate, it's not a joke, I don't appreciate his attitude or yours. It just may be some time before I return."

"Actually, Tony, I must say that that scenario is possibly the first thing I have found agreeable from you today. You needn't do me any favors. I will put you in my prayers, but I can't say that I will look forward to seeing you again until you change your approach."

"Well, Kate, a long time passed the last time we walked away from one another, and I survived fine. There's no reason to expect it to be any different this time. I just hope the neighbors don't mind the jailbirds in the area."

"Is that some kind of threat? You should talk to Gus's son, Matt… God has a plan for each of us if we just take the time to ask."

"Oh, I see, the Christian widow is concerned for the 'sin-filled divorce.' Geeze, Kate, you're as pathetic as it gets. A lonely woman hiding behind an archaic belief system that died decades ago. Spare me the preaching. I don't work well with guilt…and without guilt… God doesn't exist."

"That's where we differ, Tony. I have faced the fact I needed to change; you are running from anything suggesting such a thing for your life."

"Oh, we differ more than that. You will always be a sucker for a loser. I figured out along time ago that I'm the center of my universe. Life's a big enough hassle without carrying the world along on the ride."

Tony's head tilted to the right and his eyes narrowed as he spoke.

"I knew from the beginning you wouldn't change. You're still hung up on the crap your folks taught you. It doesn't fit any more… people who fall for it are just as much a bunch of losers as that generation was."

"I always cared about you, Tony. We have been friends nearly our whole lives."

"Yeah, right. You never cared for anyone. You cared about getting ahead and lording it over the rest of us. If everything was about you—life was great. I always knew where I stood, but you offered a place away from reality… I needed that then."

Kate tried to turn away, but Tony grabbed her right hand.

"I'm not that weak, broken little poor kid anymore, Kate. But you really wouldn't know that because it isn't about you. I won't miss you much because you never really offered much more than money."

"Where's all this coming from? I always valued our friendship… you were always important to me. We were friends, best friends. I never lied about it."

"Think again, Kate. Think again. And by the way, how do you know that Holden didn't just end it all to get away from you? Just how good was that relationship…you kind of jumped into it to get away from some tough memories? I didn't know him, but I know you, and it makes me wonder. You don't need to answer, but there's a bunch more guilt for you to chew on."

"You really hate me, don't you? I have always cared about you… but that's over. Leave! Leave before I forget what I believe."

"Gladly—I just hope you never regret this day."

Gus heard the car start up, and the roar of the engine. The rocks hit the shed as the tires ripped through the gravel and the car exploded out of the driveway. He saw Kate walk slowly to the house, seeming to wipe tears away from her eyes as she moved.

The dust settled, but Gus was unsure of how to handle the next move. He never had been too good at helping people through hard times, especially women. He cared for Kate. It was strange, because he had only known her for a couple of weeks, but she was like the daughter he always wanted. He kept washing the tractor, but his heart was in the house.

"He kinda left in a huff, huh?"

"Yes, but it's probably for the best. He is an incredibly angry man."

"I was not very nice to him. Something about him just rubbed me the wrong way. I hope I didn't hurt you by making this guy upset. I really don't want to make life rough for you, Kate. I'll be glad to talk to him if I can make things better."

"You want some coffee, Gus? This farm is far better off without Tony around, and frankly so am I. I guess you helped me see the truth about a lot of things."

"Me? I really haven't helped many people in much of anything. I always been accused of caring much more about me than anybody, and ya' know something, I think they've been right most of the time. Never really found anybody worth caring for, I guess."

"What about your wife, Gus?'

He was quiet for some time.

"Coffee might just hit the spot."

When the coffee finished running and the cookies were in place on the table, Gus spoke again.

"I really don't know how to love people, Kate. I was a good husband, never took advantage of my wife, or ever raised a hand against her. I missed her terribly after she died, but I can't really say if I ever loved her."

"I know what you mean, Gus. I needed Holden, but I struggle with lots of questions about our relationship. I'm not sure that

I didn't let him down in our marriage. I really don't know if I ever loved the man, or if I was just looking for what he offered."

Gus seemed to hear Kate, but there was little acknowledgement of her statement. He just looked at her quietly for several moments.

"I watched my folks. There wasn't much outwardly resembling love in their relationship, so I guess I didn't have much of a picture to go by. We were always friends, but I gotta tell you that as far as who was most important to me, it was me. I was always more interested in what I wanted or needed than in her. I guess that's why this is such a tough question. I've thought about it lots since her death, but don't share it much with anybody. I hope you ain't the talking type."

"Gus, Tony just spent his last few moments telling me I was a selfish, pathetic woman, and I'm not certain that he isn't correct. I was never willing to give much more than necessary to my marriage. I was always afraid to lose myself for him, and the feminist movement certainly didn't mellow me much. Do you think it's too late to change?"

"Kate, I see a lady that has a great heart, and is lots of fun. We all need to change. Maybe we can work on it together. I ain't planning on going anywhere if you will let me stay. I really like you, and that jerk Tony, probably was mad because you talked back to him. I know it hurts, but you didn't lose nothin' when he left, except some gravel. I will gladly replace that."

"Do you think we can make this farm thing fly?"

"Piece of cake. I bought a used spreader today, and got some leads on other stuff we need, the farm thing will be a snap. You just worry about getting over some of this stuff, I'll take care of the farm."

She placed her hand on his and smiled. He had no idea what to do. He was without words, but he knew he was loved.

The phone rang and brought the healing conference to an end. The participants went on to their next project, but a bond had formed. Perhaps for the first time in their lives these two lonely people had begun to experience something new, true friendship.

CHAPTER 39

Holden never ceased to be amazed at how many people bought state of the art computers without a clue as to how to use them. The computer he saw in the office was one of many throughout the company. Yet there was barely one employee who had an inkling of their potential. They had purchased a main frame networked with the other desktops and loaded with Windows 2000, etc., etc., etc.... someone had made a bunch of money on these guys, then left them wondering what to do next.

It wasn't hard to be a hero with the staff, at least the ones that were responsible for any kind of record keeping or monetary issues. He let them see just enough about his expertise to believe he could be an asset, yet never gave them the impression he should rewrite their system.

The initial training process was a waste of time. It was obvious that he would never be brought to the forefront. Both he and those in charge knew that his face had far too much potential for recognition. The first two weeks of viewing the operation was interesting, but when he was given his tour of the office, he began to see their plan.

The majority of business in Highland Transfer was illegal but like most large corporations, problems existed.

He made little effort to quickly bring efficiency into the operation. He was uncertain he would be kept around if they lost interest in his abilities, or they found out how to access the accounts in Cayman. He could control the first and hoped he would never experience the second.

The weeks passed and he noticed an amazing trend. He never had the same people working around him for more than a week. They were taking no chances.

He was given a car to drive, but he knew he was always being followed. They must have expected him to leave or go to the police. Neither was ever going to happen…at least if the numbers were in their possession.

The first order of business was to put together a program to maximize the use of the plates. He formatted a program that sorted the plates by number and date of expiration, then used shortest first to insure minimal possibility of detection. His program was an instant hit, and he became a star overnight.

Holden smirked and realized he could milk this job for a lifetime without breaking a sweat. They would never know…and the money continued to roll in as the cars continued to roll out.

*****

The job was easy but not so his time away from work. He ate nearly every evening at the Rusty Skillet, hoping to see Tom, Angela, or someone, but most nights he spent alone. He was initially concerned that Tom had linked him with the death of his father, but after speaking with him, he knew Tom blamed himself for Mickey's death and his mother's faith for their lack of a healthy marriage.

Angela was not doing well. Holden pretended to care for her, and maybe he did. Mostly he just saw her as never really accomplishing much in her life. By Holden's definition, she had never lived. He never shared these thoughts with anyone. He knew they were the truth. Sharing would change nothing.

What bothered him more was a growing desire that he might experience what her son had worried about. He was very protective of those thoughts as well. Holden decided he should try to see people differently…something other than useful tools, but he had to admit that he wasn't doing well at changing. On this night, Angela was working. At least he could have a conversation with someone he had known longer than four days.

"Why are you sitting over here in the corner? There are lots of tables with more light and a better view."

"I really don't need lots of light, I know the menu. And when you're around the view is fine."

"Smooth, Jack. You sound like some of the guys I used to fear in my twenties. They weren't the type of guys I looked forward to serving…in any manner."

"Sorry, Angela, just attempting a bit of humor…probably not appropriate. You really do look nice, and… I've missed talking to you. How's Tommy?"

The tears welled up in her eyes, and she turned away. "Sorry, Jack, I'll be right back." And she was gone.

His coffee was empty, and her outlook seemed better when she returned.

"Sorry, but I just sometimes fall apart when I think about Tommy. I haven't heard a word from him in nearly three weeks. It's usually really strained when we do talk. He blames me for the rotten life he had to live, and it probably is my fault. I was a terrible Mother in the early years. I really didn't want a child, and he picked up on it. Then, I had to be honest with him about his father's death, and that didn't go over well either."

"Honest? In what way?"

"Honest about my tears after that horrible identification ordeal."

"Tears are normal. Why should that anger Tom?"

"I wasn't crying because I had loved Mickey. I was crying because I saw in his face true death…death without hope. It really got to me."

"In whose face, Mickey's?"

"Yes, Mickey's. There was terror on that face, and I know why. He wasn't heading for the light. He was experiencing darkness when he died. I never was able to get through to him. He died without Christ. He died without hope."

"You shared that with Tom the night he was faced with his father's death? I wasn't there, but I think there would have been better ways to handle it. That's tough stuff to even believe, but really tough on a kid that just lost his dad."

"I had no choice. Tommy thought I was crying at the loss of my husband. I had stopped crying about that, years before."

"Kids always think their parents will somehow work things out...someday..." Holden tried to change the flow of the conversation...it didn't work.

"That was never going to happen. I knew that decades ago, but I had always prayed that Mickey would find the truth. Realizing that he died without it brought me to my knees. You don't believe this stuff either, do you?"

"I don't believe in adding pain to a painful situation."

"You think that's what I did?"

"Not for the sake of adding pain, but I think that's what happened."

"What about the truth, doesn't that have any merit in this situation?"

"Sometimes the truth is just a little bit too harsh for a particular moment. I guess I have learned to use other approaches than simple truth."

"You believe in the lies."

"That's a bit harsh, I prefer to think of it as compromise for the moment. Truth can always be brought out later."

"At a time when it isn't such a harsh reality?"

"Exactly!"

"Except...truth is rarely comforting. Compromise and half-truths are what we want to hear. We want to believe the best, the lies...they bring comfort but rarely bring change. Jack don't continue to live your life on the shallow surface. Look inside. Tell yourself the truth. You deserve that from yourself, not the lies."

"Who taught you this stuff?"

"Life taught me this stuff! Tough life. I nearly killed my child and myself when I was young. I told myself I deserved more than I had been given. I thought I didn't need to be responsible for what had happened...that we'd be better off dead. It was all lies. I will never again live like that. The truth hurt, but it made me change.

I needed someone to lean on. A friend told me about Christ. He helped me find the truth. I found life, not lies in His friendship. We all have to choose…it's the one decision that is each of ours alone."

"That's what I hate, Angela, that preachy stuff, the canned gospel according to whoever is telling it. You attribute everything to some being that you have never seen. What'd you get? Has life been any better? Did He help you make it big? Is your family better off? What have you accomplished that is worth a damn?" Holden did not raise his voice, but he leaned in moving his face closer to Angela as he spoke.

"You want the truth? You're a waitress in a run-down greasy spoon. It's all you've ever been, and probably all you'll ever be…not much to brag about! If I were God, I can't say I'd hold you up as my poster child as to why to become a Christian. Angela, get real, nothing ever changed, you just got used to being a failure. It's the harsh reality, the truth, and it probably would have been better if it never had been said."

"I tell you Jack, by the worlds standards I probably am a failure, but by God's I am more than the richest man without Christ. I found light, not wealth. I found peace, not fame. I found contentment, not desire for gain. I can be happy with nothing, can you?"

"Nope, and I don't think I can be happy with only God. I'm not trying to put you down. I know I said some stuff that was a little rough…but I wanted to show you what Tommy might be seeing. I really like you, Angela. I just have trouble understanding the Christian stuff." Holden watched Angela as he spoke, half expecting her to well up with tears. It didn't happen.

"Your honesty is refreshing, but you don't like me. That's a lie. You think I'm a loser. You want to sleep with me, but you don't want to know me. Jack, that's the truth. I see it, and hear it, and feel it. I don't hate you for it. I just pity you if you don't find some way to pay for it."

"Pay for what?"

"Sin! Lies are sin. I care about you and pray for you. Don't wait too long… I'll see you tomorrow maybe. In the meantime, I'll get you a waitress. I signed out before I came over to the table. Good-night, Jack."

*****

Holden ordered and smoldered while he waited for his dinner. Why did these fanatics seem to show up in nearly every area of his life? He was rarely confronted by anyone, especially a woman. He had been rude and nasty. It was for her own good. But...she saw something he was hiding. That's what unnerved him. Was he really that transparent? Maybe this guy Jack was taking over. That was absurd. He was still Holden. He still had a future with lots of cash. He still had a legacy. He had been a success. He had earned the respect of millions.

Who in the hell was this woman to be questioning him? He needed desperately to find some way to get those numbers. He needed someone on the inside...someone who could get the book back. Holden felt his life melting away. He was a caged animal. They were always watching. Eventually he would be gone too...one way or another.

CHAPTER 40

Gus had enjoyed the six weeks living at the farm. It was just like he'd never retired. He had been busy. The barn was clean, the windowpanes were replaced and puttied, the hay bales in the loft had been restacked, and the straw was moved to the opposite side where it could stay separated until it was needed as bedding for the animals.

The hog house had been cleaned and washed down, and the partitions were stacked along the sidewalls until they would be needed for farrowing or feeder pigs. The walk-in feeders were emptied and cleaned, ready for the animals. The well and the watering tanks were checked. They didn't leak and were ready to go. The yard had been dragged and mowed. The place looked like a farm.

It was late fall, and the evenings were chilled. The fragrances were unmistakable, harvest time. Gus couldn't get enough of the farm, and oh how he loved his machinery. Marty had found him a four-row John Deere planter that had been new in the early sixties, and a four-row cultivator that would fit.

As luck would have it, Marty did find a nice International 560 at a farm sale and got it for a song. Gus couldn't believe his eyes when it was delivered. It was as if Gus was thirty again. Old Marty had even put a new seat on it. Gus spent half a day with Simonize to get it shining like new. The sheds were filling up, and Kate was comfortable with Gus running the show.

Life was great. He loved it here. Kate was a big part of the story. She cooked supper for them nearly every night. They would eat in her kitchen and talk about the old days. He loved Kate almost as much as he loved the farm and she seemed to like having him around.

It was Friday night. Usually Gus would be heading for home, but this wasn't just any Friday night. Company was coming for the weekend, and Kate had asked him to show them around. At five thirty, the first car arrived. Gus wondered if Kate had any friends with short hair when the old guy got out. He had a ponytail and graying hair that was a bit thin on the top.

When Gus saw him, he figured they must be about the same age. He didn't look in great shape, but he was big enough to help if that's what he came for. He was dressed in a dark sweater and tan pants. He wore cowboy boots, and an old Timex watch. He looked at Gus and smiled.

Gus had never experienced anything like that smile. Then Gus saw the black kid get out of the driver side. Then he saw three more black kids crawl out of the back seat. It must have been a sight for the locals watching this carload of trouble drive into town. The big guy grabbed Kate and hugged her then introduced the gang (Gus smiled at that thought). Kate was beaming as she turned toward Gus.

"Gus, I'd like you to meet a great friend. This is Jack Grayton."

"Pleased to meet you, Jack. Any friend of Kate's is a friend of mine. And you seem to make her smile."

"Gus, I hear you really know your farming. This is Brian, and these guys are Will, Sam, and Nate. We're all here to work, and we want you to know, you're the boss. Point the way and we follow."

"I ain't been used to being a boss, but there's plenty to do here if we are going to get this place ready for spring work. The buildings need some sprucin' up, and the fences aren't ready for any kind of animals, but we got some time and these guys got youth on their side. Any of you worked on a farm before?"

Jack smiled. "Better ask if any of us ever worked before, much less on a farm. Truth is…this is the first time these three have been out of the city, and this is Brian's second time on a farm. I hate to admit it, but these guys have spent far too much time in jail. They all believe in the same Jesus, so we have something in common, don't we?"

"You know my son Matt?"

"Absolutely, Matt led me to Christ in a jail cell. He changed my life. He's a son to be proud of…a man without equal in my eyes. But you must already know that."

"You guys want to see the barn? I been doin' a lot of work on it. Got the machine shed put back together again, and even got some new machinery."

"Lead the way."

Brian could hardly contain himself as he toured the farm. It was a glorious fall evening, and Gus shared his love for the land. Brian showed the others how to mount the tractor, and almost melted down with enthusiasm when Gus showed him how to start it. The tractor roared to life and the eyes of the boys lost the look of the city. Each boy got to drive around the lane, while Gus stood on the draw-bar teaching him to shift on the move.

Kate watched in wonder as this gruff old man taught black gang members lessons his father had taught him over a half-century before. It was the miracle of the farm. As they climbed the steps into the hayloft, Kate heard Matt's voice.

"Anybody home?"

"We're up here in the barn. Join us."

As Matt entered the barn, Gus seemed to chill. "We'll only be up here a little bit, but you can come up if you want. You're gonna get dirty, though."

"Hey, everybody, the place seems to be a lot more lived in. This barn is incredible, did you clean it out, Dad?"

"Well, I ain't never been that good at sittin' around. Hard work never hurt anybody. Yeah, I put some time in on it. First couple of days I was kinda stiff, but a guy gets over it soon enough. Kate never said you was coming. Just said we were having company."

"I thought I'd surprise you, Gus." Kate smiled.

"Probably thought I'd leave if you told me, huh?"

"Gus, I thought I'd come too. It's really been a long time since I've seen you. Far too long."

"Connie… This is a real surprise. What'd he have to promise you to get you to come along? 'Spose you wanted to see the house. Got a coffee pot that fills itself. You'll like it."

Connie walked directly to Gus and put her arms around him. "I knew you were the man for this job, Gus. You have a gift with the farm, and you can teach lots of others so much about living. I'm sorry I've taken so long in seeing it. I really love what you can do." Then she kissed his cheek and gave him a squeeze.

Kate was certain that she saw a tear in Gus's eye, but, just like everyone in that loft, she looked away.

Gus was never one for sentiment. He had lived most of his life avoiding any kind of emotional obligations. He only remembered saying I love you to his wife once, on the day they were married. After all, some things just should be understood without all the rhetoric.

Now, within days, he had experienced loving remarks and touches from two different women. It was amazing to him. It was something he had lived without for a long time.

He almost got choked up when he felt the hug of his daughter in law. It was so warm that he almost lost his breath. On top of that…he thought that she said love…and right in front of everybody. What kind of real man lets others see him like that?

He held on tight to those emotions. He held it all back. He was pretty sure pulled it off…but it was close. He turned to the boys once again…but he would never forget those words.

"This here is hay. See, it's kinda green and smells sweet. This is the stuff that cattle like to eat. It's clover and grass, and we grow it in the fields that look like a lawn. Then we have to cut it down with a mower and bale it. After it's baled, we bring it up here to the loft and store it here 'til we need it. It's a lot of work, and a really busy time… bailing hay."

"What's this yellow hay?"

"That ain't hay, that's straw. We still have to bail it, but animals don't eat it, we use it for bedding."

Gus noticed the looks on the faces of the boys. "Bedding… break up the bales and throw it into the stalls so the animals have some place to sleep…kinda like a mattress."

They nodded and Gus knew that it was going to be a long process. "I think that's enough for now. Lets head down the ladder."

"What's that ladder against the wall? The one that goes up to the window way up there." Brian pointed to the back wall of the hay loft at a small window just below the peak of the roof.

"That's the 'crow's nest. The ladder and the crow's nest are never covered up by hay bales. It leads to the little door on the floor level, where we can drop the hay into the cow-yard as we feed the cattle. Otherwise we'd have to use the inside chute and it would be more carrying to get the hay outside. There are two doors along the side-wall too for loading hay bales, both into—and out of—the barn. The nest is the highest point of the barn and the track ends there."

"What track?"

These boys sure weren't picking this up.

"The track is the long steel bar that runs the length of the top of the loft. It is designed for the carrier to run on it, that's the big thing with the wheels and the rope attached to it. When we bale hay, the bales are loaded onto a flat wagon in the field that is pulled behind the baler. Usually two men ride the wagon and stack the bales onto it. When we bale, we will load eighty to one hundred bales, 'cause I figured out how to get ten bales to a pull."

"Pull?" Brian questioned.

"See, the carrier goes out that big door way, and when it gets to the end, it unlocks and drops down to the wagon, the rope lets it down easy if you know what you are doing. The rope runs along the track to a pulley up by the crows nest, then down the back of the barn kitty corner to the corner over there where it goes out through the floor through another pulley and down to a final pulley on the ground."

Gus wasn't certain if any of this was getting through…but he had started it, so he continued to wade on.

"The end of the rope is hooked to a tractor, we always used a little ford, but any tractor works. The rope has to be long enough to let the forks get all the way down to the wagon floor outside, and still tie onto the tractor."

"Do you use the same tractor that pulls the wagon?"

"Nope, that's why we still ain't got enough tractors. This one sits here all day and only pulls the rope."

Gus waited a few seconds. No one seemed to have a question.

"When the forks are loaded, the tractor backs up and the hay begins to rise toward the point of the doorway. When it reaches the top, it clicks the carrier and the whole ten bales slide into the loft." Gus's hands were working hard to help the mental picture.

"When the load gets just over where the men up here want it, they holler really loud and the guy outside pulls the rope, and the bales are dropped to the floor. Then the hooks are pulled back out and the guys on the hayrack get another load ready while the guys in the loft are stacking the bales. I always stacked my share, at least five per load, sometimes six, and they were stacked tight and straight."

The entire group listened and imagined. Gus had them spellbound.

"It's hard work, but when you go to bed at night, you know you did somethin'... God, I miss hay season."

"Dad, do you think we can get this farm running like that with the people you see here? We don't have much experience...and this can really be hard work."

"Hard work comes naturally to people, the desirin' to do somethin' that's foreign in a lot of circles nowadays. I see these guys light up when I talk about the tractors and the ropes and the forks, but there's a bit more to it than that. Most of the farmin' is done in the hot of summer."

"This here loft is sometimes over 120 degrees and the new baled hay is givin' off heat too...sweat runs right down the crack in your butt, and in your eyes. You drink water by the gallon and think you're gonna die, or sometimes are so tired you're afraid you won't. It ain't easy, but it's ours when we're done."

Gus wondered if he was scaring them off...wondered if he should tone it down.

"I ain't gonna tell you you'll love it, but you'll learn who you are and just what you can do...might even learn how to live together kinda like a family. We'll see about that." He looked at the crew he had before him and had his doubts.

"But hell yeah we can do it, just a matter of if we want it bad enough."

Gus knew he wasn't the only one with doubts.

"Tomorrow we're gonna clean the manure out of the old chicken house and wash her down. In the afternoon we can start clearing the grove. Some people been dumping stuff amongst the trees, and we want to be ready to mow it."

"Lets head in and have coffee, it's getting dark and tomorrow's going to come soon enough. Maybe we should try to get to bed at a decent time." Kate smiled as she realized how much like a Mother-hen she must have sounded. "I got all the rooms ready and everybody has a bed, so lets get settled."

"Kate and I got a carpenter coming out Monday to give us a bid on the first bunkhouse. Hope to put it over there right across the lane from the house. We want to get this stuff checked out this fall so we can maybe start farming in the spring." Gus started to walk toward the house. "I get kinda carried away, but farming has always been my life, guess I expect everybody to get just as excited."

"You got me, Gus." Jack smiled. "I think this is God's gift to those of us who never had the chance to enjoy his plan. I know this sounds corny, but seeing this place just makes me feel His love."

Jack panned the horizon. The sight of orange and yellow trees and the smell of fresh air truly engulfed him. He closed his eyes and breathed deeply.

"This place just puts a smile in my heart. Look at that light in the kitchen of the farmhouse, it says home. I think we should call this place 'Welcome Home.'"

They all nodded as they walked toward the light.

CHAPTER 41

Fall was Holden's favorite time of the year. The mosquitoes were gone. The summer boaters were gone. The lawn needed less trimming. The occasional fisherman was the lone glitch on the open water. His work had always taken priority, but there were still the memories of sunsets on the dock with a fishing pole by his side, a Grisham book in his hands, and nature surrounding him.

The suburbs of Chicago gave no hint of the season. The trees were a minor clue, but they changed so much later, fall was nearly gone before the dropping of the leaves. It had been months since Holden stumbled into this hell and he was uncharacteristically losing hope.

He once again considered suicide. Angela was distant if by chance he were to be in the Rusty Skillet when she was working. Tom had a new partner and rarely spoke to Holden. In the early days he made copies of all transactions with the thought that someday he would buy his freedom through blackmail. He now knew many of the local policemen were on the take. The chance of selling the information locally was a joke, the operation was too small for the big boys to care.

He was a dead man living his final days. He knew he'd been an idiot, a selfish idiot. Just like every other night he ordered room service. ESPN had the Gophers playing Michigan State, at least it would cover most of the evening hours. Bedtime was arriving sooner these days. Holden knew it was depression not age.

God must be enjoying all this, watching me squirm under the pressure.

Holden could imagine the big guy smirking and thinking of new ways to screw him over. He probably would be better dead. At least it would be over, and he could have the last laugh…he could at least be in control of his death. He knew he was too far gone to ever make it up to God anyway. All that crap about going to hell if you killed yourself didn't matter…he was going that way anyway.

He dozed off smirking at God.

*****

The phone rang as if it were in a barrel around his head. Holden nearly jumped out of his chair. The stiffness in his back and neck gave him some indication of the length of his nap. He grabbed the phone and winced at the pain.

"Hello."

"Jack, is that you? It's Angela… Did I wake you?"

"I wasn't in bed if that's what you mean. Just fell asleep in the chair."

"I heard that you were staying at the Extended Stay but wasn't sure I could reach you."

"Geeze, Angela, it's One AM. What's up?"

"It's Tom, he wants out of the job. I think he might be pushing the wrong buttons. He just left a few minutes ago, and you know how hot he gets."

"What buttons? What's he been doing?"

"He's been telling his new partner that he's heading out. Now tonight Morrey met him when he came back in and told him to cool it because the ripples were causing concern. Jack, I know Tom thinks that they killed his father, and he just might be right. Mickey knew a lot of people that were unsavory. The death was suspicious, but the police investigation found nothing."

Holden smiled…he did not verbalize his thoughts.

"Tom heard something about someone named Tony, he mentioned that name to Morrey, and Tommy said he turned red and grabbed him by the throat. He told Tommy never to repeat that name, and never to bring up leaving again to anyone."

"Calm down…the kid gets a little hot, but everybody knows it's a lot of air."

Jack could almost hear Angela pacing with the phone in her hand. There was more than concern in that voice.

"I'm afraid, Jack…do you know Morrey… Can you talk to him, and maybe work on Tommy…? I don't want to lose a son, too. I just don't have anyone to talk to about this."

"Where's Tom now?"

"I can give you his cell phone number. You can call him."

"He really doesn't like me much Angela."

"He just won't get too close to anyone. He's built a lot of walls. He respects you but doesn't know much about you. I'm not asking you to be his best friend, just to help if you can. He needs someone with some insight and common sense…someone who isn't his mother or on the take."

"He thinks I'm one of them."

"He knows you're not like them…he just doesn't know who you really are. I know exactly what he means. Jack, please. Will you help me?"

"Will you have dinner with me if I do?"

"Gladly, but I'd have dinner with you even if you wouldn't. I miss talking to you."

"I thought I really made you angry the last time we talked."

"I wasn't angry. I was honest. I thought I probably scared you off."

"I can't say that I believe the religious stuff, but I miss the relationship. It's pretty lonely here, and you two are really the only people I feel I can trust. Sure, I'll call Tom. The worst that can happen is that he hangs up…at least I won't have to eat alone tomorrow night."

"Thanks Jack, call me, I have tomorrow off."

"Sure thing, talk to you tomorrow."

The line was dead, but the phone was still against his ear. It was impossible. He missed a waitress. He was renewed after hearing her voice. He had dinner plans…he had to make a call.

*****

The Buick Gran Sport ran like a sports car and purred like a kitten. Tom loved driving, especially at night when the roads were nearly empty. It was nearly 2:00 AM, and other than a semi here and there, he had the road to himself. Tom wasn't stupid enough to really hit the gas, he also knew when you were the only car in sight, it just might be a trooper's sights your in. He had paid too many speeding tickets and heard way too many front seat sermons to want to duplicate the aggravation.

He was dreaming of a new job and a new way of life. Tom had made it clear to Morrey that he was through. The memory of their conversation flooded his memory.

"I been doin' a lot of thinking… I want out."

"Geeze Tommy, not this stuff again. Just quit thinkin' and do your job. We all got to get used to things that we don't understand."

"That's just it, Morrey. I understand it just fine. You keep trying to scare everybody into shuttin' up. It ain't gonna work. I ain't scared. I've had enough of this place."

"I'm not trying to scare you; I'm trying to tell you to shut up and quit making waves. There are expectations from people lots higher than me…they aren't the people you want concerned."

"Morrey, you got no guts. You run from shadows. I know about the cars, and all that…that don't matter. I ain't interested in spreading any of it around. I just gotta watch out for myself. It's time to leave and I'm leaving."

"I'm telling you…you don't know who you're dealing with. Sleep on it. Rethink it. It's too dangerous."

"You think I'm an idiot. I know about stuff. I know about Tony…and lots of other stuff. I…" Tommy never got to finish. Morrey grabbed Tom's shirt with his huge left hand and shoved him against the wall of the office.

"You don't know nothin' about Tony…you hear me!" He started choking him with his right hand as he lifted Tom by his collar.

Tommy moved quickly. A knee to the groin, and right cross broke the choke hold, as Tom reversed his position. He now held Morrey by the throat.

"You touch me again, and my leaving will be the least of your problems. I'm giving you one-week notice, then I'm gone." He loosened his grip, and Morrey slouched to the floor.

It was a bad scene.

Tom told his mother about it. She wasn't much help. She told him to pray for guidance and she would be doing the same thing. He figured he needed help all right, but it had to be someone he could talk to that would talk back. He had considered asking Jack…but he was in the office now…so he probably was one of them.

Tom had stewed about it for two days and couldn't sleep. He remembered his father's burned body, that terrible smell. He needed protection.

Tom had spent three hours the night before in the Police Station in Merrilville. A Sergeant Espisito and his partner spent nearly half of their shift with Tom. They had brought him coffee and a sandwich, and they wrote it all down.

Tom was really impressed at their questions. They wanted all the details. They never once acted like he was stupid or lying. When Tom asked if he should be worried about protection, they told him no one would ever know that it was him that talked. They said they would keep an eye on him.

Now today at work, everything seemed different, even better. Morrey must have seen that Tom wasn't somebody to push around, because he had made him team manager. He had a company car, and an expense account. He should have stood up earlier.

Tommy wasn't even sure he would leave, and he kind of had mixed emotions about telling the police. But he needed friends, and now he had them in both places. Morrey respected him, and the police were looking out for him. He had to tell his mom that her prayers had been answered.

Tom was approaching Merrillville on the interstate. He had told himself that he deserved a break since he had worked out some of the stuff that had been bugging him. It was nearly two-thirty and the radio was blasting. He sang along with Travis Tritt and knew he could make it big in country music if this job didn't work out. He smiled as he looked in the mirror.

He saw the lights behind him coming on fast...not to worry, he was in the right lane and he wasn't going over seventy-two. Even if it was the police, so what? The car followed right on his bumper for nearly two miles. It looked like a big car...kinda like a cruiser, but no cherries on the top. Probably some jerk looking for a fight. They'd get tired soon enough and back off.

After the second mile, the car pulled along side and just lingered beside him. Tom wanted none of this, so he told himself not to give them the benefit of looking at them. As he slowed they slowed, as he sped up, likewise. Finally, after what seemed like an eternity, Tom turned to glare...the sign in the window said, "Tony says good-bye!"

*****

The phone rang at 2:35 AM, and Holden struggled to answer. A voice that seemed familiar spoke, "Buicks can be very hazardous especially in this line of work. Careful, you might get burned," then he was gone.

"Hello...hello! Who in the hell is this... Jackass?" But the phone was quiet. Holden dialed *69, but the number wasn't available. "Cell phone," he muttered.

Holden tried to get back to sleep but remembered the other references to a Buick. He only hoped he was wrong about the message.

At 4:53 AM, the phone rang again. Angela spoke as if stricken. "There's been an accident. Can you come to the house and go with me? It's Tommy, he's in the hospital."

"Tommy?... Hospital?...slow down. What happened?"

"The car exploded; the police say the gas tank just blew up out on the road. It wasn't even his car."

"What hospital?"

162

"Mercy."

"I can meet you there. It'd be closer than picking you up."

"I just don't think I can drive... I can try someone else, but Jack, I need you right now."

"I'm sorry, that was really stupid, of course I'll come... I'm just not good at caring I guess...of course I'll come. Forgive me."

"Forgiven. We can talk on the way to the hospital."

"How bad is it?"

"Bad."

*****

Jack drove like a maniac but got there without being pulled over. As he turned into the driveway of the small house, Angela walked hurriedly to the waiting car.

"You had to fly to get here this fast."

"I didn't miss many lights."

Angela was silent for the first few moments. Holden didn't speak. Finally, she whispered through her tears. "Jack, do you think this wasn't an accident? You know what we talked about."

Holden was positive his car was bugged. He chose his words carefully. "I think that right now the only thing that matters is Tommy. Did they tell you how bad he is?"

"Third degree burns over most of his body. He's been in shock since they found him."

Angela's voice had little of the familiar vibrancy. She struggled to keep her mind from the inevitable.

"Someone with a cell phone called it in at 2:45, they sent an ambulance right away, but couldn't get close to the car until nearly 3:00 AM. Too hot."

"How'd Tom survive that kind of heat?"

"That's the thing...he wasn't even in the car. The explosion blew him out. After the Paramedics looked through the wreckage, they searched the ditch and found him on the other side of the interstate. He would never have survived if he had worn his seat belt."

"Angela, he probably isn't going to look like himself. The tissues really swell up after a burn."

Angela was quiet again for several miles. As they approached the hospital emergency entrance she reached over and held Holden's arm. "However bad it is, promise me you'll stay as long as it takes."

"As long as it takes."

*****

The hallways in the hospital were filled with carts and machines of all descriptions. Everywhere Holden looked were people in uniforms, and each of them wore a nametag.

The nurse behind the reception desk was thin and black. She had her hair in a bun under her cap, and beautiful, comforting eyes. "I'm Sam, are you here to inquire about one of our patients?"

"Tommy Parker," Angela whispered.

Holden realized that the ER wouldn't have any record of Tommy by his name. The car was registered to someone else if there was anything left. He quietly said, "The kid in the car accident."

"Of course. He's in Intensive Care on the second floor. We have no information on him, and he is only allowed immediate family visitation."

"How do we get to the second floor?" Angela interrupted.

"I'll take you right up there. Are you his mother?"

"Yes, and this is his father, Jack."

He wasn't certain that Angela even knew that she had just lied. She could repent later. They moved toward an elevator door, with Sam in the lead. The elevator was new as were most of the surroundings, but it moved at about an inch per second. Holden was glad that Tom wasn't on the tenth floor; they would have needed a lunch.

Sam spoke to the charge nurse and moved aside. The new leader politely motioned and walked to Room 754. "I'm Renee, I'll be right out here. Please don't try to speak to him, he hasn't awakened, and the body has a lot of healing to do. Rest and the medications are all we have to give. And of course, prayer helps."

Angela stopped and touched Renee's hand. "We'll be doing a lot of that, it's our only hope."

We will? Holden thought. He wasn't thrilled about the sound of that.

The room was nearly dark. The body in the hospital bed could have been anyone. His eyes and mouth were uncovered, and there were small openings for his ears. Holden was relieved that the damage was covered.

The smell in the room was medicinal. Bags of liquids hung everywhere. Something called D5W...potassium... Rocephin...all hanging on a metal rod and attached to a small pump that made a quiet gurgling noise. The pump had a small screen on the front with numbers.

Wires and tubes trailed from under the dressings in the chest area leading to other monitoring equipment. Holden could hear the labored breathing of the body in the bed.

Renee brought in a second chair and set it beside the bed. "You might just as well sit. It will be sometime before the anesthetic wears off."

"Anesthetic?"

"Just something mild to keep him asleep while we got him out of his clothes and the dressings in place. We are never certain whether the patient will wake up during prep, and that is not good."

"What are his chances?"

"The doctor will have to speak with you. I really have limited knowledge of the case at this point."

Holden had seen the charts on the desk and knew full well that the nurse had a great degree of knowledge about the circumstances. He also knew that there was an order of how things were done. She wasn't the chosen one to share with family.

He just smiled and said, "Lets just sit a bit."

Angela nodded. Her eyes never left the sight of her son. She sat numb.

Holden wondered what she was seeing. Could she see the mummy-like form, or was she seeing her child? Holden had never been close to his family. He was a realist. He saw the injuries...he saw the impossibility. He heard the lungs and knew that they had experienced fire. He saw the raw eyelids and knew what lay beneath the dressings. The body was a wonder, but the skin was an organ. Like any other organ, there was only so much injury that could be sustained before the obstacle was too much to conquer.

Holden was a realist, yet he cared for this woman. He felt the pain of a Mother watching a son's labored breathing.

Holden would stay as long as it takes. He knew they would leave alone.

Who were these animals?

The hospital emergency room was a blur to Angela. Someone spoke to them and took them to the second floor. Renee, a nurse in white took them to Tom's room. Renee also told them that prayer would probably help the situation.

Angela couldn't have agreed more. From the time that she had been phoned, until this very moment, she had been in prayer. At times Angela had spoken to Jack, but she'd had been in communion with God since the call.

Oh how she prayed that God would spare her son. Oh, how she prayed that her son had met Christ before this moment. The last time she had spoken with him about God had been a disaster. Tom was angry and not interested in spiritual matters.

The form in the hospital bed was not a comfort. Angela had seen the damage. She knew it would be a fight.

Kneeling beside the bed, Angela carefully touched the mattress as she prayed in the darkness: "*Lord in heaven, I come to you in the name of your son, Jesus the Christ. Lord, you have given me wondrous blessings. I lift to you my son, Tom. He is my only son. I love him more than anything else on this Earth, and you know that more than I.*"

The tears rolled silently down her cheek, glistening on the shiny tile.

"*Father, I have little to offer you, but what I have is and will always be yours. I know that your will is perfect, and I lay my son at your feet.*

I only ask, Father, in Jesus's name that if Tommy hasn't given his heart to you that you will not take him until he is saved. He is yours to do your will. I love you Lord. Amen.

The sun broke through the window, as Angela finished praying. The glow of the rays touched the bandages around Tommy's face.

Holden was unfamiliar with praying, especially out loud, and felt extremely uncomfortable. He continued to keep his eyes open and wanted to run from the room. He saw the sun, he felt it's warmth, he and was amazed at the scene. He wasn't sure, but he almost thought he saw Tommy smile as the sun touched his face.

He was bone tired. He was tired of pain. He was tired of pretending. He was tired of religion, and he was tired of all this God stuff. Holden stood, moving in silence to the window. He needed to look out into the world, away from this chaos. He peeked through the curtains. It was raining. There was no sun.

*****

It was 10:00 AM and Holden knew that the Paranoid Patrol would be wondering why he hadn't shown. He was inclined to tell them to twirl, but he found a phone bank and dialed the office.

"Highland Deliveries, may we help you?"

"This is Jack. Let me talk to Morrey."

"Jack, we were kinda wondering' where you were. Are you sick or something?"

"I'm sick, all right, sick of the whole bunch of you."

"Hey, what's the problem? It ain't like we sent out the National Guard or nothin'. We was worried about you, that's all."

"Yeah, worried I might get fed up with all this and take off. Kind of like Tommy was getting…but we all know that leaving isn't an option. At least not leaving alive."

"Geeze, Jack, this ain't no private line, keep it down. Where the hell are you?"

"I'm at the hospital. Tommy was in an accident last night. His car blew up. The same car you let him use for business."

The hospital? How would I know he was in the hospital? Nobody called here tellin' us nothin'. How bad is he?"

"Don't play stupid with me Morrey. You maybe didn't flick the switch, but this isn't a big surprise for you. I know he was rattling cages, and I know he was hit. I'm here with his mother, and I won't be in until this thing clears up."

Holden turned his head as an orderly approached. He dropped his voice several decibels.

"If you want to send someone to keep an eye on me, I'm in 754. But remember, I'm not Tom, and I'm not stupid. Dying is not the way I plan on leaving."

"You may not think you're stupid, but your mouth is sayin' otherwise…stay at the hospital all you need but never forget who you're talking to. Sometimes things just get too hot, and something has to explode. Those old Buicks are known to be a fire trap…gas tank could go at any time. What did the police say?"

"Haven't seen the police, but I'm pretty sure it was just another accident."

Holden hung up the phone without saying good-by. He didn't need Morrey to tell him it was a hit; the phone call at 2:30 AM was enough.

The conversation told him Morrey knew but Holden was certain Tony was behind it. Something had to be done…but for now there was Tom and Angela.

The doctor was in the room when Holden returned. He was writing in Tom's chart, and consulting with the nurse. Angela sat quietly waiting. The conversation was in whispers over a chart. Holden noticed the anticipation on Angela's swollen tear-stained face. After some time, the physician turned and walked from the room without so much as a nod toward Angela. He did not stop until he reached the nurses station.

Holden was not amused at the arrogance. The Physician's back was to the room. He was unaware of Holden's movements. He was speaking quietly to the nurse as Holden approached, and although the nurse tried to warn him, she received no more attention from him than Angela had experienced.

"Is there some reason that we were ignored in that room, or are you blind as well as being arrogant."

"Excuse me?"

"That boy's mother has been sitting in that room for the past four hours waiting for some word from an authority figure. Apparently your nurse is not allowed to give any explanation because it might take some of the spotlight from you or your title. When you finally arrive, you don't even have the common decency to smile, or nod, or speak."

The doctor made an attempt to turn his head and move away, but Holden pinned him against the counter. He looked directly into the face of the physician and continued.

"I hope you are planning some sort of consultation with the family, because if you don't start showing some compassion you might be the next one needing a room in this place."

"I realize that you are upset, sir. But threats are a bit outside of the realm of my tolerance. Please take a seat in the room and let me finish my report. I will be happy to speak with you when I am finished. The patient is my primary concern."

"Doctor, you and I both know that this boy is dying, and there is not much we can do about it except wait for the moment…but that woman is alive and hurting. She feels alone and lost, and she has no reason to feel at home in this place. Maybe if you looked past the clothes and the bank account, you might see a person that needs help, a person that is just like you except without an ounce of attitude."

"I will be in shortly."

"Actually, I have changed my mind, no…you changed my mind, we don't want you as our doctor."

"But I am his doctor."

"You were his doctor, pal. I think this is still the United States, and patients have rights. I am exercising the right to choose. And I don't choose you. Get someone else up here, and be quick about it, or we may have to call someone about discrimination." Holden spoke without hesitation.

The Physician dropped the file and walked out of the Unit. "We'll see about this."

"Nurse, could you please tell your Administrator that I would like to speak with him."

Renee smiled, and picked up the phone.

"He'll be right up, sir." She smiled as she replaced the phone and moved the chart to her desk. "You were right sir. Please don't judge our hospital on his attitude, most of us here are praying for that boy. We really do care, but we feel that it's best for the mother to be alone with him at least for now."

We will be happy to get you anything that may make you more comfortable, but we don't want to be a bother. It's a fine line we walk here in the final hours."

"Call your administrator and tell him not to bother with coming up here. I just can't stand arrogance. I've seen enough in my life to last forever. There must be some doctors that care in this place."

"I'll take care of that, sir. Just go back in and help her."

As Holden turned and walked back toward 754 he realized one year before he was no different than the doctor. He had judged people by a set of criteria that included their dress, their position, their bank balance, and their power. He knew full well that in his past he would have never looked at Angela, or Tom. He would have been trying to impress the doctor.

Frankly, Holden wasn't certain that it would change if he were to ever get to Grand Cayman. He wasn't certain if the anger had come from seeing a lack of compassion in this man or not being given the respect he felt he deserved. He knew he was filled with a rage that centered in frustration…he was not accustomed to being ignored. Was it about him or Angela?

Twenty minutes later a thin man in his mid-fifties entered the room. He didn't look at the bed. He didn't approach Tom. He knelt before Angela and touched her hand.

"My name is Dr. Tilman. These are tough hours. It's a parent's worst nightmare. I have watched far too many of these scenes and lived through one of them myself."

"You had a child that was sick?"

"I had a child that died. He would have been thirty this year. There isn't a day that goes by that I don't see his face. I can't lie to you. It doesn't look good for Tom. He has third degree burns over most of his body. He inhaled flame and has burned the airways."

The doctor turned and looked at Tom's bed, then dropped his head for a moment.

"The body has amazing healing powers, but this might be outside the realm of reality. We will of course be trying to take each problem as it arises and treat them, but we can only do so much." Dr. Tilman continued to hold Angela's hand. He looked into her face. His eyes were deep and peaceful, and when he spoke there was a calm.

"Is he in pain?"

"Third degree burns are painless, most of the nerve endings are on the first layer of skin…the third layer has none. While there are still some second-degree areas and a few first degree, he probably is not in pain. We have a drip of low dose Morphine going just in case, but it slows breathing, so we must be careful."

"He seems to be working so hard just to breathe."

"That is our concern too. The lungs are burned and will swell up. His throat is the same, so we are watching signs of inflammation in them. We also have antibiotics running to help fight infection. The first few hours will be the ones that will tell the story. We will treat the problems, and many of the people here including me, are praying for help with this. You can pray too if you would."

"Doctor, you couldn't have said anything that comforted me more. I have been praying since I heard. Thank you for your concern and thank those who join you. It's all in God's hands now."

Then end came at 4:00 PM. Tom opened his eyes and saw Holden and his mother. As they approached the bed, he spoke in a voice that was barely a whisper. The gravel tone was agonizing.

"Jack,… Tony…says… Good-by."

"Mom, He's here… Jesus… He's here."

A smile, and the swollen eyes closed for the last time. His hands twitched and the breathing stopped.

Angela stood beside the bed and wept, but said something that Holden would never forget, and never understand.

"*Thank you, Father. In Jesus's name, Amen.*"

*****

The funeral was small and poorly attended. There were a couple of Tom's school friends and maybe three friends from work, the entire staff from the Rusty Skillet, and an uncle and aunt, but the church was cold and empty.

Holden was appalled at the sight. A young man had been lost and nobody seemed to care. Had Tom's life been that much of a waste? Holden considered the pictures of the service when he had been buried. There were dignitaries and eulogies from all over the United States, and other parts of the world. The flag at the Legacy headquarters flew at half-mast for ninety days, and the President of the United States phoned a message for the service. There were tears and sympathies shared for days. Where was the sympathy? Where were the mourners? Who cared? Then it hit him. *Who cared at his funeral...* Kate and the kids, his parents? When all the show was subtracted...the funerals were much the same. Had Holden's life really counted, and what criteria would be used to measure that question? He remembered...this was how it all started. Now he realized the question was really "What is the meaning of life, any life."

Angela seemed to sense Holden's thoughts. "The celebration is not down here. The party is in heaven... Tommy's at home. This has meaning only to us, the ones left in this dreary world. I can hear the laughing and the music. If I couldn't be certain, I would never stop crying. I will see Tom again, but this time there will be no tears or pain. Life is truly only about where we will spend eternity and learning to love...the rest is just fluff."

Holden shifted in the pew and tried to give the impression of interest. There would be time to debate all of this, although it probably was a waste of time. He was working on a plan. These people would pay.

CHAPTER 42

It was May in Minnesota. The ground was warm. The land was black from fall plowing. Welcome Home had a much different look. The new bunkhouse would house twelve people. The Log home included five bedrooms…three large doubles and two larger triples. The beds were in place. The furniture was ready.

There was a large center room that had a double sliding door that opened to a deck. There was seating for up to eighteen people on couches and over-stuffed chairs, a large television and bookcase stood on one wall, a big thick rug lay in the middle with a fireplace in the corner.

The kitchen was huge. It was a beautiful place. The most amazing piece of furniture in the house was a fifteen-foot long table built with wood salvaged from the shed. It was three inches thick and covered with acrylic finish. There were no chairs, just benches on each side, and each end. Fourteen men could easily sit around it. And from the numbers of inquiries that Kate had experienced, the second bunkhouse would be needed before harvest.

The community had been initially apprehensive. Jack and Brian had visited the local churches with their stories several times. The support was amazing. Women from town had brought food as the men offered to help with the preparations. Throughout the winter, Jack and Matt traveled over two thousand miles, and given nearly one hundred different boys and men an opportunity to see the farm. The responses were different. Some weren't enthralled with the work expected, but most were excited and saw the chance to learn a new start.

Gus was a new man. He loved them all. He was beginning to see that some of these men needed something he could offer…praise. He never understood that his praise had merit, but the smiles of black inner-city boys taught him a new approach. He still had high expectations, but he now said things like "Good job." Or "Now you got it." Or "Looks good."

Matt began to see his father as a different man, and Gus saw him as a son. The walls were coming down.

The weekend after Mother's Day, the entire group gathered for a picnic and a final walk through of Welcome Home. Gus had all the machinery lined up and polished. The barns were cleaned and ready. The bunkhouse was finished. The grove was raked, and the new grass was filling in the spots where trashed machinery and appliances had been stacked. The fences were in place, and the various feeding areas were dragged and ready.

Gus hadn't been this proud of a farm since he left his own. Kate had overseen the entire project and had been involved in the decorating of the bunkhouse. The couches were leather, with a western look. There were horseshoes and bridles and halters on the walls. The tables were made from logs and leather. There were lamps with broncos on them. There was a saddle on one wall of the sitting room. The wall over the fireplace had a huge painting of a cattle drive. Each bedroom had a different style, but all were a western motif. It was incredible.

Jack and Brian arrived first. They had helped three days a week for the past three months. Matt and Connie nearly lived at the farm throughout the winter. Matt had changed from a deliveryman to a hard-working farm hand.

Connie and Kate had become like sisters. Their abilities complimented one another. Kate had the eye… Connie was a relentless office worker. Connie spent a multitude of hours working with organizations and telling the story and dream of Welcome Home. The acceptance was extraordinary. Welcome Home offered both a place to live and a place to learn life. Social Service workers, therapists, parole officers, physicians, clergy, all were looking for a facility offering more than a Band-Aid approach to men and women. Welcome Home seemed just that.

The Christian agenda was a concern for some, but Connie never compromised the dream. God had called this place into existence. It would not be forgotten or changed by man. The true healer was the head of this farm...healing was what would take place here.

Twelve clients were scheduled to arrive June 1. They had been handpicked by Jack and Matt who interviewed nearly fifty applicants.

Everyone was excited. Gus came from his little house dressed in new everything. His khaki pants were clean and pressed. He had a new plaid shirt with a pure white tee shirt shining through the V in the neck. His white hair was combed, and the beard was trimmed. He was wearing a straw hat with a green visor sewn into the front brim, and his new boots were spotless.

"Figured if were gonna have a classy place, I'd better look the part. How'd ya like the hat?"

"You look like a cross between Green Acres and Diamond Jim." Jack squeezed Gus's shoulder and smiled.

"Look at these boots...a hundred bucks, but they're waterproof and insulated. Don't get hot in the summer or cold in the winter, but...a hundred bucks? They do look pretty nice, though?"

"Where'd you get them, Gus?" Brian questioned.

"Right in town...they're Redwing. They were even on sale at a hundred bucks. Think maybe you'll need something other than those tennis shoes?"

"They've done ok 'til now, but maybe my first check I might look into them." Brian looked down at his worn Nike's.

"Hang on. I'll be right back." Gus turned and left the group. He quickly headed back to his house. Two minutes later he approached the group with a large grocery bag. As he stopped in front of them he reached out his hand and gave the bag to Brian.

"These are for you."

Brian took the bag and opened the top. He reached in and pulled out a box with a big Redwing Logo on it.

"Hope old Jack was right about you wearin' an eleven, 'cause I called and that's what he told me. Elevens…that's right ain't it?"

Brian didn't speak. He just stood holding the open box. "Gus, are you saying these are mine?"

Hell yes, you earned them. A good farmer and tractor driver like you needs boots. Those tennis shoes have seen they're better days… you can keep them, but I think you'll like these better when you get 'em broke in."

"Gus, I don't know what to say."

"Don't say nothing. Try them on and see if Jack there knows what he's talkin' about."

Tears ran down Matt's cheeks, and Connie turned her head as she sniffled.

"I was gonna get you a hat like this too but wasn't quite so sure about that."

They all laughed at the thought of Brian in a green visor straw hat…probably was best to hold off on that for now.

"Gus, are we ready to go?"

"This place is ready to run. The seed corn is in the shed, and we have everything we need to put it in the ground. We ain't gonna set any speed records but we ain't going for speed anyway, just farmin'." Gus made sweeping motions with his hands while he talked.

"I was gonna suggest that we maybe call the guy that has helped me get this stuff together. He really knows machinery. He's used to farm. That's the thing about farmin'…gets into your blood. He'd probably like to work here if we could use him… I ain't sure he's religious though."

"Well, if he's not religious, then we probably can't use him…" Jack just sat there, then that devilish smile appeared.

"Damn it Jack… I was tryin to be serious." Gus hit him on the arm.

"I'd love to meet this Marty, if you like him, we'll love him. If we all had to be perfect to work for Him, God wouldn't get much help. We have to decide how much we can pay these people."

"I got some numbers together," Connie piped in. "We can offer at least what the going rate is here in the area, and we can offer some benefits, like insurance and vacations. We are just another business when it comes to these decisions. We can take applications and do some interviews just like Walmart."

"What are the criteria that we want to use in these decisions?"

"Prayer, it always works. Let God do the selection process."

Gus just shook his head. He had always believed that "God helps those that help themselves." He shared that with Jack when they were working together. Jack told him that was an expression that wasn't in the Bible…in fact the opposite was true. God wanted men to depend on Him for their help. Seemed like the opposite of what Gus had always tried to do. He never wanted to have to depend on anyone, and he wasn't real interested in changing.

Gus or his beliefs didn't seem to offend Jack. He was always slapping him on the back and hugging him. It made Gus nervous at first. He'd heard about some of these city guys, but this guy was straight. He'd even been married. Jack shared stories that seemed impossible. Something had changed him…it could have been God.

Gus had never experienced friendship, but he really believed Jack was about the best friend that he had ever known.

The afternoon was spent in lawn chairs relaxing. Kate would have her CPA put together a business plan including costs and necessary revenue. They would decide the daily or weekly fees needed per client to cover the costs.

They would need four therapists part-time, and one full-time position to coordinate the programs. They were going to talk with Marty about his possible involvement in the farming process. They would hire three kitchen staff, and one full time position and three part-time people to staff the Bunkhouse.

Connie reported on the need for benefit programs and the tax ramifications of salaries. The process was bewildering to Gus, but the talents of this small group impressed him. Matt volunteered to oversee client spiritual growth. He asked it they all agreed that the therapists needed to be believers. It was unanimous.

Finally, Gus asked about animals. "A farm just ain't a farm without animals. Have you got any ideas about animals?"

"What are you thinking, chickens, cows, pigs, a horse?"

"Yep, all of them. People get a great feeling about doing chores morning and night. Gives them a reason to live…breathing isn't a reason. That's what's wrong…kids don't have anything to do but try to entertain themselves. Adults keep trying to get enough money, so they don't have to work…then they're so bored they'd just as soon be dead. Drugs and alcohol take the place of dissatisfaction. Being dissatisfied comes from not liking life…and not liking life comes from being bored."

"Let's hope this place can make a difference for these people." Connie said as she moved toward Gus, smiling.

"This ain't going to make the difference, but it might show them that they can accomplish something, and that kind of success is addicting. You don't need other stuff when you like life…but they gotta learn to like life. God brought me here to show me who I could be if I'd try." Brian's words brought everyone to a standstill.

It truly was the lesson of the day, given by someone that found life and hope right in this place…a small farm in the middle of nowhere. Gus was amazed. They were a generation and a world apart, but Brian and Gus saw things the same.

Maybe it was God.

CHAPTER 43

The rusty skillet was still Holden's favorite restaurant...it wasn't about the food. Nearly a year had passed since he left Minnesota. It seemed like an eternity. Tony visited Holden after Tom's death... only once. He was neither apologetic nor candid. Holden would never forget the meeting.

Tony entered Holden's office unannounced. He took a seat directly in front of the desk. The two thugs that followed Tony whenever he moved took their place on either side of the door. They were dressed nice but cheap.

"I hope we aren't interrupting your day."

"Not in the least, it is always nice to have a killer and his friends stop by. Can I get you anything...coffee, soda...a remote for a bomb?"

"Why Holden Jeffries, you have an interesting sense of humor for a dead person. It's so interesting how someone who is responsible for the death of a friend, can find justification for transferring responsibility. Tom's dead because you opened your mouth. He was killed by hired help, but you flicked the switch."

"Listen, jerk, I liked that kid. I would have protected him if I'd known what a psychopathic, pile of dog crap, you were. You think you're big time, you're nothing but a joke."

"I thought I made it clear to you Mr. Jeffries that nobody was to hear my name. I told you to keep your mouth shut. You didn't. He died. Your fault. End of story."

"You're an idiot. You got this place bugged. Your lackeys follow me everywhere. I hadn't seen Tom for a couple of weeks. Just when did you hear me give him your name, or ever speak your name? Actually, your name is the last thing I would consider sharing…it has little if any importance to me."

"Where else would he have gotten it?"

"Tom told his mother Morrey used your name in conversation. Tom said he tried to use it for leverage…he told her Morrey went nuts when Tom mentioned it." Holden waited for effect, then continued with sneer in his voice. "You think that could maybe have been where he picked it up, or is thinking outside your realm of capability?" Holden's eyes narrowed as frustration and hatred stirred within him.

"The kid didn't have a clue what he was talking about, just got unlucky because that fat slob sitting at the front desk can't keep his mouth shut."

"It really doesn't matter." Tony hissed. "Nobody mentions my name especially as a threat." He turned and smiled slightly. "You may not be solely responsible, but your leaving Minneapolis has really been a bit catastrophic on that waitress's family. I wonder how she'd feel about you if she knew the truth." Tony's dark eyes stared at no one as he considered the reaction…the corners of his mouth turned slightly upward in a wry grin…then seriousness.

"Anyway, the kid was a loose cannon. We don't like that sort of thing. He had to go. We don't play games. I heard he lived a while. That must have been painful for everybody. I heard that you were a source of comfort…sounds like the funeral was less than packed." Tony stopped as if in thought.

"Guess all of his friends must have been busy. It's sad when the community loses such an asset? With his life, maybe we did the kid a favor?" Tony turned his head toward the two gorillas, and they all had a good laugh.

"So, Tony, how'd you get to be like this?"

"What's the matter? You can't see the humor in this? You just gotta lighten up a little, Jeffries!" Tony glanced at Holden, then nodded and laughed again.

"I mean…was it your old man? Didn't care much for you, huh? That stuff really affects kids…hurts for a long time."

The laughing slowed as Holden continued.

"I heard you were kind of a pansy in school, not exactly middle line backer potential. My wife told me you were kind of a loser. You knew it too, huh?"

Holden caught a glimpse of the bodyguards—they seemed to be waiting for some sign to shut Holden up… Tony sat as if he wasn't hearing. Now Holden turned and looked directly into Tony's eyes.

"Probably told yourself you would never let anybody treat you like that again. That's the thing about power. You can buy any- thing…even fake respect. Truth is your old man had the right idea… you weren't worth his time. Bet you thought about killing him a time or two? But…that takes lots more guts than putting out a hit on a delivery boy."

Tony's smile was gone. There was little change in his expression. Holden knew he heard it all. He also knew from the color of Tony's neck Holden was on the verge of becoming a victim.

"You know something Jeffries? There will come a day when you will question why you ever made those last statements. I don't *pretend* to have power, you will see, I *do*. In the meantime, we have some people going over your little book. Seems some of my friends think the numbers in it could link to a bank account somewhere…maybe Cayman? Lots of banks there."

Now Holden fought to hold back his emotions.

"When they break the code, you're gone. Hell, you might be gone anyway. I haven't quite decided. I'd kill that waitress too… probably do that one myself, but it's more fun thinking about her trying to get over losing a son, and you having to listen to it. Bet that makes bedtime fun, huh." The laughter returned, especially from the gorillas.

Holden shuddered. His code…what a joke. A bunch of letters and numbers mixed. The code was an old pricing code he learned when he worked at the drugstore in high school. WORMSCANDY,… each letter was used in the place of a number, W=1, O=2, R=3, etc. It wasn't much of a code; he had used it for his pin numbers and to get into his house security system…experts wouldn't need much time to break it.

*****

It was late June. Holden had finished much of a new system for the company. There was E-mail at every desk. All invoices and receipts were on a new program. It gave breakdowns on nearly every accounting procedure. He set up Internet Banking, complete with withdrawal and deposit online. He linked with two investment firms, so money was constantly making a high rate of return.

Holden had to throw himself into his work to keep from insanity. As Holden loaded the data into the new system he recognized several miscellaneous deposits to bank accounts. The initials belonged to Morrey, and Tony. They were skimming some of the cream.

Holden was anything but surprised…but the level of secrecy was basic at best. These guys were small time with big money. *Maybe he'd have some time after all.*

His nights were becoming intolerable. ESPN baseball was boring. He hated both the Cubs and the Whitesox.

Angela continued to bring some light into his life, but she would not compromise her values…there would be no sex. He had come to care for her as a friend. Being comfortable as "just friends" surprised him.

He had not contemplated suicide since Tom had been killed, but…he was losing hope. He had actually thought about prayer. He needed somebody, and Angela had shared something with him that had made sense. At least as much sense as he had ever gotten out of the Bible.

Holden was sitting in the corner booth, his favorite. It was 7:00 PM on a Tuesday night. He was planning his evening…more of the same. Angela walked over and quietly laid a Bible on the table. She sat down across from Holden and said, "Read the underlined section."

"Why do you call me Lord, Lord and do
not do what I say." (Luke 6:46)

"Those are the words of Jesus. I always thought I understood what they meant. I thought he was saying, why ask me what to do, and not do what I say... I'll bet I've read that one hundred times, and never saw the truth in it. I felt like Jesus was saying don't call me Lord if you don't plan on listening and changing. I don't think that was truly what Jesus meant."

"Oh, this is one of those truth things."

"Jack, I'm serious. I see something different now. He isn't talking to those who ask for something, he's talking about anybody who calls Him Lord. See, He says, 'Why do you call me Lord, Lord.' It's about all of us who call him Lord."

"Okay, its about you, so what."

"He says, 'How can you call me Lord, and not do the things I have told you to do. In other words, how can you be a Christian and not follow his teaching."

"Got it, but what is such a big deal about that."

"Well, read on...the next section says..."

> I will show you what he is like who comes to me and hears my words and puts them into practice. He is like a man building a house, who dug down deep and laid a foundation on rock. When the flood came, the torrent struck that house but could not shake it. But the one who hears my words and does not put them into practice is like a man who built a house on the ground without a foundation. The moment the torrent struck that house, it collapsed, and its destruction was complete. (Luke 6:47–49)

"He says if we don't follow his teaching, we will maybe not be able to stand when trouble strikes. He isn't saying that He wants us to follow or else...he says he wants us to follow so we can stand against the flood. The foundation that keeps us strong comes from hearing, seeing and doing what he tells us to do. He doesn't want us to suffer. He knows if we do it His way, it works."

"Well, He sounds a bit angry with those who don't listen."

"I used to think that too. I don't now. I think he is saying 'Do what I say so you get strong,' not 'Do it or else.' He loves us and wants what's best for us, not a bunch of puppets. It hurts Him to see us fall. I hear compassion in his words, not control."

"Look, on the next page, he says not to worry about anything…"

"Yeah, that's easy to put into a book, but he hasn't seen some of the stuff that's going on in my life. Yours hasn't exactly been filled with fun the last few months either. How can he tell you not to worry and expect you to listen with the crap that's gone on lately?"

"He isn't saying that nothing bad will happen to believers, just that He can give us some answers when we need help. If He says not to worry, how can I call Him Lord and not do it?" Angela paused as if needing an answer. Holden sat silent. "I know in the world's eyes it seems unrealistic, but maybe it IS the answer. I know there was comfort in those times that came from something I never possessed."

"That was shock. You were in shock."

"Well, I'm not in shock now, and I can live with the past. He gave me a memory Tom's face at the end, filled with peace. I saw something far different in his father's eyes. The difference had to be Christ. The difference between night and day, light and darkness, it was there."

Holden had to admit it was there. "I did see something I never expected." He never told her about the sunbeam, probably never would.

"I think I'm going to try to stop worrying. And look at this last thing. Read this…

       "So, I say to you: Ask and it will be given to you; seek and you will find; knock and the door will open to you. For everyone who asks receives he who seeks finds: and to him who knocks, the door will be opened.'" (Luke 11:9–13)

Holden wasn't comfortable reading the Bible in Church... Angela was nearly shouting and pointing as she read. As Holden squirmed, Angela rolled on.

"See, we need to ask, and seek and knock when we need answers. He doesn't say 'Call me Lord and you will receive, or you will find, or it will be opened. He says ask. He says seek. He says knock. If we *need help* we have to *ask*. It's up to us. Do you see this, Jack?"

"Geeze Angela are you wound up tight or what? You got all of that out of a couple of verses in the Bible? Maybe instead of being a waitress, you should be a preacher. Do you really plan to live like this?"

"Live like what?"

"Asking God for everything. What about us having a mind of our own?"

"I just know that God said ask. I'm going to start asking. I don't know if it will be all the time. I just know that I'm going to start... especially when things aren't going well...when I'm down."

Holden hated preachers. He and Kate were members of a large Lutheran church in the Twin Cities. They rarely attended. When the kids came home from college for holidays, Easter and Christmas, the family would make an appearance for the sake of the Corporation. It was good PR to be a member of a church.

His membership worked well for both parties, the church got a great donation yearly from the family, and Holden got the "church-member" label added to his resume. He had never taken spiritual matters seriously.

Church never changed the lives of anyone he knew. The business world had no place for obedience, dependency, or servanthood. How could anyone ever be a servant and run a corporation, run anything for that matter. It was a belief system for the weak...a crutch for the multitudes that had little drive, or talent. But...the power of God had merit, and Holden could use some help right now.

Fanaticism was below him but asking for help was within the realm of comfort. Even the President of the United States has advisors. It was worth a try.

When Holden reached his suite, he turned off all the lights and locked the door. He took the phone off the hook and put it under his pillow. He got down onto his knees, put his hands together, bowed his head and began:

"God, I am aware of my misguided life. And…you and I both know that I have never been a Christian. You and I know that I will probably never change and be good enough to meet your criteria for heaven. Holden was more aware of how much his knees hurt than what he was saying. This wasn't working. He trudged on.

I really don't know why I am even praying to you, but you said ask, so I'm asking. I'm in a mess, and I just don't know how to get out of it. I know that as soon as they find out that code, I'm screwed. You seem to have the kind of power that just might be enough, and even though we both know that I don't deserve it, you said ask.

Will you help me? I've got to tell you, if I get out of this, I'd be pretty sure that it was You. I know it's a lot to ask, and if nothing happens, I understand; but it was YOU that said ASK. Thanks, Amen.

The prayer ended at 8:00 PM, it took less than two minutes, and Holden was less than enthusiastic about the prospect of help. He had even said "screwed" in a prayer. God would never tolerate that. Screwed was probably the prophetic adjective, the word for the future.

He put the phone back on its base, turned on the lights and smiled. It was incredulous, with all the negotiating training he possessed, he had prayed like a street bum. He could hear himself trying to negotiate with God. He could almost imagine the smirk on God's face. Well it was honest if nothing more.

He turned on the TV. ESPN had a boxing match, and ESPN II had a baseball game. At least it would take his mind off the last hour. At nine fifteen, the phone rang. Holden rarely had calls in his room…especially at night…he was always apprehensive.

"Hello?"

"Is this Jack Grayton?"

"Speaking. May I help you?"

"Are you an early riser, or a night owl?" It was the voice of a man. Holden had never heard the voice before, but it was deep, and sounded middle aged.

"I beg your pardon?"

"I'd love to have a cup of coffee with you, but I'm really not certain which time of the day you would prefer, evening or morning."

"Why would I want to choose any time for a meeting? I have no idea of your identity."

"I really would like to speak with you. I know that you are being watched, so you would need to meet me at a time that wouldn't seem out of your routine. But…trust me…you do want to meet me. I have a number of things to share with you that you will want to hear."

"Who are you? And how do I know I should trust you?"

"You probably shouldn't trust anyone, but you should meet me. What time is best for you?"

"I never go out at night after dinner, but I do usually eat breakfast early."

"Breakfast it is, Rusty Skillet I presume?"

"I'm not certain we won't be watched, but I'll be there by 6:30 AM."

"I will contact you tomorrow at breakfast."

Click…the phone was dead. Now Holden began to worry about his phone being bugged.

He spent the next two hours going over the conversation in his mind. This guy knew that he was a prisoner. He knew that he frequented the Rusty Skillet, but he didn't know his routine, so he must have asked around for the information. Who would he have asked?

"Angela, sorry to call so late, but has anybody been asking questions about me at the restaurant?"

"Wow, Jack, what time is it?"

"About eleven thirty…did you hear my question?" Holden was abrupt. "Has anyone been asking questions?"

"Not to me…at least not about you."

"So someone has been nosing around? What about, if not about me."

"A guy was asking about Tom, and his job. He asked if the place had a computer system. Wanted to know if it was a new system. I thought he was probably trying to see if he could sell Highland a computer system."

"What'd he look like?"

"He looked like just another salesman, wrinkled suit, slicked back hair, about thirty. He never mentioned your name. He wanted to know who the head of the office was, and who he should talk to. I told him Morrey, and he left."

"When was that, tonight?"

"Yes, about eight or eight thirty. Is something wrong?"

"I got a call...some weirdo...so I get a little paranoid. Sorry to wake you."

"I'll say a prayer for you."

*****

Holden slept even worse than usual. He dragged himself out of bed at five thirty, took a shower, and dressed as usual. He wore a pair of khaki slacks, a black mock-turtle sweater, black gold-toe socks, black wings, and a woven silk jacket. He loved clothes, and with not much else to buy he regularly abused his expense account at Marshall Field.

He dried his salt and pepper hair, added a little styling gel, and sprayed his cologne on his sweater...he was ready. As he approached his car, he felt the twinge that bothered him every morning. He always cringed when he turned to key. The motor started easily. He drove the way he always drove, and in fifteen minutes he was parking at the Rusty Skillet.

Angela was already working. Holden slid comfortably into his corner booth. Angela brought coffee and the menu.

"I think I may wait to order; someone may join me."

"Is this about the phone call?"

"Possibly, but don't worry, I'll be fine."

Ten minutes later, a large shouldered man about six foot two, middle aged with long dark hair graying at the temples and a pony-tail approached the table.

"You must be Jack. I'm Art Walters. It really was nice of you to agree to meet. You'll never pay more for your supplies again, and I know how budgets can be eaten up by those costs."

"I was afraid you might have had trouble finding the place. Please have a seat. We can get you some coffee. Lets order, before we get into the business plan."

"How's the food here?"

"Actually, it's excellent for the price. Breakfast is their specialty." Holden played along not quite knowing what else to do.

He observed the man as he ordered. He was dressed in black Dockers with a cuff, a white shirt with button down collar and long sleeves. He wore a dark suit jacket with a gray fleck pattern, and cowboy boots. On some men the boots would have seemed out of place...on Art, they fit.

He had large hands and a weathered face, but his greatest asset was his eyes. They were dark and deep, but they said peace."

"Jack, would you mind if we move to a different table? The lights bad here, and I would really like to show you some of our new items. I was so happy to hear that you are getting the system up and running. Excuse me, miss, would it be a big problem for you if we move to a table where there is a bit more light? Business, you know."

Holden was impressed. This guy was smooth.

"This will do nicely, thank you... Angela, isn't it?"

"Do I know you, sir."

"Your name tag... Angela."

"Of course." Angela looked down and smiled. "Would you like coffee?"

"Coffee would be great, and a menu, when you have time. The bacon smells wonderful."

When Angela left, Art smiled at Holden.

"This is some place. How'd you find it? It's a bit off the beaten path."

"Oh, I used to stay at the Motel next door. You said that you wanted to talk with me. I hope it truly isn't about computer supplies."

"It's a little deeper than that, but we're going to need the facade of the catalog. People are watching. I hope they don't have every table bugged, but I know the corner one is. So just look at the catalog, and we can talk about almost anything without causing a need for concern."

"So what's your story?"

"Actually, we have some mutual friends. Some you may recognize, others you probably won't. Let me introduce myself, I'm Jack Grayton from Minneapolis." Jack didn't offer Holden his hand.

Holden felt the blood rushing to his head. This was the man he had hoped never to meet. This couldn't be. Jack Grayton was a street bum, a loser, a waste of time. Jack Grayton never left Minneapolis. He never owned anything. Holden knew that he was about fifty-three or fifty-four. He knew that he was about two hundred pounds and about six feet two inches tall, with brown hair and dark eyes. It fit, but this guy didn't look like a loser. He looked like he had been around, but he didn't look or act like a bum.

"It probably is hard for you to believe, but you and I have the same name. The difference is, I have always had mine, Mr. Jeffries."

It was him. Holden had no answer. Denial was pointless. Another shake down was in the making. Holden smiled as he imagined God smirking at him saying, "you're screwed"... "Yep, prayer really works." Holden whispered under his breath.

"I want to thank you, Holden. Not for taking my identity, but for sending a man to a jail for a Bible Study. You were truly responsible for changing my life. God changed my life, but He used the money your company donated, and a man named Matt Roth to do the job. I owe you a great deal because eternal decisions bring eternal thanks."

Holden continued to shift in the booth and look at the floor.

"Jack, a lot of life has elapsed in the last twelve months... I really don't have any doubt that you're the real Jack Grayton. I should have expected you, but let's just get right to the point... I never did one thing for you."

Holden was even surprised at what was coming out of his mouth.

"I sort of wish that I was that kind of person. I'd like to be able to take the credit, but the truth is... I gave him the money, money that belonged to lots of people, not just me, so he'd get you out of jail, and my plan would not be sidetracked. I really didn't care much about his ministry or you."

"Well, God used you whether you wanted it or not. If God saw something in you, then I feel that I have to do what I can for you."

"God maybe saw something in you, but not in me. I was and still am in this for me. I never wanted to hurt you, but I am not a religious man. I am not a Christian. I am not even on His list, much less one of God's favorites."

Holden smirked at the thought of God enjoying this scene.

"If God brought something special into your life I'm happy for you. But other than trying to get away from my life and use your name to start somewhere else, I had no concern for you. Just tell me how much you want… I'm willing to listen, but I'm sort of in a jam, so I can't really promise much."

"So you think I am here to fleece you?"

"You know that I was wealthy…what should I think you want?"

"Maybe you will see that we really aren't that different. Take away some of the breaks, and you might have ended up just like me."

"I really doubt that. I made my own way. I didn't have the world handed to me. I had to work for everything I got. I worked all my life…bet you can't say that."

"Work?…not exactly…in fact biggest share of my life was spent on the streets of Minneapolis. I have been involved in crime since I learned to walk. I spent my share of time behind bars."

"Jack, I know your story. I checked it all out before I left. I know all about you. But how in hell did you find me? Does anyone else back there know?"

"I never had any reason to even look for you, Holden. I have friends in the Twin Cities. They know that I'm a Christian now."

Jack hesitated as a customer walked by them on the way to the restroom.

"Well a couple of months ago, the word came down that Jack Grayton was connected in Chicago. The friends were concerned that I might be scammin' them on the God thing, so they confronted me.

It was really hard to get them to believe me, because I'd been gone a bunch of time working on a project."

As I thought about it, I wasn't sure if I should push it anyway. If somebody was using my name, and they found out it wasn't me, then somebody might just get killed. I figured that I should check it out before I play it out. I don't drive, so I hopped a Greyhound to Merrilville, and was I surprised when you popped up with my name."

"The head of this bunch certainly knows I'm not you."

"You're talking about Tony knowin'? He's trouble…big trouble."

"But what about the rest of the people that know you…do they know who I am?"

"I'm not sure, but if they don't yet, it probably won't take long. They'll check it out soon enough. That's part of what concerns me. I know your wife, and if the news gets back to Kate about your being alive, it will cause more suffering for her. I have mixed emotions about how to handle it. I thought I would come here and try to find how God wants it handled."

"You really believe that stuff too. You think He will make a difference."

"No, Holden, I know He will make a difference. I've been in lots of jails. I have listened to situations that seem hopeless. I take the same message to each man. God is their only hope."

"Yes, but those are hopeless men. These are men that have never had training, or experience with handling situations."

"Those guys probably haven't tasted the success that you have, but how much hope do you have right now?"

"They're classic losers. Of course, they will grasp at religion for help. They will grasp at anything that has even a glimmer of hope. It's the fact that you are visiting; it's not God. They haven't had anyone so much as give a crap for years…you show up with a 'God and Pony Show' and it certainly isn't surprising that they go for it. That's where the name 'con job' came from, convicts saying anything they need to say to get what they want."

"So you wouldn't like a little help…you couldn't use a bit of hope? Sure, these guys are losers. I was a loser. I had so many people to blame for who I was that they had to stand in line. I never had a home, never had a father, never had new clothes, never was accepted by anyone that mattered. I did drugs and alcohol in the early days to help forget. I can barely remember the years from 1963 to 1972. I was in a fog. I got married, and divorced I think all in the same year."

"When I was twenty-four, I nearly got killed by a bunch of punks looking for thrills. I ended up in the hospital for three weeks and cleaned up the drug habit. That beating had given me a real reason to live, vengeance."

Jack's right hand formed a fist as he spoke. He turned his eyes directly at Holden.

"When I got out, I hooked up with a group of tough guys, and over the next three years, each of the guys that beat me, mysteriously ended up in traction. The last guy is a paraplegic. I was a tough guy. I worked just enough to keep myself in booze and betting money, selling drugs and collecting debts for the boys. I was in and out of jails at least three times a year. I was a harmless, nameless street bum...a loser. You worked downtown in the Metro Building. You probably stepped over me at least once in your life. You never even saw me."

"Sounds like you are still blaming people. What should I have done for you? What do you think you offered that would make me see you? Did you ask for money? If you had asked, I probably would have given you something. It's easy to blame the rest of the world, but you chose the streets."

"I was born on the streets. I didn't ask to be born to a single woman that got herself knocked up by some guy that made her feel important. Why do you think you should have seen me? I am a human being. We need to see people because God sees them. People don't have to offer something to be worthy of our concern!"

Holden glanced again at that huge fist.

"That's why I have come here. You are worthy of my concern. I really don't appreciate what you have done. I think it's selfish and immature, but God calls us to bring His message to those in need."

"In need? You sound like you're preaching to your loser friends. You're angry. You don't like me, but you feel guilty or something. Is that what all this is about? You need to pay back a debt to me or God."

"I am talking to one of my loser friends, you are just as lost as anyone of them." Jack smiled and pointed to the catalog. "Don't forget to look at this once in a while."

Holden looked quickly at the book and continued to read it for about fifteen seconds. He wondered if the last few sentences had been too loud. He certainly felt the pitch of the conversation had risen a bit.

"Sorry, I have just heard so much of this religious mumbo-jumbo in the past it doesn't do much for me. You need to know that I never intended to cause you problems with my selection of your identity. I needed to be someone who could not be followed. You had little potential of changing. Who would have guessed that you could have overcome your past? I think even Matt has been surprised by all of this."

"That's precisely the point. Man is always surprised by God's work. I didn't have the slightest chance of digging out of the hole. In fact, I was quite comfortable in it. There's a scripture that I use in the jails that is interesting. It's in the Book of John, chapter 5. Jesus goes to this place in Jerusalem where a large number of invalids would lie. One of the men lying there had been paralyzed for thirty-eight years. You know what Jesus asked him when he saw him? *'Do you want to get well?'* I thought that was the stupidest question I had ever heard. But do you know what the man said? You would expect "yes," but he told Christ that every time he tried, someone would get there first. He had nobody to help him. It wasn't his fault. He had an excuse, not an answer. I realized I was just like that. I had lots of excuses. I was justified in what I was doing, I really didn't want to get well. I was comfortable in the hole."

"So you think it was God who dragged you out?"

"God offered me an opportunity. He asked me to look at myself with the truth, to stop the lies and decide. Matt brought Jesus to the jail; Jesus did the work. We still have a free will. That means we make the decisions of what or who we will follow. God abides by the decision but waits for us to choose Him. God brings about situations in our lives that are major crossroads. We still choose the way we turn.

Do you really believe that you chose me by coincidence? I don't think that God works in coincidence."

"You think that all of this was God ordained? You think that God made me hate my existence so I would hurt so many people just so I can come to a crossroad. Wow, that's some God." Holden's sarcasm almost surprised even him.

"That's not even close to what I am saying. You chose to build an existence that was unfulfilling. You chose to blame others for your unhappiness. You chose to run away from it. God has been there all the time offering a way out, but you won't to choose it. That's free will. He's not responsible. He's available. We have to ask."

Holden stopped speaking. He sat quietly as the food arrived. He had asked. He had prayed. He never really expected anything from it, but here was a man that was telling him about things that he had always questioned.

Could this be an answer to my prayer? Could God have sent Jack?

"How do you know my wife?"

"I met Kate through Matt. Your company cut the funding for the jail ministry almost immediately after your death. Matt and I continued to keep it going, but it was growing so quickly, and there were so many men that needed funds for legal fees…we just ran out of money.

"Matt called Kate and asked her to talk to the new CEO. Kate called, but got nowhere. She took the ministry on and funded it personally. She also has begun a full-time project called 'Welcome Home'…a farm for people like me to learn how to live and make good decisions before we face the world on our own."

"She converted the farm? By herself?"

"No, a number of us have spent countless hours putting it together. They are putting in the crops as we speak."

"How is Kate?"

"Kate is a new person. She has found Christ, and a love for life that flows from her into everyone she meets. You would love her. Everyone does."

"Did you ever meet the kids?"

"They have been a bit suspect of their mother's decision. They drop by and help now and then, but God just hasn't finished the job yet."

"They are busy. Each of them has been successful in their field. At least they aren't hassling Kate about the farm."

"I certainly am not putting down your children, or their work ethic. I am a bit concerned that they have been taught about life from some sad people, and that is difficult to overcome without help."

"So...you think that my lifestyle taught my children the wrong path? Who says it's wrong to seek success? We have been given some talents shouldn't we use them?"

"How happy did *success* make you, Holden? Was it worth it? When you got to the top how'd it work for you?"

"So what's the answer?"

"There is no answer except a relationship with Christ. Love him and it all comes together. It's not that problems don't arise, it's just that He has answers."

"So why did you come here, to convert me?"

"Actually, I think God called me to come. I think I am supposed to help you. Are you in trouble, or something? Why are they following you and listening to your conversations? How did they find out you were here?"

"They stole my car."

"When?"

"I was on my way through this place, heading to the airport. I stopped at that Super America on the corner for gas, and they stole my car. They didn't have a clue who I was, that's just what they do...steal cars. When they opened the trunk, they found a bunch of money, clothes, and personal stuff. They got curious as to why I didn't call the police and found me."

This guy Tony...he's a real psychopath. He knew Kate from grade school. He had read about my disappearance in the paper and seen the picture. He recognized me and has been holding me hostage. I did a lot of work on their computer system, but it's pretty much done now, so who knows, I might be in trouble."

"You're telling me that the only reason they haven't finished the job is because you know computers. They're taking a chance of you being recognized for that? What aren't you telling me?"

"Jack, there's nothing you can do about it. This is the kind of knowledge that could get you killed. It already has cost too many people too much. See Angela over there?"

Holden tilted his head toward Angela.

"Her son was killed just for repeating Tony's name. You should just go back to Minneapolis and forget about me. This will probably all be done soon enough."

"I need to know something, Holden. Did you ask?"

"Ask what?"

"Did you ask God to help? Did you ask?"

Holden was quiet. He picked up his coffee and held it to his lips.

"I really never have prayed much in my life, never thought it was important. Last night, just before you called, I asked Him for help. It wasn't much of a prayer, but…yes… I asked."

"I thought so because He told me to come. What do they have on you? What aren't you telling me?"

"They have a book with some especially important numbers in it. Account numbers for financing my new life. They can't read them, but they are trying. If they ever do, I'm screwed, and God knows it."

"He wants to help. I'll get started. I'll contact you again as things happen. Angela, can I get the check?"

Jack paid the bill and was gone. Holden sat quietly for twenty minutes thinking about all of this. Then he headed for the office.

CHAPTER 44

The first two months at Welcome Home had been a blur. God had provided staff and clients in abundance. Kate and Connie had been involved for four entire days with the interview process. The kitchen had a rotating staff of seven. Other staff included four psychologists, two retired teachers, a retired physician, three mechanics and six mothers whose children were grown. All loved Jesus Christ.

The first staff meeting was much more like a prayer meeting than a business meeting. It began at 7:00 PM with prayer and praise, and then the staff was given an opportunity to share their vision for Welcome Home. All concurred that it was to be a place of family, a place to learn to grow through hard work, a place to learn the joy of loving life, and living love.

That became their motto "Loving life by living love." The clients would arrive soon, and the format of the farm was coming together.

The initial residents included three black male teens from the St. Paul area, a twenty-five-year-old alcoholic from Utah, three men in their late twenties that had been heroin addicts, two men in their early thirties and two in their late thirties with long histories of chemical abuse. And finally, Paul, a forty-year-old giant of a man from southwest Iowa. He had spent twenty-three years in prison for murder. He stated in his interview, "I have nothing to offer a world that has passed me by and feels no need to look back. I have no answers, and no complaints, but I would like to use what time I have left to make a difference in something. I have no qualifications to bring this to pass."

The committee and staff had concerns in their meeting. Paul had shown little interest in the Bible Studies at the jail, Matt had never met the man. The pre-requisite was a desire to cultivate a relationship with Christ. It seemed lacking, but the attitude seemed to have potential. Matt and Jack felt an interview would answer the concerns. Two days before opening Welcome Home, they met Paul in the library at Lincoln County Jail.

"Have you been in this jail long?" Jack asked.

"Actually, I just arrived here two weeks ago. It's kind of the last holding cell before they decide where they send me to finish my sentence."

"What's left of the sentence?"

"That all depends on what's available. I have earned a reprieve from the prison cell, but not a full pardon. The sentence has ten years remaining, and I could be free in three if I can show cause to make that decision. The trouble lies in the history of my life. I have known nothing but prison since I was a teen. At seventeen, I had a warped view of life, and I really can't be certain that my experience inside has qualified me as ready to live a new existence. I never really bought into the prison lifestyle, but I have never known much positive in my life."

"Why would you tell us all of this kind of information? Don't you want us to see a positive side of you?" Jack smiled, but only slightly. "Why aren't you telling us that you're ready to become an outstanding citizen? Why not give it your best shot?"

"I'm tired of lying. I am trying to give it my best shot. I want to change. I want to learn how to live and do something. Telling you a bunch of bullshit might get me sprung, but if you guys buy that stuff...the treatment phase may not be for the real problems. I will just end up being screwed up, but free. Free is not the only thing I want to be. I want to find some of the answers."

There was and edge to Paul's voice as he made his point.

"You guys may not know them, but somebody does... I think the only way to find that somebody is to find the person who is willing to take a chance on the true me. So if that is a problem, then you probably aren't the right people to make that difference."

"You kind of sound like you got a chip on your shoulder." Matt replied.

"I may sound like that, but the truth is, I've had enough of the political bull. You asked me why I'm not giving it my best shot. I'm telling you why…if you can't see that I guess I should just go back to the cell."

"I've heard all this crap before, even mumbled some of it to myself at times." Jack said, "Most of it is a pity party. I spent my share of time in jail, and most of it I spent planning my next move when I got out. You can want to change, and you can try to pull it off. The truth is, you either learn what we teach you, or you will be back inside for the rest of your life. And frankly, what you really are is rude. We respect what you say, but we're giving up something by coming here, and we deserve more than arrogance." Jack stood up for effect. Although he was about two inches shorter, there was little doubt he could handle the confrontation.

"You got me all wrong. I'm not trying to be a jerk. I'm forty years old, and I quit living when I was seventeen. I was breathing, but my life was about existence, not living. I know there must be something more than what I have experienced. I don't know what this "Welcome Home" place is like, but I'm willing to do anything if I can be a real person for the rest of my life."

"So what do you want out of life?" Jack asked quietly.

"What do you mean?"

"I mean, if you could write the rest of your life, how would you write it, realistically."

"Realistically?"

"Well, we aren't going to help you win the lottery, or anything. That would be an unrealistic request, but the basics—what would you want?"

"I'd like to have a job and a place to live where I could have a room with a window and a little desk maybe. I would like to get married and have kids, but not right away. I would like a place to call my own eventually. I don't want to be rich, but I want to be loved by someone…and understood. I would like to have my own clothes and cook my own meals.

Paul paused and thought for a few seconds, "This is kinda like dreaming, but I would love to drive a car, and have a garage with a mower and garden tools. There are probably other things, but those would be a wonderful start."

"What would you be willing to give for this?" Jack asked smiling slightly.

"Are you telling me you can get me this stuff?"

"I asked you what you would be willing to give for this dream."

"I would give almost anything."

"So you have some reservations, I thought you wanted to live life, to finally become something…now you want to hold back?"

"I never said I wanted to hold back anything!"

"You said, 'I would give almost anything,' that doesn't sound like you are without reservation. It sounds like you aren't willing to give it all up."

"Well, I wouldn't give up my life, but everything else is up for grabs."

"Do you read the Bible?"

"Not much, why?"

"Well, I want you to read something, turn to Matthew 7:7–8. Matt and Jack waited as Paul thumbed through the Bible before him.

"Ask and it will be given to you, seek and you will find; knock and the door will be opened to you. For everyone who asks will receive; he who seeks finds; ant to him who knocks, the door will be opened."

"There's the answer." Matt said and held his finger to the page.

"The answer to what?"

"To your dreams. It has always been and always will be the answer to enjoying life."

"So you guys are all about religion? This is a religious place, this Welcome Home?"

"I am talking about finding the answers to your dreams, and you are worried about religion. God offers you a way out of the trash heap you've been living in, and you're worried about religion." Jack shook his head in disbelief.

"I watched my mom get sucked in by that stuff, I ain't getting involved in nothing like that. I'm just not the religious type."

"So it was just noise." Jack leaned forward his face nearly against Paul's.

"What?"

"The story about wanting to find the answers and wanting to change. The whole thing about no more lies. You want to find the person who is willing to take a chance on the real you. I am offering the person who knows the real you, who created you and wants to give you a real future, and you…you're afraid to face the truth."

"I have lived twenty-three years with people who have little or no concern for life. I have been threatened and beaten. I have been swindled and cheated. I have seen it all. I assure you fear is not part of my life."

"Then you're stupid. You are willing to let some perception of your youth keep you from the only true help available."

"Perception…that religious stuff, turned my mother against my father, and they divorced. We were left with a broken home and I was without a father for most of my childhood. My dad drank a bit, and there was just no room in the church for a drinker. She turned her back on my father, and it was all because of religion. I heard them fighting about it a hundred times. If she just would have kept her mouth shut, he would never have hit her. They could have sorted things out. I don't want anything to do with a God that breaks up families."

"You blame God for that? Who do you blame for *your* troubles? I suppose that's His fault too?"

"You're kind of a smart-ass." Paul now moved toward Jack. "I never said that. Why are you trying to get me mad? Is this some kind of test or something?"

"I'm trying to get you to listen to yourself. You are thinking like somebody fifteen. God isn't responsible for the divorce. Your father hit your mother. It probably wasn't the first time. He hit you too, didn't he?"

"Sometimes, he just couldn't help it…he was always sorry when he sobered up. She just used to say stupid stuff."

"She told him not to hit you, didn't she?"

"Yeah, she tried to stop it sometimes."

"She probably tried to get him to concentrate on her so he wouldn't beat his kids. That's what mothers do. She wasn't the problem. God wasn't either. In fact, if your father had turned to God, your family would still be together. He is the author of life. He is willing to do anything to help those who call on His name. He probably kept your father from killing your mother… He says he will protect us."

"It's a nice picture, but you weren't there. You can't possibly be certain of any of this." Paul was nearly nose-to-nose with Jack.

"I can only get my perception from what I have heard, just like you. You've decided about God from what you perceived over thirty years ago. You were a kid. Kids see lots of things but aren't always the best at interpretation. I know too much about God and Jesus to believe your interpretation."

"So you think I'm a liar?"

"I think you were a kid. I want you to start thinking like a forty-year-old adult that needs help. You said you wanted help. Do You?"

"It all depends."

"Depends on what?"

"Depends on what I have to give."

"Everything."

"That's not too tough, I don't have anything."

"He wants your life. You said earlier that wasn't available."

"I meant that I wasn't going to die for my dreams. What good would that do? You can't change a life if you are dead." Paul said with a wry smile.

"That's exactly what He expects you to do. You have to die."

"You're nuts. What the hell are you trying to say?"

"Matt, what's that verse in Luke… *If any man would come after me…?*

"It's Luke 9:23, I think." Matt replied, grinning.

"Let's read that together. '*If any man would come after me, let him deny himself and take up his cross daily and follow me. For whoever would save his life will lose it; and whoever loses his life for my sake, he will save it.*'

Jack continued, "You need to reject who you are. You are to say no to who you used to be and take up your cross. Men in Jesus's day who took up their cross, didn't come back. People knew what that meant. It was over for them. It means that you must die. The old you has to die, and the *new* person that Christ brings to life, lives. It says that you must do it daily. This is no easy fight. He says that if you decide that you won't die, if you want to save your life, you will lose it. But if you are willing to give it all up, you will live. That's why I asked what you are willing to give. Salvation is a free gift, but it costs everything."

Paul hesitated before he spoke, "You think the only way to change is through Jesus? What about all the treatment centers available? Why are they bothering to do their thing if you have the only answer?"

"Treatment is only as good as the patient's willingness to see a need to change. You must see something is necessary, and that is exactly what you said when we met you. I think God has already made you aware of your sin. I think you are a broken man that has no idea of what to do. I think God has called you here, and us to you. I think we both know it's time to stop fighting Him."

"What makes you think you can read me? You know nothing about me. I've met hundreds of men that think they have the answer."

"You just answered your own question. You can't rely on men for the answer. If I were bringing you an answer, you'd have a right to turn and run. God is offering you a way out of the pit, and a future that has nothing but light ahead. I haven't come to offer you anything. I have nothing to offer, but the one who changed my life has sent me here to speak to you for him…invite you to his kingdom. The choice is and has always been yours." Jack went silent.

Matt spoke quietly, interrupting the silence. "Turn in your Bible to Revelation, the very last book, chapter 3 verse 20… Listen to what it says. *Behold, I stand at the door and knock; if anyone hears my voice and opens the door, I will come into him and eat with him, and he with me.* Christ stands at the door to your heart knocking. He doesn't say that you must do anything other than open the door. He says *anyone*, so I know that I can bring this to all men. There is only one doorknob, and it's on your side. Christ won't open the door. He can only knock and wait. If you will open it, He says He will come in, not He might, but that He will. It truly is up to you."

There was no sound in the cell. The huge man sat before them as a little child, head down in his hands, shaking quietly. Matt and Jack had seen it so many times. Men must be broken before they can be saved.

"You're right, I probably do need help. I just don't know what to do. I have been angry for so long that I can't remember the last time I smiled. What do I do?"

"You stop a minute and think about the truth about your life. What is it that you are being dishonest about? Take your time, it will come to you."

There was dead silence in the room three to five minutes. It seemed like an eternity. The noise of the fan and the fluorescent lights became louder. Matt and Jack sat with their heads bowed, both men praying.

"I am afraid to try this. What if I give my life to Him and it doesn't work, then there is nothing left? What if He can't change me? I think I'd rather not take the chance than to fail at that too. I know that I have nothing to offer God. What could He get from me? I haven't got an education. I got no parents. I always was alone, always worked it out. How can I take that chance?" Paul wiped his nose with his sleeve, and dropped his head forward covering his eyes with his hand as he massaged his forehead. Tears continued to drip on his dusty black shoes.

"If God doesn't want me then there truly isn't any place else to go. If I give up my walls I have built, if I am vulnerable again, and I fail, I just don't know if I could live through the pain."

"God has known all of this since you were a child. He can only deal with what you are willing to give Him. You must give it. You have laid this out before Him. He can deal with it now and heal it. Bow your head, and repeat after me: '*Lord, I come before you a frightened, lonely, sinner that has no place to go. I need your forgiveness and your touch. I want to follow you and learn your will for my life. I need the gift of your blood and the assurance of your Spirit. Come into my life and renew me. I ask this in the name of Christ.*'"

When Matt and Jack opened their eyes, Paul was on his knees on the floor. The tears continued, yet even with his head bowed, they saw a changed man.

Jack had seen it hundreds of times in the jails. Angry men, many of them with good reason, come to tell God off, or just make a point. God breaks through it all with a touch. Men could put up a fight, but God had the final word if they would listen.

In the first month, Paul became a leader among the men. He loved the farm, and Gus. His true passion was the tractor and working the land, which brought joy to both men. He led Bible studies among the men and attended any opportunity to study with Matt or Jack or both. Jack had spent a great deal of time with Paul in the month of June. Then on June 25, Jack spoke up at a staff meeting.

"I am taking some time off. I don't drive, so I am taking a Greyhound to visit a friend in Chicago. I have loved each of you and will cherish your memories until I return…please pray for me, as I know that the task ahead has hills and valleys. I love you all."

Gus spoke first. "Geeze, Jack you sound like you're dyin' or something, what kind of visit is this anyway?"

"I don't mean to be dramatic, but sometimes I feel that I don't tell you all what you mean to my life. I have come to realize the wonder of what we have been allowed to accomplish here."

"Jack, you are planning on coming back again, aren't you? Kate spoke in a questioning tone.

"I may be gone for a while, but I intend to be back to see the harvest if not before. I probably did get a little morbid. I just felt sad to be leaving when things are just getting going."

"It's okay but take care of yourself. We all will be praying."

CHAPTER 45

He hadn't slept the night through since his meeting with Jeffries. The arrogance of the wealthy had always sickened him. He controlled the jerk's life. It was he, Tony, who literally would decide when he had let him live long enough. He had just that kind of power.

He would have killed him that night, but Tony had plans. Holden Jeffries had not begun to suffer. There would come a day when he would know that he had toyed with the wrong man. He had hated his type for his whole life.

They always got the breaks...the athletes, the jocks with their preppy clothes and fancy cars. They never suffered. He had endured the shadow of the silver-spoon crowd for his early years, and he promised himself he would never tolerate their crap again.

Tony had brought him to his knees, and he wasn't about to let up. Holden was nothing but a hostage, Tony's hostage. Holden couldn't flush his own excrement without Tony knowing it. Yet there was this attitude. Holden had to have been in awe of Tony's power. He had to have seen it. Tony had blown away the kid without a blink. Holden had to be scared. He was just too proud to show it. It really didn't matter because pain was only beginning.

*****

Problems were something that Welcome Home had overcome before, but nothing had prepared them for this. Paul had been remanded to the custody of the farm. It was all legal...the papers had been signed by everyone but the governor, and his arrival was without incident.

Near the end of July, a Ford Taurus drove into the yard, followed by a large truck with a transmitter attached and a camera crew on board. Matt walked slowly from the barn and was met by a reporter for Channel Six News, and a camera with a blinking light.

"Is the community aware of the potential danger of the residents here?"

"I beg your pardon. What kind of danger."

"Isn't it true that your have addicts, rapists and murderers living here with extraordinarily little supervision. How do you intend to keep the residents safe on the adjoining farms, much less the people that live in the community? These are men have been incarcerated for years." The camera scanned the farmyard then came back to the man with the mike. "How can you be qualified to be responsible for their activities."

"These men are no threat. We are providing a training program to make them part of the community. There has been no instance of concern, and there is no potential for one."

"It's never an issue until it's too late. Has the community been made aware of the crimes that these men committed in the past?"

"The men have paid their dues to the system. They have been acquitted or paroled to our custody. It is an optional program for most of them. We are here to teach them to make good decisions in life. I have no concerns for the safety of the community. My wife and I live on the premises. Doesn't that say something about my trust level?"

"Are you the owner of the property?"

"No, Kate Jeffries owns Welcome Home. I am just one of the directors. My name is Matt Roth."

"I own this property, and by the way, you are trespassing."

"You must be Kate Jeffries. What do you think the community feels about the presence of a criminal element in their backyard?"

"We have found a great deal of warmth from this community. They have been involved in the renovation from the beginning. I grew up here and would expect nothing less from these people."

"So you would be surprised by any uprising from your neighbors?"

"Uprising? I would be surprised by a negative comment from them. These are our friends."

"Well, here is the beginning of a petition calling for the closing of 'Welcome Home,' signed by nearly five hundred of your so-called friends. It seems that the presence of inmates like Paul Prentiss, the murderer, has brought a change in their feelings. Guess the feeling of commitment is less than mutual. Do you plan to fight the petition?"

"I plan to ask you to leave. Nothing more."

"That certainly is an interesting approach to the problem. Rather like hiding your head in the sand, wouldn't you say?"

"I have nothing to hide, and nothing to share. This is a working farm with hard-working men and women learning in a Christian environment. We look to the future and forgive the past."

"Let's hope there is nothing to regret in the future."

"Are you speaking for yourself now, or for us?"

"I suppose we will just have to wait and see."

The camera was turned off, the crew loaded up, and they were gone. It wasn't that easy for Kate and the rest to move on. They called a meeting of the directors one hour later, everyone but Jack was there.

Kate drew in a deep breath and began. "We are here to face the situation that may be arising in our own backyard. While I have heard nothing to suggest that it is true, there just may be a petition to hinder what we are trying to accomplish, or even close the farm down. I didn't have the time to really look over the list of names, but it certainly looked official to me."

"This can't be true; the town just can't be turning against us. They were so supportive in the planning stages, and the remodeling and building phase. What do you suppose is going on? Where is all the fear coming from?"

Matt stood and quietly spoke. "We have been called to this ministry. We know that God ordained it from the beginning, and we have felt his hand upon it almost daily. There is no doubt that we are experiencing turbulence but consider the turf we are trespassing upon." He hesitated and let the others grasp the suggestion.

"We are in the midst of a spiritual war with the King of Darkness. It's not going to be fun. I personally don't feel like walking away. This is a sign that we are making a difference. Satan doesn't get angry when everything is going his way. I'm not saying that I relish the idea of going through this."

Gus had been listening intently, then stood and walked toward Kate. "I've been independent all my life. I stood against insurance companies and banks that tried to take my farm in hard times. I was farming during the NFO strikes in the sixties and remember how friends turned against friends. I didn't know God then, but I wouldn't turn from what I thought was right, and I ain't about to start now."

Never one to mince words, Gus continued. "If you people are really what you say you are, then you got much more than I ever had to fight with. Seems like you got the strongest force in the universe on your side. He either is God and is strong enough to handle this, or He isn't…guess it depends on what you believe?"

"I have no doubt that He is strong enough, and that He will fight the battles…people get hurt in battles, and I am concerned about my friends. I am not unwilling to fight. I just know there will be pain before this is finished." Matt smiled and touched his father's shoulder. "And by the way, Dad, you keep talking about what we believe—I think God called you as well as us to this battle."

Gus nodded once. "Probably…probably."

"This is pretty gloomy talk," Connie remarked, "look what God has brought us through so far. Fear is something that should have no place in this farm. Like Elijah when surrounded by the armies, God's army is present and is far greater than anything that may come at us. I think we need to thank God for the opportunity he has given us."

Each of them prayed and asked for guidance and strength. Then as one, they smiled and hugged one another, and went back to their farm. Kate knew that someone had to talk to Paul. She wished that Jack were there.

*****

The flyer that had anonymously found its way to the mayor's office had begun to pay dividends. The town had started a petition to close the dream farm down. *That witch Kate's dreams were heading for oblivion, and it was about time that she suffered a little.* Tony smiled wishing he could have been there.

He had trusted her. He was just one more piece of garbage to her uptown crowd. He burned as he thought of how she must have laughed in the early days. Holden had told him, but he knew it long before that.

The community had laughed at his family, now he would turn them against one of their very own. He would play the trump card and spread the pain as far as Chicago…maybe farther.

*****

Channel Six News played the story at six o'clock and ten o'clock, as the feature story "Can Murderers Ever Be Trusted? A small town in Minnesota says NO!" The phone rang constantly for three hours.

There weren't many questions, just a lot of comment. Everyone wanted the farm gone. Kate took the brunt of the calls since she had been the visible voice on the news.

Matt wanted to call the station and ask them for equal time, but the thought of another one-on-one with the media brought shivers to Kate.

"This will blow over soon if nothing is made of it. They want it to become a story, and it is up to us to keep that from happening." She stated with all the conviction she could find.

"What if the people continue to ask for the closing? What if it turns ugly? Even now some of the calls were potentially threatening. How do we handle the public if they turn against us?" Matt stepped to the window and looked out at the farm buildings.

"I have a better question. Where did the town people find out about Paul's history? That's confidential stuff, you don't think we have a leak here do you?" Gus wasn't the trusting type.

"I would trust these people with everything I own. In fact, I am doing just that. I don't think we have a leak, but I do believe we have some enemies."

Who ya' thinkin' of...enemies I mean. That big wig from Litany...was he peeved at you for askin'?"

"Actually, he could not have cared less. But someone did stomp out of the yard when this first began. Gus, you remember Tony that day, don't you?"

"You mean the slick with the attitude, that guy that left here all in a huff? I never really did hear you call him by name. I know he was ticked when he left."

"I have never thought of him as mean, but he was certainly nasty that day. Someone doesn't want this to exist, and at this point they have all the cards."

There was a knock at the front door. Standing in the light of the porch was a crowd of at least ten people, most of whom Kate had known for years. Kate opened the storm door and stepped onto the landing. Matt, Connie, and Gus were close behind.

The Mayor spoke first. "We are sorry to bother you this late at night, but something has to be done. The town is in near chaos over this farm."

"You are talking about the feeling of animosity toward this venture of ours. You people were open to the idea no more than forty-eight hours ago. We are still the same people all of you helped with painting and pounding nails. We sat together with in that very kitchen, and shared meals and laughter. We haven't changed, but something has."

"We didn't know you were going to bring in murderers and rapists to our community. We thought this was about helping needy people." It was obvious to Kate that the mayor had been given an ultimatum.

"That's exactly what it's about. Who is more needy than someone who has never known love and caring? We spend a great deal of time screening the clients. These people are probably far more trustworthy than some of the people who signed the petition."

"None of the people that signed the petition have a criminal record, and I resent your accusations. This could be a real time bomb, and that's not what the people want in their community."

"We aren't here to judge. We are here to bring healing to hurting hearts through learning a work ethic and a Biblical perspective. We hope to bring positive growth to this community, and we feel the community has much to offer in the process."

"That's all well and good, Ms. Jeffries, but there is to be a meeting next Wednesday at City Hall. The petition and lots of questions await your answers. I just wanted to tell you personally. The rest here wanted you to know that I am not alone in my concern. We will see you then in six days. Good night."

As the car turned toward town, Paul strode quietly toward the lighted porch. Kate was still standing by the door when he arrived on the top step.

"It really isn't a surprise you know. Whenever anyone finds out that I was convicted of murder there's trouble. The only place that I am accepted as human is in prison. I'm not here to complain. I just want you to know that this is not the first time that my presence has caused problems for people."

"This situation is not just about you, it's about the entire farm. The people want to control the client list. That job belongs to God and God alone. He called us to open this place. Paul, we feel that He called you to come here, and to live your life according to a new plan. I will not allow fear and darkness to change that. He will provide the answers."

"Mrs. Jeffries, I really think that it would be better if I just went back to prison. I'm used to the lifestyle, and comfortable there. I don't want to bring more trouble to you. I'm too old to probably make much difference in the world anyway."

"Don't you want to stay at the farm? Gus says that you seem to be a natural. Are we seeing things wrong?"

"I absolutely love this place, and that old man has given me something I've been missing for as long as I can remember. He has treated me like his son. He's gruff, but I know deep inside me that he cares. If I could choose, I would never leave this place, but I don't fit into this society anymore. They don't want me anywhere near here."

"If you want to stay, we will fight this. They're having a meeting in six days, and I would like you to go with us. I want them to get to know you."

"Kate, I'm what they fear. Do you think it's wise to throw me in their faces? They may just burn this place down or something."

"They have to see the person, not the sin. That's how God does it, he gets us involved with people so much that we can't see what they've done, just who they are. If they see you Paul, they'll know there is nothing to fear. These are good people who have been fed bad information. They will do the right thing. God knows what He is doing."

"I was serious about leaving, and still will if you think it would make a difference…but if I could choose, I would stay."

"Then you will stay. Gus needs you anyway. He gets real cranky if he has to work alone, besides, I know you are right. He really does love you."

"You think so?"

"Can't you tell?"

"Not really. I don't think I could tell if someone did."

"But Paul, we all love you. Everybody here loves you."

"You will have to forgive me. That's going to take me a while to believe."

"Well it's true."

"Thanks Kate, Good-night."

"Good-night, Paul. Thanks for coming up here. You just brought my answer. You will go to the meeting then?"

"Of course I'll go. I only hope it makes a difference."

CHAPTER 46

The door to the elevator had barely closed when Holden realized that every floor number had been pressed. He swore under his breath as he thought about the little jerk that had pulled this one. He remembered pushing all the buttons himself once in an elevator in Dayton's Department Store. There were only four floors, so it wasn't that much of a problem in those days. After the door closed on the second floor, he decided to sit back and enjoy the tour.

On floor four, the door opened, and Jack got on. On floor five they both got off and walked to room 522 where Jack produced the key and opened the door.

"Sorry about every floor thing, but this way if someone is watching they never have a clue where I got on or you got off. Keeps them guessing. I was in your room and set the radio to come on in four minutes so they will think you came home and turned it on."

"You were in my room? How'd you get in there? It's locked."

"Well Holden, there are some things that you just never forget. I know that the Lord forgives me now because I didn't take anything. It's better if we don't get much deeper in that subject. I got some good news today and wanted to share it. Your book isn't quite so lost as you might think."

"My book? You found my book?"

"Not exactly, I said it might not be as hard to find as you thought."

"So what do you know and how in the hell did you get this information?

215

"Well, I still have some friends on the inside that like me. And frankly… Tony doesn't. He's a real loner who doesn't have a friend on the lower or the upper side of the ladder. Most of the guys think he'll snap if things start to come apart. Most of them would just as soon see him gone, and they don't care how."

"How do you know they aren't just feeding you the line, Jack? Can these guys be trusted?"

"It's only one guy. I've known him for years and would trust him with my life. The information about the book just happened to come about in a conversation that was secondary. I was asking about the operation, how it works and the like. Just so happens my friend is the bookkeeper on the intake side of the autos. He's the one that inventories each auto." Jack continued to pace around the room, looking behind curtains, in the smoke detector, the phone mouthpiece…all while he spoke.

"I guess Tony doesn't really trust anyone. Every piece of paper, candy, coin, comb, window scraper, etc., in the car when it comes in, is inventoried and copied and put in a file. It's copied and inventoried by two people so Tony can be certain that nothing gets away. Then it's boxed and sent to his office in Chicago, but the copies are kept right here in the plant."

"You're telling me that there is a copy of my book right here in Merrillville? Which office?"

"That's the tough part, it could be in any one of three. But none of them are too far apart. We could get in and find it in an hour if the security is light. Truth is… I don't think Tony even remembers that he has them doing this busy work."

"We've got to get in there and get it. I will pay you whatever you say. We've got to get that book before he decides to make his move. Last time we talked I think he wanted me dead right then and there."

"The guy has some real issues, all right. His old man was an alcoholic and wasn't around much and his mother wasn't much better. He never really fit in much as a kid. Kinda the loser profile; not that I would know much about that. But he's an angry man with not much to lose. We just must get everything setup before we make any moves. We don't want him coming after you, or anyone else when

216

the bottom drops out of his plan. We need to get that taken care of first." Jack spoke quickly but with authority. He turned and faced Holden.

"You have E-mail there don't you? Well I got some ideas of how to build an offensive plan. I must go back, Kate and the gang are having some trouble, so you will have some time to get it together. Listen carefully."

CHAPTER 47

It was sweltering by Minnesota standards though it was nearly eleven o'clock at night. Kate's bedroom was unfamiliar to Connie, but she had been asked to keep track of the house while Kate visited friends in Minneapolis. Since Matt was planning to be gone, Connie had complied. She usually went to bed by ten thirty, right after the news, but staying in this house was proving anything but comfortable.

She was so uneasy sitting in the family room, watching television, she decided on trying to get to sleep early. There seemed to be movement and sound in nearly every corner of the house. They were not visible, and rarely loud, but a presence she felt frightened her. She was not usually bothered by the sounds and sensations of the night. She spent many nights alone when Matt was visiting the jails. This was different.

This is absolutely silly. I am a forty-year-old woman. I should be old enough to stay by myself without acting like a frightened teenager.

Sleep evaded her. She tossed and turned on the king size bed for nearly an hour. It was as if something was watching and waiting. At times Connie was almost afraid to open her eyes. She wished Matt were with her. She wished she had said no to this housesitting job.

Connie sat up and grabbed the remote. She switched on the television mounted to the wall in her bedroom. The Twins were playing the Angels, that wouldn't help much. She turned to channel 38 and found an old episode of "Law and Order." She loved that show, so she turned up the volume and tried to get into the plot. The room was dark except for the dim light from the TV. Shadows danced on

218

the walls and the ceiling. Connie could not rid herself of the ominous presence that seemed to be watching from the corners and the darkness. She turned up the volume, but realized it was not noise that was needed it was light. She considered turning on the overhead light in the room but chose to try a different source.

"Father, I come in the name of your son Jesus the Christ. I am feeling alone as I lie here in the darkness. I feel the lack of your light in this place, and the overwhelming presence of darkness here with me. Lord I know that darkness cannot exist in the light. Father light this room with your presence. Light every corner of this room, and drive darkness away, give me peace and joy in this place. Amen."

Connie opened her eyes and the room had changed. There was no fear, no presence, it was like a humid summer day when a front passes and the air becomes cool and comfortable. Connie smiled. She sat up to fluff up her pillow. As she glanced at the window, an approaching automobile on the road cast light on the lawn below.

From the corner of her eye she noticed something move. *What could that be? Was that a figure that darted across the shadows?* She knelt and looked closer. In the window, she could see the reflection of the TV screen, but outside the reflection, in the darkened window, she could see the lawn. Once again she thought that she could make out movement. The car passed and, darkness again took control of the landscape. Only the shadows from the periodic moonlight broke the blackened scene. Connie looked at the sky. Large clouds hid any hint of moonlight. She peered into the night for nearly ten minutes. She saw nothing more. Connie glanced around the rest of the farmyard and noted a light in the barn. She wished she had more knowledge of what to expect from the farm at night. Perhaps the light was always on.

Then she saw it again. This time she was certain. A black form of a man moved across the yard. She could not make out the form. There was someone out there. Should she go out there? What if it really was a prowler? She needed to think this through. She breathed deeply and phoned Matt.

"Matt, sorry it's so late, did I wake you?"

"Connie, is that you? I…maybe was dozing. Wow! It's eleven thirty, are you okay?"

"I'm fine, but you know how much of a twit I am about not sleeping in my own bed."

"It's great to hear you, but it makes me feel guilty that I'm not there. This conference thing could have been done another time or never…if I had known you were apprehensive."

"It just gets a little eerie at night. I was pretty messed up for a while. I said a prayer, and it's okay now, but I looked out the window and thought I saw someone move. I think someone is walking around on the yard, and it's late."

"Connie, the sows are close to farrowing. Paul may be checking on them. If one of them is having babies, he may be up all night. I should have told him to let you know if he would be outside. Is there a light on in the barn?"

"Yes, in the lower left window. At least one light is on."

"That's it! I bet it's the sows."

"I thought about going out there and checking it out, but I decided it might be better to call and see what you thought about it. I'm glad I did, now. I would have looked like an idiot walking around out there this late at night."

"I can come home if you want. It's only a forty-minute drive from here. I really don't care if I miss tomorrow."

"That would be nearly as silly as me calling you in the middle of the night. You already paid for the room, and it's stupid to give that up. I'm fine. I would have taken you up on that about twenty minutes ago, but I'll be fine now. Matt, what do you think about all that spiritual battle stuff? I mean…sometimes it sort of gets to me, I think."

"This whole farm issue is frustrating. I think about that stuff sometimes, sometimes it almost frightens me."

"Well, I think it affects me sometimes. I felt a presence tonight that was almost real. I could feel it close to me…looking at me. I was just about to freak out, and you know that's not like me, but then I prayed for God's light, and the feeling is gone."

"Connie, I should never have come to this conference. Are you sure you are okay? You're certain that whatever it was, it's not there anymore?"

"I am fine now. Of course, it is also nearly one hundred degrees outside with 100 percent humidity. I don't have a clue how Gus can stand sleeping in that little shed on nights like this."

"Do you have the air on?"

"Sure, but even with that on, it's uncomfortable."

"I know, but that gives you a good reason to call Dad and have him come into the house. Tell him that you are concerned about him sleeping in this weather and you would be more comfortable with him in the house."

"I'm not going to get him up to tell him to come in and baby-sit his daughter in law. I love Gus, but he's been asleep for hours. I feel lots better knowing about the pigs."

"Connie, I'm coming home. You got me all messed up with this spiritual stuff. Listen to me. I want you to check all the doors and windows and turn the air up, so you are comfortable...even if you have to turn it to sixty degrees. Lock the door to the bedroom, and I will be there in less than one hour."

"Matt, seriously, you don't have to come home. I am not afraid."

"Connie, just do what I say, it'll be me that you hear in an hour knocking on the door."

"Are you sure that's what you want to do… I'll be fine."

"I was tired of this conference anyway. I'd much rather be sleeping beside you than lying here all night worrying about you. Would you like me to call the police? They could just swing by and check stuff out."

"Absolutely not! Don't call the police, they'll really think I'm nuts. It's probably just an overactive imagination. I'll be fine. Tomorrow morning, this is going to seem silly. I'll be waiting...don't speed! I love you."

"I love you too...go right now and check the doors. See you in a bit."

Connie threw back the sheet and headed for her door. The house had four doors that opened to the outside, and one that went directly into the basement. She was certain that all of them were already locked. She smiled as she rounded the stairwell and peered into the darkness of the first floor. Matt would be home soon, she felt mixed emotions at that thought. It would be wonderful to have him close, but he was missing the conference."

The light above the stove in the kitchen was always on. She was comforted by its glow. It would be much easier to negotiate the darkness with even a little light. As she started down the stairs she stopped. *What was that? It couldn't be.* But yes, she felt it…a breeze. It was not much of a breeze, but a slight movement of the air around her, she shuddered as the nerve endings on her skin reacted to the movement.

She leaned forward and squinted. In the faint light she realized the curtain in the window at the base of the stairs was fluttering. Her mind began to race, of course she had closed all the windows, as she looked closer she saw the broken glass on the floor. There was movement to her right. She noticed a shadow on the wall to her left, it moved and was gone?

This was not happening. It could not be…someone was in Kate's house. She froze on the step and heard a creak from the floor below. The door to the basement had been moved. She knew the sound and fear sent a shiver through her being…*who was there?*

She had to move, she had to think… "Who is down there? What are you doing in this house? Who are you?" She yelled out with all the courage and determination that she could find within herself.

There was no answer. There was only quiet…deadly quiet. Suddenly the light above the stove went dark. Then she saw it, definite movement from the darkness below her. It was coming her way. She turned and lost her slipper on the carpeting, running up the stairs, her long legs taking two steps at a time. She must lock her door. She must keep him out. She hurled herself into the bedroom and slammed the door grabbing for the lock as it closed. The lock slid smoothly into place.

Connie turned out the TV and grabbed the phone. She hit the redial key. The solid hardwood door exploded into the room. In one movement, even in the total darkness, he was on top of her. She could feel his weight and his strength. She let herself sink under his weight, then lunged with all her strength at his throat with her left hand. She caught him just below his jaw on the right side of his face, the force of the blow moving him to his left and changing his balance.

With one quick move, Connie slid free and jumped to her feet. As she began to move away from the bed, he reached back with his right hand and grabbed her shoulder length hair. As she turned, she saw the knife in his left hand, and brought her knee up into his groin as he slashed across her chest. She could hear herself wheeze, as her lungs seemed to burst. She grabbed for his face and clawed with all her force as the knife once again found its mark. Suddenly, the darkness was leaving. Light began to fill the room…the brightest light that Connie had ever seen began to approach. There He was with arms open. There was no pain; there was no more darkness. Connie was home.

*****

As he turned into the farm he recognized the lights he had been watching for the last quarter mile. There were ambulance lights and police lights everywhere.

The house was completely lit, and Gus was sitting on the front step with his head in his hands. Matt slid to a stop and slammed the car into park as he threw open the door of his Taurus.

"Dad, what's going on?"

Gus stood and grabbed his son by the shoulders, "It's Connie, Matt. She's been murdered. I heard it all. She's gone—killed. Connie's been killed. I was sleeping, and he cut her up. I should have been watching. I should have stayed awake and watched. I'm so sorry, Matt, I wasn't watching. I fell asleep, and now she's dead.

"I just talked to her. She can't be dead…just talked to her less than an hour ago. I came home because she called me. She can't be dead."

Matt struggled out of the grasp of his father and ran for the house. His head was swirling, his breathing, short gasps. He nearly ran into two officers and a third man in handcuffs. With the light behind them, Matt didn't recognize the prisoner immediately, but as he turned to let them pass his worst fears were confirmed, Paul, and he was covered with blood. Their eyes met. Paul turned away.

Matt was unable to move. He heard his father's voice explode in anger. Gus screamed and was able to hit Paul twice in the face with his fists before the officers dragged him off.

"I treated you like my son! How could you kill her? You talked about God and Jesus and being changed. You killed Connie. You killed her! I loved you both. How could you kill her?"

Gus sank to his knees in tears, his shoulders heaving under the pain. Matt turned and ran back down the stairs to his father. He knelt beside his father and wrapped his arms around his shoulders.

"I left her alone too. I should have been here. She was my wife. I should have stayed here. It's not your fault, I should never have left."

As the minutes passed, the tears subsided, and they sat on the driveway side-by side.

"She called me about eleven-thirty. She feared something. She said she saw some movement on the lawn and heard noises. I told her to call you and have you come into the house and sleep." Matt was speaking to Gus, but neither of them acknowledged the other.

"She wouldn't hear of waking anybody, so I decided to head home. I thought Paul was probably taking care of the sows."

"He knew that Connie was alone in that house. He heard you leave. He saw the light on in the bedroom. I found him in the house!" Gus was still steaming. "They were right... I never should have trusted that son-of-a..."

"You found, Paul? I thought the police found him. I called them when I had been on the road for about ten minutes. I just felt like I should have them check things out, and I knew I would be another half hour at best. They said they would send a car. What made you go to the house?"

"I just woke up, heard the dog making a racket. Went to the sink to get a glass of water and saw the kitchen light go out. I got a little worried, and went to put on my pants and shoes, then headed for the house. As I walked out of the door, I heard a bunch of doors slamming in the house, so I ran up there. Every damn door I tried was locked, finally found the side door open, but it was all over by then. He was already done."

"You found Paul in Kate's room?"

"Hell yes, he was in the room! That murdering SOB was crouched right over her like an animal. He was talking to her and crying like a baby, still had the knife in his hands. If I'd had a gun, they'd be haulin' his carcass out too."

"Did you talk to him? Did he say anything to you about why he did it? Why would Paul kill Connie?"

"He asked me if I saw who did it. He said he was trying to save her. They never confess. Of course, he'd say he didn't do it. What's he going to say? I'm telling you he was still on top of her, and he had the knife in his hand. What more proof do you need? The Sheriff didn't even blink. He cuffed him the minute he saw all the blood and heard about the knife. He said the same thing, probably never thought he'd get caught."

"But dad if he was guilty why didn't he run? Why did he stay to get caught? Did he say anything else?"

"He said he found Connie on the floor and saw someone leaving through the window. The window was open, and the screen taken off…that's how he got in. Paul had just been in the house the other night talking to Kate. He probably opened the lock then to get everything set up. And think about this…if there was someone else, where is he? How'd he get away? Like Paul isn't big enough to rip apart almost anyone that comes at him? I'm telling you Matt, he's damaged goods. You just can't change damaged goods."

"Well, I think that God changed this man, and I'm not about to condemn him before I know for sure it was him. Connie said she felt evil around her when she called, and I don't think that sounds like Paul." Matt was trying to think, trying to be reasonable.

"She's gone, Dad, and I want to find who killed her as much as you, but I want to find the guilty man, not just any man."

"I was there, Matt. I saw it. I want the right man too. We have him."

"I hope you're wrong. I'm going into the house now. Are you going to be okay?"

"Are you sure you want to see that?"

"I've got to, Dad."

"Go ahead, I'll be fine."

The inside of the house was chaos. There were men everywhere with brushes and powder, and flashlights and cameras, and tweezers and on and on. Matt saw the open window and realized how vulnerable Connie had been.

His eyes burned from the tears, and his mind ached from the memory of her voice. He would never hear it again. He saw a slipper on the stair and called one of the detectives over.

"Was this slipper here when you entered?"

"Excuse me, but you are not part of the team. You should not be in here."

"Connie was my wife. I drove here after she called me less than an hour ago."

"Where were you staying? Was it the Bell Hotel in Fairmont?"

"Yes, the Bell! How did you know that?"

"The phone was off the hook, and someone had dialed the Bell Hotel and never hung up."

"She must have hit the redial to call me when she was in trouble. If only I had stayed here, if only I had stayed..."

"I've been involved in three of these cases in the past. This guy would have waited until you left, no matter what. This guy was a predator and they just never change."

"How can you be certain it's Paul? He said he saw someone else and tried to stop them."

"We pulled his record, had it faxed to us before they took him out of here. Read it for yourself."

The paper was shiny fax paper, but easy to read. Paul Prentiss, murder suspect, was found at scene with knife in hand. Suspect stated at capture that he found victim and saw a man running away from scene. No evidence of third party was found after investigation. Prints on knife belonged to Prentiss and victim. Blood type at scene matched victim and suspect. Death caused by slashing chest of victim and puncture wounds to lungs.

"That case is twenty plus years old. It's like reading the same scenario. These guys are cons. They'll say what you want to hear, all the time planning their attack. I'm sorry Sir the Judge made a mistake, and it cost you your wife."

"I trusted him with everything. He was an incredible worker and seemed to be a deeply devoted Christian. I just can't believe she's dead."

"I have heard that more times than I care to remember. These are the toughest cases. Young people should never die like this, I'm sorry. We probably will want to talk to you. You possibly were the last person to talk to your wife, and she may have said or done something that will help us. We still plan on investigating this, although we believe with certainty that we have the right man. You asked about the slipper, why?"

"The last thing I told Connie to do was to go downstairs and check all the locks and doors. It looks like she left that step in a hurry. He probably was in the house even while I was on the phone. She had to be scared to leave the slipper there. I wish I had never left the house."

Matt realized that he had not seen his wife. He had been there for nearly an hour. He wasn't certain if he wanted to see her, yet he had to be strong.

As he reached the top of the stairs he recognized the fragrance. The odor of blood was heavy in the air. As he entered Kate's bedroom he was brought to his knees by the scene. The bed and the walls were covered with blood, and bloody foam was on the floor directly beside the bed. A man in a uniform noticed him sink and hurried to steady him.

The voice behind Matt said, "Sorry sir, if I had known you were coming up here, I would never have let you come alone. You probably shouldn't be here. The memories last a long time when it's someone you love."

"Where did you find her body?"

"Right there by the bed. She put up quite a fight, looks like she almost got away"

"Where the foamy red is?"

"Yes! When the lungs are punctured, the bleeding is sometimes foamy from the air. I'm sorry, but this is not good for you. We should go."

"If there is that much blood on the floor, was she face down?"

"No, they found the suspect kneeling over her, she was face up."

"There usually is a lot of blood when the stabbing is close to the heart."

"But if the body was face up, wouldn't the blood be in two spots, one on each side of her, not one large spot."

"Blood flows under the body, especially this much blood."

"What are these footprints leading toward the door?"

"It could be one of the officer's prints, there have been a lot of people tramping around up here. We took pictures before anything was touched, so we will see if there are prints anywhere, but it probably is just from the traffic."

"Where is her body? Can I see Connie?"

"The funeral director took her to the chapel. He told me to tell anyone that wants to see her to come into town. He just wanted to clean up the body before anyone sees her. We were finished with our investigation."

"Did you check under her fingernails in case she clawed him? She was always so particular about those nails. She never had dirty nails. Did you check them?"

"I'll be happy to check, Sir."

The detective moved quickly across the room and spoke with an elderly man in the corner. They both turned abruptly and moved toward Matt.

"I'm Senior Detective Adams. I understand you have some questions."

"Did they check Connie's fingernails before she was taken into town."

"I checked them myself, nothing there. We want to cover every option. It is sometimes harder when the suspect is apprehended during the crime. We don't want any loose ends either. You needn't worry, Mr. Roth, we might be a small group, but we have several detectives with a great deal of experience in these matters. I began in the Minneapolis Police Department, along with two of our junior detectives. We will be busy gathering evidence for quite some time. If you have any questions, don't hesitate to bring them to us."

Matt walked wearily to his Taurus; it was already nearly 5:00 AM. He wanted to drive past the mortuary just in case there was a light on. The Chapel was open. Matt opened the door and heard the bell ring in the back to warn the staff if someone had entered. From the back of the building came a rather large man with a loving smile and graying hair.

"I'm Ned Ritter, can I help you with something." As he moved closer. He saw Matt's face and eyes and spoke before Matt could answer. "I hope that you didn't mind that I brought her here. It's just that I felt she had been through enough. I could tell by her dress and her hair that she would never want to be seen unless she looked perfect. I would have wanted someone I loved taken out of there. I just asked if it would be okay. They were all so busy that they really didn't care. You are Connie's husband, Matt?"

"Do I look that bad, or how do you know?"

"You actually look a lot like your father, Gus. I spoke with him for a short while when I arrived. He told me he was Connie's Father-in-law."

"Can I see her? Would it be okay?"

"I have her in the back, she is just in a robe, but yes, you should probably spend some time with her. I will show you the way. Spend as much time as you need."

The first fifteen minutes were the worst. Matt laid his head on her stomach as waves of tears and anguish moved over him. He had experienced grief when his mother died, but never like this. All his plans, all his hope in this life, all his love centered in their relationship, and it was gone. Grief washed through him like waves on a beach.

He saw her face, and felt her hand, it was cold, but he recognized it. He knew she was dead. It was not supposed to be like this. He remembered how she had warned him not to get involved with inmates. Now she was dead, and he was alone. *What would life be like without her to love? Oh, how he would miss this woman.* Matt couldn't see it, but all heaven grieved with him.

At 8:00 AM, Matt emerged from the room. Ned was still there in his office, waiting.

"Do you drink coffee? I went down to the bakery and picked up a couple of donuts. My wife isn't too happy about the bakery only being a block away," he rubbed his stomach, "but they have good stuff. Would you like to sit a while?"

The coffee was wonderful, and Matt hadn't realized how hungry he had become. "This really hits the spot. Can I ask you something?"

"Anything."

"When you brought Connie here, did you clean her fingernails? She grew up with brothers and she put up a fight. I think she would have clawed her killer if she got the chance. Did she have anything under her nails."

"As a matter of fact, she did. I am sort of a fanatic about that kind of stuff. I kept the scrapings and put them in a baggy. I figured if the sheriff department ever came asking, I'd have it for them."

"Ned, can you keep a secret? I asked the detective about her nails and he assured me that he checked them. Either he didn't want to look stupid, or he just doesn't care. I would prefer if you don't let them in on what you found. Just put it in your safe, and if we need it later we'll have it."

"As far as I'm concerned, whatever was with Connie belongs to you."

"We will have to make some plans soon about the ceremony. When do you think we should have it?"

"I didn't bring her here so that you'd have to use our chapel. I just wanted to get her out of there. You are welcome to have any Funeral home pick her up if it would be more convenient for you."

"Ned, you know Christ, don't you?"

"He's my best friend."

"Then she'd want you taking care of her. How do we go about it?"

"Maybe you should contact friends and relatives and see what the best time is for them; then we'll talk. By the way, her small toe was severed. Did the detective say anything about that to you?"

"Nothing. Do you think it was done at the time of her death?"

"Right after she died...some bleeding, but not like if she had a beating heart."

CHAPTER 48

The news brought a smile to his face. Watch that town blow up when the media hears about the murder. Fortune had really smiled on them. Not only had the killing been as planned, but "ex-con Paul" had shown up as if scheduled. He was found hovering over the body, weapon in hand. It was if it had been scripted.

It was impossible to know if the media in Chicago would pick up on it, but friends in the Twin Cities talked of pictures and on location remote coverage.

Tony was ecstatic. Initially he had been bothered by the identity of the victim.

The plan was to kill Kate. He could have brought some pain to Holden in his last few days and gotten even with her for leading him on all these years. Fate sometimes twists events to fit even better than planned. Kate and the entire fanatical bunch would watch as their dreams caved in around them. *There was plenty of time to deal with Kate.*

The phone rang at his desk. He strolled from the window and picked up the receiver.

"This is Tony…" His smile widened. "Send him in."

The huge bodyguard entered the office and took a seat to the left of the desk.

"Nice job; sounds like you got out clean and left the jail-bird hangin' big time. What the hell happened to your face and neck?"

"She fought 'til the end. Even got me with her knee in the groin. But I did just what you said, cut her right across the chest and then through the lungs. She dropped pretty fast after the second cut."

"I want all the details. Did you get the toe?"

"Got it right here in a baggy. Why's it such a big deal?"

"Word in the joint is that old Paul cut the little toe off the girl he killed. It was never made public because they didn't want to get some copycat thing going. That will be the nail in his coffin. I'd love to see the faces on the crew when word of that reaches them. See, it really pays to do your homework. I know that '*turn the other cheek*' attitude they profess. They'll all want to believe he's innocent. He'll never be able to get out of this one." Tony pulled a huge cigar from the wooden humidor on his desk and clipped the tip.

"You won't ever see Minnesota again. Those little police departments want a quick, clean case, and we just gave it to them."

"I brought the tape, too."

"Cool, I can't wait to show it to Mr. CEO. I called him about a half hour ago, he's going to be at the warehouse office within the hour. Let's head out."

*****

Holden had a bad feeling about the call. He was certain Tony was behind the meeting. He had no option but to play along. Jack said something about Kate having some problems with her project. He was aware of the farm but knew little about the problems.

Holden had begun his work on the final chapter of this nightmare. He reached the office about ten minutes before the meeting and picked up a cup of coffee at the breakroom. He noticed a gentleman with a slight build and rather coarse reddish hair, seated at one of the tables. He was wearing thick glasses and a pocket protector with a computer logo on it. He didn't stand out from the rest of the office workers. His clothes were inexpensive, and he wore shoes from some discount store, but he was intently staring at Holden.

After leaving and then returning to prove his theory, Holden was certain. This guy had some reason to be interested in Holden. He made a mental note to locate his office right after the meeting.

Holden passed Morrey in the hall on his way to the meeting. Morrey walked right past him as if he didn't exist. Holden felt the end of his tenure at Highland was just around the corner.

As he entered the office, Holden scanned the area. There was no sign of Tony and his two sidekicks. Maybe this was about something else. He had barely set his coffee on the desk and taken a seat when the side door opened. The king and his court entered.

"I see you still need to work on that knocking thing. Please come in."

"It is always wonderful to visit with the former husband of a former friend. Are they treating you well here?"

"I have no complaints. I am certain that as far as a hostage situation goes, this is nearly as comfortable as it gets. The food is excellent, and expectations seem to be lessening and time flies by. Thank you for asking," Holden's sarcasm seemed to go unnoticed. "Now is there a point to this meeting other than your presence. What the hell happened to the 'Gorilla in the mist' over there? He looks like a truck hit him. A truck with fingernails." Holden was sorry he had mentioned it when he saw the sardonic grin. "Actually, it almost seems to have enhanced his looks. With any luck the scar tissue will hide most of his face."

"Every time we visit, I am taken with your humor. I look forward to the day when I will have the time to genuinely appreciate it."

"I hope you aren't saying that you don't appreciate it now."

"I took the liberty of having a VCR delivered to your office. I'm certain you've been wondering why it's here?"

"Can't say I even saw it. I just got here myself. I stopped for coffee on my way."

Holden was shaken as both Tony and the Gorillas smiled a nauseatingly knowing smile.

"I have a little film that I would like you to see."

*****

Holden recognized the bedroom. The furniture was new, but the dormered walls and the windows were forever etched in his mind. He and Kate made love in that room, in the first year after their marriage.

Kate took him home to visit the farm and help her make some decisions about renting the land. Holden was far more interested in getting her alone in the house than in the details of the farm. He remembered pretending to listen to her. He acted as if he was interested in helping with the leases and the rent, when all the time he was studying the body inside those jeans and that sweatshirt.

He had always been that way. He knew the words to say, the way to act to impress people. He cared nothing about others, never had and wasn't certain that he ever would. It was always about him. He had watched the tape in horror.

When he first saw the body, he thought it was Kate. Now he was ashamed that he had been relieved to find it was someone else.

Tony had laughed as he told about the plan. "All the time we had planned to kill the 'Widow Jeffries' instead we got the preacher's wife. Turns out to be even a better story." He had watched Holden, knowing that he would make the same mistake.

Tony beamed as he saw Holden flinch. He laughed as the scene unfolded on the screen. He saw Connie lying on the floor face down. There was blood on the walls and a huge red circle under the body. Her hair was covering her face, long shoulder length blondish hair. It was caked with blood and sweat. As the movie continued, a hand reached from behind the camera and moved the hair revealing the face of Connie Roth. Her eyes were closed. He had seen that look on Tom when he died, she was a believer.

Holden knew he would never forget that blood spattered face. He knew now where the bruises had come from on the bodyguard's neck and face. The film ended as the camera panned the room and then was held in a position to show the face of the killer. The face was the same man that shared the room with them. He had a sick smile and specks of blood on his cheeks.

As the room went dark and the lights were turned back on, Tony showed Holden a plastic bag with a grizzly treasure inside. A human toe had been cut off and placed in the bag.

"It's interesting how toes never decay, they stay like this forever. They dry out, but in one hundred years they will look just about the same. It makes a nice memento, don't you think? I only wish it could have been your wife's, but nonetheless, this will do. Look closely and always remember what happens when you underestimate your competition."

The death was nauseating to envision, but the snickering of these animals as they relived their victory was nearly more than Holden could tolerate. He sat quietly until they left. They had no concern. They told him everything. They knew it didn't matter. Holden didn't exist. He was dead to them. He was nothing. He had no power. He was nothing to fear.

Holden knew they were right.

Now as he sat in the dark of his hotel room, he was again faced with the pain of the truth. He was a selfish man. He had never loved anyone as much as he cared about himself. It was evident in all that he had done. He built a corporation to glorify himself. He built a fortune to glorify his name. He lived his marriage for the sake of self-gratification. He pretended to care for others. They bought it… but he knew the truth. He offered things to his children in the place of his love. He blamed every problem on others. He was a success, and most of all, he was always right.

Now he sat in darkness. He felt the emptiness of his life all around him. He was never satisfied with his treasure. There had never been enough. He blamed work, and family, and life for the chaos of his existence. It was clear as the lies were stripped away, it was him. He was the problem.

An entire life of toil had been wasted. That waste caused pain for nearly everyone pulled near. He wanted to kill Tony and the goons, but he knew they were only part of it. They could be punished for what they had done, but it would solve nothing. They weren't the problem. It was him; he was the center of his world. He had been a success in the world, a failure in life.

If only he had seen this before all these people had been hurt. If only he would have told himself the truth long ago. Things could have been different. As he sat in the dark, he knew that even the money meant nothing, it would solve nothing.

Holden knew wherever he went, an unhappy, selfish man would go with him. He was looking forward to that day when he would turn the key in the ignition, and it would all be over. It had all been a lie.

He could hear God laughing. He knew the truth...he was *screwed*.

*****

As Holden floundered at the very bottom of his life, in an unseen world Satan laughed. As Holden felt the truth upon his shoulders, in another world of light, God called upon his Angels to guard him. They anguished with Holden in his pain. Life begins in truth.

CHAPTER 49

Kate and Jack arrived at "Welcome Home" within hours of Connie's death. They found Gus in the fields cultivating the beans. The house was a crime scene and the farm was in mourning. Channel Six News and three other news teams were camped in the hay field across the road.

The story was Headline News by the morning edition. Pictures of anything that moved or could be described found their way to the breakfast, lunch and dinner hours of the entire listening audience.

The arrival of Jack and Kate brought new speculation. Paul's mug shot had been incorporated into almost every part of the story. The previous interview added to the innuendo. The news anchor stating, "Let's hope there is nothing to regret in the future," was played with the pictures.

The mayor and the council members were quick to point out they had seen this coming. They felt badly, but the guilt must be placed on those who brought this element into their community.

The Sheriff had stated flatly that they had evidence that supported their arrest of the suspect. He would be arraigned within the hour. It was an open and shut case. Kate closed the farm immediately upon her return. The clients were sent to other treatment centers. The employees were told this was a temporary closing, but much would depend on the findings of the investigation. Kate declined an interview, and Jack stated that he had no reason to comment on the guilt of their client.

At 1:30 PM, Matt, Jack, Gus, and Kate met at the bunkhouse table. Jack broke the silence.

"I was coming back to help with the meeting. I heard that things were getting tough back here. Matt, I am so sorry. I will miss Connie for the rest of my life. I know that doesn't help, but it is true. How are you doing through this mess?"

"I am numb. I spent some time with her in the chapel. I tried to sort it all out, but just can't get it into my head. I will never talk to her again. I had so much to tell her."

"Matt, I should never have asked her to stay at the house. I think they were after me. Nobody knew she was staying there. I only wish it had been me. How can I ever say I'm sorry for this? I loved her. She was my best friend, a sister I never had, I am so sorry."

"Kate, it's not your fault. Each of us could blame ourselves. It doesn't help. God was there. He knows the truth. If He wanted it some other way, it would have happened some other way. I feel like my heart has been ripped out. I fall apart when I think about our last phone call." Matt looked absolutely in ruin as he spoke.

"You said that you talked to her just before all of this happened. Was she frightened? I was here, right here. I could have maybe stopped this. Why didn't she call?" Gus spoke as if he was still in shock.

"We talked about calling you, Dad. She didn't even want me to come home. She said that she had felt some kind of presence in the house. She prayed and it had left. She was not afraid, but she had seen somebody moving around in the yard."

"She said that? She saw someone walking around. Why didn't she call the police?"

"I told her it was probably Paul. I figured the sows were farrowing and that he was up with them. I didn't think it was a killer."

"It probably was Paul. He was the killer."

"They said you found him in the room, Gus. Is that true?"

"He was crouched over Connie's body. He still had the knife in his hand. There was blood everywhere. He was crying and holding her head in his hand. I will never forget that scene. I thought he loved us. I should never have trusted him."

"Dad…was Connie…did you see…" Matt stopped. He tried swallowing hard. He placed both hands over his eyes and then to his mouth. It was as if the pictures in his mind would not let him speak. There was no sound in the room for several seconds as Matt pulled himself back from the island in his heart. "Did you see Connie lying on her back when you walked in?"

"Yeah, looking right up at her killer." Gus nearly spit out the words.

"But what if Paul stumbled onto the scene after someone else had killed her? What if he were trying to see if he could save her? The blood on the carpet is one big round spot. If she fell on her back with the wounds in her chest wouldn't the blood be in smaller pools on each side of her body. This almost seems like she fell face down."

"Matt, he killed her. There was no sign of anybody else. Have you checked his history to see how he killed the last girl? That's too much of a coincidence. It's hard to swallow, but he killed her."

"It may have been. There was lots of anger going on around this town about us being here. It's pretty easy to find out the background of a criminal right on the Internet. After all, some people wanted this placed closed."

"Has anyone gone to see Paul? Has anyone heard his side?" Jack asked changing the subject.

"I was in town, but I just couldn't bring myself to visiting him yet. We have to get him a lawyer." Matt answered as if he was ashamed.

"Why would we get the killer of one of our family a lawyer? Let him get his own damn lawyer. We aren't responsible for his case, he is! Let him worry about it. Let him rot in that place."

"Gus, I know you loved her. We all loved her. Connie would want us to find out everything about this. We will talk to Paul. If he has no answers, he's on his own. I know you want the killer punished as much as anyone…we have to know for sure."

"Jack—I know for sure. I saw it with these eyes. He killed Connie. You'll see."

"I really hope that's not true, but it fits what we have seen. Kate, have you heard from that friend of yours lately? I think his name is Tony."

"I haven't seen him since he stormed out of here months ago."

"Why was he angry?"

"I accused him of being rude to Gus and asked him to apologize. He refused and became belligerent. He said some really nasty things about me, and the farm…he also said that he hoped that the neighbors wouldn't mind the jailbirds in the area."

"You're sure about that, Kate?"

"I remember it vividly because that's what made me get the community involved."

"Do you think he was angry enough to hold a grudge?"

"I can answer that one," Gus interrupted, "That guys face was as red as my socks. He was peeved big time. I wouldn't put much of anything past him as fast as he exploded. He hated it when Kate seemed to take my side instead of his. I had been a little rude myself, so I felt kind of bad."

"What had you said to him?"

"I was kidding him about his long hair. He had a ponytail."

"That wasn't it. A storm had been building in our relationship for the last couple of times that we had been together. This was just the ending in an ongoing saga."

"Maybe it wasn't the ending for him."

CHAPTER 50

They found Morrey's body in his car. There was a case of French wine on the seat and a dozen roses in a box on the floor. A hose connected the tailpipe to the rear window.

His secretary and long-time lover was tied up and gagged in the trunk with a bullet hole through her heart. She was wearing a full-length mink coat and nothing else. She had one rose tucked into her hand. A simple case of murder/suicide, open and shut.

He was buried in a plain box with no headstone. His family did not attend. There were less than ten mourners, all from Highland. Morrey was gone. He had gotten greedy and stupid. He had been ordering wine, and flowers and who knows what else from the Internet and using company money. He was stealing and flaunting it.

Tony couldn't have made it clearer. He had watched every move.

Morrey was an idiot. Tony had set him up with some of the extra money. The rules had been simple. Don't get greedy. Stupid people just don't listen.

When the money in his account dropped, he transferred more in to keep the balance looking as if there had been no activity. The loser shipped most of the stuff to his girlfriend's address. Tony watched it all. He waited until he was certain it wasn't just a single mistake, then set up the hit.

It was so easy. They picked up the woman, took her to the warehouse, and shot her. Then the picked-up Morrey and let him open the trunk to find the surprise. While he was still gasping from the sight of his lover, they gave him a single injection of Succinyl Choline in upper quadrant of his left buttock. He was paralyzed in less than two minutes, eyes open. His breathing was somewhat shallow, but the boys knew that he would still take in enough carbon monoxide to end it before the shot wore off, and if it took longer, that was better.

It was nearly perfect, they got to watch him die, and he was watching them laugh at him. The drug exists naturally in the body, so it is impossible to trace. Some of the fun was lost because the police were so inept at investigating. It was some of their best work.

Tony smiled as he contemplated the final days of Holden Jeffries. The jerks in the office still hadn't come up with anything from the notebook pages. He had been on them for some answers. He suspected they weren't really qualified to break codes.

The cars were rolling through faster than ever, and the money was rolling in. He had hoped to watch Holden squirm, but it probably wasn't going to happen. The guy was like having a time bomb around. He was too smart, and eventually he would cause problems. It was going to be nice to have him gone.

*****

Night after night he saw her face hidden by her hair. He had not slept more than an hour at a time for more than three weeks.

Jack was gone and probably wouldn't return for some time. Morrey had been killed, and the offices were there to be picked. Holden knew he had to go in alone. He had scouted the red head's office and watched him come and go. The guy never worked nights. If he didn't go soon, he knew that he would not be able to pull it off. He had to go tonight.

CHAPTER 51

The funeral was over. The church had been packed. Connie had been a quiet servant who had touched the hearts of many. The many people who had shared their stories comforted Matt. The friends left to return to their own lives. Then the finality of death touched the survivors.

Matt and Jack spent a great deal of time at the jail talking to Paul. They retained the services of one of the best criminal lawyers in Minnesota, but Paul's depressed state worried them. Now nearly three weeks after the murder, another bombshell had exploded.

Jack and Matt set up a meeting with the attorney and Paul for their weekly planning session. It was nearly two o'clock, and the 1:00 PM meeting was supposed to be in full swing, but no one had seen the attorney.

"Are you certain that you set the meeting for one; this guy is never late." Matt asked. "I spoke with him last Friday, and we agreed on Tuesday at one. I even called and confirmed it yesterday."

"Then there has got to be something wrong."

"Let's get Paul in here anyway and run over some of the plan."

"I'd much rather just get him to open up. I hate it when he just sits staring at the wall."

"He said he didn't kill her. What more do we need? The rest is up to Peterson. He's the lawyer."

"Something is missing. He is not comfortable with something."

"Jack, we have some big problems in this case. I know that Paul didn't kill Connie, but the police are comfortable with their perpetrator. They already believe he's the guy. They just played around at investigating the crime." Matt stated remembering the eyes of the investigator when questioned.

"Then we have no witness except Gus. I am not an investigator. This is way over my head. I love you Jack, but I think it's over yours too. I just don't think anybody really cares. They want him convicted, pure and simple."

"But, Matt, you know the scripture. *'You shall know the truth, and the truth shall set you free.'* I think the more we find out about all this the closer we get to freedom. If God knows that Paul is innocent, the answer lies in the truth. I believe we need to be here, but God will do the work of protecting the innocent."

"Sorry, Jack. You're right we just need to trust Him."

Paul entered the library and sat at the table across from Jack and Matt.

"Paul, how are you doing through all of this?"

"I'm okay."

"Are you able to eat, and sleep?"

"I eat some, but I don't sleep too much."

"You need to try to sleep."

"Guys go home. Leave me in this jail. I should never have tried to change my life. I need to pay for the crimes I committed. That world out there just doesn't fit me. I am worthless out there. I tried to be part of something, and I got your wife killed. It isn't ever going to end. I'm a killer; that will never change. I'm a killer."

"But that was a long time ago. You paid for that."

"You say that I paid for that, but who are you to pardon me. I can walk from these walls, and outside I will always be a killer."

"It wasn't your fault, Paul. You were an innocent bystander."

"Then why am I in this jail? They were right… I should never have come here."

"But you are changed. God made you a new creation. You're not the old Paul. Remember that prayer? You asked Him for help. You asked Him to lead your life. You told Him you loved Him."

"I remember it all, but I don't think He's ready to forgive me quite yet. It's not that I don't believe in His power, it's that I do. I know that He is still angry with me. I need to pay the full price."

"You haven't paid it, Paul. Through Christ, it's paid, He paid it. Remember, it's not about how good you have been or how bad you have been, it's about who you follow. He hasn't left you or forsaken you. He will still help us in this…we just need to trust. He can make something good come out of this if we believe."

"Then maybe that's the problem… I don't believe enough."

"Then you need to pray for that. He will provide if we ask."

There was as creaking as the door to the library opened. The guard was followed by James Peterson, Attorney at Law. As the guard made his way back to the door Jim took a chair beside Paul. When the door was locked, he began to speak with guarded tones.

"I have just spent the past two hours with the County Attorney. They wanted me to come up to speed on the evidence against us. We know about Paul's fingerprints on the weapon, and the blood stains on Paul's clothes. We know about Gus's eyewitness of Paul over Connie's body. But there was something that has just been brought forward that may be a major problem if I can't keep it out of evidence. Connie's small toe on her left foot was severed apparently with the knife."

Paul pounded his hand against the table and inhaled through gritted teeth.

"It just can't be. Who would have known that? They couldn't know."

"What are you talking about Paul? Settle down, you must settle down."

The guard reached the table with handcuffs ready and his nightstick in his other hand. "What the hell was that? Is everything okay?"

"We just got some news that was not the best. I'm certain that everything will be okay. Paul, you are going to be okay, right. Everything's okay, right?"

"I want to go back to my cell. That's where I belong."

Paul stood, keeping his head down and was escorted back through the door to his cell.

"The other murder...the girl's small toe had been severed. It happened to be on her right foot, but that probably won't matter to the jury. I am writing a motion to suppress the evidence. I wouldn't count on that happening. The details of the first murder were not made public. This will not be easy to fight."

"Did they find Connie's toe?"

"Not yet. That helps, but not enough."

"But these are just similarities. Really nothing is the same. Did they find the other victim's toe?"

"Yes, it was on the scene. Paul apparently was high on LSD at the time and had no idea what he was doing. But juries don't look much past the obvious...this is not good news."

"Counselor, do you think that Paul killed Connie?"

"I rarely can afford the luxury of considering guilt. I must say I think this is a set up, but whoever is behind it has a lot of knowledge. It's information that has been hidden in police reports for years...not easy to get."

"What can we do?"

"I will keep working on this, but we sure could use a break."

"Jim, I almost forgot. When I went to see Connie's body on the day she was killed, I asked Ned if she had anything under her nails. I know she would have scratched anyone who was trying to kill her. I had asked the detective about it, but he said that he had checked her nails and they were clean. Ned did not agree, in fact, he cleaned under them when he prepared her body, and put the scrapings in a bag in the case that the Police came inquiring. At this point they have not."

"Matt, are you nuts? That's hiding evidence." Jack was horrified at actions of his friend.

"Actually, that is not at all what it was. This is a grieving husband that has been through a lot. There will be no problem getting this into trial. Let's just hope Ned kept the bag. We certainly can use the evidence but unless we can match it up with someone's DNA, all we can prove is that it isn't Paul's." Jim tried to smile as if relieved. "But it is something...it's more than we had before."

"I really hate to do this, but I need to be gone for a couple of days. Matt, can you hold down the fort. I have some unfinished business. I hope to be back in a week."

"Jack, what's more important than this case? We really need you here. I have a tough enough time when it's the two of us."

"I have a friend that just might be terminal. I promised I would try to help him through his fight. God hasn't forgotten Paul. He will be with you.

"I hope so, Jack."

CHAPTER 52

The offices were dark, except for the night clerk. The TV blared loud enough you could have driven a car past the door and he probably wouldn't have heard it. Holden felt like he'd watched one too many James Bond movies. He was dressed in black from head to toe. He was wearing a black stocking cap that had already begun to make his scalp itch. He had camo face paint to finish the look. He chuckled at how he must have looked. He headed in the direction of 'Red's' office.

Entering the doorway, he stopped dead, no alarm. The ball game on TV was in the seventh inning, and though twenty-five feet of empty office space was between them, he was aware of the score and the full count on the batter.

Holden switched on the flashlight placed it into his mouth. He moved quickly toward the desk listening ever so closely for any sign of movement. He gently opened the large lower right desk drawer to find it filled with hanging files. He moved them to each side and saw nothing thick enough to be his book. He moved to the top right drawer. It was filled with assorted junk. No book. Each drawer offered less potential. The desk was clean.

Holden rose directing his attention to the file cabinets on the back wall. There were two cabinets each with five drawers. He found records of nearly every transaction for the past five years. There was plenty of evidence of Highland's theft ring, but still no notebook. He found a listing of every employee in the company, with background checks intact, still no book.

As he opened the top drawer in the final cabinet he heard a doorknob click. The game was still on, the volume rose as the door began to open. Holden doused the flashlight and dropped to his knees behind the tall backed leather desk chair. He was out of sight, but in no way hidden. His heartbeat like a damaged hard drive…he tried to keep calm.

As the door opened the overhead light flicked on. The stark office, now fully lit, had no potential for cover. Holden's heart was in his throat. He was not going without a fight. He grabbed the flashlight in the palm of his hand. He leaned forward on his toes and readied himself. He heard movement. The light above his head clicked off, and the door closed.

Holden held his breath. He looked at his watch. The luminous hands showed midnight. It was probably just an hourly check of the rooms. He waited another five minutes. Then slinked back to the cabinet.

His search was futile. He was no farther than he had been when he began. The office was void of more hiding places.

Just because this guy is one who files everything, doesn't mean he has the stuff. I just must keep looking.

By three AM, Holden had searched three offices. Four more times the rooms had been lit, surveyed, and left for another hour. Holden had come to rely on the process to tell him how fast he was moving.

On the fourth office, Holden got a surprise. As he began to open desk drawers, he noticed a five-by-seven picture of Tony's bodyguard in a full-dress Marine uniform. As he checked out the other photos, the gorilla was in them all. This was his office.

In the second drawer Holden hit pay dirt. He didn't find his book, but he did find a large manila envelope with "Mn" in the corner. Inside were ticket stubs for a recent flight to Minneapolis, a car rental contract, a VCR tape, and the small plastic bag with a gruesome reminder of his work.

Holden took the photo from the frame and put it into the envelope. He folded the envelope and placed it into his black vest. At four AM, Holden slipped out of the office building, and took the bus to a familiar street. In less than ten minutes, he was standing on Angela's unlit porch.

He knocked lightly. There was no movement. He knocked again with more force. He waited two minutes. He was about to try one more time, when the light of the front room lit the stoop. Holden instinctively ducked behind the shadow of the door. Angela seemed startled as she opened the inside door.

"Jack, is that you? It's after 4:00 AM, what are you doing here?"

"Angela, can I come in for a couple of minutes? It's important."

"Of course."

"And could you turn out that light?"

She clicked the switch and stepped back as Holden entered the solace of the darkened room.

"I really can't tell you much. You have to trust me."

"What are you talking about, Jack? Let's go into the kitchen, you can tell me about this there. I'll make a cup of coffee."

"I don't have that much time. I must get out of here before light. I want you to promise me to do something before I go."

"Are you leaving for good? Is that it…are you in trouble or something?"

"I have been in trouble for a long time, but I think I'm close to being one more victim of Highland Transfer. That's not the problem. I can take care of that. I have something here that I want you to keep for me. Don't look into the envelope. Put it someplace safe…very safe. Don't give it to anybody unless he tells you he is Jack Grayton. I will have someone pick it up. This is very important." Holden grabbed Angela's shoulders. "Will you do it? A man's life depends on it."

"Jack, is this money? I won't have anything to do with stolen money."

"It's evidence of a murder. I can get word to him to pick it up. Will you do it?"

"I believe you. Nobody will ever know unless I hear your name."

"It's not money, I promise. Maybe someday I can come back and tell you the whole story. Until that time, you must believe that I never meant to hurt you. You have been so important in this last year. You really are something special." Holden had forgotten about holding Angela's shoulders…he relaxed his grip. "I have never met anyone like you. You are not about religion you are about love. That makes you the most amazing person I have ever met."

Holden leaned down and kissed Angela lightly.

"If things had been different, I would never let you go." He whispered.

"Jack, you mean a lot to me. I know God is not finished with you yet. Please be careful, I do love you."

"Don't turn the light on when I leave."

Angela touched his face. He turned and walked into the darkness.

As Holden approached his hotel, he saw the beginnings of light in the eastern sky. He turned up the back street and checked out the alley. There was nothing new on either side. He had not gotten off at the regular stop. He chose to walk three extra blocks in the case that they had followed.

On his walk, he dealt with the loss of the money. It meant little to him anymore. It would have been nice to start over as a rich man. He had spent his entire life building that fortune, now he almost felt relieved. He was relieved because the old him was gone. He cared about someone.

Fifteen months earlier, he would never have taken the chance to get that evidence to Angela. It was just what he thought he should do. He probably would not step over Jack on the sidewalk now. He probably would have been really interested in Matt's plan. He may have even learned to love his wife.

That was it, love, he was learning to love. He was about to smile when the glove covered his mouth. The sickening smell of chloroform was the last thing he would remember.

CHAPTER 53

The days on the farm were not the same in the aftermath of the murder. Late summer in Minnesota is usually a beautiful time of the year. The corn was nearly seven feet tall. The second cutting of hay was in the barn. The oats were ready to harvest. The long days offered more sunshine than clouds. Welcome Home was empty.

The new buildings and the new equipment now seemed to have lost their gleam. Most of the animals had been sold so the outbuildings were nearly empty. The machinery sat idle. There was grass growing along the edges and in the middle of the driveway, and in the fence lines. The familiar sounds of laughter and joy were a distant memory.

Kate spent most of her hours in the house. She still could not bring herself to sleep in her bedroom. Gus spent every waking moment in the fields. He was determined not to lose the crop. Matt had made a promise to himself to find the truth about the death of his wife. Brian went back to the Twin Cities to work with a shelter until the farm reopened.

Kate busied herself as she had seen her mother do three to four decades earlier. There was breakfast for Matt and Gus by 6:00 AM. She would take coffee out to the field at 10:00 AM, lunch was at 12:30, coffee at 2:30, and supper at 6:30. It was busy work, but the refuge of routine brought comfort.

As Gus brought the windrower into the yard and pulled up to the gas barrel, he sighed with remorse. The farm, his beautiful farm, was already starting to show neglect. The tractor is a great place to think, but sometimes it had been too heavy.

He loved Paul like another son. Gus saw amazing things in him. Gus never wanted Matt to be anything but himself, but he knew that the farm just wasn't in him. Paul thrived in the outdoors. He loved hard work and was usually one step ahead of Gus. He learned effortlessly.

Gus saw Paul as the future of the farm. He remembered the first day that he put Paul on the planter. Gus was very particular about the rows; they had to be straight. He always said, "Every Sunday the folks drive by these fields and they make judgments about our farm by looking at the crops, crooked rows means something is lacking, and it usually goes with the rest of the operation as well."

Now as he had spent the weeks cultivating and pulling weeds, he had marveled at the level of pride that Paul had put into his work. His rows were perfect, and everything else had the same attention to detail. Gus wished a thousand times it had all been a bad dream. It wasn't.

Gus had vowed never to talk to him again. As he sat on the MTA, and smelled the earth and the grain, he was changing. He loved the man. He loved Connie. He didn't know what to do. As the gas was running into the tank, Gus began to pray...he was not accustomed to this, but the words just started to flow.

"God, I know that I have done lots of stuff that has made you mad. It ain't like I blame you either, 'cause I blew it lots when I was young. You still love me and are willing to forgive me for that, am I supposed to do that, too? I mean, it ain't like I killed anybody. Paul killed Connie... I'm not even sure why. That's different isn't it? We aren't supposed to forgive that stuff are we? I know you even told us about that in the Ten Commandments, so that's one of the big ones. That's why I'm asking. I don't know much about praying, but my heart is really hurting right now, and I miss talking to him. I just don't know what to do. I don't know how you will get your answer to me, but I'll wait to find out what to do. I just don't want to forgive someone who shouldn't be forgiven... okay...you'll tell me what to do won't you? Okay, I'll wait."

Gus finished filling the tractor and crawled off. He headed toward the house for lunch with Kate. He looked forward to the chance to talk. Jack was gone again, and Matt was so busy with the investigation, he rarely saw anybody anymore. He walked into the entryway, hung his cap on the hook, untied his boots, removed them, and headed to the bathroom to wash up.

"How does the oats look? Is it fully headed?"

"Looks like we'll get a great crop. Only got thirty-five acres, but it will probably be enough to store some for feed if we ever get animals back again. Should get a bunch of straw bales too, great bedding for sows."

"Sounds like it's still a farm in some ways. I wish I could get the excitement back; I just don't seem to have it anymore. It is great to hear some good news anyway. I remember as a girl the oats harvest signaling the end of summer. School can't be far away when we're baling straw."

"Kate, do you think we will ever open this place again? I'm thinkin' chances are slim."

"I can't think much past this afternoon. I would love to open it again, but I think the town would really be up at arms unless we can prove Paul innocent."

"What if he isn't innocent? What if he did it? I swear I saw it. What do we do if he is guilty?"

"You mean with the farm?"

"The farm and all the other stuff…what do we do?"

"All what other stuff?"

"I don't think I can ever forgive Paul. I really liked him, but he's a killer."

"But Gus, he was a killer before he came here too, and you forgave him, didn't you?"

"But he paid the price for that. He was in prison for a long time."

"Not really. He is no different than any of us. His sin is just a lot easier to see."

"He is different. He murdered two people."

"But one of them you feel that he paid for."

"You know what I mean. We never killed anybody."

"All of us have killed someone. Christ was murdered for what we've done. We are all responsible for that death. All of us are killers. God was willing to forgive us. If we refuse to forgive others, we are saying we're better than God. You may choose to never talk to Paul again, but you must forgive him if you are a Christian."

"You really believe that? We killed Jesus? I wasn't there."

"Gus, think about it! I'm not trying to condemn anybody. You asked... I am telling you what I think. I can't tell you what to believe, just what I believe. You got to figure it out for yourself. Let's eat."

Gus finished windrowing early. He took a shower and headed for town. He wasn't sure about visiting hours, but he was going to find out.

"Visiting hours are Tuesday and Thursday from 1:00 to 3:00 PM, and all Sunday afternoon."

"I don't s'pose there's any chance of seeing anybody tonight. I work most of the time during the day."

"They're having dinner now. Who are you looking to see?"

"Paul Prentiss."

"He hasn't had many visitors. What's your name?"

"Gus Roth." Gus dropped his head wondering what he was doing there. "Tell him Gus wants to talk to him."

The jailer came back in ten minutes, smiled and gave Gus a form to fill out. "Just sign it. We can't let you in, so you will have to talk to him through the glass. The door is just outside here and to the left."

Gus was unaccustomed to jails. The thought of going into some little room in this place was less than appealing. The last time he saw Paul, he wanted to beat him to a pulp. He really wished he had put this off a day or two.

The room was ridiculously small divided into three small glass alcoves that reminded Gus of voting booths. There was a phone attached to the wall to the left, and a small stool built into the floor so visitors could sit. He felt fortunate that he was alone. *How could anyone share intimate stuff if someone were right next to you on a phone?*

Paul entered the room followed by a guard. He was handcuffed to the railing to his right, and then allowed to pick up the phone with his left hand. The guard told him he would be right outside the door. He smiled at Gus and pointed at the phone. Gus realized that he had just been sitting there like an idiot while all this was happening. He grabbed the phone and put it to his ear.

"I really didn't expect you to ever visit here, Gus. I am so sorry about Connie. I have been praying that you would come since the first night they brought me here. Forgive me, Gus. I should never have come to the farm."

"Why did you kill her?" Gus blurted out almost before he thought about it.

"I know how it looked. And really, I probably was responsible for her death. I didn't kill Connie, my being there got her killed. I knew there might be problems, but I stayed anyway. Gus, I'm sorry I let you down. I never enjoyed anything more in my life than working with you, and that selfishness is what caused Connie's death. Forgive me."

"You didn't kill her? That's Bull Shit, pure and simple. I saw you over her body?"

"Gus you've got to believe me. She was already stabbed when I found her. She was lying face down, and I could hear her gurgling like she was trying to breathe. I had to try to save her. I didn't care how it looked. I had to try to save her. I'd do it again. I turned her over and saw the knife lying under her. I picked it up so I could turn her over. She died right there in my arms. Gus, I see her face and the blood in her hair every time I try to close my eyes." The pain in Paul's face said far more than the words. He looked pale and haunted as he continued.

"When you came in, and the police were there. I knew how it looked. You must believe that I'm guilty of being stupid, but I never would have hurt anyone that lived there. I loved them all. You were all my family."

Gus spoke after a long silence. "How did you get into the house? How did you know there was someone in there?"

"I was trying to help in the farrowing stalls, so I was up anyway. I saw lights on and walked around the house to check it out. I figured nobody would see and Matt was gone. There was a window broken from the outside. I didn't like the looks of it, so I decided to check it out. There was lots of door slamming and noise. By the time I got to the room, it was all over. I didn't see anybody. There had to be tracks because there was blood everywhere."

"Why didn't you tell me this?"

"There was nothing I could say that night. I wished I was dead when you hit me. Gus, you are the only Father I have ever known. I need you to believe me. I promise that I am telling the truth. Someone else killed Connie. He had done it before too because he knew what he was doing."

"If it was somebody else, where did he come from? Who was he? See, it doesn't make sense, and you been in jail for killing somebody already. Everybody in here says they're innocent."

"Gus, I understand. I killed a girl when I was a stupid kid. I was high on LSD. They say I was like a crazy animal when they found me. They probably were right. I'm not trying to get out of here, and I'm not asking you to do anything for me. I am telling you that I could never have killed Connie. I would have gladly given my life for any one of you on that farm. I tried to save her, and I would do it again. The only thing I want is for you to believe I am who you thought I was, then you can go. What does your heart tell you? You must be hurting if you are the man I think I knew. You know I didn't do it...you wouldn't be here."

"I'm just so screwed up, Paul. I hated you. I wanted to hate you forever. I thought that would make up for her death. I thought if I could make you hurt, it would stop hurting for me. It's just gotten worse. I can't come up with one reason that you would do this thing." Gus paused again. "You really didn't kill her? I just want to know the truth. It wasn't you?"

"Gus, it was about me, but it wasn't me. I'm sorry that I ever brought this pain to your life. I didn't kill her. I wish I knew who did."

"Then we gotta find out who did it. I ain't buyin' it being your fault. If you didn't kill her you aren't any more at fault than me. I wasn't watching the way I should have been that night neither. Matt was gone, and I let her down by not watchin'. That don't mean I killed her, no sir, I didn't do it and neither did you. We just gotta find out who did. I feel like a real rear end, the way I treated you."

"It's okay, Gus. I would have probably done the same thing. I probably would never have come to talk to you. That took a lot of courage."

"Kate told me to come. I'm glad I did."

"Don't worry about me, Gus. I've lived in these places as long as I can remember. I know there's no way I'm getting' out of here, but it's okay. I feel so much better now that we talked. You're sure you believe me?"

"Yeah, I really do. I ain't about to let them keep you here. We got a farm to run. I'm gonna find a way. Maybe I'll even pray more and see what comes."

The guard entered the room. "Gotta end this, sorry."

Paul stood and was led out of the room. Gus sat a minute to get himself together. He was so happy that he had come. He stated flatly, out loud, "Thank you, Father."

*****

Holden was alone in a taxi when he awoke. The driver was looking in the mirror with a smirk on his face.

"Welcome back. That must have been some party."

"What party?"

"The guys that put you in the cab and paid your fare told me you had a little too much of something at the party. Said they hoped you would be awake by the time we hit the airport."

"Airport, what airport?"

"They said you probably wouldn't remember. The tickets are supposed to be in the briefcase at your feet."

Holden grabbed the case and opened it. There was a letter tucked into the upper pocket. Jack Jeffries was typed on the front. Holden opened the letter slowly finding a single sheet of paper. "Wait to be paged at the airport. Follow instructions, we'll get you out of here. Jack"

The driver pulled up to Terminal three at O'Hare, got out and opened Holden's door. "Have a great flight. Hope you don't get a headache from that stuff. They took care of the bill. You need any help…are you okay?"

"I'm fine. I can make it from here."

"I almost forgot…your bag is in the trunk."

The driver opened the trunk and pulled out a small roller suitcase.

"Guess that's it then. Bon Voyage."

"Thanks."

Holden was hardly dressed for travel. He had no passport or money. He heard an announcement on the loudspeaker.

"Jack Jeffries pick up the phone in the waiting area of terminal four for a message."

Holden hurried to the bank of phones ahead and to his left. The house phone had no dialer. He picked up the receiver and waited. The operator asked, "May I help you?"

"This is Jack Jeffries; I believe you have a message for me."

"One moment… I'll connect you."

"Is this Mr. Jeffries?"

"That's correct."

"Meet me at the bar just off the ticketing area in Terminal Three. I know you. Just pick a table."

Holden suddenly began wondering who this was. "Maybe it wasn't Jack. Maybe it was a set up."

Thoughts began to run wild in his head.

Holden headed for the bar. Five minutes and a brisk walk later, he was seated at a table to the right of the door. There was space to exit, but he was out of sight of the general traffic flow. Seven minutes later a man dressed in a sport coat with a white shirt and dark tie, asked if he could join him. Holden had never seen him before.

"We've had quite a time finding you, Mr. Jeffries. I am here for a mutual friend, Jack Grayton. We waited at your hotel nearly all night. We were just about to head out when we spotted you walking. Sorry for the chloroform, but we wanted you out of there and had little time for questions. The sun was starting to rise, and we weren't the only ones looking for you."

"How do you know all this stuff?"

"Jack is a great guy. Lots of people really like him. He's helped several us out of some tough jams. Anyway, the word was, you were dead after tonight. We had the plan together, so we put it into effect."

"I was in the offices looking for some of my property. It got later than I expected."

"Everything is ready. Your plane leaves in two and one-half hours from gate G11. You must be there two hours ahead of time to board. There are clean clothes in the black bag. You probably should change. There is a razor in there too. Your passport picture shows no beard. You should probably shave before you board. The rest of the information is in the manila envelope. Jack said to tell you you're in his prayers. Take care, and don't waste too much time. You got a lot to do in a half hour."

"Can you get a message to Jack? Tell him to go to Angela's house there is a present there for him. It's urgent that only he goes. She will give it to no one else."

"I'm not sure I will see him again, but I will certainly try to give him the message."

"Listen, this is even more important than me getting out of here. He has to get the message."

"Okay, okay, I'll tell him—now get going."

He stood, then disappeared in the crowd. Holden picked up the new briefcase and headed for the men's room.

Shaving in the restroom was more of a challenge than Holden had imagined, but fifteen minutes later he was clean-shaven. The clothes were wonderful. Black silk trousers and a silk mock turtle sweater from Johnston and Murphy. He had new gold toe socks and Italian loafers. The jacket was lambskin in a dark brown color. Everything fit perfectly.

Holden felt as if he walked out of a nightmare instead of the men's room. He found his ticket, flight 1297 to Grand Cayman leaving at eleven thirty from gate G-11. The passport was with the ticket, and copies of his book were tucked in the bottom under some travel folders. He flipped through the pages and found the account numbers.

The dream was alive. He had been given a gift from someone he had both pitied and despised eighteen months before. Under the copies of the book he found a letter addressed to 'Holden."

"If you are reading this, they found you. Thanks to people that you will never know, and God's help, we have been able to put this together. I am giving you a new life just as you gave to me. I want you to know that I am grateful for your gift. Someday I pray that we will meet where there are no deadlines. Please Holden, find the answer, I want to have you as a friend for eternity. I think we could have really hit it off. Love in Christ, Jack"

The plane lifted off at eleven thirty-five without incident. Sixty-two miles away an investigation had begun. A red Buick Grand Sport had exploded on a parking lot at the Extend Stay Hotel in Merrillville. There were parts of the car, and parts of the passenger in a six-hundred-foot radius. The car was reported to belong to Jack Grayton. It would be some time before the identity was certain.

CHAPTER 54

"**G**us, there is really not much more that we can do. The investigation report points directly to Paul. We need something new, a break… I can't see how to win without it.

"I am willing to give another statement sayin' I was wrong. I know Paul wasn't the guy. The skin under Connie's nails proves it wasn't Paul. That should be enough."

"It's all circumstantial evidence. It proves that Connie didn't claw Paul, not that he's innocent." Matt was venting his own frustration. He was no investigator, yet he felt that it was his job to find an answer. "We feel strongly from the bloodstains that Connie was face down initially. That would support Paul's claim that he turned her over to try to help her, but even if they buy face down, the prosecutor will say he was just checking to see if she was dead. The knife only has one set of prints on it. They belong to Paul." Matt stood and walked to the window. He stared out into the world wondering how all this could have happened.

"There are so many other footprints on the carpet that we can't really get anything from that, and even the ground by the broken glass was too hard to make any prints. We would love to find an angle that would prove something positive, but there just isn't anything."

Gus was not one to give up. "Matt… God saw the murder, and He has all the answers we need. We should at least pray about it, don't you think? I ain't particularly good at that, so I think we should do it together. We can get Kate to help. What do you think?"

"I think it's a great idea, I'll go in and see if Kate's busy. Maybe we can do it right now."

Matt walked toward the house and was nearing the gate when they both noticed the black Grand Prix turn into the driveway. They recognized Brian immediately and headed toward the car.

"Hey buddy, I can't think of anyone I would rather see come home. We've really missed you. Are you here to stay a while?"

"I'm not too sure what I'm doin', just had to bring some news by. Have you heard anything about Jack?"

"Actually, I was about to ask you the same thing. We haven't heard a word since he left three weeks ago. I sort of wish he'd get back. The investigation is kind of bogged down and he always has such a positive attitude. I miss his friendship."

"Gus, I didn't think you'd be here, in fact I watched all the fields to see if I saw the M or 560 out there."

"Ain't you gonna give the old guy a hug? Seems like you've been gone forever. We sure could use a good tractor driver out here. Harvest starts soon, and I could use the help, I ain't beggin' but I will if it would help."

"Can we go in the house?" Brian asked. "I got some stuff to share, and I'd like to have all of us around. Is that okay?" Brian's eyes showed the weight of the last few weeks. The boyish grin was gone.

"You look pretty serious. Is it more bad news?"

"I'd really like to talk about it when we're all together."

"I was just going in there anyway. Let's go have a Coke or something. We can at least celebrate your arrival. That's great news."

"Yeah, Kate always has the coffee on. It is so good to see you."

Gus wrapped his big arm around the lanky black boy and walked with him and Matt toward the house. Kate was opening the screen door.

"Brian, seeing you is the best thing that has happened this week." Kate instinctively hugged him ignoring his discomfort with the gesture. "You have got to sit and tell me everything you've been doing."

Brian gave Kate a half-hearted smile as he entered the house.

"I've missed you guys too, but I got some pretty bad news."

"Let's sit. It can't be all that bad now, can it?"

They all sat at the kitchen table, as Kate got some coffee and cookies, and a Coke for Brian. Brian waited for Kate to finish and take a chair.

"Let's pray… *Father bless this food and this fellowship, in Jesus's name, Amen.*"

"I just found out about this yesterday morning. The guys on the street heard it first and knew I would want to know. Jack has been killed in someplace near Chicago."

There was no sound around the table as Brian pulled a newspaper clipping from his shirt pocket.

"It's from the Chicago Sun Times, over a week ago. *The police were called to a possible car-bomb explosion at the Extended Stay Hotel in Merrilville, Illinois this morning. There have been reports of as many as fifteen minor injuries to neighboring occupants of the hotel and other buildings as windows were shattered by the blast up to two city blocks away. Police report the death of the driver of the automobile, however no positive identification has been confirmed. The automobile is reported to be registered to a Jack Grayton of Minneapolis. Grayton had been a resident of the hotel at the time of the explosion. Details will follow as available.*"

"They're not certain that it was Jack. And we really don't know if that's where he was visiting. I am not ready to believe it was Jack." Kate said after a short silence.

"Brian has there been any more information on this?"

"The word is that some of the brothers in Chicago have some inside information about Jack. Seems he was working for the wrong people. They say he has been involved for a long time. It's a car theft ring…some heavy dudes. Anyway, the boss of this place had a hit out on Jack, and that's for sure. They said there isn't enough left of the body to ever get ID."

"That doesn't make any sense. We all knew Jack. Is there any one of you that thinks he could still have been working on illegal stuff? I for one just won't believe that."

"I learned a big lesson from the Paul problem. I saw it with my own eyes and was wrong. I ain't jumpin' to conclusions again. If there is no positive identification, then I still believe he's alive. And if it turns out to be him, I will never believe he was dirty."

"Brian is there any way to talk to these people. This doesn't add up to the Jack we knew." Matt seemed serious.

"I can try to get you hooked up with one of the guys. He's been coming to the Bible studies, but he may be reluctant to let you in on much inside information."

"It would be strictly confidential. There's got to be something to the story. I don't believe it's our Jack."

"Matt, don't you think you might be a bit out of your league heading for the Chicago area. What makes you think they'd tell you anything? If you go you should take Brian with you. He probably is more comfortable in that setting, having lived in the city all his life."

"I'd go with you. That might make a difference on how much information I could get. These guys got no reason to lie. Something is going on, and I would like to know what it is too."

"I would leave tomorrow if we could find out enough to know who to talk to."

"I'll be right back."

Brian got up from the table and went outside with his cell phone.

"Do you really think he's dead?"

"I pray he's not, but who knows, Kate. He was a very private man, and he hasn't been too willing to share much lately. I still will never believe that he was involved in anything illegal..."

"I think it's a great idea to check it out. Taking Brian makes sense too. Kate and I will be fine here." Gus added.

"Let's just see what Brian finds out."

Brian entered the kitchen after approximately ten minutes.

"I got some names. There's a place called Highland Transfer that is the front for the business. It's right there in Merrillville, but we are going to have to be careful. This isn't the first explosion. Seems another guy was killed the same way. The police aren't going to be much help either, word is some of them are on the payroll and don't like people nosing around."

"I'm not so sure you two should go. This sounds like trouble to me."

"Kate, I think it's what were supposed to be doing. God will take care of us. We need to get to the bottom of all of this. For some reason I feel called to visit this place."

"If Jack is dead, and something happens to you two, I don't think I could take the loss. Something about it scares me."

"I would never hurt you, Kate, but I have to do this. I want to leave tonight."

CHAPTER 55

The money was waiting; it worked just like he had pictured it in his mind so many months before. Holden transferred one hundred fifty thousand into a personal checking account and found no one to question his ID's. He could transfer the rest at any time he desired. Jack Grayton was just another millionaire enjoying Grand Cayman.

The chaos that had been his life in Merrillville was all but a distant memory. He was free and rich and working on happy. It was all worth it now. This is what life is about. He was ready to live a little. No more job, no responsibility, no questions, no need to answer to anyone.

Holden found a luxury penthouse overlooking the bay. The rear patio offered a view of the sunset. The sound of the waves and the smell of the ocean brought memories of winter vacations in Mexico and body surfing with his son. The afternoon sun reminded him of the few times he and Kate had sat on their deck and watched the sunset over their lake. He walked the beach in the mornings and contemplated the future. Nightlife was of little interest. Empty days lacked the passion for life that he had always found important.

He missed the Rusty Skillet. He certainly didn't miss the food, or the job at Highland, but something was missing. He had never considered this. He was just as lonely with all the money as he had been in the Extend Stay, or the Blue Roof Inn. He had all the stuff... hot tub, sauna, pool table, big screen TV...but baseball was baseball, ESPN was still ESPN even on a big screen.

He needed a friend. It had been thirty-five years since he had trolled for women, but he needed to find the missing ingredient. He didn't want any commitment, just some company. A little feminine attention would certainly add a dimension.

Holden spent the afternoon shopping. He would need something that was classy, but not flashy. He found a dark burgundy, silk mock turtle sweater with elbow length sleeves and cream-colored silk and rayon slacks at an exclusive men's store on the strip. The salesman helped him with a pair of Italian woven leather shoes in a burgundy color, and socks that matched his slacks. The belt was simple, with a gold buckle. He got his hair styled at a salon and headed home to get ready.

The shower was a welcome break. He stood absorbing the mist for nearly twenty minutes. He shaved and brushed his teeth, added a small spray of cologne, and contemplated himself in the mirror. He felt much different than he looked. He nearly hung everything back up and called Domino's.

The "Blue Lagoon" was a high-priced nightclub on the east side of the island. Holden took a cab and arrived about eight. He ordered a drink and sat enjoying the sunset from the corner table. The music was far too loud to enjoy and was too "with it" for him to recognize. *This place must cater to a younger crowd.*

Holden was becoming extremely uncomfortable. Who was he trying to kid? He was fifty-three years old. He was out of his comfort zone, and he was clueless about what women wanted anymore. He had opened a door for a woman, only to have her snap at him something about his condescending attitude. This was a mistake. He had lived his entire life with one woman and a job that kept him from extracurricular activity. There would be other nights. He would enjoy a dinner, and head back to ESPN. As he finished his brandy Manhattan, a young woman approached his table.

"Are you waiting for someone?"

"Actually, no, I am enjoying the sunset and the view... And you?"

"I was supposed to meet a friend here, but it's getting late."

"A man?" Holden asked.

"Excuse me?"

"The friend, is it a man?"

"No, a girl friend of mine. We were meeting here after work."

"What kind of work do you do?"

"I am a teller in a bank here. Banking is big business in Cayman."

"Have you been there long?"

"About four years. I moved here from the west coast. I heard it was a nice place to forget about life for a while."

"Did it work?"

"What?"

"Did you forget about life?"

"Not really. Would you like another drink? I'm going to order one." She asked.

"Perhaps, but let me buy you a drink, it would be my pleasure."

"That's not necessary but thank you."

"Excuse me, could you get the lady something, and I'll have another of these. So you haven't found the answer yet."

"The answer? To what?"

"To getting away from the past, to leaving it behind."

"No, actually it came with me. I can't get away from me. I keep coming along wherever I go." She giggled slightly.

Holden liked her smile...but she was young enough to be one of his kids.

"Aren't you afraid of being picked up in a place like this."

"You're new at this, huh?"

"Sort of. Is it obvious?"

"You look the part, but you care too much to have done much of this. You ask questions that are too deep to play this game."

"What game?"

"Okay, this is a free one. I am here to pick up guys like you. I get a nice dinner, a couple of drinks, some laughs. You get to feel a tight body and have sex, and nobody gets hurt. You give me a couple of bucks for a cab, and tomorrow night I find someone else."

"You're a prostitute?"

"I'm a bank teller that needs a few extra bucks. I don't do this twenty times a night. I got a kid that needs clothes, and food, and I

269

got a loser husband on the west coast. No, I'm not a prostitute, I'm poor. The dress and the shoes are for show. The body is real, and it is my ticket to having a life."

"Doesn't it get to you to be used by men? Can you really live with yourself doing this?"

"Doing what? Having sex with a man who doesn't care about me? I had a husband who was no different than any of the men I sleep with. I had a father that cared nothing for my mother. You're kind of judgmental aren't you? Tell me you weren't trying to hook up with a little something sitting here in this bar. You are no different than any other man. You all want one thing, and the woman under the skin is just one more thing you want to possess until you are fulfilled."

"Actually, I was just like that. I have always been just like that, but I don't want to do that anymore. The truth is that this is wrong. I was looking for a relationship without commitment. That's no longer possible for me. I don't know you, but I do care about you. I would love to know your story. The rest is all wrong for me."

"You're serious. I can see it in your eyes. How come you aren't married?"

"It's a long story, not one I want to share. Could we have dinner? My treat, no obligations, I would just like to get to know you. You remind me of my daughter."

"I would love to join you, but the sex is no problem for me if you change your mind."

Holden woke at six AM with a splitting headache. Three Brandy Manhattans were far past his limit. It felt as if each time he moved his head his brain was crashing into his skull. The night, however, had been wonderful.

He dined and danced with a beautiful young woman and learned much about himself. He knew now he was never going to be happy alone. He withdrew $5,000 cash from his account and placed it in her hand. She had offered herself a number of times. He declined.

She kissed him passionately when they parted, and he nearly changed his mind. He could see his daughter in her eyes. It was wrong. He could have done it, but he didn't, he didn't step over her in the street. He saw her. He saw a person.

CHAPTER 56

The knock on her door startled her. She had been resting after a long day at the Rusty Skillet. Work wasn't what it used to be. The memories of Jack's visits still brought a smile to her face, but the knowledge of his death had opened wounds that she thought had long since healed.

Did I make a mistake by closing my intimate life to this man? I know with all my heart God is clear about sex outside of the marriage bed. Should I have given him some hint of her interest? Was there any interest? I saw something extraordinary, yet was it love? He cared for me too. It doesn't matter he's dead.

The explosion claimed one more of the people she loved. The article stated no positive identification, but he was gone.

As she opened the door she was still engulfed in the questions of her thoughts. She really hadn't considered what she was doing. The sight of his face took her breath. She pushed the door aside and rushed to him engulfing him with her arms.

"Jack, you're alive…you're alive! The paper said you were dead. How did you manage to get away? They said you were dead."

The embrace overwhelmed Holden. He pushed her away slightly, grabbed her shoulders and tried to get her attention.

"Dead? What are you talking about? What paper? Who said I was dead?"

"I'm just so thankful you are alive. I have been praying for something to bring some light back into my life. I never expected this.

"You need to tell me about the death!"

271

"The paper's here on the table. I'm sorry I grabbed you, but I thought you were dead."

Holden devoured the article.

"Has anyone come asking for the package?"

"Nobody has knocked on my door since you left that night. I have no one left in this town that cares."

"Angela…we need to talk."

CHAPTER 57

Kate spent a lot of time with her flowers. She had heard nothing from Matt. Five days had dragged by. Gus was busy as ever in the fields. The crops were wonderful. The workload almost more than one man could handle. Kate had become a true believer in prayer.

God wanted to lead, and she was ready for it. She could not explain the paradox. It gave a sense of control.

As the fields called for more time, God provided Marty. Gus had considered having him work for "Welcome Home" Marty had declined because of his job. One week ago, he just walked in. Kate was not surprised. She loved God more than she had ever loved anyone.

Kate was in her garden. She did not notice the car. The visitor was nearly upon her before she saw her.

"I hope I didn't startle you. I thought you heard me drive up. Forgive me."

"I was just deep in thought. May I help you?"

"My name is Angela Parker. Are you Kate Jeffries?"

"That's right, I'm Kate. Should I know you?"

"We have a mutual friend. I have something to share with you."

"I'm nearly finished here. We can go into the house. Would you like a cup of tea or something?

"That would be wonderful, it's been a long trip from Merrillville."

*****

273

It had been just one dead end after another. Even with Brian along, lips were tight. The mention of Jack's name turned heads, but nothing had been offered as an explanation. Highland Transfer was an empty warehouse. Nobody was willing to admit they had ever seen the place. Matt had heard a name of a waitress who befriended Jack, but she was no longer employed.

The site of the blast looked like a war zone. The hotel closed for two weeks and the street just reopened to traffic.

The police allowed Matt to see the pictures, but none recognized a photo of Jack. It was like a story that never happened. Matt and Brian had prayed for hours in the hotel room asking for leads. It all seemed futile as they packed. A man with reddish hair and pocked face followed as they walked to the car.

"I've heard you've been asking some questions about Jack Grayton."

"That's true. Do you know Jack?"

"You aren't from around here. How do you know Jack?"

"Jack works with us in Minnesota in a Recovery Center. We really need to find him. He's our friend."

"Looks like you're heading out for good."

"Not much reason to stay. So…do you know something?"

"It's a long story. This is no place to try to talk. I'm taking a chance just standing here. I'll meet you at a bar called the Hitchin' Post. If you want to know more, head west and watch for it on your left. I'll be there in half an hour."

The man left without another word. He just kept his eyes on the ground as he walked. He crossed the parking lot and left in a blue van. Matt and Brian looked at each other, shrugged, and finished packing.

As they headed west, the cell phone rang. Brian was driving, so Matt answered.

"Kate, is that you? I was planning on giving you a call. We should be on our way home soon. We are having a meeting with one more character here in a couple of minutes. I really don't know what to expect from it. What's up?"

"Matt you will never believe what just happened. The answer we've been looking for just came walking up the driveway. She has evidence that proves without a doubt that Paul is innocent. I haven't watched the film, but she has Connie's toe. Jack gave it to her to bring to us."

"She...who is she? Where is she from...around there?"

"Her name is Angela, she's from Merrillville."

"Angela...is it Angela Parker?"

"That's right, how did you know that name?"

"We've been looking for her here. She was a waitress at a restaurant. She and Jack were good friends I guess. Did she tell you how she got to know Jack?"

"No, she just brought the evidence. She told me that Jack gave it to her to give to us, and then she left."

"She left? Did you get the license number of her car? Did she tell you where she was going?" Matt was speaking faster than Kate could answer. "Kate, we may need her for the trial. We must find her. See if Gus can drive you into town to at least look around."

"I'm sorry Matt. I didn't think about that. I was just so happy to hear the story and have a way out of this that I guess. I'll run out to the field and get Gus. We'll find her if we have to get police blockades set up."

"I gotta go. We just got to the Hitchin Post."

Kate hung up the phone. She grabbed her keys, pulling the door behind her. She turned the key in the lock. She began to turn as she heard the voice.

"Kate, it's me. I didn't want it to happen like this, but it's me."

She stopped, never looking at the voice.

"Holden...?"

She turned slowly. Then sank like a rock to the step.

"Kate..."

"Holden, I don't understand. How can you be alive?"

"I've been working some things out. I am so sorry to just drop in on you, but I'm not certain how to do this."

"You're not what?" There was a silence that seemed to last forever.

"This can't be happening! You've been hiding for the last two years? I don't understand. You couldn't have put us all through this. Holden how could you do this? Nobody could be that selfish."

Holden stood with his head down, his eyes to the ground. He had never considered Kate's side of this. He knew that she would be bothered by his death, but he had been so engrossed in his own situation he never considered her pain.

"You're right, Kate. I would give anything to go back and do it differently. I know I hurt a lot of people."

"STOP, JUST STOP! Nearly two years of pretending you're dead, and you are sorry. That's supposed to be enough. You think all you did was hurt a lot of people? Some of us you did more than hurt...me...you shattered. You ran away and left me to work through the mess. You left me."

More silence, Holden said nothing.

"Where have you been? Why didn't you call? You made us all go through hell. We all thought you were dead. Holden, we buried you. How can you show up here? How can you even show up here? You may be alive Holden Jeffries...but not to me. Turn around and walk away...don't ever come back! Not today or ever... I wish I had never known you. I'm going to try forgetting I ever did."

CHAPTER **58**

Matt and Brian entered the bar from a side door. The place smelled of beer and stale cigarette smoke. Their new friend sat at a corner table with a bottle of Bud, a glass, and a worried look. The clientele reacted to the bright light as the door opened returning to their world as the door closed.

Matt and Brian took a seat, and each ordered a Coke. The story that unfolded before them was almost more than they could comprehend. The man with the pocked face and the strawberry hair was named Joe. He worked inside the office of Highland Transfer. He had worked his way up the ladder gaining the respect and trust of those who matter. There actually were two Jack Graytons. One had entered the story nearly a year earlier than the man with the cowboy boots. The original Jack Grayton just showed up at the Highland Transfer without much fanfare. He was a classy dresser and a smooth talker that seemed chosen take over. He seemed to be protected, receiving a tremendous amount of attention from those in control.

Joe filled them in with a lot of sorted details. "I didn't like the guy… I wasn't the only one. He was too quiet, to smart." Joe's voice was drowned out by the cheers at the bar. The place smelled like men, working men. The smoke hovered just overhead it's fragrance penetrating everything in the place. Matt could barely make out the television behind the bar, but something had brought a roar. Joe ordered another beer. Matt and Brian declined another Coke, but added the beer to their tab.

"I had no idea the cowboy was Jack Grayton 'til I received a call from some of his friends. They suggested we be available to help the new Jack in any way possible. Jack was from the Twin City area and had some mutual friends in Chicago. We were to keep a constant watch on the Computer Jack. We were to take care of him.

Secondly, there was some information that had been taken from Computer Jack's car. It had to be found."

Matt interrupted. "Slow down… I can't keep track of who's who."

Computer Jack is the first guy. He really isn't Jack Grayton. Cowboy Jack is the guy with the power in the right places.

"Okay, got it…go on."

"I knew all the stuff that came in with the cars. The stuff was easy to find. This Computer Jack was in trouble. Cowboy had to get him out of town. Timing had to be right. We were working on it when they found Morrey dead."

"Morrey? The boss of the company?"

"Yeah…official statement was suicide. We knew full well it was a hit. Morrey had been spendin' money like he had six months to live, turned out less than that. Cowboy insisted Computer Jack be followed everywhere. We were to check out his car inside and out every day." Joe turned and waited. "Ya followin' this?"

Matt smiled. "So far I'm with you." Brian nodded.

"Morrey's dying was a statement. Don't screw around with company funds." Joe gestured with his right index finger…he pulled it across his neck like a knife.

"Morrey was a dumb-ass, but he was loved. Everything was in an uproar." Joe's voice was nearly a whisper.

"Somebody musta had some inside track on this Tony guy 'cause on the night that it was supposed to come down, all hell broke loose. First, Computer Jack didn't come out for his usual ride to dinner. We cased his hotel, nobody. All we could do was watch the hotel and wait. A man dressed in black appeared from the shadows some time about two AM. He was almost impossible to see.

He disappeared beneath Computer Jacks car. Took only seconds. Gone quick as he came. I wouldn't believe it if I wasn't watchin'. This guy was good, really good."

Joe stopped and motioned to the bar. "Another Bud…you guys want anything?"

"No, we're fine, you go ahead."

Joe waited until the bartender left to continue. Matt wondered if Brian was following all of this.

"Time was runnin' out. There's a bomb in the car. We got no clue where Cowboy is, it's between four and five in the morning. My pager goes off. It's one of our guys we sent out looking, I call him on his cell, he tells me Computer Jack had just stepped out of a bus three blocks away."

"I sent three guys out with instructions, I stayed to watch the car. This whole thing could blow up any time. Five minutes later, a black Lincoln pulls up about ten feet from the car. Three men get out, they pull a fourth guy outa the trunk. He's wearin' a black leather jacket…got long hair pulled into a ponytail in the back. He seemed dazed, but awake. They put him in the driver's seat. He just sits there. I could see his eyes, open. They go back to their car it backs up real slow. The lights are off, but I see Cowboy Jack walking from the other direction. I think, *What the hell is he doing here. He wants us to get his friend out of town, then shows up here.*" Now Joe was leaning forward like he didn't have enough time or energy to finish.

"I thought somebody dropped the A-Bomb. Noise like I never heard and heat like a rocket engine. Stuff was flyin' around everywhere. Windows broken for two blocks." He flung his arms across the table for effect.

I was behind a stone garden wall across the street. I ducked as soon as I saw the flash. Still got nicked." He stopped and raised his hair showing the small scar. "My ears rang for ninety minutes. When the fire slowed down I look around. No Lincoln. I couldn't see Jack neither. The guy in the car was history. Sirens from every direction.

"But Jack, where was Jack?"

Found him on a lawn about a half a block from the blast. He was burned and bloody from the metal that had ripped into most of the front of his body. I didn't waste time looking for a pulse. Dead or alive I had to get him out of the there. I carried him three blocks through the alleys. I used his cell phone to get some help."

"Ol' Tony went out with a bang. Seem's like Morrey wasn't the only one fond of buying on the web."

"Who was this Computer Jack?" Matt asked after a moment of silence.

"He was just some sucker who got his car stolen by Highland. He was runnin' away from his life I guess. Guess he's some big wig out of Minneapolis. He was pretending to be Jack Grayton."

"You're sure he's from Minneapolis?"

"Absolutely, probably would have worked if it wasn't for some of the real Jack's friends being in the here, and if he hadn't left his keys in the car. Biggest joke of all, the guy's wife turns out to be a friend of both Jack and Tony. Tony knew her in school, and Jack was working with her on a farm somewhere."

"Did Jack mention the guy's name?"

"It's something real weird. Can't remember for sure."

"Is it Holden… Holden Jeffries?"

"Yeah! That's the name, Holden Jeffries. Leave it to the rich people to have two first names. You know him?"

"Thought I did."

"The kicker is…the real Jack got him a plane ticket out of the country. He's layin' in the sun somewhere enjoying his money."

"You said you took Jack away from the blast. Where is he now?"

"He's at a place close to here. He doesn't remember much. He's pretty beat up. We been scared to take him to a hospital 'cause of his name. We figure the police like him for the blast. He ain't getting a whole lot better so I figured I'd better try to get some help for him." Joe lit a cigarette, inhaled deeply and blew a perfect smoke ring toward Brian's head.

"I don't want anything to happen to him. I just didn't know what to do."

The room was in the basement of a run-down tenement house. It was clean, but still smelled musty. There were lights that hung from the ceilings on cords. The smell of cigarette smoke was heavy in the air. Matt, Brian entered the room and were sickened by what they saw. In a small metal bed that sat against a green painted wall lay their best friend. It was almost impossible to recognize him, except for his eyes. Matt would always recognize those eyes.

The swelling of Jack's face made him look like some kind of alien. He had cuts from the glass and metal on the entire front of his body. There was evidence of infection on several of the larger wounds.

"Does he still have a fever?"

"It comes and goes."

Matt noticed a smile come to Jack's face when he heard his voice.

"I knew you'd find me. I'm not doing so well. I think I look worse."

"I've seen you look better. Helps on the way."

"This man has to be seen by a doctor."

Matt dialed 911.

"Send an ambulance to 1601 Wickenburg Street."

"Do you want us to dispatch the police?"

"Not at this time."

"It's on its way."

Matt hung up, and dialed Kate.

"Kate, we found Jack. He was near the blast. He is really messed up, but we have an ambulance on the way. The story is unbelievable, but Jack's alive, and most of the rest can wait." Matt hesitated, considering his next sentence.

"Thank God. I just don't think I could take another death right now."

"There's something I need to talk to you about, but I want to wait until I see you in person. As soon as he can travel, we'll be heading back home." Matt waited.

"Are you okay, Kate? Are you crying? Is something wrong?"

"You get Jack on the mend. Don't worry about me. Take care of Jack."

CHAPTER 59

K ate was so happy after Angela's visit. Then like one more cloud, Holden had been standing at her front gate. It was as if an unseen pernicious evil had been unearthed within her soul.

She had no elation that he was now alive. She had no joy that her husband had returned. He had chosen to leave. She preferred him dead. She was crying when she called Gus into the house.

"Are you okay, Kate?" Gus was never comfortable with women's tears. He always felt that he should fix the problems, even when he wasn't certain what they were. "Can I help? What's wrong?"

"I am sorry to make you uncomfortable, Gus. It's just that I need you to get this tape to Sheriff's Office right away. No, take it to Paul's lawyer. It has evidence that he will want to see." She continued to wipe her eyes as she gave directions. "And Gus, the bag has Connie's toe. I nearly faint every time I think about it. Jack sent it back to help us."

"Jack! You heard from Jack?"

"No, but he is alive. Matt called. He got a tip from someone who knew that story. He was near the car, but not in it"

"How did Jack get a hold of this evidence? If he's still in Chicago…how'd he get it to you?"

"I don't know how he got it. He has some connection with this whole thing. Right now, getting Paul out is all that matters. I would go, but I'm just a mess."

Paul was released two hours after his lawyer received the new evidence. Channel Six news was on hand with Live Cam. A sketch artist's rending of the real killer was released to the media in the entire Midwest. Twenty-four hours later, Vincent Langley was apprehended, near Omaha, by the Highway Patrol. He was stopped for speeding.

The phone rang at Kate's house at 8:30 AM. It was Inspector Cas Thomas of the FBI. "I hate to bother you this early in the morning Ms. Jeffries. Would it be possible to stop by and ask you a few questions? Perhaps you can shed some light on some developments."

"I am not exactly presentable at the moment. If you give me an hour, I should be able to see you."

"Fine, I will plan on meeting with you at nine thirty."

The doorbell rang exactly at nine thirty-one. Kate answered dressed in jeans and a sweater. She had taken time to put on makeup and touch up her hair with a curling iron.

"I'm Inspector Thomas"

Cas Thomas was thirty-three years old. He was about six-foot five and had enormous shoulders and hands. He wore a crew cut but it was gelled, so it gave a hint of his age. He was dressed in a deep blue suit with black trendy loafers."

"Won't you come in? We can sit here in the kitchen."

"The kitchen would be fine. I can lay some of these papers on the table."

"Would you like a cup of coffee? I was just finishing my first cup."

"Coffee would be nice."

Kate set the blue Lenox cups on the table and brought a plate of homemade cookies.

"You said on the phone that you have some questions. I hope there is no question as to the identity of the real murderer."

"Actually...we have the murderer in custody. The questions revolve around the tape itself. Where did you say it came from?"

"A middle-aged lady named Angela Parker just showed up in my front yard and told me that Jack Grayton had given her the tape. I had never seen her before, but I believe her story."

"We printed the tape and did find two sets of prints from females. One we believe to be yours and a second that we feel are Angela's."

"So what is the question?"

"We found three other sets of prints on the tape case that do not fit your story."

"Is one Jack Grayton's?"

"We have Jack's prints on file, they are not on the tape. We found the prints of a thug named Vincent Langley. We have him in custody for the murder. We isolated the prints of a known underworld figure named Tony Minelli. He works out of the Chicago area and actually grew up in this area."

"Tony Minelli? Are you certain about that? I knew Tony from my early years in grade school. I spent a great deal of time with him right after I moved back here. We were friends."

"There was another set of prints. We traced them to the name Holden Jeffries. Ms. Jeffries, I am not certain that your husband died in that accident two years ago." He watched for the change in Kate's expression.

"I know that he is alive. Holden stopped here."

Kate glared at the young Inspector.

"I believe that if you find Angela Parker, you probably will find him too."

"You didn't share that with any of the law enforcement people?"

"This has been less than comforting to me. I buried my husband and worked through the loss. I haven't talked to the police. I haven't talked to anyone since I sent Gus in with the evidence."

"We showed Vincent a picture of Holden, he recognized him, but called him Jack Grayton."

"How can you believe anything a killer says?"

"Vincent was running for his life. He was forced to kill his boss. He knows what will happen to him in prison. We offered him a lighter sentence and protection for his information. If any of it is false, the deal is off," Cas stated.

"I see. He has a lot to lose by lying."

"Exactly. He said Tony was holding Holden hostage for over a year near Chicago. He had planned to kill your husband. He also said Connie's death was a mistake. Tony wasn't aware that you were out of town. You were the target. He had been paid to kill you, Mrs. Jeffries. Why would Tony want you murdered?"

Kate's eyes flashed anger as she spoke. "Inspector Thomas, do you expect me to believe that my husband has been the victim in all of this? Do you think that it was all a mistake? Holden was not kidnapped from the Boundary Waters. Whatever discomfort the decision brought into his life pales in comparison to the pain that he has inflicted on the rest of us."

"I am only sharing what we know. I am not excusing the actions of anyone involved."

"And you want me to believe that this sociopath Vincent was after me and got Connie by mistake? That he was a hired assassin sent by a man that I called my best friend for most of my preteen and teenage years. This is absurd!" Kate slammed the coffee mug onto the table sloshing its contents onto her hand. She winced in pain.

"Tony was a lonely man with a painful past. I'm not certain of anything."

"Mrs. Jeffries, we do know for certain that Vincent has killed before. We believe he was responsible for the murder of Angela's son, and maybe even her husband. Both were killed in single car accidents. Both cars mysteriously blew up. There was also a death of one of the Department Managers at a place called Highland Transfer that has Vincent's signature on it. He is not new to killing for hire."

"But to kill Connie by mistake? I guess I don't want to believe in that kind of evil. Where is Tony now?"

"If we can trust the testimony of Vincent, and that certainly is debatable, Tony is dead. Vincent states that he was killed by the mob. He was blown up in a car bombing. We know about the bomb, but there wasn't enough left of the scene to identify the car, much less the passenger."

"Matt Roth is in Chicago now. He went there with a friend from our farm to find Jack Grayton. Jack is in a hospital. He was hurt in a car bombing. He may have some information that can help. I will give you his cell phone number."

"I think that may help. This story has far too many unknowns. Did you or Holden know Jack Grayton before Holden left?"

"Jack Grayton was in jail most of his adult life. Matt Roth helped him find Christ in a Bible study in a county jail somewhere near the cities. Holden's company did donate money to Matt's ministry, but Holden never got involved."

"If Vincent is telling the truth, Holden was using Jack's name in Chicago. I don't get it. You said that Jack was hurt in Chicago, why would he be in the same place as your husband? And why would your husband come back at the same time Angela comes here with evidence from Jack?"

"I really don't care. I have told you all I know. My husband's last two years is something in which I prefer to forget. If there is nothing else. I would like to be alone."

Inspector Thomas stood, offering his hand to Kate. "It has been a pleasure to meet you. We will find out the answers to all of this."

She did not shake his hand.

"I don't want to know. I would appreciate it if you would just go."

"Are you going to be all right?"

"I think the days of my being all right are long gone."

CHAPTER **60**

The IV antibiotics and fluids brought Jack to life almost instantly. They were planning his return to Minnesota on his fifth day in the hospital. There were few lingering effects from the explosion. His hearing was almost fully recovered, and the cuts and scrapes were healing nicely. The police had found the evidence they needed and were now investigating the deaths of both Tom and his father.

The new information made it almost impossible to overlook the problems of the past several years in Merrillville. Four men in the police department had been indicted on charges of conspiring to defraud, and more were expected to follow. The testimony of Holden Jeffries and some interesting computer files were bringing down the house. Highland Transfer had been closed, but the new evidence was pointing fingers at prominent men in both city and state government.

Since Vince had crossed state lines when he murdered Connie, the FBI was at work and heads were rolling. Jack read the paper from front to back daily and enjoyed every victory. Patience was not his forte.

"I'm thankful that you folks are here, and I cannot tell you how much I appreciated your hospitality, but it's time for me to go back home." Jack smiled as he spoke to the nurse.

"Your release depends on your doctor's orders. It's his decision when you are discharged."

Dr. Williams entered the room moments later. He listened intently to Jack's chest and heart; then probed the wounds checking the stitches and the reddened areas. There was little conversation.

Before Jack had time to ask questions, the doctor stated, "Looks good, we will be discharging you today if you have someone here that can sign a release form."

"That was pretty easy, I thought I was going to have to get rough." Jack laughed. The doctor didn't.

"I will attend to the paperwork, in the meantime, we will have nursing remove the IV tubing and let you take a shower. Then you can get dressed."

Two hours later Matt, Brian and Jack were in a car headed toward Interstate 80 and Minnesota.

"How is Kate taking the Holden situation?"

"She is not doing well," Matt shrugged. "Gus says she has barely left the house. I am really concerned about her."

"Has she talked to Holden?"

"I don't think she has talked to anyone. I phoned her to tell her thanks and to fill her in on your progress. She seemed interested in your situation and said she was praying. I asked her about things there. She found a way to say good-by." Matt shook his head in concern.

"She is hurting. We must try, but you realize that we may not be able to change her heart. She has the right to react in any way she chooses. God allows it. We have no right to act differently. We can pray for her though. These are tough times." Jack shifted in the seat as he spoke.

"But don't you think she's wrong? This isn't the way Christians are to act. Don't you think we should tell her that?"

"Nope… I think that's what the prayers are all about. I think we are to pray for her spirit. We are to pray that those walls will melt around her heart…that her heart will become soft and pliable again. We are to pray that God's Spirit will be able to touch her. Whatever comes after that is His responsibility not ours. When we pray like that we don't have to keep score." Jack smiled as he spoke.

"It would be harder for me to pray about Holden. I only know what I have heard about him." Brian interjected.

"Got some problems with Holden, huh Brian?"

"How can you not blame Holden? Look at what he caused with his selfishness." Matt's face was serious again.

"If it weren't for Holden, Matt here wouldn't have had the money to continue his ministry. I may still be living in the street or be dead. And you, Brian, where would you be? I don't condone what he did, but God used it for good. In the midst of darkness there is light. He wants us to join Him…not direct Him."

Matt sat quietly listening, yet not in seeming agreement. "Holden Jeffries used me and the ministry to find an identity for his charade. He is a corporate wolf that will wear any mask necessary to make and impression. I don't know who you met, but the man I knew was pretty wrapped up in himself."

"What's he doing back here then? I know for a fact that he was given a ticket to Grand Cayman. He was put on a plane and given back his dream. Why do you think he's back?"

"You saw him in Chicago, right Jack? What was he like?"

"He was like a man in jail. He had nothing left to hold up as himself."

"Do you think he's a believer?"

"I think God is working on him. I think that this whole process has changed his outlook. Death can be a tremendous eye-opener."

"I must be honest here, Jack. I'm angry with this man. He's lost nothing. Look what we've lost. Look in the mirror. See the scars. You have them on the outside, mine are on the inside. How many of them were direct result of his deception?"

"Each of us must face the truth of our lives. I have deceived many. I have no pretense of sanctity. I am fortunate to have been found because Holden Jeffries is a Saint next to me. The details are not important. The fact that I have been forgiven is all that matters. You must decide your feelings about Holden Jeffries. I am impressed that you are willing to be honest about your feelings and not take the 'religious approach.' Take it to the Father. He can deal with the truth."

"I know the answer. I'm just not ready to hear it yet."

CHAPTER **61**

K ate had not washed her hair in three days. She wasn't certain when she last changed her clothes. It was of little consequence. The return of Holden had opened wounds closed for nearly forty years. The farmhouse that she loved now held memories of a drunken father, and a dying mother.

Kate could feel the oppressive presence of the past in every corner of the house. She knew in her heart she had let her parents down. She had always been a selfish woman.

Everything had been fine until she left home. She had left her mother and gone to college. It was the last time she saw her well. After her mother died, she left her father alone in this house. She wasn't willing to sacrifice her future. He died alone. She looked in the mirror it was her. She was the problem. She was incapable of a relationship, she never had one with her father, never wanted one with her husband. She was alone in her house. It was nearly 8:00 PM. The truth was tearing at her soul.

"I hate you, God! I was better off before I ever met you. You promise new life and joy and peace. What a joke. When is that coming? When is anything good coming? All I have seen is pain. It has always been pain. I gave up this farm and all that I own to start a place for people to get to know you. Where were you, God? Is it because I really make you mad? Is that why? I hate it!" Kate grabbed the crystal pitcher she inherited from her mother and hurled it against the wall. Splinters of clear glass exploded in all directions.

"My best friend was killed right here in this house. And what about her? She believed in you too! She loved you. How could you let her be killed? Some guardian you are."

Kate paced the floor, fists clenched, head tilted up. God was wrong...she knew it.

"I don't want to keep doing this. I hate my life. I hate my husband. I hate this farm. I want out! I've had enough. I don't even think you hear me. I don't care anyway. I just want to die."

Kate fell to the floor in her kitchen. The house was totally dark. Tears puddled beneath her sagging head. She was broken. She was alone in a house that had witnessed the death of everything she had held dear. Now she had offended God. Death would have been a relief.

The light began in the corner of her kitchen and slowly illuminated most of the room. Kate lifted her head, her burning eyes not knowing what to expect. They were all there. Her mother and father and Connie. They were seated at the kitchen table facing her. It was not a dream, yet it was not exactly real.

The three figures nearly glowed, but there was no fear at their presence. Kate rose to a kneeling position hesitant to speak and ruin the scene.

"That was some show you just put on kid. You still have a way of expressing yourself that leaves no doubt where you stand." Kate's Father smiled as he spoke to her.

"You saw that Dad?"

"We were all wondering how much more you would take until you finally were honest with yourself. You have been playing the role of the strong woman for nearly five decades. In the early years you had anger to keep it intact. Then you surrendered to God and we knew it was just a matter of time until the flood."

"I was really angry. I said some nasty things. I am sorry that you had to hear all of it."

"At least you're done pretending. You can build a relationship on a foundation of truth. God was involved in this. He wants you to be real. You know that he really doesn't react much to what we say. It's what's in our heart that concerns him."

Kate's mother broke in, "Kate, it was never your fault. You didn't cause my death, or the death of your father. What he has just told you is true. You must start with the truth. You gave us so much pleasure with your mature attitude. You were always a good student and always followed the rules. We could never have asked for more from a daughter. We loved you more than you could have ever guessed. Never blame yourself for anything concerning us. We love you. That's the truth!" Both her mother and father were nodding as she finished.

Connie sat listening with that loving smile on her face. "I really miss you, Kate. But knowing that you will be here with me makes it easier. You must be strong and real after this because Matt hasn't faced himself. His day is nearing. You are an important part of God's plan on Earth. He would never have brought you to this point unless that was true. From this day forward, praise him for all your circumstances, even the ones that are difficult to understand. All have purpose, all have merit, some are painful…but all are worth it. We have been allowed to visit to tell you this. You know we love you but realize that no one loves you like Jesus. We must go, but we are with your spirit always."

"Please stay. Please stay. Please stay." It was four-thirty in the morning and Kate's back felt like it was breaking. She had been lying on the kitchen floor in a puddle of tears and saliva. She opened her eyes and the kitchen was in total darkness. She could barely make out the table that was less than three feet away. Had it been a dream? Probably, but it was from God. She was no longer angry. There was no blame. She was whole for the first time since her mother had passed away. She knew the truth, and she was free.

She stood with a smile and said, "Thanks Lord, I am sorry I shouted at you, forgive me."

"*I already have.*"

CHAPTER 62

Holden left the farmhouse with no clue where to go. He wasn't sure what he had expected from Kate. He tried to think. The force of her words was still cutting.

He wondered if men and women ever really enjoyed each other. He recognized the sign on the Motel and turned in. He and Angela had checked into separate rooms the night before. He wondered if he had made a mistake coming here. Angela could never have kept his existence secret. He had hoped to find an answer back here.

As he opened the door to his room, he heard Angela's voice behind him. "Are you back already? I expected this to take some time."

"It was probably not the way I should have handled it. Kate didn't take it well. She never wants to see me again."

"We always say that."

"I think she really meant it. Her exact words were, 'I wish I had never known you. I'm going to try forgetting I ever did.'"

"Did you apologize?"

"Yes, of course, it just made her angrier. Angela, I think trying to put something together that never existed is a mistake. I've decided to tell the whole story. Then I'm leaving. That is, if I don't end up in jail."

"I think you should take one day at a time, let God handle this."

"Whatever you say, Angela."

CHAPTER 63

Inspector Thomas gave Holden the opportunity to tell his story for the fourth time. He was becoming disillusioned with the process. It had been six days since he and Angela had brought home the tape.

Holden had heard or seen nothing from Kate or anyone from the farm. At 2:00 PM on day seven, the door to the small room in which he had spent the last several hours burst open.

"Inspector Thomas, I am Jack Grayton. We spoke on the phone. It is a pleasure to meet you."

Holden could hardly keep from smiling. He had missed this man. The wheelchair seemed to be for the sole gratification of those who were with him. Even with the obvious injuries, his eyes said that he was back on his game.

Jack had a large wound on his forehead and another on his left cheek. There were some bruised areas and cuts on his hands, and the black youth pushing the wheelchair seemed concerned whenever Jack moved. Holden was certain it was going to be a chore to keep this man in this two-wheeled jail for long.

Matt Roth entered the room seconds after the wheelchair. Holden remembered an office in Metro Building. He noticed Matt's face and realized he was probably on the same mental journey. Holden nodded. Matt turned his head pretending not to notice. Holden was not surprised. He had seen the film of Matt's wife. He suddenly could no longer look at Matt.

"No one informed me that you would be arriving." Thomas stated with almost a questioning tone.

"Thought it might be better to arrive unannounced. We weren't certain if we would stop or not along the way. Drove straight through. Hello there, Holden, I heard you had come back to the states. I thought you were gone for good."

"Some things don't work quite like you expect them to. It wasn't the future I had anticipated."

"Inspector Thomas, why is Holden still here? You must have all the information by now? I hear he even brought some discs for you."

"We are still in the routine questioning mode. There are a lot of loose ends that need to be tied up." Thomas spoke with agitation in his voice.

Holden barely let him finish. "We have been over everything at least four times. There is nothing more that I can tell you. It is all the truth. That's why the answers are always the same. Check the story out, you'll see."

"Inspector, we have testimony from an eyewitness that will probably help. I am afraid that you will just have to take my word for it though, he will not be available for testimony. It could be hazardous for him. The information may fill in some of the blanks." Jack tilted his head as he spoke.

"You can't withhold the name of a source from the FBI, that's a federal offense. You could be put into prison for even suggesting it."

"I doubt that. I will share them with you if I am given immunity from prosecution. Like I said, at least you would know the *rest of the story*." Jack mimicked Paul Harvey

"You can't make a deal in a Federal case. You have to tell us what you know."

Matt had been standing quietly watching the bantering. "Sir, we are not trying to be disrespectful. We appreciate your dilemma. What we know is confidential information given to us by an unnamed source. If you want to go to Merrilville and dig, perhaps you can find the same source. We will share what we know. We will not share our sources. It is that simple."

"And just who are you?" Thomas snapped.

"I am Matt Roth. Vincent Langley murdered my wife. I have spent a great deal of time tying up some loose ends of my own. We will not be intimidated. You have all the information you need to bring those at fault to justice. The rest is only to put the story into perspective. The choice is yours."

Thomas stormed out of the room. Two other police officers turned and followed. The door slammed.

Holden spoke first. "I do feel obligated to do whatever it takes. I know I caused all of this. Matt, I am so sorry about Connie." Holden did not turn his eyes toward Matt.

"I'm not certain Matt is ready to hear that yet. We spoke a bit about it on the way home. Wounds like these take lots of time." Jack tried to smile for the comfort of both men.

"I still don't get why they killed her. Connie had never done anything to anyone." Matt's eyes looked deep into Holden.

"Matt, it was because Tony hated *me*. He sent Vincent here to kill Kate. Connie was in the wrong place at the wrong time. It's my fault she died. Tony wanted to hurt me. Hell, none of this would have happened if I hadn't tried to run."

"Tony killed because he hated." Jack's head turned from Holden to Matt. "He hated Holden's reputation, and he hated Kate's rejection and faith. Evil will always try to kill truth. Tony hated the happiness Kate was finding in Truth. He had to contemplate his own spiritual life. It was easier to kill."

"But why Connie?" Matt was in tears now. "She never ran away! She never dated a psychopath! She never was selfish! Why kill her? I have always trusted God, but I think he was wrong here. The innocent paid the price."

"Kinda like Jesus." Brian spoke almost to himself.

"It's true." Jack whispered. "His ways are not anything like our ways. He took Connie home and left a big hole here, but it was not in vain. He never does anything in vain."

Matt turned and slowly walked out of the room. Brian followed.

Jack turned slowly toward Holden. "I forgive you Holden, someday Matt will too."

"I can't get the picture of Connie out of my mind. Nothing like any of this was supposed to happen. I just wanted to leave it all behind and start over."

"It's pretty amazing how things start to roll when we turn from truth. Have you seen Kate? She's a different person."

"I saw her, yes. I don't think there is any future here for me. If they ever decide I can go… I'm gone."

"You don't learn real fast. That isn't what all of this was about. Too much has been paid to run away."

"Jack, I don't have any answers anymore. I really am dead. I died in that canoe and a thousand times since."

"Sounds like a perfect time to get to know Christ. Have you talked to him about this?"

"It doesn't work like that for me. I don't fit into that mold like you do, Jack. I need to work through this myself. I appreciate all that you have done, and I am glad to see you."

"I think the truth is that you are the closest to getting better than you have been your whole life."

CHAPTER 64

Kate opened the door. Matt, Brian and Jack stood on the step beaming. Gus, who had been waiting in the house with Kate, was smiling as he saw the joy in her eyes. She hugged each man and kissed him on the cheek.

"Come in," she motioned, "I wasn't certain that I would ever say that again."

The smell of home cooking and pie filled their nostrils and beckoned their entry. It was like Thanksgiving and Homecoming wrapped into one. The men seemed almost as excited as Kate.

Gus pulled his hands out of his pants pockets and patted each man on the back. They all walked slowly into the kitchen talking in the small talk of good friends.

"We've got one more bit of good news." Gus said as if it was killing him to wait.

"I don't think we deserve much more." Jack replied with a smile.

From the darkened family room stepped a near giant of a man. Paul had been waiting for the introduction. There was hugging and hand shaking and high fives.

"I don't know how to thank you for all of this. I never would have been out of this without you guys." Tears rolled lightly down Paul's cheeks.

Jack backed away and smiled. "I knew you were innocent, but Tony had it pretty cut and dried. It would have been quite a fight even with the testimony of my friends in Chicago, if Holden hadn't found that tape."

"But the tape came from you. The lady said Jack sent the tape." Paul questioned.

"Wrong Jack! Holden was using my name as an alias. Angela knew Holden as Jack, that's why she said that. She is a believer too."

"How did Holden get the tape? Why would Tony take the chance of getting caught?"

"Angela told me the night when the car exploded, Holden brought the tape by her house and told her to keep it and give it only to Jack Grayton. He tried to get it to me so I could bring it back here. I got a little too close to the explosion. I never got the package."

"So how did it get here?"

"Holden took a chance and showed up at Angela's door one day. When he heard about the blast and the newspaper story, he figured I was dead. He decided to deliver it himself. It was Holden that got you out so fast. Actually, it was a pretty courageous thing to do."

"Well, Jack, it's nice to hear that someone likes him." Kate said curtly. "I can't quite see that side of Holden."

All the heads turned. Jack said quietly. "Kate, you know I love you. I have considered you a friend since the day we met. But you can't have spent much time with Holden if you think he is still the man you used to know."

"That's true, Jack." Kate's eyes flashed as she spoke. "And I don't intend to change that. Holden is dead. I was there when he was buried. I am a different woman than when we were married. I have no need for what Holden Jeffries was or is. If God has changed him then He will find him a future. Paul, you may owe Holden some gratitude. I'm sure that Jack can tell you where to find him and Angela. And understand, nothing makes me happier than getting all of us together again in this house. But Holden will never be a part of my life again, ever."

CHAPTER 65

Gus had never been that good at figuring out women. He was sort of angry when he left the house. Kate had seemed so happy at the beginning. Then Jack had brought up her husband and the party was over. He remembered the times in his own marriage when things didn't seem to work too well. Usually it was all his fault. He was always wrong.

No big surprise…women are the ones that decide when to be mad, and they're the ones who decide when to get over it.

Gus had hoped to enjoy the evening with his friends. There had been enough stuff to be upset about around here, most of it had come out okay. *Why get so upset and cause more problems?* He knocked on Kate's door.

The door opened slowly, and he saw her face. It was obvious that Gus was not the only one that had spent a restless night. *Why do women have to be so emotional?* He wished he had stayed in his house.

"Gus, come in. I'm sorry I look like this. I just can't seem to get it together right now. Sit down, I'll make some coffee."

He watched Kate struggle to make a pot of coffee and realized he had misjudged the situation. He had come here to tell her to grow up. Now he didn't have a clue what he was doing.

"It sure was nice to see the guys last night, huh?"

"I was so looking forward to it, Gus. Then Jack brought up Holden, and I got all upset. I messed up the whole thing. I just can't seem to get through this. Gus, do you think I'm being stupid? Do you think I'm wrong?" Her voice seemed almost distant.

There it was: the question he had never expected. He had come here to tell her she was acting stupid and that she was wrong. Now what?

Women, how can they always do this? He wondered.

"Kate, I never been too good at givin' much advice. I ain't been too many places. I know farmin' pretty good…but that's about it. I just see that you ain't happy much anymore. It would sure do me some good to see you smile like it was natural, not like it hurt."

"I can't pretend, Gus. I keep falling apart. I don't want to be like this. I don't know what to do anymore."

"Well, you are a Christian woman, aren't you? Have you been prayin' and stuff? Isn't that supposed to help?"

"It doesn't seem to work very well right now. Sometimes I even question where God has been in all of this. I am not mad at God; I just wonder if He has turned His back on us."

"You may not be mad, but that sort of sounds like you don't trust Him much. I don't pretend to be no big time Christian… but God always seemed to have His own way of doin' stuff. I never expected Him to ask me for my advice. I just figured He had His own reasons and I shouldn't bother worrying about His stuff."

"But what about when it hurts? Is it supposed to hurt all the time?"

"Seems like we're the ones that decide if we hurt. I know that lots of stuff has happened, but it ain't been all bad. We lost a friend, but we found a new one in Paul. We got Jack and Matt and Brian all back. Some of it has worked out. I try to look at the good stuff. It helps it hurt less. See, we decide what to think about."

"But I thought I was getting over it. I thought I was getting stronger. I heard God's voice and he even helped me with lots of pain I carried from when I was a little girl. Then this Holden thing last night and it's all back. I really get tired of being a mess."

"So what's really messin' you up? Is it that Holden ran out on you?" That wasn't even close to what he had wanted to say. He really wished he could be somewhere else.

"I really don't know if that's it. Seems like I used to believe everyone had run out on me at some point in my life. That's what

God helped me realize wasn't true. But Holden is different, I always trusted Holden."

"Trusted him how, was he unfaithful?"

"See, that's it. I'm not sure about anything anymore. I thought he was faithful, but he ran away and pretended to die just to get out of his life."

"Isn't that stuff Holden's problem? I mean, isn't what Holden has done something he has to face? Why pick up all that baggage too?"

"What baggage?"

"Just because Holden was stupid, why do you want to take the blame?"

"But Gus, he left. What does that say about our marriage? What am I supposed to think about how he felt about me? Don't you see? He didn't want me."

"But if his leaving means he didn't want you, then does his comin' back mean that he does now?"

"He came back to help Jack and Paul. Jack said that last night."

"So if there could be a reason other than you for him to come back, couldn't there be some other reason for his leaving?"

"Gus, sometimes you just don't get it!"

"That's exactly what I been trying to tell you. I ain't smart enough to get it!"

They just sat not saying a word. Gus picked up his coffee cup and took a sip. Kate turned her head and looked out the window. She had no answer to the questions.

Gus spoke first. "Kate, I lost my daughter-in-law, and you are about the only female in my life that matters. I ain't sayin' you're stupid, but sometimes the stuff we tell ourselves ain't the only way to look at it. You ain't getting' any happier, and it makes me sad. I didn't come here with answers… I just came 'cause I care about you and what you are. It don't matter to me if you forgive Holden or ever talk to him again, but I see someone who needs to deal with this to get better. I ain't much help, but I will always be here if you need me. Thanks for the coffee."

"Gus, you're wrong."

He was not surprised by the statement, most of his life he had been wrong. He knew he never should have come.

"You really do get it. I think you are one of the most intelligent men I know. I will consider what you have shared with me. I love you, Gus. You are the father I never had."

She leaned over and kissed him lightly on the cheek.

Gus hadn't seen it coming. The kiss brought total discomfort, but her words and touch were already filed forever in his memory. He nodded slightly and headed for the door.

"I, uh, do love you, Kate. I only said that to one other woman in my whole life. I gotta go get some work done."

Kate stood and watched this man is his Osh Kosh bib overalls leave her house. She had never been happier to hear the word love from any other soul in her life. She needed so badly to be loved.

Holden Jeffries had most of his clothes packed when he heard the knock on his door. He was really tempted not to answer. The door opened letting in the afternoon sun. It took a moment for Holden's eyes to adjust. Jack's face was a welcome sight.

"I just thought you might need some company. Have you heard anything from our favorite FBI agent?"

"Come on in, Jack. Inspector Thomas just left. I guess he must be tired of hassling me. I'm a free man. I'm heading out as soon as I can get packed."

"What about the insurance company, and Litany Systems? Are there any repercussions from the charade?"

"The insurance company was pretty happy to get their money back, and the premiums I paid all those years will never pay now, but they want nothing to do with me anymore. I guess Litany feels about the same way. Hell, seem as if nobody wants much of anything I offer. You probably heard about Kate; she wants me dead. I feel that way most days myself."

"I used to think about suicide lots. Even had the gun in my mouth once. Never could quite pull the trigger. Are you sure that leaving is the answer? It didn't do much for you before."

"I'm not certain about anything anymore. I got all this money, and I could care less. I put a million in the bank here in an account for Kate. I won't move it into her account until I'm gone. I guess most of the reasons to come back are taken care of, seems like it's time to go."

"Well, Holden, sometimes what seems right is far from it. Have you ever wondered why I was near the explosion? Ever wonder what I was doing there?"

"You were saving my life. I can't figure out why, but I know you did it. Most of the time I think I should thank you." Holden managed a smile.

"You want the truth."

"If you want to share it."

"You know that I have been born again. I follow Jesus Christ, and it is the most important part of my life. I spend a lot of time in prayer and reading Gods word. I sometimes hear His voice. He changed my life."

"I can attest to that fact. What does this have to do with the car?"

"I left the farm here to head to Chicago. I left my friends and had quite a little 'self-righteous farewell' with them before I left. I really had no clue how much self was involved in what I was doing."

"You came there to help me. Don't be so hard on yourself, no one else really cared."

"That's the way it looked. If I face the truth, I was sort of putting on a show. You need to understand, I wasn't aware of it, but I had that God Groupie thing going. Then when I got to Chicago and felt the power of having people nearly jumping when I talked. I fell right into the trap of it. It nearly got me killed."

"Were you looking for me, or what?"

"No, actually I was suicidal, I guess. I was convinced that God wanted me to sacrifice my life so that you could live."

Jack had a lump in his throat as he spoke...he stopped for a moment and looked away.

"I decided that if the police found a body in the car with fingerprints that matched the name Jack Grayton that would end it. I thought God had sent me there to become a sacrifice for you. It made perfect sense to me since I was such an *"important"* part of God's plan. Don't you see how self-serving all of it was? I wanted to be known as the man who gave it all up for someone who had hurt him. It was a deception from Satan. It was a lie I wanted to believe.

Even though I had studied God and was aware of the teachings... I was duped."

"But you weren't in the car."

"I was walking up to the car. I didn't even see the car backing away from it. I was on a mission. I was in *sacrificial mode* nothing would change my mind. Thank God for His understanding of my stupidity. He let me learn a lesson about getting out front, not following. The explosion probably should have killed me. It sort of seems like you are doing the same thing."

"That's Bull...?" Holden snapped, his eyes squinting.

"It's easier to leave and hope people will think or say nice things than to stay and face the trials. Tell me you don't think about what they will say when you transfer in that money."

"You can't tell me all your motives are true."

"What do you think I was just telling you? My motives are sometimes totally selfish. What I was telling you is that it's wrong, you could get hurt doing it that way." Jack whispered.

"Pain seems to be the emotion of choice in this world. You're a Christian and you can't figure it out. How in the hell can God expect me to get it straight?"

"He doesn't! I never said I couldn't figure it out, I said I got messed up. I figured it out when I gave my life to Him. The answer is to follow. It never changed. I just decided to lead a while. It must be more of Him and less of me to work. I just got that mixed up a bit."

"But you have been a Christian a long time and you still get messed up. How can I ever make it? I don't want to change. It's not that I don't believe in God. I have even seen some of what He can do, but these are problems about my life, not religious stuff."

"He wants to work on the things of life. It has nothing to do with religion. It's about a relationship with you. If you think it's about perfection think again. He's perfect, you Holden never will be."

"So you have a relationship with God?"

"Yep, He cares about me and I love Him. It's the most important thing in my life. I learn more in my time with Him than in anything else I do."

"How'd you get to be friends?"

"After Matt prayed for my salvation, I wanted to know Christ and God and even the Holy Spirit. I just told Him that I didn't love Him and wanted to learn how to do it. He even taught me how to love Him. I couldn't even do that."

"How did you know it was happening?"

"That's easy, I began to love God and all He stood for. That was nothing like I had felt before. I asked, He delivered. If I had asked him about you and the car bomb rather than trying my own thing He would have handled it too. I just got in a hurry and decided to think for myself."

"What if I don't measure up? I really don't deserve much from God."

"None of us do. If we got what we deserved we would all go to hell. He took care of that too. You just need to fall down and tell Him the truth; you don't have a clue of how to get up."

"How can just saying some prayer really matter? It's too easy?"

"If it's so easy to tell the truth, why have you been lying to yourself for so long? This isn't about talking; it's about sharing your true heart."

"I know I have no place to go...nobody cares. Is that what you mean?"

"Have you had enough of life according to Holden Jeffries? Then it's time to find some real answers."

"I am tired of the old ways. I truly am not the best at praying."

Holden knelt by the bed. Jack placed his hand on Holden's head, and they prayed. The tears streamed down the cheeks of a former CEO, and a street bum.

The brothers in Christ spent the next hour sharing and laughing amazed at the similarities of their lives. Holden thanked and asked forgiveness from Jack for the answers in his life. Now there was joy in his life, joy that had no source other than his true Father.

Holden felt as if he had come home.

Jack left as the sun was falling, promising to call Holden before he hit the rack. Holden wanted to share it with the entire world. He walked to Angela's room and knocked. There was no answer. He headed back to his room and unpacked the suitcases. He would stay until he knew it was time to leave. He knelt and prayed, this time alone.

Father, thanks for never giving up on me. I know that I insulted you and your son for years by my actions and my words. You had every right to leave me behind. I have no right to expect anything from you, yet you have touched my heart and lifted the weight of my life. Never leave me Lord, I want to learn to love you. In Jesus's name I pray.

Holden stood and wiped tears from his eyes. He had to tell someone. He found his keys and grabbed his jacket. She may just to throw him out, but he was not leaving without a fight.

CHAPTER **67**

It was amazing. An old man who had spent most of his life tending cattle and sheep, lifted some of the burden in her heart. Gus had turned some of Kate's thoughts inside out with his questions. She had not stopped thinking since he left the house.

Kate paced the floor as she thought. She had never considered that the feeling of others had perhaps been the basis of their unacceptable responses. *Had he loved her?* She remembered the early years when he relished her presence. He would put his arms around her and pull her close to him and bury his nose in her neck. He seemed to cherish every scent and touch that she offered. She was ashamed to admit that she was rarely warmed by those moments. She feared that he was manipulating her. She often turned away and left him standing. There were requirements for her affection. She would not be used.

"God, is this pain ever going to end!" Kate wept as she confronted her past. *It wasn't just the intimacy; I was afraid to let down my guard...to just love him. I had to be careful. Did I drive him to leave? I never asked him what he thought was missing. What kind of relationship did we have? We were two people living together with a certificate that said married. Our lives were separate.*

Just how different was it when he left?

Kate opened her Bible to Mark 8:34–38. *"If anyone would come after me, he must deny himself and take up his cross and follow me."*

"Deny myself? Lord can you help me change? Will you help me?"

The doorbell brought Kate from her thoughts.

CHAPTER 68

Angela had agreed to drive. Jack had been waiting in the hotel lobby when she returned from her walk. He was smiling and shared the news about the new Holden. Angela was so excited that she hugged him right there in the lobby. Jack explained that he needed a lift to the farm to share the news about Holden with Kate. Angela was a bit concerned about seeing Kate again, but offered to drive and wait in the car.

The door to Kate's house opened to reveal a smiling face. Jack saw the change.

"I haven't seen that look for a long time. Has God been talking to you?"

"I think that's exactly what's been happening. What brings you here?"

"I just left Holden's hotel room and thought I would share some of what I experienced. Can I come in?"

"Who's in the car?"

"It's Angela. She said she would wait."

"Jack Grayton you have the worst manners of any man I know. Do you think it is normal to let people sit out in the car? I will not hear of it. You go ask her to join us, or I will."

"I think that's a great idea." Jack stated flatly.

"Go get her, Jack."

"No, I think it's a great idea for you to go out and invite her in."

Kate didn't hesitate, just stepped past Jack and walked briskly to the car. Jack was amazed moments later to see them walking together toward the house. Kate's arm was around Angela's shoulders.

"I will not hear of it. You are welcome in my house any time. In fact, if you continue to stay in town, I would love to have you as a guest. The hotel is nice, but nothing like a home."

Angela did not answer, only smiled.

The coffee was fresh and of course there were cookies at the table.

"You said that you were with Holden. How is he doing?"

Jack turned quickly and looked at Kate. He smiled as he spoke.

"He has decided to follow Christ. I think he has had enough of trying to work things out himself. We all know that feeling."

"Holden prayed?" Kate questioned with a look of disbelief.

"We actually prayed together, but I saw his heart. It was real."

"Oh...it's not that I don't believe you, it is just that I feel somewhat jealous that you have been offered an insight into this man that I never was given. I only knew the shell."

"Unfortunately, that is not all that rare in a marriage." Angela offered. "I have never been allowed to share those feelings either."

"Sometimes we need to be the vulnerable one. I shared some of my weakness with Holden and let him know that he was not alone. If we are not willing to be transparent how can we expect others to take a chance?" Jack waited. Silence followed. All seemed to be contemplating the coffee more than the statement. Kate lifted her head and looked at Jack.

"Do you think there is a chance that we can put it back together? There was a time when we loved each other. Do you think anybody ever makes it?"

"Kate, I have never been married, but I know that God designed marriage. If He planned it, then it can work if you will share it with Him."

"Will you go with me to see him? I really want to try again."

"I can think of nothing I would rather do than help two of my best friends look for a future. When do you want to do this?"

"I will take a quick shower and get some makeup on, then let's go."

CHAPTER 69

Holden was certain that he was doing the right thing when he started the car, but as he drove toward the farm he began to doubt.

How could Jack be so open? How could he afford to take the chance of letting others see? Jack had little care for the accolades of men. Holden would change. He had help in Christ. *Wow, that really sounded preachy.* He never thought like this. He turned the car around and headed for the farm.

Holden was within two miles of Welcome Home when he saw the lights blinking. A four-wheel drive tractor lay in the left ditch, and a blue Taurus sedan in the other. A farmer was waving his hands like a wild man.

"They came over the hill. With the sun going down they must not have seen me. I had my lights on. The car hit the left wheel and then flipped into the ditch."

"Have you called an ambulance?"

"I don't have a phone."

"Use the one on the seat of my car" Holden pointed as he flung open the door and headed toward the Taurus, "Just dial 911!"

Holden approached car. There was no fire. The wheels were still turning as they pointed skyward. Then Holden saw her. Angela was lying in the grass on her side.

"NO!" He screamed.

He rushed to her, kneeling and listening for breathing. He saw her eyes open and felt a rush of joy.

"Don't try to move? Was there anyone with you?"

"Jack…and… Kate. Have you found them? Holden, ARE THEY ALL RIGHT?"

Holden crawled toward the car. He saw the blood on the window of the driver's side and knelt to look inside. He saw movement on the passenger side as Jack pulled himself from the car.

"Holden, she's hurt pretty bad, we have to get her out of the car, I can smell gas. She's breathing poorly. I think my legs broken, but I'm okay. Get Kate out."

Holden struggled with the door handle. Everything seemed to be in slow motion. He pried the handle downward and slowly opened the door. Kate was suspended by the seatbelt, and blood was dripping on the velvet roof. He knelt beside his wife and prayed as he worked.

Don't let her die, Lord. She isn't the one, take me. Don't let her die!

Suddenly the farmer was inside the car on the opposite side. "We can lower her down together. We have to be careful. Is she alive?"

"I don't know, but we have to get her out of here."

The farmer turned off the switch to the motor and they locked hands under Kate's shoulders, then Holden nodded, and the farmer snapped the seat belt. Kate's body fell to the ceiling and Holden pulled her out of the door and into the grass.

"Holden?" A faint smile came to her lips. "How did you find me?"

"I was coming out to talk to you. Lay still, you're going to be okay."

"Holden, I'm so sorry I said I wanted you dead. I was so nasty to you. Forgive me."

"Don't try to talk, Kate. I forgive you. I still love you. I have always loved you. I just got the important things mixed up. It's going to be different. I want to come back Kate."

The entire time that Holden was talking, he was holding tightly to the wound on Kate's right arm. It was still bleeding through his grip. He was certain that the glass had cut an artery Holden knew time was short.

"I was coming to tell you I wanted to start over. Can we start over, Holden? You have always been the only one. Even when I was angry, I think I loved you. Let's start again, just us. Let's not worry about working, just us."

Kate's voice was weakening. Holden jumped up still holding Kate's arm. "I need help here!" He pulled the belt from his pants and tightened it around Kate's arm. She winced

"Where's that ambulance?"

"It's got to be coming soon, they said soon!"

The farmer was covering Angela with his coat and looking after Jack while they waited for help.

"Holden, don't worry, just stay here by me. I'm getting cold."

He lay beside her and pulled her close. He buried his nose in the hair around her collar and wept. He could hear the siren now and knew it was closing. Kate smiled as she felt the breath of her husband on her neck.

"I always loved that," she whispered, "we didn't do enough of this."

Holden continued to hold her tight. He could feel the change. He knew she was gone. He just couldn't let go. He wept for the opportunities he had squandered, lost forever for the sake of a career. He wept for the past. He wept for the loss of future. He wept for his own pain and the pain he had brought to so many others. He wept for the years they had known and never shared. He wept because nothing else that made sense.

The hand upon his shoulder startled him. He looked up as a bearded EMT with deep eyes lightly touched his arm. His face was weathered but strong. Holden felt as if the world had stopped turning. The sun still shone, the clouds still rolled, but sound was muffled, something was different. He felt as if he was losing consciousness, he had to hang on."

"She's dead... I felt her die before you arrived."

"Let me have a look." The voice was so deep it surprised Holden. "She needs my help. Could I get you to release her just for a bit? I need to have a look. Don't be afraid...just trust."

Holden released Kate and slid away. The uniformed man worked quietly first looking for a pulse on Kate's neck, then checking the wound. "Could you get a blanket from the rig, she needs to be covered. The rig is right over there. She is just sleeping, just trust."

Holden turned and headed for the ambulance, trying to find some of the hope the EMT was demanding. He knew Kate was dead. One more time he had earned God's wrath. The blanket was just inside the door. He grabbed it and turned back toward the car.

"There it was again, something changed." The light seemed different, the sounds around him were clearer. He noticed the two other EMT's working with Jack and Angela. He hurried around the car to Kate's body. She was alone. Her head was propped up on a blue uniform. There was no wound in Kate's arm. She smiled. She smiled at Holden as he approached.

Holden stopped. He could not take another step. He was afraid the dream would end if he got too close. It couldn't be. He looked at the car, the blood was gone from the fabric in the roof. There was little blood anywhere. Moments before it had looked like a war zone, hadn't it? She was dead, wasn't she? The EMT, the guy with the eyes and the voice like thunder, where was he? He had to be close by, he had to know what was going on.

"Holden, is that you? How did you find us? How did you know about the accident?" Kate still seemed to be struggling for breath.

"I was coming to talk to you, coming to tell you I love you." Holden nearly whispered, hoping it wasn't a dream. "Are you okay, does it hurt anywhere?"

"My head hurts, and I'm cold, but seeing you makes it worth it. I was coming to find you. Angela and Jack, are they okay?"

"They're being attended to" Holden lightly placed the blanket over Kate and lay down beside her. He pulled her close and breathed in her scent. "I'll just try to warm you up a bit until they get over here."

Kate smiled as she felt the breath of her husband on her neck.

"I always loved that," she whispered, "we didn't do enough of this."

"We will Kate, if it's what you want, we will. I have been so blind for so long. It's a chance to start over Kate, can we? Can we start over?"

"I was coming to ask you that exact question. You have always been the only one. Even when I was angry, I think I loved you. Let's start again, just us. Let's not worry about working, just us."

"Just us, Kate...just us.

CHAPTER 70

Darkness has its own clarity. Holden sat quietly on the step of the Freeborn County Hospital as the events of the day replayed in his mind. He had asked the other paramedics about the man with the dark eyes.

They looked puzzled. "Only two ride in a rig."

No one remembered the blood. The farmer didn't even remember helping Kate out of the seatbelt. It was as clear in Holden's mind as the streetlight above him.

Jack never batted an eye. "Angel, or maybe Christ himself. Not sure. Probably not Christ, he's not coming back 'til the end. Had to be and Angel."

"Except, nobody remembers anything about the bleeding. I held that arm myself. I felt that warm blood ooze out of her. I'm telling you I can still smell it, Jack. She died. I felt her die in my arms. She was dead, Jack, dead."

"What did he say to you? The EMT, what did he say exactly?"

"He asked to see Kate."

"That's all?"

"He said 'don't be afraid, just trust.' Then he told me to go get a blanket."

"Jesus said that. He said 'don't fear, just trust' when he brought a girl back from death. They all laughed at him when he told them she was just asleep. He said to the father of the girl 'don't fear, just trust.' That's where it came from. It was from God. You are a blessed man Mr. Jeffries. She probably was dead."

Jack had patted him on the shoulder and smiled. That had been hours ago. Holden just wished he could be as certain about all of it. He returned to the hospital room wondering where the rest of his life would lead. The night was quiet again. Holden could only smile. He was excited about what lay ahead, and so very tired.

Kate's whisper got his attention. "I was hoping you'd come in before you left."

"I'm not going anywhere. At least I don't plan on it if you were serious today."

"I want to start over. I want to know all about you, Holden. I know it will only make me love you more. I was a fool for so many years, I want to do it differently." Kate turned her head toward Holden and smiled.

"No more separate worlds, no more separate anything. I haven't a clue where I'm going, but I don't want to ever go back. Kate, I never was much of a husband or father, but there's still time."

Kate reached out and took Holden's hand.

"Actually, Holden, we have eternity."

E P I L O G U E

Jack was not surprised about the angel. He knew God loved Holden Jeffries. He knew God had a call on his life. God needed men like Holden Jeffries.

Kate was discharged from the hospital after five days. "Welcome Home opened within one month. Kate remained CEO but refused to move into the house. Jack and Brian shared the farmhouse, and eventually talked Gus into joining them. Within the first year the farm expanded to thirty-six clients and has grown to sixty to date. The average length of stay is twelve months, and the cure rate stands at over 80 percent. The farm continues to produce crops and livestock. The clients are paid a wage for their labor. The results have been so impressive that media and law enforcement officials frequently visit the farm.

The death of the entire staff of Welcome Home takes place each morning of every day as they take up their cross. Their smiles say dying is the only way to overcome life.

Holden Jeffries continues to have questions, but he spends a lot of time with the most powerful being in the universe…that's another story.

ABOUT THE AUTHOR

J. Michael Koppen has lived a storied life. His career as a pharmacist and executive coach has spanned five decades. He is an artist, a musician, a poet, and an author. As a mid-life believer in Christ he established a Bible study in his hometown county jail meeting every Monday night for over thirty-five years. He served annually for a decade in Guatemala as pharmacist with Helps International, a surgical mission team of volunteers from across America. Jim has traveled the world extensively with his wife and friends. He has always been a storyteller both in his writing and in music. He has three adult children and eight grandchildren. Jim and Kandis, his wife and childhood sweetheart, divide their time between rural Minnesota and southwest Florida.

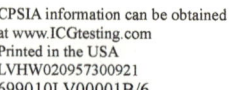